WILDER LOVE

EMERY ROSE

Copyright © 2019 Emery Rose

All rights reserved.

Cover design: Najla Qamber, Qamber Designs & Media

Editing: Ellie McLove, My Brother's Editor

No part of this book may be reproduced or transmitted in any form or by any means, electronic or mechanical, including photocopying, recording or by any information storage and retrieval system, without written permission from the author.

This is a work of fiction. Any names or characters, businesses or places, events or incidents, are fictitious or have been used in a fictitious manner. Any resemblance to actual persons, living or dead, or actual events is purely coincidental.

❦ Created with Vellum

For Aliana Milano. Love you, boo. xoxo

Playlist
"Grizzly Bear" – Angus & Julia Stone
"The Devil's Tears" – Angus & Julia Stone
"These Days" – Samuel
"Sorry" – Nothing but Thieves
"Dream" – Bishop Briggs
"Consequences" – Camila Cabello
"Skyscraper" – Demi Lovato
"Dancing With Your Ghost" – Sasha Sloan
"Baptize Me" – X Ambassadors, Jacob Banks
"Love Me Anyway" – Pink, Chris Stapleton
"Someone You Loved" – Lewis Capaldi
"Nobody Knows" – The Lumineers

PART I

BEFORE

1

Remy

Hope is a dangerous thing. It makes you wish for things you can't have. I thought mine had died in a shitty apartment in Detroit when I was twelve, along with the frayed threads of childhood innocence I'd still been clinging to. So, it surprised me when I woke up that morning feeling... hopeful.

Maybe Mom's words, uttered more times than I could count, would finally come true.

"You'll see. Everything will be different here."

It might have been the tangerine clouds or the palm trees swaying in the summer's breeze outside my bedroom window. Whatever the reason, hope bubbled to the surface like it used to when I was a kid and didn't know any better.

Our new apartment building was on a hill, desert-dry grass sloping down to fenced-in backyards behind terracotta-roofed white stucco houses. It reminded me of photos I'd seen of seaside Mediterranean towns. Slightly shabby but with an old-world charm. Nothing like the derelict neighborhoods we usually ended up in.

Don't get too attached, Remy.

Even so, I wanted to capture the moment, preserve it in a photo. Digging through my backpack, my hand wrapped around my most prized possession. A 35mm Canon Rebel. Everyone wanted digital cameras, but I preferred using film. It felt more authentic. I had found the camera in a pawn shop in Tulsa and begged Mom to buy it for me. I'd never asked for anything before. She gave it to me for my fourteenth birthday. Two weeks late, but still, she'd gotten it for me. And now it went everywhere with me.

Kneeling on the mattress I'd shoved against the wall last night, I hung out my open window and snapped photos. Of my first California sunrise. The palm trees. Beach towels hanging on a wash line. Three surfboards leaning against the back of a house. Then I stowed my camera in my backpack for later and rummaged through my still-packed duffle bag on the floor, eager to get out of here and explore my new town.

I threw on a faded orange bikini under cut-offs and a swim team T-shirt from a Midwest college I'd never attended and shoved my feet into my beat-up white Chucks. Grabbing my skateboard and my backpack, I made a quick stop in the bathroom. It was so small my knees grazed the bathtub when I sat on the toilet.

My sneakers squeaked on the linoleum as I crept across the living room. Dylan was still asleep on the sofa, his face smashed against the back cushion, his long legs tangled in dark blue sheets. I watched him sleeping for a few seconds, debating whether to wake him then decided against it. I wanted this time to myself. To see the ocean on my own. To capture the memories in dozens of photographs.

Shouldering my backpack, I closed the apartment door quietly behind me and jogged down the metal staircase attached to the side of the building. Our apartment was on the second floor, the parking deck below us, and two more stories above ours. Late last night after we unpacked, Dylan and I had climbed onto the flat roof of the building and smoked a joint. He had scowled for the camera, a blunt clamped between his lips, a hazy halo of smoke hanging above his head. My moody, broody twin was catnip for good girls who fell for bad boys. They wanted to fix him. Tame him. Make him love them. They would fail. Falling in love with Dylan would only break their hearts.

I stopped at the bottom of the staircase and watched a guy across the street slinging a surfboard into the back of a white Jeep Wrangler. A few years older than me, he had a golden tan and disheveled light brown hair, sun-streaked and curling a little where it met the collar of his faded-out blue T-shirt.

He looked like summertime. Like a California dream. *Golden.*

If I captured him in a photo, it would go in my beautiful collection.

He caught me watching him and gave me a smile. This really beautiful chilled-out smile that made my stomach somersault.

"How's it going?" he asked as I ventured closer.

"It's all good."

"Just moved in?" He squinted at the second floor of our building as if he knew we'd just moved into that apartment.

"Just passing through." I didn't know why I said that, except that it was usually true. We never stayed in one place for long.

"On your way to where?" he asked as if he was genuinely interested.

"Something better." It wasn't true. It never was.

He cocked his head and closed one eye as if he was about to let me in on a secret. "It doesn't get any better than this."

I believed him. It probably didn't. "Guess I'll have to take your word for it."

"Or maybe you'll find out for yourself."

"Maybe." Although I doubted it.

He glanced at the skateboard under my arm. "Where are you headed?"

"The beach." After I said it, I wasn't sure if he was talking about where I was headed after Costa del Rey, which I didn't know, or where I was headed at this moment. I looked down the narrow, winding street, as if I had a plan of action. I had no idea where the beach was from here. I had a lousy sense of direction, something Dylan found baffling.

"Well... catch you later." I hopped on my skateboard and took off down the street. It was better to beat people to the punch. I hated being left behind. Better to be the one who did the leaving.

He called after me, but I didn't hear what he said. I was already gone, cruising down the street, my wheels eating up the asphalt. White-washed houses, palm trees, and hot pink tropical bushes zipped past. Bougainvillea, I'd later find out—that was what the tropical bushes were called.

At this early hour, it was quiet, the town still sleeping. Bathed in an amber glow, Costa del Rey was a dream town. Like something from a movie set. But I knew better than to get too attached. We never stayed in one place long enough to put down roots. We were ramblers. Free spirits, Mom called us, as if that made us special. She always claimed it was something everyone wanted but were too afraid to be. She was wrong though. People wanted to feel like they belonged somewhere. Like they'd found a home. But I never bothered arguing with her. She wouldn't listen anyway.

In my peripheral, I saw the Jeep following along beside me, music drifting from the open windows. It was chilled-out music, bluesy with some soul. This guy was the quintessential cliched surfer dude. "If you're headed to the beach, you're going the wrong way," he said conversationally.

Well, that didn't surprise me.

"Is it far from here?"

"A five-minute drive."

"So, at the speed you're going..." Sloth speed.

"A hell of a lot longer." He didn't sound particularly bothered by that, like he had all the time in the world and this was no inconvenience.

"Are you headed in the right direction?"

"In a car, yes. On foot, no. It's a one-way street and you're headed east."

"I'm following the sun."

"Okay." I thought I could hear his smile, but I wasn't looking at him, so I couldn't confirm that.

"I'll give you a lift," he said finally.

"Do you always offer rides to total strangers?"

"Only the ones who are beachbound before seven in the morning."

"How do I know you're not a serial killer?"

"Leap of faith."

"I've already used up my lifetime quota of those."

He laughed, and I joined in as if it had been a joke. I wasn't looking at him. I was scared it would be too blinding. Or that he'd see too much. Hood rat. White trash. Slut. Whore's daughter. Smokin' hot. I've heard it all. I wasn't ready to chance it that he'd see the same thing other guys did. I don't know. Maybe I wanted him to see something good in me. Something that went beyond the outer package.

"A beautiful girl like you... why, you can get anything you want," Mom always said. *"You'll see, baby. You'll see how far beauty can take you in this world."*

Sometimes I thought my beauty was more of a curse than a blessing. It attracted attention. In my experience, the *wrong* kind of attention.

"My name's Shane, by the way."

"Remy, by the way."

"Remy," he repeated, testing it out.

I was named after Remy Martin. Mom claimed it was top shelf, like me. I'd have to take her word for it. Our last name was St. Clair. Dylan and I suspected that she'd made it up because she thought it sounded fancy, although that had never been confirmed.

"What's your best stroke?" he asked.

My best stroke? Oh right. I was wearing a swim team T-shirt. "Butterfly." It was the first one that came to mind. I couldn't swim the fly to save my life, but I lied all the time.

He chuckled. "Good try. But I'm not buying it."

"What gave me away?"

"Your spaghetti arms."

I snorted. "I don't have spaghetti arms."

"You don't have swimmer's shoulders either."

I hazarded a glance at Shane. He had swimmer's shoulders. They were wide and tapered down to a narrow waist. He was lean and lithe, all muscle without an ounce of fat. I quickly averted my gaze, focusing on the street in front of me. Too much goodness inside that Jeep.

Mom always said if something seems too good to be true it usually is. Which explained her track record for sabotaging anything that seemed *too good*. Sometimes I worried that I'd turn out to be just like her.

The Jeep rolled to a stop at an intersection. I kicked my heel against the tail and skidded to a halt, the board grating against the asphalt. Should I go left? Right? Or back the way I came?

"Come on. Get in," he said, seeing my indecision. "My conscience won't rest if I let you fend for yourself."

I hesitated. Probably because I wanted to get into his Jeep. I was always hesitant about accepting the things I wanted. They usually came with strings attached. He leaned across the seat and pushed open the passenger door, a further invitation to hop in and let him take me wherever he was going. Tempting.

I gnawed on my lower lip, considering his offer. I should be scared. Freaked out about accepting a ride from a stranger. Just because he was gorgeous on the outside didn't mean he wasn't ugly on the inside. Beautiful people did bad things too. But my internal warning signals weren't going off. Not that I would call him safe, exactly. My heart was doing dangerous things. Harmless? I knew better than to think that about anyone.

Call me crazy, I climbed into the passenger seat and stowed my skateboard in the footwell between my legs, my backpack in my lap. I wasn't always known for making the best decisions. I'd done a lot of stupid things in my life. Maybe this would be one of them.

"Thanks," I said as he started driving.

"No problem."

Now that I was inside his Jeep, the space felt too small. Too intimate. It smelled like coconut and candle wax. I leaned my shoulder against the passenger's side door and absently chipped away at the dark polish on my nails.

He reeled off a few letters and digits that jumbled in my brain. What was he saying?

"My license plate number. Text a friend. That way they'll know where to look for the buried body."

"You're a rookie at this serial killer gig, aren't you?"

"What gave me away?"

All I could do was laugh.

Minutes later, gravel crunched under the tires as he pulled into an empty lot. The scent of the sea was stronger here and I thought I could hear the sound of the surf, but I couldn't see the beach.

"Do you surf?" He cut the engine and took his keys from the ignition.

I shook my head. "I've never been in the ocean. Actually, I've never seen it before," I admitted.

I could feel him staring at me like that was something he couldn't imagine.

"Well, thanks for the ride." I backed away from the Jeep, ready to turn around and bolt.

"Hang on a sec and I'll walk you down."

"Oh, you don't have to do that." But I wanted him to. I wanted to walk with him. So, I waited.

"It's purely for selfish reasons." He grinned and took his board out of the back. Then he stripped off his T-shirt and tossed it inside the Jeep, his movements casual like it was no big deal. Which it wasn't. Shouldn't be. But I couldn't breathe. My gaze swept over golden tanned skin stretched over bone and muscle and drifted lower to that V and a fine dusting of golden hair. The happy trail that led to whatever he was hiding under those boardshorts. Jesus. What was wrong with me?

He gave me a mischievous grin like he'd read my mind. I quickly averted my gaze, pretending I hadn't just been checking him out.

I fell into step with him and we made our way along a sandy path through scrubby bushes and tall grass that swayed in the warm breeze. My skin was sticky from the salty air and I could taste the ocean on my lips.

My arm brushed against his, sending a jolt through my body, delicious shivers running up and down my spine. I took a deep breath, trying to rein in my galloping heart.

Chill out, Remy.

"How is it you've never seen the ocean?"

I shrugged. "I've never lived near a coast."

"Where are you from?"

"Everywhere and nowhere. I've moved around a lot." I cleared my throat, wanting to steer the conversation away from my crazy life. "Why did you say it was purely selfish? Before?"

He smiled but didn't answer the question. We came into a clearing at the top of a bluff and there it was, stretched out below us—the Pacific Ocean. The sea hugged the sky and it was hard to tell where one left off and the other began. The colors were muted and hazy, like a vintage photo. I watched in fascination as the waves built and grew and then crashed, spraying the air with whitewater, the tide rushing up to the golden sand and retreating again. The ocean was infinite, stretching out beyond the horizon, seagulls circling above it. I thought the water would be blue, but in this light, it was steely gray, the waves churning up a mossy green. Seaweed, I guess.

I took a deep breath of sea air. The thunder of the waves silenced the voices in my head, drowned out the ugly, and made me feel at peace in a way I never had before. I didn't know if it was because I was standing next to the golden boy with honey-brown hair and sculpted muscles, or if it was the ocean itself that made me dream of possibilities rather than only seeing obstacles. It was the closest I'd ever come to a religious experience.

I felt so small but not in an insignificant way.

Home, I thought. I've found my home. Which was a weird thought for a vagabond like me.

"Because of that," he said quietly, not wanting to break the trance I was under.

"Because of what?" I asked, still staring at the ocean, barely conscious of the smile tugging at my lips.

"The look on your face. I wanted to be the first person you saw the ocean with."

Oh. I dragged my gaze away from the scenery, to him. Up close, I could see that his eyes were hazel, swirls of green and brown flecked with shards of amber. There was a hint of stubble on his chiseled jaw like he hadn't shaved in a few days, and his nose was peeling. For some reason, I found that peeling nose adorable. More human, less godlike. My gaze lowered to his mouth, his lips slightly parted and a little bit chapped. His tongue swept over the full bottom one before he gripped it between his straight white teeth.

What would it feel like to have those lips pressed against mine? What would he taste like? Warm sunshine and the sea?

"Dude. What up?" A male voice from behind us broke the spell we were under and I turned to look at two guys with surfboards under their arms.

"How was J-Bay?" a guy with curly blond hair asked.

Shane grinned, his attention diverted from me to them. "Fucking awesome."

"No doubt. Saw you snagged a third in the event. Nice one, dude. And what's this I hear about you wrestling a Great White?"

"The tales keep getting taller," the guy with a blond buzzed-cut said.

"You're a fucking legend."

"Don't feed his over-inflated ego. They were seals."

"Seals with fins," Shane scoffed.

The guys shared a laugh and Shane put his hand on the small of my back, bringing me into their circle.

"Remy. This is Travis. He can't be trusted." He jerked his thumb at the guy with a buzzed-cut and then to the other one. "And his brother Ryan. Don't trust him either."

"Such an ass," Travis said.

Shane slung an arm around my shoulders like he was marking his territory. "Stick with me."

"Better the serial killer you know?"

Shane winked. "Exactly."

"How did you two meet?" Travis asked. "Did you go out last night?"

"You're such a jealous lover. And no, I found Remy on the side of the road hitchhiking. The rest is history."

Ryan bobbed his head like this was nothing out of the ordinary for Shane, like he picked up strays every day. "Wouldn't surprise me."

"You believed the Great White story too," Travis said.

Ryan shrugged. "You never know. Shit happens in Shane's world."

"A case of hero-worship," Travis said. "You're shameless."

Shane tsked and shook his head. "There he goes, getting jealous again."

"I know, right?" Ryan said as we descended the wooden staircase to the beach.

Shane and Travis were discussing the direction of the wind and the size of the swells in surfer lingo. Hollows and tubes. Left and right breaking.

When we reached the bottom of the staircase, I toed off my Chucks and leaned down to pick them up.

"Nice to meet you," I told the guys, giving them a little wave. They echoed my words and I pushed through the soft sand, striking out on my own. When I reached a spot that felt just right, not too close to the staircase or the empty lifeguard stand, I dropped my board, backpack, and shoes and sat cross-legged, collecting the soft sand in my hands and letting it sift through my fingers.

Shane backtracked and stopped in front of me. He had thin white scars on his shins, I noticed before I lifted my eyes to his. "How long are you sticking around?"

"Not sure."

"If you're still here when I'm done surfing, I'll give you a lift."

"Thanks."

He turned to leave then doubled back again as if he'd forgotten something. "Do you want to catch the fireworks tonight?"

Oh my God. He was asking me out. I shouldn't say yes. I really shouldn't. "Yeah. Sounds good."

Shane crouched in front of me. "Cool. Give me your phone." I dug through my backpack and came out with my cell phone. A pre-paid flip phone from Walmart. In other words, a burner phone.

"Are you a drug dealer?" Shane joked when I handed it to him.

"That's my side gig. Kind of like your serial killer gig."

He chuckled as he entered his information and pressed the call button, so we had each other's numbers. Cutting the call, he handed my phone back to me with a smile. And I died just a little.

"Catch you later, Remy," he called over his shoulder as he headed toward the water.

I watched him paddle out to where Ryan and Travis were. He looked at home out there, straddling his surfboard. Relaxed, like he was in his element.

When he caught his first wave, I couldn't tear my eyes away from him. He zigzagged across the top of the wave, doing cutbacks, his body bent low over the board and riding the wave for all it was worth. He caught air and did a one-eighty—his board stayed underneath him like it was an extension of his body.

I was all jazzed up just from watching him. Like a vicarious adrenaline rush.

Zooming in with my camera, I snapped photos of him as he rode wave after wave. Stealing pieces of his soul without him knowing it. It was so beautiful. Poetry in motion. Zipping across the waves with so much speed, grace, and flexibility I was in awe. I watched the other two surfers for a comparison. There was none. Travis was good, Ryan was just okay. But they were nothing like this guy. I knew he was special. I knew he was good. Like, really good.

For one, he was a bigger risk-taker than the other two. Shane left it all out there, not holding anything back, yet he made it look effortless. I noticed that other surfers gave him the right of way. Dropping back when he was charging a wave, like a show of respect, a nod to the fact that he was the superior surfer.

I didn't know how long I sat on the beach. Long enough for the sun to get stronger, the heat more intense. For the surfers to multiply and the beach to get crowded. The ocean color changed, the sunlight making the water sparkle like thousands of blue and green diamonds.

I could watch them surfing all day long. Not them. *Him.*

My stomach growled, reminding me that I hadn't eaten since last night. Reluctantly, I left my spot on the beach and trudged across the sand. When I reached the top of the stairs, I turned around for one more look. From this distance, I couldn't be sure, but I thought he was watching me leave.

Did I really have a date tonight?

"Where've you been?" Dylan licked the peanut butter off the steak knife he had used to make his sandwich. His dark hair stuck up all over, an imprint from the nubby sofa fabric on his left cheek.

"I went to the beach. It's amazing. You're going to love it."

He threw the knife into the sink, the metal blade clattering against the stainless steel and leaned against the speckled brown countertop.

"You went without me?" He sounded hurt and angry, his usual tone these days. I missed the Dylan who used to laugh so hard tears sprang to his eyes. But that boy was long gone.

"The ocean is still there. It's not going anywhere."

He scowled and took a bite of his sandwich. I cleaned off the knife he used and made my own sandwich, leaning against the counter next to Dylan to eat it. Except for the beige walls, everything was brown—the cupboards, the linoleum floor, the countertops, the refrigerator. It smelled like bleach and the lemony scent of cleaning products. This apartment was cleaner and nicer than the dumps we usually lived in. It was also more expensive. That worried me.

"What's it like?" he asked, finishing off the last bite of his sandwich. In a better mood now that he had some food in him. He chugged milk straight from the carton and wiped his mouth with the back of his hand.

"It's beautiful. Even better than the photos."

His dark brows raised in surprise. Usually, I felt the opposite. Photos were better than real life. But this time the photos didn't do the ocean justice. Photos have limitations. They couldn't capture the sound of the surf. The scent of the sea air. The power and the vastness of the ocean.

"Wanna go check it out?"

He nodded and graced me with a rare smile. His smiles were heartbreakingly beautiful, but the smile slipped off his face so quickly that I was left wondering if I had imagined it.

I shoulder-bumped him. "What's wrong?" I asked because I cared. I cared so fucking much. We used to be so attuned to each other, almost reading each other's thoughts. There was a time that we could communicate without words. Our secret twin language, Mom called it. But lately, he'd been slipping away from me. Putting up an invisible barrier. And it killed me that we didn't talk like we used to.

He pushed off from the counter and faced me, his arms crossed over his bare chest. He'd gotten bigger over the past few months—leaner and meaner, with broader shoulders, and defined muscles.

"I don't want to leave." His gray-blue gaze met mine. Dylan had storms in his eyes, like there was something always brewing just beneath the surface. "I'm staying here. I'm not moving again."

He clenched his jaw and narrowed his eyes on me as if daring me to dispute his words or point out that it was never up to us. I nodded in agreement like it was within our power to make that kind of decision. "Sure."

"I mean it," he gritted out, his voice low and angry, his body coiled with tension as if I'd just told him he couldn't.

"I know you mean it. I'm on your team." I held his gaze, reminding him that we were in this together. His shoulders relaxed, and he rubbed his hand over his face.

For all that we've been through and for all the times that Dylan could be moody and broody and shut me out, our bond was still strong. Sometimes, I needed to remind myself of that. If we didn't have each other, where would that leave us?

"Let's get out of here."

I finished my sandwich and followed Dylan into the living room. He pulled on a ratty gray T-shirt with a ripped collar and stuffed his feet into his high-tops. Skateboard under his arm, he strode to the door, desperate to get out of this apartment and see his new town. The one he'd chosen by marking the map with a purple Sharpie while we were driving, headed west from Little Rock.

"You wanna go clear across the country?" Mom had asked, laughing. She had been in a good mood. She was always happy when we were on the move. You could always tell when she was getting ready to leave. Mom got restless, complaining about the people or her bartending job or the nosy neighbors. She'd get that glimmer in her eye, like she was imagining far-off places where everything that glittered was gold. She used to have the power to make us believe that the next town would be like Disney World, only better. We'd stopped believing her around the same time we stopped believing in Santa Claus. But she acted like she didn't notice our lack of enthusiasm. Maybe she didn't.

Dylan had pointed to the map. "I circled the name of the town. That means we have to go there. Those are the rules."

Mom raised her brows. "Since when do you play by the rules?"

"Since today." He crossed his arms over his chest and set his jaw, waiting for Mom to agree.

"Well, okay then. Costa del Rey here we come. We'll just make a pit stop in Vegas."

I groaned but Dylan was too excited to let it dampen his spirits. We spent four nights in Vegas. Dylan and I watched TV in the motel room and ate food from the vending machines. He scored a six-pack of PBR and a dime bag of weed from a group of guys throwing a bachelor party and came back to our room drunk and glassy-eyed. We didn't see Mom until the fifth day when she turned up at six in the morning, with raccoon eyes, in a skin-tight black sequined dress and six-inch heels.

"Look who's a big winner." She pulled a wad of hundreds out of her bra and fanned them under our noses. "We're gonna celebrate in style. But first we need to get outta here."

I didn't ask why. I didn't want to know. I suspected that she hadn't won the cash at the craps table or slot machines. But I didn't question it and neither did Dylan. When it came to Mom, there were some things we'd rather not hear about. We saw enough to draw our own conclusions. So, we hit the road, laying rubber as she peeled out of the parking lot of the shitty roadside Vegas motel, the manager running after us, waving his arms in the air and shouting obscenities. Mom left him in her dust without a backward glance. She blasted the music and sang along to rock ballads and heavy metal.

We took the scenic route to California. She drove us through the desert, on roads where we didn't see another car for miles. Skinny-dipped in a lake under the light of a moon while me and Dylan sat with our backs leaning against the pine trees and watched from the corner of our eye to make sure she didn't drown. She splurged on surf and turf for three and a bottle of champagne for one before I pocketed the rest of the cash. If I hadn't, she would have blown six months of rent money on a shopping spree for random shit we didn't need that would inevitably end up at the pawn shop.

Before Dylan and I went to the beach, I checked on Mom. She was still asleep, the blinds drawn, the room plunged in darkness. The scent of stale cigarette smoke hung in the air. She stirred, and cracked her eyes open, trying to bring me into focus.

"Baby?" she croaked, her voice hoarse like she hadn't used it in a while. "You okay?"

"Yeah, Mom. I'm good. Dylan and I are going to the beach. Did you need anything?"

She mumbled something I didn't catch and closed her eyes again, curling onto her side. I watched her sleeping for a few moments. Dylan and I had inherited her black hair, high cheekbones and skin tone. Tawny, like we always had the start of a suntan even when we didn't. She once told us that she was part Cherokee, but Mom said a lot of things and they weren't always true. Dylan and I didn't know who our father was, or anything about her life before she had us. Whenever we had asked, Mom always said it wasn't important, that kids just needed a mom.

Sometimes it felt like we didn't even have that.

2

Remy

Shane was wearing a white T-shirt that said: Live Fast, Die Shredding, frayed cargo pants with the hems rolled up and Vans. He was straddling a shiny black and chrome motorcycle —a Triumph, according to the logo—and smiled at me as I walked toward him. Like I was someone special and he was happy to see me.

"Are you okay to ride on the back of a bike or would you prefer to go in the Jeep?"

"The bike," I said without hesitation and was rewarded with a smile.

"Come here, Firefly." He crooked his finger and held up the helmet in his hand.

"Firefly?"

"You remind me of the blue ghost fireflies."

"Are they here? In California?" I looked around as if they might light up the sky.

"Nope." He grinned.

Well, okay then. I stepped closer and he put the helmet on

my head, securing the strap under my chin. How many other girls had worn this helmet? How many other girls had ridden on the back of his motorcycle?

"You ever ride on the back of a bike before?" he asked, putting on his own helmet.

"Nope."

"Another first. Wish I could have them all."

I wish he could, too, but it was too late for that.

"Do you want to go somewhere with me?" he asked.

"I thought we were going to the fireworks?"

"We are. They're down at the pier but it gets crowded. I know a better place. Off the beaten track. But only if you're up for it."

"Since I don't know where you're taking me, how do I answer that?"

"Do you trust me?"

I smiled. "No."

"A leap of faith?"

If he asked me to jump off a bridge with him, I'd be right beside him. "My second one today."

"Brave girl." He gave me a mischievous grin. "Climb on and put your feet here." He pointed to the chrome foot pegs. "I'll drive safely."

I climbed on behind him and he reached back and pulled my arms around his waist. "Hang on tight."

He didn't have to tell me twice. I never wanted to let go. The engine rumbled beneath me, my body humming from the vibrations and then we were off.

"Where are we going?" I asked as he led me across the street—we'd parked in a lot next to a library about twenty minutes from Costa del Rey—and up a winding tree-lined drive to a fancy hotel. It was pink sandstone and looked like something from the 1920s. "This is what you call off the beaten track?"

He laughed and took my hand in his. It was warm and strong and callused, probably from surfing.

"Just pretend you own the place," he said as we waltzed right through the front doors and across the marble lobby dotted with potted palms and orange trees. I was wearing a skull print tank top with ripped jeans and my beat-up Chucks, finger-combing my wind-blown mane. Nobody would ever believe that I belonged here or that I'd even be a guest at a hotel like this. It dripped with money, the guests milling around wore designer clothes and the scent of expensive perfume filled the air.

I glanced at Shane in his surfer-dude clothes, his expression chilled, yet he exuded confidence.

"Good evening," he said as we breezed past a man in a hotel uniform.

My palms were starting to sweat. Shane was unflustered, greeting hotel employees with a good evening and a charming smile that stopped the words from coming out of their mouths.

We exited through a set of French doors onto a stone patio set up with rows of Adirondack chairs occupied by guests waiting for the fireworks display, sipping cocktails and champagne.

"Oh wow," I breathed, as we weaved through the people sitting on the lawn in front of the hotel, with a prime view of the ocean. It was the view that made my heart beat faster. Shane guided me along a coastal trail that snaked its way along the bluff and I imagined myself falling over the side. Down, down, down, I'd go, my body crashing on the rocks below. Did everyone do that—imagine themselves falling off a cliff or down the stairs?

We were alone out here, and it seemed strange that nobody from the hotel would venture out of their comfort zone and strike out on their own. But people liked being catered to, they liked their luxuries and fancy surroundings. Shane and I found a spot on a patch of scrubby grass with an unobstructed view of the ocean and the twinkling lights of the towns along the coast.

"From here, we'll get to see fireworks from two different towns. The Costa del Rey fireworks are that way," Shane said, pointing left. No sooner were the words out of his mouth when a burst of red, white and blue lit up the sky.

"I should have brought cocktails and canapes," he joked.

"We could have enjoyed them before you tossed me over the cliff and buried my body."

"But first, I wanted to give you this." He swept his hand across the night sky as if the view and the ocean and the fireworks exploding in the distance were all his to give me.

"You have a Mona Lisa smile," he said a few minutes later.

I turned my head to look at him. "What does that mean?"

"Mysterious. Hard-won. It makes me want to do just about anything to see your smile."

"I get the feeling you don't usually have to work that hard."

"I get the feeling you're worth it."

I wanted to tell him that was the nicest thing anyone had ever said to me. Instead, I just smiled. "Tell me a secret."

"I've wanted to kiss you since the minute I saw you."

"That's not a secret."

His lips curved into a smile. "No?"

"No. So obvious." This didn't feel like my real life. Girls like me didn't meet guys like him. This kind of thing—this night, being with him—it was fleeting. I knew it couldn't last, so I decided to make the most of it.

"Mmm." He leaned in and wrapped his hand around the back of my neck, pulling me closer. I closed my eyes as his lips touched mine and everything around us went quiet. Like that moment of calm just before thunder strikes and lightning splits the sky in two. His tongue swept inside my mouth, gentle but demanding, and my fingers gripped his hair, tugging him closer. He pushed me onto my back, and we made out on the scrubby grass on a bluff above the sea, like we were the only two people in the world. I could feel every inch of his toned muscles and the scruff on his jaw rubbing against my skin. I breathed him in... the sea and sunshine and limes and something that was just him... masculine, intoxicating. I was dizzy from his scent. Even though his mouth was on mine, our tongues tangling, I wanted more. And more. And more.

Boom.

My veins throbbed, and my heart exploded.

Neither of us cared that we were missing the fireworks display.

I wasn't sure how we'd gone from kissing to laughing so hard my stomach hurt to baring the secrets of our souls, but we had. "Tell me something you've never told anyone," I said. "Something big and important."

He pushed his tongue through his teeth, contemplating how much he was willing to tell me. The fireworks had ended a long time ago, explosive finales up and down the beach, a backdrop for our kisses and conversation. Shane told me he was a surf bum. I told him I was an amateur photographer. Guys always thought I was older, and I knew he did too. He thought I was in college and I didn't set him straight. A white lie that I'd worry about later. I told myself that I just wanted one night. One night of magic. Because that was what it felt like, being with Shane. Magic. He had this capacity for joy that I envied, and he made life sound like one big adventure. I wanted to go along for the ride.

When he learned the truth, I knew he would view me differently. I wasn't ready for the night to end. I never would be.

I loved his face and his tousled, messy hair, his easy smiles and the sound of his voice—low and husky and when he laughed, it came from somewhere deep inside him.

We were lying on our backs now, looking at the stars, my hand clasped in his. It was odd, this feeling that I'd known him forever, and I was somewhere I belonged.

"When I was nine, my mom was killed by a hit and run driver," he said. I listened without interrupting because he was telling me something important. "We were cycling. On our way home from school. It was an ordinary October day. Blue skies. No forewarning that this was the day my life was about to change. A white van came out of nowhere. Ran the stop sign and didn't slow down. It was all so surreal and at first, I didn't even realize she'd been hit."

"Even now, twelve years later, I'll see a white van and get this sick feeling in my stomach. I try to get a visual of the driver... Are you the one? Are you the fucker who killed my mother and didn't have the decency to stop and help? It kills me that somewhere out there, that driver is eating or sleeping or watching a movie... just going on with their lives."

I squeezed his hand and rolled onto my side, propping my head on my hand. I traced the curves of his gorgeous face with my fingertip. So boldly. As if he was mine and I was free to do this. I wanted to find the right words to make him feel better, to make it okay, but for something like this there were no words. "People suck."

"Not all people." He turned his head to look at me. "Tell me something about you, Remy."

I'd just been telling him all about me, but I'd left out most of the crappy stuff. There was so much shit in my crazy life. I flopped onto my back and stared at the dark sky, trying to think of what I could tell him. Something as big and important as what he'd shared with me.

"I..." I cleared my throat. I've never told this story to anyone.

"When I was twelve, we lived in this shitty apartment in Detroit." Oh God, I couldn't believe I was telling him this. "My mom had a boyfriend. His name was Russell." He was a drug dealer, but I didn't mention that. Bad enough I was spilling my guts to Shane. "He used to call me pretty girl and he was always watching me, you know?" I shuddered at the memory. "One night... he came into my room and accused me of stealing his cash. He said I'd have to pay for that."

"What happened?" he asked quietly. I could feel the tension in his body.

"He tried to... you know..."

"Rape you?"

"Yeah. But I screamed at the top of my lungs and I bit him." I'd always been scrappy, a hood rat with self-defense my priority. Living with Mom was dangerous. Russell had backhanded me, and I flew against the wall and then he was all over me again, his sour breath on my face, his meaty palms on my skin.

"My brother heard us, and he came after Russell with a baseball bat. He just kept swinging and swinging, beating the shit out of Russell. We ran and hid behind the dumpsters. But the thing is that he was right. We had stolen his money. So yeah, I guess that's, um..." I cleared my throat. "Not a very good first date story. Not that this is a date." I squeezed my eyes shut, wishing I could reel back my words. Or better yet, change my entire history. "I shouldn't have told you that."

I side-eyed Shane who had been quiet for too long. "What are you thinking?" I asked, chipping at the dark polish on my nails.

"I'm coming up with creative ways to kill Russell."

Our crazy night of beautiful kisses and ugly stories, laughter and sweet moments, came to a screeching halt when Shane parked his bike in front of his place and helped me off the back, wrapping his arms around me. We kissed each other dizzy until our lips were raw and swollen. "Come home with me."

I wanted to. More than anything. I was all set to say yes when he pulled back and brushed a piece of hair off my face. "How old are you, Remy?"

I'd already worked out that he was twenty-one. "I'm... older than the date on my birth certificate."

His eyes narrowed, and he took a step back. "What does that mean?"

I couldn't lie to him, not when he'd asked a direct question and not when he was waiting for an honest answer. "I'm sixteen but I feel so much older."

"*Sixteen?*" He gripped the back of his neck and looked up at the sky. His laugh was harsh. "Fuck. You're not even legal."

3

Shane

It had been one week since I last saw Remy, and I'd like to say that I'd forgotten all about her, but that would be a lie. I'd been so pissed off at her for feeding me lies that I didn't even know what to believe about the night we'd watched the fireworks. Was anything she had told me the truth? It didn't matter. This was exactly why I steered clear of committed relationships. I never went around spilling my secrets or confiding my deepest thoughts to total strangers. No, I was the guy who hooked up, moved on, and avoided messy emotions. All my time and energy were devoted to my surfing career. So, I needed to forget about Remy, the lying temptress.

Anyway, I was sitting on my board—I'd brought The Stubby Bastard today—talking shit with Oz. He was a high school friend with zero ambition and no drive. Back in high school, he claimed he wanted to be a pro surfer. Not happening. For one, he was lazy as shit and spent his days playing video games and getting high. Occasionally, he made an appearance at his job. His parents owned an organic juice bar. Everything in SoCal was organic.

Now he had the brilliant idea of becoming a surf blogger. This was his half-assed attempt at an interview. I doubted he'd ever commit it to memory or type it up on his laptop, so I was just blowing hot air. Talking about a day in the life of a pro surfer.

Let's face it, I was living the dream. How many other guys got to travel to the best beaches in the world, chasing after killer waves for a living? The only cloud in my silver lining, if you could call it that, was the pressure to win. Now that I had sponsorships, I couldn't afford to slack off. My most lucrative deal was with HartCore, a local surfing apparel company that I signed a multi-year six-figure contract with. To them, I was a brand. It was all about the bottom line. Surfing had never been about the money for me. But dreams cost money, and I needed sponsorships to be able to live my dream. So, money was a necessary evil.

Other than the occasional stress, life was good. I had four weeks to train for Teahupo'o, considered to be the most dangerous break in the world. The waves were heavy and glassy, breaking over a sharp coral reef. To be honest, I was scared shitless. I'd be stupid not to be. The Tahitian wave was terrifying. A wave could kill you. The coral reef could rip your skin to shreds. The scar on my back was proof of that. Despite the fear, I was stoked. The fear factor amped up the adrenaline rush, and that was what I lived for.

"So, you have a training schedule?" Oz asked. "I thought you just surfed." He scratched his head, baffled by the concept that you had to put the work in if you wanted to be good at something. I didn't just want to be *good*. I wanted to be the best. "What did you do yesterday?"

"I surfed. Indo Boarded my ass off. Did an intense interval session at the gym and finished the day off with hot yoga."

"What would you do if you couldn't surf anymore?" he asked, presumably for this blog post he would never write.

"I'd die." I was serious. Not surfing was inconceivable. Surfing was my life. I *lived* for it. I wanted to still be chasing waves at ninety. I wanted to be world champion. So, sitting around talking shit with Oz wasn't getting me any closer to achieving my dream. I eyed a bump on the horizon. It was going to be a good set, I could tell. "Are you ever going to start this blog?"

He bobbed his head. His long brown hair wasn't even wet, proof that he'd been sitting around, drying in the sun like a lizard. "Yeah, sure. Tomorrow."

Slacker.

I caught the next wave. A long, fast, bowling right. It never got old. The rush you get from a good ride. And that was when I saw Remy. Her wild waves of jet-black hair lifted in the breeze as she walked away.

When she reached the top of the staircase, she turned around and even from a distance, I could see those damn ocean eyes. Aquamarine rimmed by long, black lashes. I had never seen eyes like hers before.

Get her out of your head. She'll only fuck with it.

For the next few hours, I worked on developing my favorite moves—aerials, tailspins, and 360-degree cutbacks. I zoned out everything around me and it was just the waves and me, competing against myself.

After a good day of shredding, my body was all loose and relaxed, my mind at peace. Until I stopped by my dad's surf shop to pick up some wax for my boards.

The bell over the door signaled my entrance and she lifted her head from behind the laptop, her eyes on the door. The fuck? I stared at her then scrubbed my hand over my face as if that would make her disappear. Nope. Still there. Standing right next to my dad. She was wearing a cobalt blue Jimmy's

Surf Shack T-shirt. This was starting to feel like a joke, and the laugh was on me.

"Shane. This is Remy. My new employee."

His new employee. Holy mother of God. My gaze narrowed on her. "What the hell are you doing here?"

"It's nice to see you again too," she said calmly.

"Did you know this was my dad's shop?"

"How could I have known? I didn't even know your last name. I'm not one of your groupies or whatever..." I glared. She planted her hands on her hips and exhaled loudly like *I* was putting *her* out. "I needed a job. And I looked everywhere. Nobody was willing to give me a shot..."

"Why did *you* give her a shot?" I asked my dad.

He gave me an amused look, enjoying my little exchange with Remy. My dad had a sick sense of humor. "I had an ulterior motive. Hiring Remy will benefit you."

"I doubt that," I muttered.

He set a stack of photos on the counter. "She's going to work on your videos too. We're shit at it."

Grudgingly, I flipped through the photos. They were good. Better than good. And they were all of me. Which was... flattering? Weird? Fuck if I knew. "So, you're not a groupie? Just a stalker?"

She rolled her eyes. "Don't flatter yourself. I'm not stalking you."

"Remy wants to learn how to surf and I volunteered your teaching skills," my dad said, barely holding back his laughter.

I glared at him. "Not happening."

He was chuckling as he went to assist a customer with a wetsuit. Remy came around from behind the counter and I tried not to notice her mile-long legs in those tiny shorts, but I was all too fucking human, so I noticed, and I committed the sway of her hips and the shape of her ass to memory.

"I taught myself to skateboard," Remy said, refolding a stack of T-shirts that had been rifled through. "I can teach myself to surf."

"It's not the same. You can't just—"

"I wasn't asking for your opinion."

"I wasn't offering to teach you to surf."

"But you did offer... a week ago." She turned to face me, pinning me with her eyes. A person could drown in those eyes. "I'm still the same person."

"You lied to me."

"I didn't lie."

"You misled me."

"And yet I was more honest with you than I've ever been with anyone."

It was the same for me. I'd never told anyone all the things I'd confided in her and that pissed me off. "You should have said something."

You should have asked sooner, dumb shit.

"Maybe I just wanted..." She bit her bottom lip. Kissable lips—bee-stung, naturally pink-tinted, and pillow-soft, if you must know. I'd forgotten how beautiful she was. No, that was a goddamn lie. I remembered. She didn't have the kind of beauty that snuck up on you. No, it was like a sucker punch to the gut. Boom. One punch and it knocks the air out of your lungs. "Never mind."

I strode out of the shop without saying goodbye to my dad and without the fucking board wax, the original purpose of my visit.

4

Shane

"WHAT'S UP?" I ASKED, PULLING DOWN THE GARAGE DOOR. Tucking my cell between my ear and shoulder, I locked the door to keep my prized possessions safe—thirty surfboards and my Triumph Bonneville.

"Ryan said he saw you carrying rocks this morning," Trav said. "What was all that about?"

"Just getting my rocks off. Are you plying me for my training secrets?"

"Friends share."

"It was my dad's idea," I said, watching a car pull into the parking lot across the street. The motion detectors kicked in, triggering a fluorescent light that illuminated the drunk woman stumbling out of the car. "To help deal with the fear factor so I don't lose my shit if I wipe out in a heavy wave."

"Share Jimmy's infinite wisdom."

"It's going to cost you."

"You can have my first-born."

"You're cold, Ice Man. It's simple, really," I said, distracted by the scene across the street. If I hadn't known this was Remy's mother, I wouldn't pay any attention. But I had seen her coming out of their apartment a few days ago. The pitfalls of living across the street from the girl you were trying to forget. The same girl your dad, in his 'infinite wisdom' had hired to work in his shop. "Find a rock that weighs you down and keeps you underwater, so you can walk the ocean bottom. Stay under as long as you can."

"Nice one," he murmured, and I was certain Travis would be out there tomorrow morning walking the ocean bottom. He was my best friend, but he was also my competitor. Sometimes it was a strange dynamic.

"Hey, I'll catch you later." I cut the call and pocketed my phone.

A lit cigarette dangled from the woman's hand, her feet unsteady in fuck-me stilettos, her skirt so short it barely covered her ass. The man walking up the stairs behind her slapped her on the ass, eliciting another laugh from the woman. "You're a naughty boy."

He growled. "You're about to see just how naughty. You like it dirty, Rae?"

"The dirtier the better, baby." She tossed her lit cigarette over the railing, unconcerned about the potential fire hazard.

The apartment door swung open, and Remy stood in the doorway.

This is none of your damn business. Just walk away. But I didn't. I stayed, and I watched from across the street, in case she needed my help.

"You need to leave," Remy said firmly, standing her ground, her arms crossed over her chest.

"And who are you, doll face? You gonna join the fun?"

"Party's over. Like I said, you need to go."

"I don't need my own daughter telling me what I can and

cannot do." I detected the hint of a Southern accent in her mother's voice.

"You got a kid, Rae? You never said nothing about no kid. How old are you?"

"Sixteen. Now hit the road." Remy was tough, but her voice quavered, giving her away. I saw her vulnerability in the way she covered her chest with her crossed arms. And I thought about her Russell story. She wouldn't have made that up. It made me nauseous to think that some asshole had messed with her.

"Like he wants a scrawny kid, Remy. Get over yourself. He wants me. Don't ya, baby? You know I can make you feel good."

"I'm out of here. You never said nothing about a kid." He turned tail and left, pushing Remy's mom away when she tried to grab hold of him.

"Remy... you're just an old spoilsport." Her mom pouted, her voice whiny like a little kid's. "Why are you ruining my fun?"

"Mom, just come inside. Get some sleep." She grabbed her mom's arm and tried to drag her into their apartment, but her mom pushed her away, darting out of her reach and stumbling back against the railing.

I watched the man leaving, keeping my eyes on him until he got into his car and pulled out of the lot. And that should have been the end of it. He was gone, and she didn't have to worry about him anymore. I turned to go.

From across the street, I heard the sound of a scuffle, her mother's voice loud and shrill.

"Shh, Mom. You'll wake up the whole neighborhood."

"I don't fucking care," she shouted. "All I wanted was a night of fun. Is that too much to ask? And now you went and ruined it... you had no right..."

"Mom, get inside. Please," Remy pleaded.

Clearly, she needed help. I crossed the street and climbed

the stairs two at a time, assessing the situation as I neared their front door.

"You okay, Remy?" My gaze moved from her face to the nail marks on her arm.

"We're fine." She tried to grab her mother's arm and get her inside again, but her mom shook her off and turned around to look at me, her eyes raking over me from head to toe. "Well, my, my, my... what do we have here?" she asked, closing the distance between us. She ran her hand down my chest like I was her toy boy. "And who are you?"

Her hand ventured lower, close to my crotch and I moved it away, keeping a strong grip on her wrist and capturing the other one as she reached out to touch me. She smelled like cigarettes, gin, and cheap perfume.

"A neighbor. Just checking up to make sure Remy is okay."

"How... sweet of you. Are you going to tie me down?" She winked. "I bet you like it rough, don't ya, baby?"

Fuck me. I released her hands and took a few steps back, my eyes on Remy. She wouldn't look at me, wouldn't meet my eyes. Embarrassed by her mother's words. Her cheeks were flushed but her shoulders were squared and back straight, chin held high. She was too proud to let me see how much this affected her. Remy's mom lit another cigarette and took a deep drag. She blew the smoke into my face and laughed. Her red lipstick was smeared, the thick kohl eyeliner smudged, and one of her false eyelashes had come unglued. She looked like a broken doll.

"How about you get inside and sleep this off?" I said.

"How about you tuck me in, sugar?" She pushed out her tits, running her hands over her body as if it was an invitation for me to do the same. No doubt about it. Remy was her daughter. She had the same high cheekbones and skin tone and I could see that, at one time, her mother had been beautiful. But she had been around the block more than a few times and her beauty had been ravaged by hard living.

"This is how it's going to work. I'm going to help you into the apartment and make sure you get into bed. Your daughter doesn't need this kind of shit in her life. So, you're going to do as you're told. Get inside." My voice was firm, brooking no room for argument.

She rolled her eyes and staggered to the door that Remy held wide open for her. I followed, uninvited. Remy tried to shut the door, blocking me out, but I shouldered my way inside. No way was I leaving her to deal with this on her own.

"I've got this, Shane," Remy said through gritted teeth.

I ignored her. Her mother kicked off her shoes as she crossed the living room floor and took another drag of her cigarette, the smoke hanging over her head in the stuffy room. Their apartment was depressing as fuck, the only furniture a threadbare sofa and a battered coffee table littered with pizza boxes, PBR cans, and overflowing ashtrays.

"Mom, you need to put out the cigarette," Remy said as her mom flicked ash on the floor. She wrestled the cigarette out of her mom's hand and put it out in an ashtray filled with lipstick-stained butts.

Her mom spun around and slapped Remy's face, the sound ringing out in the quiet apartment. "I'm the mother, you little brat."

I grabbed her arms and held them behind her back. "Don't you ever lay a hand on her again," I gritted out.

Her shoulders sagged, defenses down, and she started crying. Like everything she did, her sobs were loud and melodramatic. She deserved an Oscar for this performance. I released my hold and she lurched forward, cradling Remy's face in her hands. The woman had the art of manipulation down to a science. "I'm sorry, baby." She sniffled. "You know I didn't mean it. I love you."

"I love you too, Mom." Remy pulled her mom into a hug and stroked her hair, trying to calm her down.

"You need to go," Remy said, her gaze meeting mine over her mother's shoulder.

"I'm not leaving you to deal with this alone."

"She's my mother." Her words were quiet but powerful. Despite everything, Remy loved this woman. She felt the need to protect her, rather than the other way around. Remy's eyes pleaded for me to go. To accept that I wasn't wanted or needed here.

"You'll be okay?" Stupid question. This was so far from okay I didn't have a word for it.

"We'll be fine."

I ran a hand through my hair, debating. Not wanting to leave her to deal with this on her own but knowing that she didn't want me to witness her mother's behavior.

"Go," Remy said, her voice strong and clear.

Reluctantly, I walked out of her apartment and closed the door behind me, leaving her to deal with her mother on her own. What the fuck had just happened? I waited on the other side of the apartment door, listening, but it was quiet inside. Remy hadn't looked scared. Which made me think it wasn't the first time she's had to deal with something like this.

If she needed my help, she had my number. She could text or call if things got out of hand with her mother. Although I doubted she would ask for my help.

I lurked outside her door for another five minutes before I turned to go and ran into a guy who vaguely resembled Remy. "Why are you standing outside our door?" he asked, immediately on the defensive.

"Just trying to help."

His eyes narrowed with distrust. "Trying to help," he repeated, looking from me to the closed door then back at me. "We don't need your help."

With that, he shoved past me, went into the apartment and slammed the door shut.

It had been an hour since I'd seen Remy and I was still thinking about her. Worrying about her. Hoping she was okay. I was out on the back deck, lying in my hammock, looking at the stars and thinking about *her*.

Sliding my cell out of my pocket, I typed out a text and deleted it. Typed and deleted. Until finally, I hit send.

Shane: If you want to learn how to surf, I'll teach you. I've got a board you can use.

A few minutes later, I followed it up with another text.

Shane: Meet me outside tomorrow morning at 7.
Firefly: Why are you offering to do this?
Shane: Do you want to learn how to surf?
Firefly: I can figure it out on my own.
Shane: Meet me at 7.

At seven-thirty in the morning, there was still no sign of Remy. I texted her and got no response. So, I went surfing without her. And I should have left it at that. But later that afternoon, under the guise of visiting my old man, I drove to the surf shop with two boards on my roof rack. Just in case.

My dad was standing outside the shop, talking to the guy I'd seen outside Remy's apartment last night. Her brother if I had to guess. The first thought that popped into my head was that something had happened to Remy. The guy strode away, and I watched him leaving before approaching my dad.

"Is Remy okay?"

His brows raised. "Is that why you stopped by? To check on

Remy?"

I rubbed the back of my neck. "Nah. I came to see you."

"Uh huh. So, you don't care where she is or what she's doing."

"Nope."

He chuckled. "Okay."

With that, he went back inside the shop. I exhaled loudly and followed him inside. "Where is she?"

"Surfing."

"She doesn't know how to surf."

"She and her brother rented boards. Said they'd give it a try. She watched some videos on YouTube."

He couldn't be serious. "Videos," I scoffed, following him inside the shop. "She can't learn how to surf by watching videos. And you just let her go out there with no lessons? Nothing? Is she alone out there?"

"There are lifeguards on the beach."

I speared my hand through my hair. "I offered to teach her."

"She mentioned that."

"And did she say why she stood me up this morning?"

This was an all-time low. I was pumping my dad for information about a sixteen-year-old girl who had become an obsession. When it came to girls, I never had to chase them. On tour, bikini-clad girls trailed after the surfers. They were mine for the choosing. Yet here I was, hung up on a high school girl. This couldn't be good.

My dad studied my face. I looked so much like the younger version of him it was ridiculous. "Nope, she didn't say," he said, his mouth twitching with amusement.

I had no idea what he found so funny and I didn't hang around long enough to find out. Five minutes later, I was down at the beach, my board under my arm. When I was a grom, I used to surf at this break, but not anymore. It got too crowded and rarely got any hollows.

Today, there were some decent, gentle-breaking waves, perfect for a beginner. I spotted her out there, surrounded by groms. She was alone, isolated from the pack. I watched her from the shore for a while without her knowing it. She was straddling her board, all that caramel skin on display.

As if sensing she was being watched, she turned her head and her eyes met mine. There was no way to pretend I had just happened to be here, so I paddled out to where she was. I could see her pebbled nipples through the thin fabric of her bikini top and my dick stirred to life in my surf shorts.

Down. Stay down.

"Checking up on me?"

"How's it going? Have you caught any waves?"

She nodded. "Yeah. It hasn't been pretty. I ate a ton of sand and drank half the sea."

I laughed. "Getting ragdolled is all part of surfing. It's half the fun. Are you having fun?"

She grinned. "I love it. Your dad's a good teacher."

That lying sack of shit. I chuckled and scrubbed my hand over my face. "He taught you, huh?"

"The basics." She laughed. "I felt like an idiot."

"Did he make you paddle and do pop-ups on the sand?"

"Yup. I didn't ask him to teach me," she hastened to add. "Dylan—my brother—and I rented boards after I finished my shift. Your dad said his conscience wouldn't rest until he made sure we'd be okay out here." She side-eyed me. "I guess you both have a conscience."

"Guess so. It's a pain in the ass sometimes."

"Better than not having one at all. Some people don't."

"I know," I said quietly.

"Yeah, I guess you would." She chewed on her bottom lip and stared off into the distance, giving me her profile. "Look, I appreciate you trying to help last night but next time just stay out of it."

I snagged on to the words 'next time.' "Does that kind of thing happen a lot?"

"No," she said firmly without meeting my eye.

She was lying. When her mom had slapped her last night, Remy hadn't been shocked. There were no tears. No hurt look or accusation in her eyes that begged the question of why her mother had done that. She was used to her mother's outbursts and physical abuse.

"I couldn't just stand back and let her hurt you."

"She didn't hurt me. Afterward, she felt bad." She shrugged one shoulder. "She just had too much to drink. No big deal."

No big deal.

That had abuse written all over it, yet Remy was defending her mother's behavior. Justifying it and chalking it up to drinking too much.

I took a deep breath of sea air. The ocean was my home. Surfing was my religion. I felt it deep in my soul. I had wanted to give this to Remy. Offer it up like a gift, as if it was mine to give. That was why I had offered to teach her to surf.

"The next wave has your name on it," I said.

She grinned. "I thought it said Shane."

"You thought wrong. Let's see if those spaghetti arms can paddle for this wave."

"Pfft. I'm stronger than I look." She made a muscle. I laughed. She rolled her eyes. "You probably wouldn't even be able to keep up." That made me laugh harder. She was already gone, paddling hard for the wave. I sat up on my board and watched her.

She caught it a bit late but managed to get to her feet. She was up for all of five seconds, teetering until she lost her balance and came off the board in the white water. But as she paddled back out to me, she had a big smile on her face.

"Did you see that?" Her smile was radiant, her voice jubilant. Well, at least I knew one thing that made her happy.

"I saw it. You'll be catching air in no time. How did it feel?"

"Amazing. Surfing is such a rush."

"Careful. It's highly addictive."

She caught a few more waves, chosen by me, and I tried to explain what to look for when choosing the perfect wave. Remy was a fast learner, and listened to everything I told her, taking it all on board.

Now, she was lying on her stomach on the surfboard, trailing her hand through the water, her chin propped on her other hand. She turned her head, so her cheek was resting on her hand, her gaze on me. The sunlight made her skin glow, her eyes almost translucent. Lulled by the gentle rhythm of the ocean, our boards floating close enough that we could reach out and touch each other, it felt intimate. Even though there were other surfers out here, it felt like we were the only two people in the world.

"I love this," she said softly.

"Surfing?" I dragged my gaze away from her face and sat up on my board, my eyes on the horizon.

"And the ocean. It makes me feel... at peace, you know?"

"Yeah, I do know." There was nowhere else I'd rather be than in the ocean. "I always feel better after I surf, no matter what's going on in my life. Every single time, it works like a charm."

I hoped that would be the case for her. I wasn't sure what was going in her life, except for what I had seen last night and a few things I'd picked up from our conversation the night we hung out together. She'd moved around a lot. Nothing in her life felt permanent. Or reliable. And her mother... I didn't know what to think of that woman.

"I can't wait until it storms."

She let out a contented sigh. Funny girl. But I had always loved the storms too.

5

Remy

MY EYES SNAGGED ON A POSTER OF SHANE IN THE WINDOW OF Jimmy's Surf Shack as I locked up my bike. A few days ago, I'd found the bike at a garage sale for twenty bucks. It was the old-fashioned kind—sky-blue with a saddle seat and no gears. I rode it everywhere, exploring Costa del Rey and getting lost along the way. I rode to the pier, the marina, explored the beaches and parks, the neighborhoods in the canyon with mountain and sea views.

As I passed a mirror above the sunglass display, I did a double-take. My skin was tanned to a nut brown from my morning surf sessions and swimming in the sea every day. But what really caught my attention was that I looked... happy.

Every morning for the past month, I woke up at sunrise and crept out of the apartment before anyone else was awake for a morning surf session with Shane. Mom had gotten a bartending job and didn't get home until two or three in the morning. Knowing her, she'd managed to find the roughest neighborhood and the diviest bar, but she had a job and that was all that mattered. Dylan had gotten a kitchen job as a dishwasher at a seafood restaurant at the marina. Say what you will about the St. Clair's, we were resourceful, our survival instincts strong. At least we weren't dumpster diving for our food in Costa del Rey.

"Get ready," Jimmy said at quarter to five.

I wasn't sure I could have ever been ready for this. A line was already forming outside the door. Jimmy's Surf Shack, in conjunction with HartCore, the local surfwear company that sponsored Shane, was hosting a one-hour signing at the shop today. A free poster of Shane for each of his adoring fans for as long as supplies lasted.

"Are they all girls?" I asked, trying to hide my dismay.

"Looks that way."

I sighed. Shane looked relaxed, with an easy smile, like he did this kind of thing every day. I guess he did. It was part of his job. I spent the next hour seething with jealousy as Shane posed for photos, his arm around willowy blondes, brunettes, redheads, and signed his autograph. Sure, there were a few groms and some giggling tweens, but his fan base mostly consisted of girls in their late teens and early twenties.

I watched him from behind the counter as a girl stuffed a slip of paper into his pocket. How many cell phone numbers had he collected? Would he hook up with any of them? I rang up a woman's purchase of a HartCore wetsuit for her son and handed him the free ballcap with the HartCore logo that came with every purchase made during the signing. The kid grinned at me and put the ballcap on backward over his shaggy blond surfer hair. He was about ten or eleven and someday he'd be a heartbreaker.

"I see you down at the pier surfing sometimes. With Shane Wilder." His eyes lit up when he said Shane's name. "Someday I want to be just like him."

"You want to be a pro surfer?" I asked, smiling at him.

"Yep." His eyes strayed across the shop to Shane. "He's a mad surfer. Like, how does he do those aerials? I've been working on them all summer, but I can hardly catch any air."

"Yeah, he's pretty great. He practices a lot."

He nodded, a serious expression on his face. "How many hours?"

"Um..." I was now the resident expert on Shane Wilders surf training.

"Honey," his mom said, laughing. "Stop badgering the poor girl."

"It's okay." I looked at the boy. "I'd say four to six hours a day in the water and then he does a lot of other training. He says Indo Boarding is really good for surfers."

His eyes widened. "Wow. Okay. That's what I need to do. Well... see ya around."

"See you. Good luck."

He gave me two thumbs-up.

After the boy and his mom left the shop, I looked over at Shane again. He was kind of a big deal, I guess. A god on a stick. He could have any girl he wanted, and I wondered why he had chosen me that day.

Since then, I had been friend-zoned. Which was for the best, really. I didn't want to get hung up on a guy like Shane. On the first night, I had told him far too much and had been too honest. I regretted that now. What had I been thinking? I hadn't. I'd just let it all pour out, this inexplicable need to show him who I really was and see if he still liked me, despite that. Most guys just wanted to skip the talking part and move on to sex. Shane hadn't been like that. He'd asked me questions and listened to my answers like he actually cared about my opinions. But not only had I told him too much, he had seen Mom in action. It wasn't her at her worst but from the outside, I could only imagine how it looked.

6

Shane

"You ready for Teahupo'o?" my dad asked over dinner—grilled salmon, wild rice and salad from the garden. The sun was just setting, and we were sitting on the back patio where we ate most of our meals whenever I stopped by for dinner.

"Guess we'll see when I get there. My training has been going well and I'll have a few days beforehand to study the waves before the heats. I'll just go out there and do my best. Try not to piss myself," I joked.

"Not many people get to say they surfed the fabled Teahupo'o."

"I'm lucky as shit." There was no denying that.

"World's your oyster." He sounded wistful like he did when he was thinking about my mom or his dreams that had died right along with her.

"Do you ever regret giving it up?" Every few years I asked him this question, wondering if his answer would ever change.

"Nope. My heart wasn't in it anymore. Competing is stressful. If you're not there mentally, physically, and emotionally, you've already lost before you even paddle out. But I don't have to tell you that. You handling the stress okay?"

I cracked my neck. "It gets to me sometimes, yeah. I mean, this is a whole other league than the QS. Some of those guys I'm competing against are my heroes. Sometimes the crowds and the travel and the little shit gets to me, but when I get out there, I forget about all that. It's just me... trying to catch the best wave and surf the best I can."

That was my spiel, the same thing I told journalists who interviewed me. I wasn't lying, but I was glossing over a few things, making myself sound more chilled than I was.

He chuckled, detecting the veiled lie. "You're doing good. Find your Zen, exhale the bullshit."

"Did you see that on a bumper sticker?"

"Facebook," he joked.

Sometimes competing brought out the worst in me but I didn't want to talk about that with him. My dad didn't have a temper like I did. He was more relaxed, more easygoing, let things slide off his back. I didn't always know how to do that but was always striving to be a better version of myself.

"So, what's the deal with you and Peony?" I asked, steering the conversation away from me.

My dad snorted and took a pull of his beer. "Her name's Poppy."

"I knew it was a flower."

He shrugged one shoulder. "We're keeping it casual."

I read between the lines. *She's not your mother.* It would last three months, tops. His longest relationship since my mom was six months. Which had prompted me to move out of the house at nineteen. Our three-bedroom bungalow was close quarters, and we liked our own space.

My dad and I hung out on the back deck for a while, chilling out and talking about life and surfing. After a day of shredding, my body was loose, my skin tingling from the sun I caught, and I was getting drowsy. Another good day. That was how I measured my life. When the good outweighed the bad, I was winning.

When I got home, I lay awake in bed, thinking about my flight to Tahiti tomorrow, and one of the most challenging contests of my career so far.

My cell beeped, and I grabbed it from the bedside table, checking the screen.

Firefly: They'll be able to see me from Mars now
Shane: That's the idea, Firefly
Firefly: You didn't have to do that. You shouldn't have.
Shane: My conscience...
Firefly: It's loud
Shane: Keeps me up nights

Why had she only just noticed the lights and reflectors I'd attached to her bike? I sat up in bed, my back against the headboard.

Shane: You're not out riding now, are you?

I waited for a response but got none. Damn that girl. I scrubbed my hand over my face and groaned. It was midnight and Remy was out there alone, riding a bike.

Remy: I'm home now. Night Shane. And good luck.
Shane: Night Remy. And thanks.

A niggling feeling settled in my gut. I stared at the ceiling for a few minutes then I got up and pulled on a pair of gray sweatpants and a T-shirt. The street was dark, and clouds obscured the moon. I used my phone flashlight to guide my way across the street. Her bike wasn't there.

Twenty minutes later, I watched from the staircase of her building as she cycled up the hill and turned into the parking lot.

She hadn't seen me sitting here. I raked both hands through my hair and I waited for her to finish locking up her bike. She stopped short when she saw me, her hand flying to her chest. "Oh God. You scared me."

"The fuck were you doing, Remy?"

She sighed. "Why are you here, Shane?"

"You lied to me." *Again.*

"I didn't want you to lose sleep—"

"Why were you out riding so late?"

"I couldn't sleep."

"Why not?"

She gnawed on her bottom lip and shrugged one shoulder.

"Why couldn't you sleep?" I wrapped my hands around her wrists and tugged her closer, so she was standing between my legs. Then I remembered that she was only sixteen and I was commando in gray sweatpants that left little to the imagination. I released her and scrubbed my hands over my face, stifling a groan.

She sank down onto the step next to me and leaned her shoulder against mine. I inhaled her scent—green apples and summer rain.

"I hate goodbyes, you know? Goodbye is the saddest word in the English language."

"Where's the good in goodbye?"

"Exactly. So, I'll see you soon. And I won't worry about you or think about you at all. You won't even cross my mind."

"Ditto. Will you surf without me?"

"You'll be with me in spirit. Like a drill sergeant barking orders. Paddle harder. Find your center. Blah, blah, blah."

I laughed, and we sat in silence for a while. A comfortable silence. Remy never felt the need to rush in and fill up the empty space. I liked that about her.

"What's it like? Riding the big waves?" she asked moments later.

"It's like... facing your own mortality." I hadn't meant to say that but with Remy, I don't know, I always voiced my innermost thoughts. Told her the things I never told anyone. "It really makes you think about life and death. And I think that's one of the reasons I chase those waves... and maybe it's the same for most surfers. So many people are just surviving, not really living, you know? And riding a big wave makes you feel so alive. It's an incredible experience. I don't know how to describe it."

"Yeah," she said softly. "I know what you mean. There's a big difference between living and surviving."

We contemplated that for a few minutes and then, without saying another word, she stood up and she climbed the stairs to her apartment. It was something I'd come to learn about her. Remy would always try to be the first to leave. She was scared of being left behind.

7

Remy

"Fuck," Dylan muttered when Mom strutted into the kitchen in a skirt that barely covered her ass and a top with a plunging neckline. I stared at the cleavage on display and the red stilettos on her feet. The slash of red lipstick and the fake lashes. Mom looked like a hooker because, let's face it, she was. I poured her coffee into a travel mug and pressed it into her hand.

"Mom, you can't wear that to our school," I told her, watching our fresh start vanish before my eyes. The first two weeks of school had gone okay. No major drama or trouble. That was about to change, I could feel it. Whenever Mom got involved, things went from sugar to shit real fast.

She ignored me and looked at Dylan. "What's his name again?"

"You're not meeting him," Dylan said, jamming his empty cereal bowl in the dishwasher and slamming it shut. "So, it doesn't fucking matter what his name is."

"He's your guidance counselor, baby. He wants to meet me. Of course, it matters. My boy is gifted. Imagine that."

It was true. Dylan was smart, and Costa del Rey had noticed what other schools had overlooked. Kids like us slipped through the cracks all the time. And guys like Dylan—he was bad news wrapped in a pretty package. Stumbling out of the girls' locker room, a cheerleader trailing behind with mussed hair and kiss-bruised lips. Smoking under the football stadium bleachers. In the middle of fights in the parking lot. That was where you could usually find Dylan. But he knew better than to push the limits too far. We couldn't afford to have the school administration nosing into our business.

Before Mom shooed us out the door, I grabbed a coat from her closet. A trench coat. Which would look ridiculous. SoCal weather never seemed to change—warm, desert-dry, with eternal sunshine even on the cloudy days. But if she would agree to wear the coat, it would be an improvement over her current ensemble.

Instead of getting into Mom's beat-up old Honda, Dylan kept going, right past the parking lot, striding up the street to God knows where. We usually rode our bikes to school, so I had no idea where he was going.

"Dylan St. Clair, you get back here right this minute," Mom screamed. Every now and then, at the most inopportune moments, Mom acted like a mother. "I will hunt you down and you *will* get in this car."

My gaze swung across the street. Somehow, I knew, just *knew*, that this display would not go unwitnessed. Why wasn't Shane out surfing already? He was waxing a board inside the garage, and the door was open. He wasn't alone either. Travis was staring at the spectacle that was my mother.

Mom lit a cigarette and sat on the hood of her car. She prodded me with a red-painted fingernail. "Talk to your brother and haul him back here, sugar." She smiled, but the smile wasn't aimed at me. It was for Travis and Shane. Fuck my life. I chased after Dylan, wishing I could just keep running. Shane was a *good* thing, and I didn't want him to keep seeing how messed-up my life was.

"Dylan. Wait up." I grabbed his arm to stop him. He shook me off and lowered his head, rubbing the back of his neck.

"I can't deal with her shit."

"It's going to be okay."

He huffed out a laugh. "Everything will be different here, right?"

"We just have to get through the next two years, Dylan. Then we'll be free to go wherever we want. To do whatever we want."

"Feels like a lifetime." Sixteen and he sounded so weary of life already.

"I know. But we can do this. We're in this together, remember? Don't give up now. Stick it out with me. I can't do this without you." I wasn't only talking about this morning, but he knew that without my having to explain it.

His shoulders sagged under the weight of the promises we'd made each other. He would do anything for me and I would do anything for him.

I cleaned out the garbage in my locker—white trash, so freaking clever—and stuffed it in the dumpster. Welcome to another day at Costa del Rey High.

I grabbed the books I'd need for my morning classes and stuffed them in my backpack, slamming my locker shut.

"Here you go, babes." Sienna pressed a Starbucks drink into my hand.

I tried to force it back into her hand, but she refused to take it. It was the third time she had done it this week and now I felt obligated to reciprocate. I couldn't afford overpriced morning beverages. "You need to stop doing this. I told you—"

"It's Frappuccino. Not my firstborn. Get over it." She flashed me a big white smile. Sienna was one of those effortlessly pretty SoCal girls with perfect blonde beach waves, a golden tan, and cute designer clothes. I'd been to enough schools to recognize the popular crowd within five minutes of stepping foot inside the door. Judging by appearances, Sienna belonged in that clique. Yet she had befriended me on day one.

"I'm in the market for a new best friend," Sienna had said.

"What happened to your old best friend?" I'd been immediately suspicious and skeptical of her motives.

"She met an untimely death."

"Did you bludgeon her with a blunt object?"

"I killed her with my withering glances."

I had laughed, and we'd bonded over our taste in music—90s grunge. And our favorite movies—old-school horror and Alfred Hitchcock.

Six weeks later and she was bringing me Frappuccino, inviting me to hang out at her pool, watch movies at her McMansion, and occasionally she stopped by Jimmy's Surf Shack on Saturdays when I worked. It had been a long time since I'd bothered making a friend at school, so it was nice to have one. What wasn't so great was the crowd Sienna used to hang out with, the kids she grew up with.

My drink flew out of my hand and splattered on the floor. I jumped back, my shoulder slamming into the lockers, and looked down at the puddle at my feet in dismay. *Shit.*

"Oops." Paige held her fingers over her open mouth, her baby blues wide and innocent. "Now look what you've done, skank."

I gritted my teeth and dabbed at the coffee stains on my Pearl Jam T-shirt with the napkins Sienna pressed into my hand. The cold liquid seeped into my Chucks. There was no hope of salvaging them.

"You're the skank," Sienna said.

"Poor Sienna. Still bitter over losing Tristan to me?"

Sienna laughed. "Trust me. He's no prize. In fact, you two are perfect for each other. Speaking of the devil."

"Slumming it, Sienna?" Tristan asked, wrapping his arms around Paige from behind. She leaned back against him with a smug smile, but his dark eyes were on me.

"Au contraire," Sienna said. "I've upgraded."

"Better clean up your mess, dirty girl," Tristan told me with a smirk that seemed to be permanently etched on his stupid face.

I flipped him the bird. He was laughing as he steered Paige down the hallway. She was wearing her little blue and gold cheering outfit, he was in his football jersey. It was the Friday before Homecoming, and it was Spirit Day at Costa del Rey High. Rah rah fucking rah.

As I'd suspected, Mom's school visit had repercussions. Rumor had it that she had made a play for the guidance counselor. That in itself would have been bad enough but what she had done next was the worst possible thing that could have happened. She had shamelessly flirted with Tristan Hart, and he had gone right along with it because he was cruel, and he was calculating. Every school had a Tristan Hart—handsome, rich, thought he was God's gift. Guys like him were dangerous. They used people as playthings, were used to getting whatever they wanted, and had never heard the word no. Unfortunately, I had drawn his attention.

Tristan Hart watched me all the time.

8

Shane

"Kai," I yelled, my voice carried away by the wind.

"What?"

I slowed down, and my mom caught up to me, riding on my left.

"We should call the baby Kai." I held my arms out to my sides, riding without hands. "It means ocean."

She smiled, the dimples in her cheeks making an appearance. "I love it. Hands on the handlebars, Hotshot."

I grinned. "Race you home."

"Stop and look before you cross," she yelled after me.

The white van came out of nowhere, flew right through the stop sign without even slowing down. "Shane!"

I veered sharply to the left and braked hard, flying over the handlebars and landing in someone's front yard. Wheezing, I rolled onto my back and stared up at the puffy clouds in the blue sky, the wind knocked out of me. My heart was pounding so hard I could hear it in my ears.

"Are you okay?"

I blinked up at the woman standing over me. "I'm good."

Her eyes widened, and she covered her mouth with her hands. "I'll call an ambulance. Everything is going to be okay."

My brow furrowed. What was she talking about? "I'm fine." I jumped to my feet just to prove it. But she wasn't looking at me.

"Take me with you," Remy said as I straddled my bike. She had just appeared out of nowhere. That was her though. She moved like a ghost. My blue ghost firefly. Rare and fleeting.

"You don't know where I'm going." Neither did I. I was just going for a ride with no real destination in mind.

"It doesn't matter where you're going. I want to go with you."

A sane man would say no. Before she had turned up in her ripped jeans and hoodie, her hair braided and hanging over one shoulder, being alone was exactly what I'd wanted.

I handed her my spare helmet and revved the engine while she adjusted the chin strap.

When she climbed onto the back and wrapped her arms around me, I closed my eyes briefly. Why did it always feel so right? Without giving myself time to dwell on it or change my mind, I pulled away from the curb. We rode through the dusk, the sky inky blue, the daylight hours getting shorter. It was October, but summer was still lingering, the breeze warm.

And we just kept riding. Zipping up the coast, a blue moon ghosting over the ocean, Firefly's arms wrapped tightly around me. She was a wildcard, this girl, with her ocean eyes and heartbreaking smile. But still, I wanted her. Every broken piece of her.

An hour... or two... who knows how long we'd been riding before I steered us home. Remy followed me up the stairs and into my apartment. I didn't invite her, but I didn't uninvite her either.

She scrunched up her nose when I suggested ordering sushi. "Raw fish?"

"Have you ever eaten it?"

"No."

I grinned. "Another first. We're eating sushi."

"Oh my God," she said, wiping her runny nose with a napkin. "You could have warned me."

"I told you to go easy on the wasabi," I said, laughing as she dabbed her watery eyes. Watching Remy eat sushi for the first time had been hilarious. I'd conducted a blind tasting, feeding her across the island with my chopsticks. After I fed her uni, she spit it into her napkin and drank two glasses of water, declaring that she'd never trust me again.

"Did your mom like sushi?" she asked, leaning her elbows on the countertop and resting her chin in her hands.

"My mom was a vegetarian."

"Tell me more about her."

"She and my dad met when they were fourteen. He asked her to marry him when they were sixteen." I laughed. "They got married right out of high school and had me two years later. We used to travel with my dad when he was on tour. They didn't like to be apart. Not even for a day. When I was seven, they decided that I needed to go to school and not be homeschooled anymore. I was so pissed, but they were adamant. And... I don't know... my mom... she was a lot like the female version of my dad. A hippie chick. Totally cool. Laidback. She was one of those people who made the world a little brighter. A total optimist."

Remy gave me a little smile. "Did she surf?"

"Yeah, she did. After she died, we had a paddle-out. It's like a memorial for surfers. Hundreds of surfers showed up. We scattered her ashes in the ocean. My dad used to say, 'Let's go hang out with Mom.' That was his way of saying we were going for a surf."

"Your dad's great."

"He is." I could still remember how lost he'd been after she had died but he had plastered on a smile for me, trying to hide how much his heart was breaking and the emptiness he could never fill. My parents were soul mates, best friends, and everything in between. Even as a kid, I had known their relationship was different than the ones my friends' parents had.

"Tell me a story, Firefly."

She tapped her chin, thinking. "When I was seven, I found a kitten hiding under the bushes outside our house. We lived in Savannah and we rented the house. It was a nice house, like a farmhouse, with a big front porch and a swing on it. We all had our own rooms and the lady who owned it, she was like a grandmother to us while we lived there. She lived in the house too. Anyway, the kitten was gray and white. So pretty. And her fur was so soft. She looked like she was hungry and lost and looking for a home. So, I took her inside and I begged my mom to let me keep her. She said I could. I was so thrilled. So excited that I had something of my own. But all I ever called her was 'Cat.' I didn't even give her a name. She used to sleep with me at night, curled up in a little ball right above my head." Remy smiled at the memory. "I loved that cat more than anything."

"And whatever happened to Cat?" I asked, knowing this story wouldn't have a happy ending. Remy's stories never did.

"Dylan and I were at school one day and we got called to the principal's office. Mom was waiting for us. She hustled us out of the school and into the car. It was all packed up with our things. She said it was time to move on. She didn't even let us say goodbye to the lady who owned the house. Her name was Dot, short for Dorothy. She used to make us sugar cookies and homemade biscuits with gravy and fried chicken. Dylan and I wanted to stay, but we never got a vote. Anyway, that day... Mom took off and she just kept driving and driving with the music blasting. It was country music and it made me want to cry or punch a wall. I hated it. I still can't listen to country music. And I kept begging her to go back for Cat because if we left her behind, she'd think we didn't love her. Mom said we'd get a new cat when we got to wherever we were going. But cats aren't replaceable, and neither are people." She gave me a sad little smile. "I guess that wasn't such a happy story, after all."

"That's your new goal in life. Create some happy memories."

"I already have," she said softly. "Years from now, my stories will all have happy endings."

If only that were true. In Greek mythology, Remy would be the siren, and I would be the sailor lured by her voice to shipwreck on the rocky coast. Yes, it was that fucking tragic. I had fallen for a girl who was too young for me. A girl who was tragic and beautiful and broken. She fucked with my head, got under my skin, and changed the tempo of my heartbeat. But on that night, the twelfth anniversary of my mother's death, we were blissfully unaware of what fate had in store for us.

9

Remy

A SHADOW BLOCKED THE DECEMBER SUN ON MY FACE AND ARMS caged me in, a hand planted on either side of my head on the brick wall behind me. I opened my eyes to Tristan's—dark brown like his hair. The scent of his shower gel and cologne filled my nostrils, his minty breath skating over my face.

"What are you doing?" I feigned boredom, so he didn't think he had the upper hand. Kurt Cobain's voice filled my ears, the song "Where Did You Sleep Last Night?" playing on high volume.

His dark eyes studied my face intently and he tugged out one of my earbuds. "What's your deal?"

In the pines, in the pines...

"No deal."

He smirked and wrapped a piece of my hair around his fingers, yanking it hard. Tears sprang to my eyes from the unexpected pain. "I bet you like it dirty, don't you? Just like your mama." Tristan pressed the length of his body against mine, pinning me to the wall, his erection pressing against my stomach. "She wanted to get down on her knees and suck my cock. How about you, little lamb? You want some of this?"

"I'm not my mother," I gritted out. I shoved at his shoulders, but the wall of muscle didn't budge. "Get the hell away from me."

His smirk turned into a lazy grin. He dipped his head and sunk his teeth into my earlobe, sucking on it before he released it. "One of these days, I'm going to find out."

"You will never have me." My voice rang with conviction, my gaze on him unwavering. My body, my choice.

"Never say never, little lamb. I'm going to use you up and then I'm going to toss you away like yesterday's trash."

Using all my strength I shoved him away. He staggered back a couple steps, enough to give me some leverage. I kicked him in the shin and stomped down on his foot. Hard. His hand wrapped around my throat and he tipped up my face, so my eyes met his. "You don't want to pick a fight with me."

"Leave me alone and we won't have a problem."

He released me and took a step back, his gaze raking over my body before returning to my face. "Why would I do that when this is so much fun?"

Tristan was laughing as he walked away backward. He shot me a finger gun and then he spun around and swaggered across the near-empty school parking lot to where his friends were waiting for him. Guys like Tristan always traveled in a pack.

I pressed my sweaty palms flat against the wall, using it to hold up my shaky legs. I didn't want to give him the satisfaction of seeing that he had affected me. My heart pounded in my ears. A tendril of fear snaked its way through my body and squeezed the air from my lungs.

What did guys like him see when they looked at me? Did I have slut tattooed on my forehead?

"Nice piece of ass," one of the other guys said, snickering.

Well, that answered my question, didn't it? I was a piece of ass, nothing more.

"She's mine," Tristan growled. "Nobody else gets to touch her."

Mine. I hated that possessiveness. That ownership. His supreme confidence that anything and anyone was his for the taking. I was a person, not an object. My nails dug into the palms of my hands. Tristan Hart would *never* have me. I wasn't his for the taking.

Dylan showed up two seconds after Tristan's BMW peeled out of the parking lot and disappeared from view.

"Where have you been?" I asked, my movements jerky as I yanked my bike out of the rack.

"Had something I needed to take care of."

My gaze swung to him. He swept his tongue over his lip and caught the blood, spitting it onto the grass. If we survived high school, it would be a major achievement. I didn't even bother asking him what had happened.

We both had our own battles to fight. I could handle Tristan Hart on my own.

"I don't really see what the big deal is," Sienna said, adding a dash of cranberry juice to her latest concoction. "There's no minimum age for falling in love."

"Nobody is in love," I lied, spinning around and around on the leather stool until I got dizzy. As if that could shake off all these feelings I had for Shane. It was like being given a taste of your favorite food and then having it snatched away before you ate your fill and being told you could never have it again. That was the price I'd paid for the little white lie about my age. "We're just friends."

"Sure you are." She rolled her eyes and slid a drink across

the polished mahogany bar in front of me. "Try it. It's my Christmas special."

Sienna watched my face as I took a sip. Whoa. The liquid burned my throat and heat pooled in my stomach. "What's in this?"

She waved her hand at the bottles of alcohol. "A little bit of everything."

We were in the library of her mock Tudor. The rooms were cavernous, all dark polished wood, leather furniture, and Oriental rugs, fresh garlands and soaring Christmas trees in every room. A tapestry hung on the wall behind Sienna—fair-haired maidens frolicking with forest creatures. I studied it for a moment as I sipped my lethal cocktail. It looked like it belonged in a medieval castle, not in a SoCal McMansion, a new-build pretending to be something it wasn't.

"Why were you with Tristan?" I asked, the alcohol giving me liquid courage. "Why would you ever fall for an asshole like him?"

She shrugged, her red cashmere sweater slipping off one shoulder. "I thought I was in love. He's one of those guys who will say or do anything it takes to get what he wants."

I'd already figured that out.

"At first, he was really sweet. He used to leave cute notes in my locker and he was really attentive. Like, walking me to class and bringing me little presents or those brownies I love with the fudge icing and walnuts..." She chugged the rest of her drink and coughed, pounding her chest with her fist. Tears leaked from her blue eyes. "Maybe next time I'll go easy on the Cointreau." She tapped her finger against her chin, contemplating this.

"Our parents wanted us to be together. It felt more like a mergers and acquisitions deal."

"What happened?" I asked, feeling like I had a personal stake in this story.

"It was like a switch turned. Right after we started having sex, he started making all these comments. Like, how I had to lay off the brownies because I was getting fat."

My jaw dropped as I stared at the willowy blonde across from me. "Asshole."

"He said a lot of shit. And at first, I fell for it. I started to believe all the stuff he said, you know? Like maybe he was right about me. I was cold and unlovable. My butt was too big..."

It was easier to believe the bad things people said than the good things. I knew that.

"I was watching my parents one day and it hit me. Someday I would be my mother. Botoxed, popping Xanax, and downing bottles of oaky Chardonnay every night because my husband had traded me in for a newer model. It's a badly kept secret in the Woods house." Sienna gave me a big smile. "So, I dumped Tristan's ass."

"And how did he take it?"

"He spread rumors about me. Haven't you heard? I have an STD that I picked up from sleeping with the entire football team of a rival school. Now I'm an untouchable at Costa del Rey High. Fuck him." She held up both middle fingers.

"Fuck him," I said, downing the rest of my drink and slamming the glass on the bar. Even rich girls like Sienna had dysfunctional families and got bullied. I used to believe that people with money didn't have to deal with shit like that but not even they were immune.

"So... tell me more about Shane..."

An hour later, buzzed on Sienna's Christmas specials, I raced through the streets of town under the cover of darkness, the cold air stinging my cheeks and numbing my hands. As I cruised past Tristan's brick colonial lit up like the Fourth of July, I raised my middle finger. "Never," I shouted to the wind. And then I laughed because I was a little bit drunk and brave and defiant.

"That's your dream? To be world champion?" I asked, although it didn't really come as a surprise. I already knew that Shane wanted to be the best.

"That's the dream." He was staring up at the sky as if envisioning it. Clouds covered the moon and stars tonight, so I made star-shaped designs on the night sky with my flashlight then set it on the blacktop. An arc of light illuminated the graffitied wall across from me. *I WAS HERE* in bold black letters, with a skull and crossbones.

Real original, Dylan.

Shane was sitting cate-corner to me and nudged the toe of my Chucks with the toe of his Vans. "How about you? What's your dream?"

I leaned my back against the rough wall, popped a piece of watermelon bubblegum into my mouth, and contemplated his question while I chewed. I was usually too busy trying to survive day-to-day life to give much thought to my future. But I knew what I would do if I could. So, I guess that made it a dream.

"To travel the world and see all the exotic places. And take photos of all the beautiful and ugly and interesting things." I wanted to go to all the beautiful, exotic places he went, but I didn't say that. I lifted the camera from my lap, brought his face into focus, and pressed the shutter. The flash went off, capturing the shot. I grinned. "I've just stolen another piece of your soul."

"Add it to your collection. Pretty soon you'll own my whole soul."

"The photos of you surfing will go into my beautiful collection." I said it without stopping to think how it could have sounded.

"What about Travis and Ryan? They belong in the ugly collection?" he teased.

"I never take pictures of them. Only you." I should have been embarrassed to admit that. But I wasn't. It was true.

Meeting up on the roof had become our thing. I'd text him and tell him I was up here and then I'd wait to see if he joined me. Every time the metal door opened, revealing him on the other side, my heart skipped a beat. Pathetic.

Shane leaned forward and grabbed the camera.

I got onto my knees and lunged for it, but he held it out of reach and batted my hands away. "It's only fair I steal a piece of your soul."

"Since when is life fair?" I settled back on my heels.

"It's not. Smile for me."

I stuck out my tongue. He snapped the photo. I rolled my eyes. He snapped another one. I blew a big bubble that popped in my face. The camera kept clicking, the flash going off until I covered my face with my hands. "Stop. You'll waste all the film."

"Photos of you would never be a waste of film," he said, his voice low and hoarse.

I lowered my hands and stared at him. He licked his bottom lip. I wanted to kiss him. Taste him. Breathe him in. Run my fingers through the waves of his sun-bleached hair. Lick his tanned skin. It was starting to feel like a sickness. A dull ache that never seemed to go away. Wanting him so badly and knowing I couldn't have him was the sweetest torture.

He was still looking at me, our eyes locked and I was holding my breath as I leaned in, my upper body tilting toward him as if I was being pulled by an invisible magnetic force.

The door burst open and Dylan strode across the roof, his eyes darting from me to Shane, narrowing with distrust. Dylan's eyes were a little glassy and a lot bloodshot, the scent of weed clinging to his clothes.

"Are you okay?"

"It's all good," he said, his eyes still on Shane who he hadn't been formally introduced to yet. I got to my feet and stood next to Shane who handed me my camera.

"This is Shane. Shane, Dylan."

Dylan ignored the introduction, rudely dismissing Shane who said it was good to meet him. He jerked his chin at me. "You got your keys?"

I fished them out of my pocket and tossed them to him. Keys in hand, he stalked away like the world had done him wrong. I watched him go before I turned to Shane, tempted to apologize for my brother but deciding against it. If he wanted to act like an asshole, that was his problem.

"I need to pack for Rincon," Shane said, heading for the door. I used to be so good at leaving. Now I always stayed too long. I trailed after him, my flashlight leading the way, and sighed as he held the door open for me. Ducking past him, I jogged down the stairs.

"Merry Christmas, Shane." We had stopped on the second-floor landing, and that moment of intimacy we'd shared on the roof only moments ago had been snatched away.

"You too. Will you be okay?" I hated it that he looked so concerned. This wasn't how I wanted him to look at me.

"I'll be great. It's Christmas. It's magical. My mom always makes it really special." What a load of bullshit. Sometimes she did, sometimes she forgot to buy us presents. I gave him a big smile. He wasn't buying it, I could tell, but he let it go.

He glanced in the direction of my apartment door and I thought he might say more, but all he said was "Catch you later" before he jogged down the stairs. I let myself into the apartment and joined Dylan on the sofa. We stared at the tree we'd put up last week. We decorated it with multi-colored lights, cheap red baubles, and glitter-encrusted reindeer. Dylan had thrown tinsel at the tree from across the room like he was pitching for the Dodgers. It looked like a drunk-ass tree, tilted too far to the left, but if you squinted, it looked okay. Festive. At least we had a tree this year.

"So, what's the deal with you and that surfer?"

That surfer. "We're just friends. He's a good guy." I shoulder-bumped him. "You could try being nicer, asshat."

"Nicer?" He sounded puzzled by the concept. As if he truly didn't know that he'd been rude. Sometimes he acted like such an ass.

"Yeah. Nicer." We were quiet for a few minutes and I was thinking about my conversation with Shane which prompted me to ask Dylan the same question. "What's your dream, Dylan?"

I expected him to ignore the question, so I wasn't really waiting for an answer, just lost in my own thoughts and too lazy to move my ass off the sofa.

"My dream is to make shitloads of money."

I turned my head to look at him. He was still staring at the tree, his face pensive. He smelled like boy sweat and laundry detergent and beer, but I didn't think he was drunk. "So, you want to be rich? That's your dream?"

"You're saying it's not a good one?"

"No. It is. I guess." But I couldn't hide my disappointment that his answer was so unoriginal. "But *how* do you want to get rich? Like, what's your passion? What do you love doing?"

"Getting high. I fucking love getting high."

I sighed loudly. "Whatever. Forget I asked." If he became a drug dealer, I would strangle him with my own two hands. Even though he hid it well and you'd never guess it, Dylan was smart and would have no problem getting into any college he wanted. As long as he didn't blow it.

The front door opened, and I held my breath, waiting to see which version of Mom we'd be getting tonight. Last week I was walking on eggshells because every little thing I said or did had her flying off the handle. The week before that she was Suzy

Homemaker, whipping up homemade meals that didn't come from a can or the freezer. She'd scrubbed, mopped and cleaned every inch of the apartment until the surfaces gleamed and the scent of stale cigarettes was almost eradicated.

Now, she called to us from the kitchen, her voice normal. Not keyed up or flat. Just right. "Who wants hot chocolate?"

Dylan jumped up from the sofa and headed into the kitchen with me trailing behind. "Hey Mom. I'll put these away," Dylan said, nudging her away from the grocery bags she'd set on the counter.

"Thank you, baby." She pulled him into a hug and kissed him on the cheek before holding him at arms-length as if just seeing him for the first time. "Look at you. My handsome boy is all grown up. When did you get so tall?" She laughed, and he shook his head, chuckling. Mom on a good day still had a knack of bringing a smile to Dylan's face. He loved her, protected her, fought for her, and felt like he was supposed to be the man of the family. If Mom noticed that Dylan smelled like beer and weed or that I reeked of Sienna's Christmas cheer, she didn't mention it. Our house rules were lax. No curfew, nothing off limits to us, no minimum age restrictions.

Mom pulled me into a hug and held me too tightly and a little too long like she needed my strength, while Dylan unloaded the grocery bags and put the food away. I didn't pull away until she released me. I never pulled away from Mom's hugs. Pathetically, I craved her affection. You never knew when it would be the last one.

"I love you," she said and kissed me on the forehead.

"Love you too, Mom."

She clapped her hands together and did a little shimmy. "We need some Christmas music. Liven up the place. Get in the spirit."

Fun Mom was home. We drank hot chocolate with marshmallows and ate store-bought sugar cookies shaped like Santa

Clauses and microwave popcorn drizzled with butter, singing along to the Christmas carols on the radio. The TV played in the background—a cheesy black and white movie about a guy who tries to commit suicide and gets rescued by an angel.

The movie must have inspired Mom. She regaled us with tales of Christmases past, painting a Norman Rockwell-worthy picture of our happy holidays.

Mom was a liar.

She wanted to see the world through rose-tinted glasses. She actually believed that was the way it had been when I knew for a fact that the Christmas we were twelve was the shittiest Christmas ever. The heat had been turned off because Mom hadn't paid the utilities. Detroit in the winter was fucking cold.

Mom had conveniently forgotten why we'd left Detroit. Dylan hadn't. His hands were balled into fists, his eyes stormy, jaw clenched but he kept his mouth shut and didn't say a word.

"Hey Rem," Dylan said after Mom said goodnight and disappeared into her bedroom. I was headed to the bathroom to brush my teeth and turned to look at him. If I had the money, I'd buy him a pull-out sofa. It still bothered me that he had to sleep on a shitty sofa that was too short for him. His clothes were in an old dresser we'd found at Goodwill. I'd tried to make it look better by painting it glossy black, his favorite color. It was a fail. The paint was chipping, the cheap wood veneer showing through. But he told me he appreciated the effort, so that was something, I guess.

"Yeah?"

"I like math." He was staring at the Christmas tree again, hands locked behind his head, his long legs kicked out in front of him. "I love figuring out equations. That shit comes easily to me. It's like a language I understand. And when I figure out a difficult problem that others struggle with, it feels good, you know? So, I don't know...I guess that's my thing. Math makes a hella lot more sense than people do. Numbers don't lie. They don't dick you around or make you feel like shit. And they don't break your heart." His voice was so low, the pain seeping out of every word, that it made me wonder if he'd ever had his heart broken. If he knew how that felt.

Of course, he did. He wasn't talking about a girl breaking his heart. He was talking about Mom. She'd broken his heart and she kept on doing it. Her actions hurt him. We'd both become skilled liars, so good at hiding our feelings and making excuses for her that it had become second nature to keep it all inside.

Dylan didn't share much but when he did, it felt like he'd given you a gift you should cherish. He'd given me a little piece of his soul, knowing he could trust me with it. My heart expanded in my chest until it was almost painful, a lump forming in my throat that made it impossible to speak.

I loved his guts.

I wanted to hug him, reassure him that everything would be okay, but we didn't do that anymore. We'd gotten too jaded and too old to hug and it was just awkward now, so I forced a smile and said goodnight, leaving him in the living room that doubled as his bedroom.

On Christmas Eve morning, I woke up to gray skies and rain, a text from Shane, and a gift outside the front door. It was wrapped in blue snowflake paper and the card had my name on it. I looked across the street just in time to see Shane leaving, a duffel bag slung over his shoulder, the ends of his hair sticking out of a slouchy gray beanie. He was wearing a blue hoodie, and gray sweatpants slung low on his narrow hips. He looked effortlessly cool and gorgeous and it was easy to see why girls would throw themselves at him. I'd heard Travis talking about all the girls on tour. Bikini-clad groupies who followed the surfers around to events. They even had a name – pro ho. I was under no illusion that Shane lived like a monk but whenever he left to go anywhere, I always felt a pang of jealousy.

What if he met someone his own age, fell madly in love, and forgot all about me? I was pretty sure this infatuation was one-sided. Unrequited love. God, that was sad.

Before he got into his dad's surf van, he looked up at my apartment as if he sensed me watching him. I smiled, and he returned it, and for a few seconds, our eyes locked. He was sunshine on a rainy day. Summertime in December. And I was the stupid girl foolish enough to fall in love with him.

Then, just like that, he was gone.

Five months ago, I didn't even know he existed. And now... I couldn't imagine my life without him in it. I knew it was dangerous to think like that. Nothing in this world was permanent. How long would he stay in my life before he decided it wasn't worth the hassle?

10

Shane

"You're playing with fire, dude," Travis said.

I ignored him, my eyes on Remy as she paddled out to us, battling the waves in the impact zone, that determined look on her face that I'd come to know so well.

"Duckdive," I yelled, motioning with my hand as she faced a set of waves. Shit. I raked my hands through my hair as I watched her get pushed back and then I lost sight of her in the white water. Worry and panic swirled in my gut. Finally, she emerged, shaking her head and retrieving her board, getting it underneath her in time to tackle the next set of waves before she got slammed.

Jesus Christ.

There was a solid six-foot swell today with gaping barrels breaking on the shore. After last night's storm, the waves were big and consistent. The stuff of my wet dreams. But I shouldn't have let her come out with me. Now I felt responsible for her safety.

"I don't get it," Travis said, watching me watch Remy fight to paddle out to us. "You've got chicks throwing themselves at you, and you're hung up on this one? I get it. She's hot. But she's *sixteen*."

"Are you here to give me shit or to surf?" I asked, a bite to my tone that I'd chalk up to jet lag after our flight from Australia if it wasn't for the fact that he was right.

Remy joined us in the lineup, looking slightly worse for the wear, but she gave us a little smile.

"How are you holding up?" I asked. "You sure you're okay to surf this?"

"I'm great. It's all good."

"You're still a beginner."

She arched a brow. "Your dad said you were a storm chaser when you were just a grom. I'm sure I can handle it. Besides, the best way to learn anything is baptism by fire."

Yep. That all smacked of my dad's logic. "What other lies has my dad been feeding you?"

Remy laughed and straddled her board like me and Travis were doing. Earlier, she'd been lying on her board and got a mouthful of seawater, so she'd learned from her mistake.

"How's school?" Travis asked Remy. "What are you now? A freshman?"

Shithead.

"I'm a junior. What are you now? A second grader?"

I laughed. He rolled his eyes.

Our chat over, we concentrated on surfing. A few cowboys were in the lineup now, whooping it up every time they caught a wave. I kept my eye on them, making sure they didn't pull any stupid stunts.

I had just ridden a set of waves in and turned around to paddle back out when I saw Remy paddling for a wave. It was hers. She caught it. One of the cowboys dropped right in on her.

"The fuck, man?" I shouted, motioning with my hands for

him to back off. He either didn't hear me or didn't give a shit because he was going for it and had too much speed to back off now. Remy tried to correct herself and get out of his way, but it was a train wreck waiting to happen and all I could do was stand by and watch. She tombstoned, her board flying straight up into the air. I undid my leash, pushing my board onto the sand.

Sprinting through the shallow water, I swam out to where her board was getting thrashed. I dove under the water, untangling the rope wrapped around her leg. When I'd freed her, I pulled her to the surface, holding her body on top of mine like I was a life raft keeping her afloat, one arm wrapped around her and the other one hanging onto her board, so it didn't smack her in the face.

She coughed, a stream of saltwater pouring from her nose, and her body went limp in my arms. "We need to get you out of here."

I helped her onto her board, instructing her to paddle in while I swam next to her. When we reached knee-deep water, she stood up, her legs wobbly as if they were about to fall out from under her. I undid her leg leash and planted her board in the sand next to mine. "Sit down for a minute."

Without putting up a protest, Remy lowered herself onto the sand.

I knelt in front of her, pushing her matted hair off her face. "You okay?"

She rubbed the back of her head, her hand coming away covered in blood. She stared at it for a moment, looking confused as if she wasn't sure where the blood had come from.

Fuck.

"Let me check your head, okay?" I looked into her eyes, needing her permission.

She swallowed hard and nodded.

I knelt behind her, trying to be as gentle as I could. I parted her hair, matted down with blood and seawater. There was a three-inch gash on her head that looked like it might need stitches. That son of a bitch. My fingers brushed over it lightly, but I heard her sharp intake of breath that told me it hurt like hell.

"We need to get you to the ER."

Travis had joined us to assist and nodded in agreement, his face serious.

"No. I don't need a hospital. No doctors. I'm fine. I just need... just give me a few minutes. I'll be okay."

"You might need stitches."

She shook her head, trying to hide the way that action made her wince.

"You need a doctor," Travis said, his concern for her well-being genuine. "You don't want to mess around with head injuries."

Remy shook her head again, adamant that she wasn't going.

"If you're scared, I'll be with you. You can hold my hand. Whatever you need. But we need to get you—"

"No. I can't go to the hospital," she said, her voice quiet but resolute. "Even a quick trip to the ER is expensive."

She wasn't scared. She was worried about the money. If she even had health insurance, it was probably a shitty plan. I exhaled. "Don't worry about the money, Remy. I'll—"

"No," she said forcefully. "I'm not going to the hospital."

I exhaled loudly, knowing I couldn't force her to go if she didn't want to.

"Is there someone you can call? Your mom or something?" Travis asked.

He didn't know about her home situation because I'd never told him. It was none of his business and I knew that Remy wouldn't appreciate it if I betrayed her confidence.

"No. It's okay. I'll just... I'm fine." She stood and took a few steps up the beach.

She swayed on her feet and I steadied her with my hands on her upper arms.

"Whoa. Head rush." No sooner were the words out, she pulled away from me and bent at the waist, vomiting on the sand while I held her hair back, Travis shaking his head, his expression grim like this was bad. All kinds of bad.

She straightened and tried to muster a smile. "Well, that was gross."

"Just sit down for a minute." I applied gentle pressure to her shoulders until she did as I asked. "I'm going to take care of you, okay? It's all good." I turned to Travis. "Look after her for a minute."

"Where are you going?" He looked panicked at being left alone with Remy. I nearly laughed.

"I have something I need to take care of," I said, already walking away.

I waded back into the water, my gaze focused on the asshole who had dropped in on her as he rode another set of waves in and hopped off his board in knee-deep water. I advanced on him and crossed my arms over my chest. He was wearing a HartCore wetsuit and looked vaguely familiar.

"The fuck was that? You dropped in on her. That wave was hers."

He smirked. "You talking about the muffrider?"

Fucking douche. I smacked him upside the back of his head. A warning.

He shoved my shoulders. The little shit. The smirk was still there but his eyes had hardened. "I'd think twice before picking a fight with me. Do you know who I am?"

"I don't give a fuck if you're the pope. You didn't even come to check and see if she was okay. You did *nothing* to help. What if I hadn't been here? What if nobody else was here to help her?"

"Remy St. Clair isn't worth fighting over. Girl's a cock tease. White trash."

"If I ever see you at this break—"

"What are you going to do? Beat me up? Oh, and by the way, I'm Tristan Hart. And you're my daddy's golden boy. Watch your fucking step."

A hand wrapped around my bicep and Travis dragged me away. I shook off his hold and jabbed my finger at the asshole. "Brush up on your surfing etiquette."

He was laughing as he paddled back out.

"Hey," Travis said, jostling my arm to get my attention. "Shake it off."

I ground my teeth. "You saw what he did."

"Yeah. He's a little shit. But it happens all the time. He's not worth losing your shit over. Come on. Check on Remy," he urged.

I took a few deep breaths and tried to calm the fuck down. Asshole. Figures he was John Hart's son. John Hart was a pompous ass. Unfortunately, I needed his money. I was a brand and I couldn't afford to lose my cool with that douchebag. He'd known that all along. He also knew Remy.

Remy was already climbing the stairs, using the railing for support, the board under her arm. Stubborn girl.

"You need my help?" Travis asked, his eyes darting to Remy who looked like she was struggling.

"Nah. I've got this. Get back out there." I knew he was dying to get back out there.

He clapped me on the shoulder before he headed back to the water. "Call if you need anything."

I jogged across the beach and up the stairs, catching up to Remy on the path that led to the parking lot. I took the board out from under her arm and side-eyed her. She was shivering, her arms wrapped around herself for warmth, her gait unsteady. Being in a wetsuit, a chilly April wind blowing, wasn't helping matters.

When we got to the parking lot, I propped our boards against the side of the Jeep, opened the hatch and told her to sit down. I rummaged in the back and came out with beach towels and my hoodie, instructing her to peel off the top half of her wetsuit. Her hands were shaking so badly she was having trouble with the simple task.

"Remy," I said softly.

"I've got it," she said. "It's fine."

But it wasn't fine, so I did it myself, peeling the wetsuit down and wrapped a towel around her, then got on my knees in front of her and peeled off the rest of the wetsuit. Her skin was covered in goose bumps, her lips blue.

I grabbed another beach towel and wrapped it around her legs, then pulled my hoodie over her head. When she figured out I was trying to dress her like she was a toddler, she pushed her arms in the sleeves and hopped off the back of the Jeep.

Remy grabbed her backpack and brushed past me, in a hurry to get out of here now. I did a quick towel change out of my wetsuit and into shorts and a T-shirt and climbed into the driver's seat, cranking up the heat as she pulled on leggings over her wet swimsuit. She reached for the hem of my hoodie to take it off, but I stopped her with my words.

"Just wear it for now. Until you warm up."

"Thanks." She pulled the sleeves over her hands and gripped them with her fingertips, wrapping her arms around herself again. I handed her a bottle of water and she thanked me, taking a few sips. "Just drop me off at home and then you can come back."

Yeah, that wasn't happening.

I drove her home. Nobody was there. What was I supposed to do? Just let her fend for herself? I waited for her to change out of her bikini because that was wet too. While she was in her bedroom, curiosity got the best of me. I checked the refrigerator and the cupboards—empty except for a few condiments, cans of Spaghetti-O's, a jar of peanut butter, and milk—and sifted through the stack of bills on the counter addressed to Rachel St. Clair. Final Notices. I speared my hand through my hair, reminding myself that this was none of my business. I had no right to look at someone's mail or nose around in their kitchen.

Crossing yet another line, this one illegal, I stuffed the utility bill in my pocket and wandered into the living room. It was slightly cleaner than the last time I'd been here. A set of sheets and a pillow were stuffed into the corner of the threadbare tweed sofa, a pile of dirty clothes next to a black-painted dresser against the opposite wall with a TV sitting on top of it. It was quiet in the apartment and I called out her name, worried that she'd passed out.

When she didn't answer, I ventured down the hallway and stopped outside a closed door that I guessed was the bathroom. It sounded like the shower was running.

"Remy. You okay?"

No answer. The water stopped, and I returned to the living room, so it didn't look as if I'd been lurking right outside the door.

I gave it five minutes then asked the question again.

"I'm fine. I'm just..." Her voice sounded faint.

"You're just what?"

The door opened, and she came out into the hallway, a cloud of steam billowing behind her, her face pale and her lips colorless. I grabbed her upper arms before she hit the floor and guided her to a sitting position. "Put your head between your legs."

She did as I said and took deep breaths. We sat there for a good five minutes before she lifted her head.

"I'm better now." The color had returned to her face, at least. "I was just trying to warm up. I thought the shower would help. And I felt gross. From the saltwater and…" She let her voice trail off and swallowed hard. "I'm sorry about all this. You should go back. I know you love surfing after a storm."

Water dripped from the ends of her wet hair down the turquoise hoodie I'd given her for Christmas. It matched her eyes. "I'm not going to leave you like this."

"I'll be fine."

"You need to stop saying that. You're not fine, Remy." I wasn't just talking about her head injury or the dizziness. She averted her head, knowing what I meant and finger-combed her hair then gathered it into a ponytail and secured it with the elastic on her wrist.

She leaned her head against the wall and turned her face toward me. We were sitting in the hallway, side by side, our legs kicked out in front of us.

"Your eyes look greener today," she said. "Green apple green."

"It must be from the scent of your shampoo."

She laughed because that made no sense. Her stomach growled, reminding me that she'd thrown up earlier and there was no food in this apartment.

"All that talk of green apples made me hungry," she joked.

"How are you feeling?"

"Not bad. I just have a headache."

"Did you take Tylenol or anything?" I asked, looking toward the bathroom.

"No. I checked the cabinet but couldn't find any."

Of course not. They probably didn't have a first aid kit either.

"You can stop playing nurse now and get back out there," Remy said after I'd cleaned the gash on her head—she'd barely winced—and gave her Tylenol.

"Are you trying to get rid of me?"

"How did you guess? You've eaten your weird breakfast. Now you're just being a slacker."

"Avocadoes aren't weird."

She bit into her green apple. "They are when you smash them and stuff them into a sweet potato."

I watched her eat the entire apple, core and all. "And that's not weird."

She shrugged and held up the stem. "It would have been weird if I ate the stem."

I laughed and shook my head. "So, how do you know Tristan Hart?"

"From school."

There was more to it, I could tell she hesitated, not wanting to tell me everything.

"I didn't realize you knew him," she said.

"I don't know him. His dad owns HartCore."

"Of course, he does. I should have figured that out." She sighed.

"Does he hassle you?" I asked, remembering his words. What I really wanted to know was if she had ever hooked up with that douche.

"No. I have nothing to do with him."

Why did I get the distinct impression that she was lying?

Remy was cagey sometimes. She kept a lot of secrets. Peeling back the many layers of Remy St. Clair was a challenge. She only shared small parts of herself but unlike a lot of girls, she didn't go out of her way to only show herself in the best light. She wasn't trying to impress anyone or pretend she had her shit together.

No. Remy was unapologetically herself. She didn't flirt. She didn't act coy. She didn't give the impression that she gave a shit what anyone else thought about her. I loved that about her. Even though she kept secrets, she was the most honest person I'd ever known. She was *real*.

"Well, as much as I'd love to hang out and watch you eat acai bowls or whatever is next on your menu, I have to get to work." She stood to go.

"You should rest."

"You're great at giving advice and not taking it, aren't you?" she asked as we walked down the stairs.

"I have no idea what you're talking about."

"Hossegor. Your rotator cuff. How's your shoulder?"

"Good as new."

"Sure it is."

After I dropped off Remy, I headed back to the break. Tristan Hart was gone.

"Where's the douche?" I asked when I joined Trav in the lineup.

"You're gonna love this," he said, chuckling under his breath. "Not long after you left, the douche got slammed by a wave. Broke his board."

We both laughed.

"Karma. What a bitch," I said. Time to get down to business.

"Don't even think about it," Trav said, eying the same wave I was.

"Got my name on it." I took off, paddling hard and caught it before he did.

"Asshole," he called after me. "Karma's coming for you."

I flicked my head back, a little move to get my hair off my forehead, like an asshole posing for a pin-up in a magazine.

Karma was a bitch.

11

Remy

MOM FORGOT OUR SEVENTEENTH BIRTHDAY. NO CARD, NO GIFT, no Happy Birthday. Nothing. Dylan and I bought half a dozen cupcakes—chocolate with buttercream frosting—and a box of sparklers. We took them up to the roof and got high and shared a six-pack, watching the sparks of light in the darkness until the sparklers fizzled out and Dylan snuffed them out in an empty PBR can. I was on my second cupcake when the door burst open and Sienna appeared.

"Seriously? You're partying without me? I came bearing gifts." She handed Dylan a bottle of whiskey she stole from her dad's liquor cabinet and tossed a wrapped gift in my lap. I handed her a cupcake and Dylan cracked open the whiskey and chugged it.

"You're welcome," she said, glaring at him.

"Thanks, Princess." He gave her a lazy grin.

Sienna rolled her eyes. "You're an ass."

I looked from Dylan to Sienna. "Am I missing something?"

"No," they said in unison.

He rolled another joint and lit it, taking a drag before he passed it to Sienna. "Don't say I never gave you anything."

She muttered something under her breath I didn't catch, making me feel like I'd definitely missed something. A few weeks ago, Dylan had gotten a new job working for a pool cleaning company. One of the pools he cleaned was Sienna's. I didn't ask if he cleaned Tristan's pool or any of the others in that neighborhood. Ever since the day Tristan and Shane had that run-in at the beach, Tristan had stopped hassling me.

He hadn't mentioned the incident, and neither had I. Which suited me just fine. Today had been our last day of school and with any luck, I wouldn't run into him all summer.

I opened the birthday present from Sienna—a Starbucks gift card and a Nirvana T-shirt that I vowed to wear every day. We hugged and shared another cupcake. It made me nauseous.

After we drank half a bottle of whiskey and smoked the joint, Dylan came up with the brilliant plan to go to the beach. I lent Sienna the new bikini I bought with my discount from Jimmy's Surf Shack, blue with a hot pink floral print, and wore my old faded orange suit. Sienna had never been inside our apartment and if all my edges weren't blurred and the filter on my life so hazy, I would have been embarrassed.

We cycled to the beach, and Sienna rode on Dylan's handlebars.

Drunk and high, the three of us were swimming against the tide in the moonlight. I was sure we were all going to drown.

Dylan was floating on his back, singing "Black" by Pearl Jam. He sang it to the empty beach and the endless sea and the silver moon. His anger and hurt seeped into every word. He couldn't see my tears. He couldn't see me breaking for him. I was just a broken shell of a girl, trying to keep my head above water. He was just a boy, trying to figure out how to be a man and keep us both afloat.

It was such a strange, sad, bittersweet night. But despite

everything—our absentee mom and all the crap with Tristan and my unrequited love for Shane—I loved our California life.

The next morning, I roused Dylan from the sofa. "Go away," he muttered.

"I know the best hangover cure."

The ocean healed. Shane and Jimmy swore by it. After Dylan and I surfed for an hour, my headache was gone and so was my queasy stomach.

When I walked into work a couple hours later, Jimmy wished me a Happy Birthday. He hadn't forgotten. I nearly cried when he gave me a Polaroid camera and I used up half the film on photos of him. If I wanted to see what Shane would look like in twenty years, all I had to do was look at Jimmy.

"Where are you taking me?" I asked Shane, putting on the helmet he handed me. I acted as if it mattered where we went. But it didn't. I would go anywhere with him.

"For a belated birthday."

He took me to Oceanside and we ate tacos. I asked him about Rio—he'd just returned from a surfing event in Brazil—and he tried to paint a picture for me with his words but ended up handing me his phone. I scrolled through the photos he'd taken, ninety percent of them had ocean views. After we ate, we watched the sunset from the pier, our arms resting on the railing.

I watched Shane's face as he stared at the ocean, his mistress, like a lover would—with longing and a smile on his perfect lips. He turned his head to look at me and the smile was still there. His eyes looked green today. I wondered if that meant something.

He pulled a small wrapped box out of the pocket of his

frayed cargo pants and set it on the railing. I just stared at it like it might bite me if I touched it. "What's this?"

"Your birthday present."

I blinked. Once. Twice. Three times. It was still there. "You bought me a birthday present?"

"Are you going to open it or just stare at the pretty wrapping? Quick. Before that pelican snatches it up." He sounded amused but a little bit embarrassed that I'd made no move to open it. We were both staring at the box now like it was a ticking bomb. He wasn't joking about the pelican. It was perched on the railing only a few feet to my left. I grabbed the box before he could swoop in and claim it.

It was pretty wrapping paper—midnight blue with silver stars. The box was light. Small and square. I turned so my back was against the railing and there was less chance of the gift falling into the water. I was holding my breath as I unwrapped it and then I lifted off the lid and gasped. A gold circle around a silver anchor on a gold chain. I lifted the necklace from the box and studied the medallion.

"Do you know what the markings mean?" he asked.

I looked at the engravings in the gold circle and shook my head. "They're the coordinates for Costa del Rey."

"It's beautiful. I love it," I said finally, realizing that it had been a few long moments of silence.

He huffed out a laugh. "That's good. Because I can't take it back."

The necklace had been made just for me. Tears stung my eyes. I couldn't believe that he would go to all this trouble. That he would have something made especially for me. I flipped it over and read the engraved words on the back: *For Firefly, so you never lose your way home.*

I smiled. It was a joke, kind of—he knew about my lousy sense of direction. But I thought the words had a deeper meaning. Like, *he* was my home. I don't know. I just wanted to believe that.

"Here," he said, taking the necklace from me. I gathered my hair and held it in one hand and he leaned in close. His head dipped as he clasped the necklace around my neck, his callused fingers brushing against my skin. I closed my eyes and breathed him in. He smelled like summertime. Like the sea. And something that was just him. Clean and manly and intoxicating. I missed him. I wanted to touch him, kiss him, press my lips against the smooth tanned skin of his neck. I opened my eyes as he lifted his head. My fingers traced the necklace and I sucked my lower lip between my teeth. His eyes flitted over my face. We were so close I could see the flecks of amber in his irises.

"Remy," he said hoarsely.

"Shane," I breathed.

He shook his head and exhaled loudly, then he took the box and wrapping paper out of my hand and tossed them in a nearby trash can. I wasn't sure why he'd thrown away the box, but it didn't matter. I wouldn't need it. I had no intention of ever taking off this necklace.

"Thank you. For the birthday present."

"You're welcome."

We walked past a man fishing from the pier and he gave Shane a two-finger salute. Shane had talked to him earlier, asked him if the fishing was good and what he'd caught. That was the big difference between us. He could talk to anyone. He was the kind of guy that other men liked. Secure in his masculinity. Friendly. Confident. Relaxed. He was comfortable in his own skin.

And I was like a moth drawn to the flame.

12

Remy

I knocked on my mom's bedroom door. "Mom, we need the rent money."

On the other side of the door, I heard a man's voice and my mom giggling.

"Shouldn't you be at school?"

I rolled my eyes. It was August. "It's summer break."

A few weeks ago, Mom said she was ready to move.

"We need to shake things up. We need a change. Everything will be different in Santa Fe. You'll see."

It was two against one this time so instead of moving, Mom took off for a few days and left us to fend for ourselves. It wasn't the first time she'd done it and wouldn't be the last. But we never told anyone when she disappeared. It was better to have an absentee mom than no mom at all. Mostly, we were self-sufficient. But now the rent was overdue and there was only so much dodging we could do.

"Mom, I need you to pay the rent today."

"You're just an old worrywart, Remy. I told you I'll take care of it. The sun is shining. Go do whatever it is you do. Have a good day, sweetie," she sing-songed.

I sighed. When she got like this, there was no point fighting her on it. She wouldn't pay attention. I blocked my ears as she moaned and giggled, somehow simultaneously.

Oh shit. Jerry made a beeline for me as I climbed out of Shane's Jeep.

He stopped in front of me and ran his hand over his combover, his murky brown eyes trained on my face and not my boobs which I appreciated. Thankfully, Jerry was an okay guy, not a creeper. But still. He wasn't running a charity organization. "I've left a few messages for your mother, but she hasn't responded."

No surprise. Mom was MIA and had been for a week. But I didn't want him to know that. "I'm sorry. She's been so busy with work."

Liar. She lost her job a few weeks ago. On purpose, Dylan and I suspected.

He scratched his head, trying to decide whether to believe me. There were sweat stains under the arms of his short-sleeve white dress shirt. "If I don't get the rent today, I have no choice but to start the legal proceedings." Poor Jerry. He looked like he regretted having to say those words. Like he actually felt sorry about it.

"I understand. I'll make sure she pays it today." My stomach sank. How was I going to keep that promise?

Jerry nodded and glanced over my shoulder. *Shane.* Oh God. He was still here, waiting in his Jeep with the windows rolled down. Now he knew that our rent was overdue. I wished the blacktop would swallow me up. Shame burned my cheeks as I watched Jerry return to his office. Shane came to stand next to me.

"How much do you need?"

"I'm not taking your money, Shane."

"How much do you need?" he repeated. His voice was strained like he was barely hanging onto his restraint. Tension rolled off him.

At this point, I had no other options. My mother was MIA. We needed a place to live and for Costa del Rey, this apartment was cheap. Dylan and I had looked for something else, but everything was out of our budget.

I winced as I told him the dollar amount. He didn't even blink. He jerked his chin for me to follow him and I did, right up the stairs and through the door to his kitchen. I leaned against the kitchen counter and waited for him while he went to get his checkbook in the bedroom. Or the living room. Or somewhere. He'd left a trail of sand across the white floorboards like he did wherever he went.

Pressing the heels of my hands into my eye sockets, I stifled a groan. Why? Why did this shit always happen in front of him?

I lowered my hands and grabbed a green apple from the fruit bowl. Might as well throw that on my tab. Room and board. My eye caught on an invoice, tucked under the fruit bowl and I peered closer. I slid the fruit bowl aside and stared at the name—Rachel St. Clair.

Shane returned with a check, his eyes darting to the bills clutched in my hand.

"You paid them?" I didn't know if I was pissed or grateful. How had he known? How had he even gotten these?

Shane didn't answer. Of course, he'd paid them. I should have known that my mom hadn't.

"I can't believe you," I shouted. I slammed out of his house and jogged down the stairs.

"Remy," he called.

I sprinted across the street and up the stairs to the second floor, my keys clasped in my hand, the metal digging into the skin.

I unlocked the apartment door and slipped inside, trying to shut it behind me. To close him out. He held his hand against the door, preventing me from closing it in his face.

"Shane. Just go."

He forced the door open and followed me inside, slamming the door behind him.

"You still need the rent money."

"Not from you, I don't."

He ignored me and set the check on the coffee table.

"I'm not a charity case."

"I know you're not."

"How many months... how long have you been paying our utilities?"

"It doesn't matter."

"It matters," I yelled. I stopped and took a breath, fighting to regain control of my jumbled-up emotions. "Why would you do that? You can't go around doing that for people."

"It's not a big deal."

"Yeah. You keep saying that. But how would you feel if someone did it for you?"

"What am I supposed to do? Pretend I don't give a shit? Let them shut off your electricity because your sorry excuse for a mother doesn't pay the fucking bills?"

"My mother is doing the best she can," I said through gritted teeth. It wasn't true. Not really. She could do a lot of things better and different. My mom was not perfect. She wasn't always a great mother. But she was ours and she was all we had. I wouldn't let Shane or anyone else talk bad about her.

Shane ran a hand through his hair and looked around the apartment. "You shouldn't be living like this." I hated to see it through his eyes. The ratty sofa. The sheets stuffed into the corner. The coffee table with ring marks and cigarette burns, an ashtray filled with butts because my bonehead brother had started smoking cigarettes now. Dylan's dirty clothes tossed into a heap on the floor. We needed to clean the place. It reeked of desperation and neglect. I hated that Shane saw so much. I didn't need or appreciate his judgment.

"What gives you the right to look down your nose at me? To treat me like... white trash."

He pinched the bridge of his nose and took a few deep breaths. He was probably counting to ten, but he wouldn't make it that far. Despite his best efforts, he never did. Not when it came to me. "You are not white trash and you know damn well I've never treated you like you were. So cut the shit, Remy."

"I hate the way you make me feel."

"How do I make you feel?" He moved closer, his eyes flitting over my face, from my eyes to my lips. I swallowed hard, pressing the palms of my hands flat against the wall I was leaning against.

"Jealous," I whispered. "And angry. And..." I squeezed my eyes shut. I wanted him so badly it hurt.

"Remy." His voice was low and hoarse, and I could feel the heat of his body, his nearness, even though we weren't touching. My lips parted. I wanted to beg him to kiss me. But I couldn't. I wouldn't. Maybe he didn't even want to. I opened my eyes and looked into his.

"I wish..."

"What do you wish?" he asked, his eyes locked onto mine.

I wished that I didn't want him so much. That everything didn't have to be so hard for us. That the playing field would be even. I wished that he would touch me. I wished that I'd never been touched by anyone else before him. I wished so very many things.

"Am I the only one or do you feel it too?" I whispered. I

squeezed my eyes shut. I'd said too much. Made myself too vulnerable. I waited for him to walk away.

The backs of his fingers brushed over my cheekbone and across my lips. I opened my eyes. His body shifted, leaning into me, his hand braced on the wall next to my head. He hooked his finger in the strap of my tank top and slid it up and down, his eyes never leaving my face.

"It's wrong." His voice sounded strained. Even as he said the words, his hand gripped my hip, his thumb rubbing the bare skin just above the waistline of my shorts. The feel of his rough, calloused fingers on my skin sent shivers up and down my spine. I couldn't breathe. I was afraid to move. Afraid that he'd stop touching me, pull away, and that the look of lust in his eyes would disappear. "So fucking wrong."

"I've been saving all my kisses for you."

He groaned, sounding like he was truly in pain, and pressed his forehead against mine. We were heaving, breathing the same air. "Don't tell me things like that."

"It's true." He dragged his thumb across my lower lip. "Kiss me." I was pleading. Begging now. And I didn't care. I needed this kiss like I needed the air I breathed. I needed *him*.

I thought he would tell me it was wrong again. But he didn't. His hand glided down the side of my neck and into my hair. And then he dipped his head, his mouth only inches from mine.

When our lips met, I closed my eyes and wrapped my arms around his neck, running my fingers through his thick hair, still damp from the ocean. He kissed me softly. Then he pulled back, and I nearly wept, thinking he was going to stop. But in the next moment his lips were on mine again, and his arm snaked around my waist, tugging me closer.

His tongue swept against my lips, parting them, and slid inside my mouth, our tongues tangling. I arched into him, and pressed my breasts against his hard chest, the unmistakable feel of his hard length against my stomach letting me know that he was just as affected by this kiss as I was. When he deepened the kiss, a moan escaped my lips and he let out a growl, low and guttural.

His hands glided down my back and palmed my ass. Then he lifted me off the ground and I cinched both legs tightly around his waist, our bodies molded so close together that not even a sliver of space remained between us. I could feel his heart thumping against my chest. I never wanted this kiss to end.

But in the next moment, my feet hit the floor with a thud as the front door swung open. Shane took a step back, putting some distance between us, and ran his hand through his hair. I couldn't look at his face. I was too scared I'd see regret. Or guilt. Or something I didn't want to see. So, I didn't look at him. I leaned against the wall, my legs trembling, and tried to control my breathing. My heart was beating too fast. Half-dazed, I swept my tongue over my lips, tasting him. He tasted like the sea and like something else—something intoxicating. Heady.

Dylan paused in the doorway and his gaze swung from me to Shane before he strode past us. My brother had the best sense of timing.

"What happened to you?" I asked, taking in the bruise on his cheekbone and the dried blood on his knuckles.

He ignored my question and picked up the check on the coffee table, accusation in his voice as he asked, "Where did you get this, Rem?"

He knew the answer. "Shane."

Dylan stalked over to us and held the check in front of Shane who crossed his arms over his chest and made no move to take it.

Dylan ripped the check into tiny pieces and tossed them in the air. They rained down like confetti. "We don't need your money. I got it covered."

Shocked at his words, my mouth dropped open. "Where did you get the money?"

"Don't worry about it."

"Dylan. Where did you get the money?"

My question was met with stony silence.

His gaze was narrowed on Shane. They were locked in a silent battle of wills, and I had broken our code, airing our dirty laundry in front of Shane, an outsider in Dylan's eyes. "I got it covered," he repeated, in case Shane had missed it the first time.

Dylan's body was coiled with tension, his gaze hard and jaw locked as he stared at Shane. This was ridiculous. Dylan was waiting for Shane to leave, his body language screaming that he wasn't wanted here.

Shane glanced at me then strode out the door. I sighed as it closed behind him and turned my attention to Dylan who was rooting through the dresser for some clean clothes. He was shirtless, his six-pack and the ink on his skin on display. Lyrics from Eminem's "Love The Way You Lie" were tattooed across his ribs.

He didn't even have a space of his own. That was why he only came home for a shower or the occasional meal. But when Mom was gone, he stayed here. Slept on the sofa so I wouldn't have to be alone in the apartment. He never said it, but I knew that was why he did it and I loved him for it. But he was keeping so many secrets from me. I'd heard so many rumors about him at school, that he was banging the housewives of Costa del Rey for money.

My twin. The one who should be confiding in me. Yet I knew next to nothing about his life or where he went or what he did. Now he looked like a human punching bag. Why?

"I'm gonna hit the shower."

I grabbed his arm to stop him. "Whoa. Hang on. Please tell me you didn't do anything illegal."

He exhaled loudly. "We fucking needed the money and I got it just like I said I would. It's you and me. We're in this together. We don't need help from anyone else. Remember?"

I took a deep breath and released it. This was Shane we were talking about. Not a stranger or an outsider. But Dylan was right. It didn't feel good accepting charity from anyone, not even Shane. Bad enough he had paid our utilities. I hated that he did that for us. Hated that he needed to. If I told Dylan, he'd find a way to repay him. I didn't want that either, so I kept my mouth shut about it and I nodded. "Yeah. I remember. Are you okay?"

"You don't need to worry about me and you don't need to worry about the rent anymore. I've got it covered."

"Dylan—"

"I'm doing this for us. Mom's gone, and I don't give a shit if she comes back. It's just you and me. Are you with me or not?"

"I'm with you." But where we would we be if he ended up in juvie? He hadn't assured me that whatever he'd done was legal.

"Nobody else needs to know our business. As long as we have each other's backs, everything will be okay."

I nodded, not because I actually believed that everything would be okay but because I knew he needed me to be on his side. To know that I had his back as much as he had mine. And as he walked away, I wondered when my brother had grown up. When had he become a man? Only a year ago, he'd been a surly sixteen-year-old boy scowling at me for going to the beach without him. Now he was shouldering the weight of the world. He'd gotten bigger and stronger and far more dangerous.

Desperation drives people to do things they'd never dream they were capable of doing.

"You better email me and text me and keep me posted on everything," Sienna said. She was dressed for bed in a champagne silk camisole and short set. "I can't believe he's doing this to me."

"You might have fun." My attempt to cheer her up was feeble at best. I didn't want her to leave either. Finding out that her dad was shipping her off to an East Coast boarding school for our senior year had hit me hard. I would have no allies at Costa del Rey High now. Dylan would be taking classes at the community college. I would be alone. With Tristan Hart and his merry band of assholes. But that was me being selfish.

"Oh yeah, right. Fun," Sienna said. "The place sounds like an institution. You've seen the glossy brochures."

"Propaganda," I said.

"Exactly."

She shoved a handful of popcorn into her mouth and tossed a Starbucks gift card into my lap, her eyes never straying from the TV screen. I tossed it back into her lap and watched Grace Kelly spying on her neighbor on the fifty-five-inch screen in Sienna's lilac bedroom while I sipped the lychee martini we had whipped up at her dad's bar. It was our third one.

A loud crash drew my attention to the open window.

"*Fuck.*"

Dylan lay sprawled across the floor, laughing like a maniac. He stood up and stumbled over to the bed, his eyes narrowed on Sienna.

"What are you doing here?" I asked, my brow furrowed in confusion.

"Came to say goodbye to the princess." His words slurred. "My kingdom for a kiss. Or a kick in the nuts." Dressed in black from head to toe—black T-shirt, black jeans, unlaced black combat boots, he looked like the villain in Sienna's fairy tale.

The mattress dipped under his weight as he crawled up the bed and knelt over her. He lit a cigarette and blew the smoke into her face while I stared, dumbfounded, trying to put all the missing pieces of the puzzle together. She plucked the cigarette from his lips and took a drag then shoved him away with her foot. He landed on the floor with a thud.

"Ow. Your floor's hard as shit."

His arm reached up and she handed back his cigarette like they did this song and dance every night of the week and were so attuned to each other, no words were necessary. I crawled over Sienna and stared at my brother. He was sitting on the floor next to her bed, his back against the wall, blowing smoke rings into the air with his eyes closed.

I glared at Sienna. "Whatever happened to confiding in each other?"

"It's... we're..." She sighed. "He's your brother. Your *twin* brother. It just felt weird telling you. Nothing is happening though."

Dylan snorted. "That's for damn sure. I'm Sienna's dirty little secret," he mumbled. "Not good enough to use the front door. Or meet her parents."

"That's not... you know that's not true, Dylan."

I scrambled off the bed but not before downing the rest of my martini and slamming the glass on her bedside table.

"Babes—"

"No. We were supposed to be friends. I told you about Shane and all this time you've been keeping this from me? This is why I don't trust people. Every time you let them in, let them get close, they screw you over."

"Why do you think Daddy's sending her to boarding school?" Dylan said, his voice bitter.

"Dylan, don't. Please..."

"Please what? I never got a fucking vote, Sienna." He laughed harshly. "But then, who would want another St. Clair bastard running around in the world, right?"

My eyes widened in shock. "*What?*"

Tears poured down Sienna's cheeks. "I'm sorry," she whispered. "I wanted to tell you. I was going to... I didn't want to get in the middle of you and... Dyl—" She was crying so hard her words garbled. I crawled onto the bed and wrapped my arm around her shaking shoulders. Dylan was holding his head in his hands.

Save our souls.

13

Shane

EARLY SATURDAY MORNING IN OCTOBER, AND CONDITIONS WERE perfect. We were on dawn patrol—me, Trav, Ryan, Cody Shaw was down from Huntington Beach, and even Oz was out here today. A gentle, steady offshore wind blew into the face of the wave and lifted it up. A big beautiful swell. And here we were, straddling our boards like a bunch of slackers, watching Remy zip across the wave and ride it all the way in. Like she owned the damn thing.

"Damn, but she's hot," Oz said, his head swiveling like an owl as he followed her every move. "She's a honey trap."

"Keep your eyes off her," I growled.

Travis snickered. "You had plenty of time to think about the honey trap in Peniche."

I punched his arm. He punched me back. Peniche was a sore subject. We'd just come back from an event in Portugal. It had been a shit show. My board had snapped in two when I rode a thick-lipped beast. The next day, the ocean was like a lake. I did my damnedest to get in a decent ride, but there was only so much you could do, and I didn't even move on to the semi-finals. Which pissed me off. I'd had a fairly good season but nowhere as good as I'd hoped. That was the thing about surfing though. You couldn't predict what the waves or the conditions were going to be like or prevent injuries. I'd come into the season with a sore shoulder, my rotator cuff—again—and even paddling out had been painful. But still. I'd take the bad with the good any day.

"We're still the luckiest sons of bitches I know," Trav said, echoing my thoughts.

"Damn straight. Beats working for a living."

"I wouldn't know," Oz said.

We all laughed at that one as Firefly joined us in the lineup, a triumphant smile on her face. "You're all proud of yourself, aren't you?" I teased.

"Yep."

"You should be. You're extraordinary."

"Extraordinary?" she asked, raising her dark brows.

"Extraordinary," I said with a smile before I took off, paddling for the next wave. I rode the energy all the way in.

Win or lose, life was fucking good.

I leaned my shoulder against the doorframe and watched Remy as she studied the framed photos on my living room wall. Most of them had been taken by her. A photo of In-And-Out. Costa del Rey at dusk. The pier at sunset. She'd given them to me for my twenty-second birthday. There were other photos that she hadn't taken. One of my mom. Another one of my parents together. And one of Remy that I took with my phone. She was sucking on a cherry-red lollipop, her lips wrapped around the round tip. Candy porn for my walls.

She hadn't been aware that I was taking the photo until it

was too late to stop me. The camera loved Remy, but she didn't love it, unless she was behind the lens. Remy spun around and clasped her hands in front of her, her eyes roaming over my living room—the braided rug on the hardwood floor, the gray sectional, the glass coffee table. My apartment wasn't anything fancy, just a place to sleep and hold my things between my travels. My dad kept telling me I needed to buy a place, invest in real estate instead of paying rent. But my rent was cheap, and I hadn't gotten around to buying my own place yet.

"Why are you here, Firefly?"

"I missed you."

"Really." I pulled her down onto the sofa next to me. "What did you miss? Because I just saw you this morning."

She swept her tongue across her lower lip, her eyes lowering. "Did you wear those gray sweatpants for me?"

I propped my bare feet on the coffee table. "You shouldn't be looking at my gray sweatpants."

"Then maybe you shouldn't go commando."

I pulled her into my lap, so she was straddling me, a risky move considering I was commando in gray sweatpants. Whenever she was near me, my dick stood up to attention. I was still trying to stay on the right side of that imaginary line I knew I shouldn't cross. Kissing was okay. We couldn't go past second base. Jesus. I sounded like a high school kid. Junior high, even. I was regressing.

She cradled my face in her hands. "Kiss me like it's the end of the world. Kiss me like you'll never see my face again."

I didn't want to live in a world where I'd never see her face again. My hands glided down her back and cupped her ass. "I don't kiss on command."

"How many girls have you kissed since you last kissed me?" She rolled her hips, grinding her body against my erection. My punishment for not giving her what she wanted.

"I didn't keep count." My hand tangled in her hair and I

pulled her head down, nipping at her lips. She sunk her teeth into my lower lip and then she sucked on it.

"I hate you."

"I know." I smiled. "I hate you too."

I groaned when she snuck her hand inside my sweatpants. Her warm hand wrapped around my cock and she squeezed.

"Remy." My voice sounded strained and desperate. Begging for release but knowing I should stop this.

"Tonight, it's my turn. This is allowed."

We were making up the rules as we went. My turn. Her turn. This was allowed. No penetration. My hands made swift work of removing her flannel shirt and tank top, exposing her white lace bra. That was allowed. My T-shirt was tossed on the floor. That was allowed.

She returned her attention to my starving cock, and gripped the shaft, running her thumb over the wet head. I cursed when she squeezed, then began pumping, her hand so warm so perfect. My hands explored her curves and silky skin and it was all I could do not to come within the first few minutes. With each torturous tug, she rolled her hips, grinding her body against mine. Our breaths came out in little pants and my head fell back against the cushion, my vision blurring as my semen came out in hot spurts, covering my abs.

Since when did a hand job nearly have me blacking out? Remy cleaned me off with my T-shirt from the floor and wrapped her arms around my neck, kissing me hard on the lips. I flipped her onto her back and pulled down her leggings, my finger trailing over the wet spot on her white panties. Her body trembled under my touch, and a moan escaped her lips. Just my mouth and fingers. We weren't crossing a line.

14

Shane

"Just think..." Travis said, his voice raised to be heard over the thumping bass as we weaved through the people crowding Cody Shaw's living room. It smelled like sweat and beer. We stepped outside onto the deck and I took a fortifying breath of cold night air. "In three years and five months, Remy will be of legal drinking age. In five months, every guy at this party including me can legally—"

I punched his arm to stop him from finishing the sentence. Thinking about Remy with anyone who wasn't me was... well, unthinkable. "Shut up," I growled, taking a pull of my beer.

Travis shook his head. "When it comes to her, you have zero chill."

"Hey guys." Two blondes greeted us, drinks in hand, big smiles on their faces. Once upon a time, they might have been my type. Now they looked too plastic fantastic, too perfect. Bland, like all their edges had been smoothed.

Cody hobbled up behind them and slung an arm around each of their shoulders. He was drunk off his ass, his leg still in a cast from when he fractured his left femur in a free surf in Oahu. "These are the guys I was telling you about. They're legends. Fucking legends. My boy Shane is the eleventh best surfer in the whole fucking world, ladies. And Travis is trailing close behind at lucky number fourteen. Show 'em some love, ladies." Cody winked at us before he stumbled away, stripped naked and joined his girlfriend in the hot tub, hanging his leg over the side as she straddled him. It looked awkward as fuck, but they made it work.

"Trailing close behind," Travis grumbled.

I wasn't too thrilled about number eleven either. Eleven was not number one, not even close, but next year would be my year. "Told you you'd be chasing me."

He punched my arm, payback for having done the same to him, and turned his attention to the girls.

They were talking about God knows what, their laughter telling me they were enjoying themselves or doing a good job of pretending. I checked my phone and read the text from Remy. It was only eleven o'clock. I wasn't drunk. I was okay to drive. Decision made, I texted her back and pocketed my cell.

"Happy New Year. I'm out of here," I told Travis, not waiting for his reply. He muttered something under his breath that sounded like 'jailbait' and 'pussy whipped.'

I got in my Jeep and drove from Huntington Beach to Costa del Rey. At quarter to twelve, I was parked outside her friend Sienna's enormous Tudor-style house, waiting.

She climbed into the passenger's seat and smiled at me. "Hello lover."

I winked. "Hello trouble. It's you again."

"Trouble follows you. Or maybe you seek it out."

I was starting to think that was the case.

I drove to the beach and parked, grabbing towels, a blanket, an extra hoodie, and a flashlight from the back of my Jeep as if this had all been planned in advance rather than an impromptu New Year's Eve visit. Remy didn't seem surprised we'd ended up here. It felt right, somehow, like this was where we needed to be to ring in a new year. I tossed her the hoodie and she pulled it on over her black sweater. I draped my canvas jacket over her shoulders and she shrugged it off, handing it back to me. "You'll need it. You're only wearing a shirt."

"I'm warm-blooded."

"Why *are* you always so warm?"

"I have a big heart."

She laughed.

I put the jacket back over her shoulders and we walked to the beach, the light of the flashlight guiding our way. When we stopped at the top of the staircase, she tucked her arm in mine, bracing against the wind coming off the ocean. The sky reeled with stars, the night cold and crystal-clear.

"Happy New Year, Remy."

"Happy New Year, Shane."

She wrapped her arms around my neck and kissed me. A slow, dirty kiss. Her lips were cold, her mouth warm. She tasted like lemonade. Like dirty secrets and hidden pleasures. There was a darkness inside Remy that I could taste on my tongue.

We spread the towels and blankets on the cold sand and she sat between my legs, her back leaning against my chest, my arms wrapped around her, so she wouldn't feel the cold. It was slightly warmer down here on the beach, the bluffs protecting us from the bite of the wind.

"Tell me something good," she said.

"Next year... *this* year, I'm going to be the world champion. Tell me something good."

"This year I'm going to turn eighteen and then I can go anywhere and everywhere I want, taking pictures of all the beautiful and the ugly and interesting things."

"You can come with me." I said it half in jest, but the idea appealed to me.

"You can put me in your pocket and take me everywhere. Let's never say goodbye, okay?" Her voice sounded small and sad, her words swallowed up by the night and the sound of the waves crashing against the shore.

I kissed the side of her neck and she cupped my jaw, turning her head to look straight into my eyes, searching for an answer, for some kind of forever.

Neither of us could make that kind of promise but I made it anyway. "We'll never say goodbye."

She turned around to face me and sat back on her heels in front of me, flattening the palms of her hands on her thighs. "I love you, Shane."

I brushed a piece of hair off her face. In the moonlight, her skin glowed paler, like she was cut from marble. A beautiful face with perfect symmetry and flawless skin. But more than that, she was tough and strong and resilient. Funny, clever, brave. And I loved her.

"I love you too, Firefly."

Her lips curved into a smile and without warning, she launched herself at me, her hands on my shoulders. My back hit the hard sand and her body landed on top of mine. She was laughing, although I had no idea why, and then she crushed her mouth to mine. My hands were everywhere. On her ass. Tangled in her hair. Brushing her thighs.

She was rocking against me, my cock lined up with her pussy, these little whimpers and moans coming from her lips as I nipped and sucked and bit those bee-stung lips. I released the lip I was sucking on and flipped us over, so she was underneath me. Which made everything so much worse and so much better, depending how you wanted to look at it.

I thrust into her between our clothes, dry-humping her on a freezing cold beach on New Year's Eve. Her kisses were hungry. Open-mouthed and sloppy. There was no finesse in this at all. Her fingers trailed through my hair, her short nails scraping over my scalp, her legs wrapped around my waist. My dick was so hard and so erect, it was painful.

I needed to be inside her.

No. No, I didn't. I couldn't.

This was bad.

Fucking hell.

I pulled back, trying to slow it down and catch my breath. We were thirty seconds away from doing something we might regret. Our hot breaths came out in puffs of smoke, our chests heaving. Her eyes were heavy-lidded, lust-laden, her cheeks rosy from the cold but hot to the touch like she had a fever. My fingertips traced the curves of her face, her straight nose, her kiss-swollen lips, as she stared up at my face, her lips slightly parted.

"You're beautiful, Remy St. Clair. So fucking beautiful."

Her eyes filled with tears. They spilled down her cheeks. Silent, fat tears she didn't try to wipe away. She averted her head and just let them fall and one by one, I kissed them away, catching each one on the tip of my tongue. Cupping her chin in my hand, I kissed her lips, her salty tears mingling with the sweet taste of her, my tongue delving into that darkness inside her.

"You taste like the ocean," I said, my voice drugged with lust. Even her tears turned me on.

"You taste like home." She threw her arms around my neck. "I want to drown in you."

"SOS," I muttered against her lips.

I was still lying on top of her, my hips between her thighs, still hard as a rock, my balls heavy and swollen with need. If it was cold out here, I didn't notice. Like an addict who needed his next fix, I sought the warmth of her mouth again. Our tongues tangled in a dance, and there I went again, dry-humping her into oblivion. I was so close to shooting my load, it was pathetic.

One word fell from her lips. *"Please."*

I squeezed my eyes shut and with all the restraint I could muster, I gritted out, "No."

"Give me something to believe in."

I pulled away and knelt over her. "This... isn't what you need."

She pushed herself up on her elbows. "It is though. *Please, Shane.*"

I didn't know what it was. The hope and the desperation in her voice. Her ocean eyes so trusting, like she actually believed I could make everything better for her. Or the fact that I was having trouble remembering why we weren't supposed to cross these lines. The world she had been raised in was fucked up. What we had... what I felt for her... wasn't.

Ask any man what his greatest weakness is, and if he's being honest, he will tell you it's a woman. Not just any woman. The one woman who is capable of bringing him to his knees. The one woman who has the power to destroy him. Rip his beating heart from his chest. *Ruin him.* I knew that Remy was capable of doing all those things.

My greatest weakness was, is, and always would be, *her*.

I wasn't sure why I didn't see the bright side of loving Remy. The sunshine and rainbows and unicorns. I just knew our love was never destined to be like that. And yet, here I was, an active participant in my own destruction.

"It's cold. We're on a beach."

"Your big heart is keeping me warm. It's perfect. We're right where we need to be."

Right where we need to be could get me arrested. It was reckless and careless and beyond stupid. But did that stop me? Nope. I was a thrill-seeker. An adrenaline junkie. I couldn't do what I did for a living if I wasn't willing to take risks, to push myself to the limits, and take a leap of faith.

But the prospect of sex with Remy was like going over the

falls of a giant wave. The water pitches over the top with you in it. You're weightless and it's quiet for a while, but you know what's coming and you think, oh shit. Next thing you know it's like a grenade goes off right next to you. There's a big bang and the water pressure squeezes you. You have no control over your own body. Arms and legs being pulled in all different directions. You're tossed and turned and flipped around, all topsy-turvy. Then you hit bottom and you know which way is up and you swim toward the light and your head breaks through the surface and you try to breathe.

Yeah, it was like that.

15

Remy

IT WAS WRONG TO ASK THIS OF HIM. I KNEW HE HAD A HARD TIME denying me anything I wanted. I knew it would tear him up inside, make him question his lack of judgement. But I asked anyway. I wanted him to put it all on the line for me. To give me something to believe in.

I pulled the blanket over him to cover us on our bed of cold, hard sand. We were alone on this beach. Under the stars and the moon, the waves crashing like cymbals, beating in sync to the rhythm of our heartbeats.

"I'll wait for you," he said, taking one last stab at trying to stop this before it went too far. "You're worth the wait."

Hearing those words, spoken with so much sincerity, should have been enough for me. The tortured look on his face, his heart and mind at war should have prompted me to push him away. But I was selfish. And I was greedy. I wanted it all. Right now. I wanted his everything.

"I want this. Us. Everything."

His eyes searched mine as I undid his jeans. He hissed

when I wrapped my hand around his cock, as if I'd done it hundreds of times before. It was hot, smooth and velvety, and hard as a rock.

"Remy," he said, his voice strained. His eyelids fluttered closed, torment etched on his features as I gave it a squeeze and circled my thumb over the slit, catching a drop of pre-cum. "*Fuck.*"

He knelt over me and unzipped my jeans, pulling them down my legs with my underwear. Then he took off my boots and left my socks on so my feet wouldn't get cold.

"This is so romantic," he said as he pulled a condom out of his wallet and pushed down his jeans, so they were around his knees.

"I don't want romantic. I don't want easy. I just want you."

He shook his head. "SOS."

We laughed, and I watched in fascination as he rolled the condom over his erection. He settled his narrow hips between my thighs, his face hovering above mine.

"So fucking beautiful," he murmured.

My heart thrashed in my chest.

The first thrust was almost too much. My body tensed, and I held my breath, trying to adjust to the fullness. He stilled. "Open your eyes, Remy. Look at me." I opened my eyes and looked at his face. It calmed me. I loved his face, his hair tousled and messy, falling over his forehead, and his eyes locked on mine. "Now breathe."

I breathed and relaxed my muscles as he rained soft kisses on my lips, my neck, my jaw. He started rocking his hips, moving inside me carefully and gently, like he didn't want to hurt me. It almost made me cry again, this gentleness. My throat burned from holding back the tears, but if I let them fall, he would misread them and think it was because he was hurting me which he was, but not in that way.

My hands lifted to his face, and I rubbed my thumbs over his cheekbones. He looked down at me, his eyes hooded.

"You're going to break my heart," he said, his voice husky and his face serious, as if he'd suddenly had a premonition. As if he was seeing into the future and knew what it held.

"Or maybe you'll break mine." That seemed more likely, but I didn't want to think about broken hearts or Russell or Billy who called me hot and got me drunk then bent me over the hood of his car. Or Tristan who played mind games with me.

I lifted my hips to meet his, my muscles clenching around him as he glided deep inside my walls. He groaned, and something inside me unfurled. I tightened my grip on his shoulders, and his thrusts became harder and faster, hitting a spot over and over that made me cry out, my breaths coming out in little pants.

"I think I'm going to…"

Oh. *Oh God*. A loud moan escaped my lips, and I fell apart.

Shane cursed, and seconds later, he collapsed on top of me, his body shuddering with his release.

He buried his face in my hair and for a few long seconds, neither of us moved.

"*Fuck*."

When he pulled away, it started to sink in. What we had done and what this meant. Would he regret it? Resent me for asking him to give me this?

He stood up and pulled up his jeans while I scrambled to get dressed. Without his body to keep me warm, I was suddenly freezing. I lay down on the towel to pull on my jeans then sat up and stuffed my feet in my boots. He gathered up the towels and the blanket, bundling them under his arm. While I just sat there, afraid to look at his face and see something I didn't want to see.

He held out his hand to me. I lifted my eyes to his face.

"Come home with me."

I took his hand and he pulled me to my feet. He pressed a gentle kiss on my lips that felt like a promise and not like regret. Our drive back to his place was quick and silent. We kicked off our shoes in the hall and left a trail of sand from his door to the bedroom. It was warm and cozy inside his apartment, quiet except for the hum of the heating. Inside his bedroom, silver in the moonlight, he undressed me, his hands warm caresses on my skin. He gave me one of his T-shirts, soft and faded blue, and we slept.

I loved him. Hopelessly and tragically.

16

Remy

"I wish that was my tongue," Shane said, his voice low as I licked the salt off my lips from my virgin margarita.

"Me too." I grinned and took another bite of my fish taco—uncharted territory for me, the girl who had claimed she hated fish when I met Shane. Turned out that I loved fish tacos.

Or maybe love changed everything—food tasted better, colors more vivid, the sunrises brighter and the sunsets more hopeful.

The sky glowed pink, the sea breezes lifted my hair, and the heat lamp warmed my skin. Shane was watching the ocean. I would forever be losing him to it. But he was here now, sitting across the table from me on the outside deck at the marina, his leg pressed against mine, his index finger absently stroking my pinky.

His gaze returned to my face and he bit the corner of his lip in that sexy way I loved. He was gorgeous. With a hint of scruff covering his square jaw. Little lines around his eyes from squinting into the sun. A year-round tan that never seemed to fade. *Golden.*

But I was losing him to the world again, and the ache of that loss made me feel rudderless. I knew it was dangerous, loving him the way I did. Like he was the North Star, the only one in the universe who could guide me home.

"Do you want to come with me?"

"Where?" My heart soared.

"After you graduate, you can travel with me."

My lungs ceased to function. I was holding my breath, waiting for him to tell me he was joking, that he hadn't really meant the words.

He leaned forward, his eyes pinned on mine. Swirls of green and brown flecked with amber. "I promised you we would never say goodbye. I want you to come with me."

"And what will I do?"

"Take photos of all the beautiful and ugly and interesting things."

"How will I pay my way?"

"I have an idea." His eyes gleamed with excitement. We were planning a future. Together.

He told me about his idea on the drive home.

I was all pumped up about the future, buzzing with excitement, the possibility of forever so close I could almost reach out and touch it.

"If you need anything while I'm away, my dad will be there for you."

"You haven't told him anything, have you?"

He sighed loudly as he unlocked his door and pushed it open, gesturing for me to go in ahead of him. "No. But it feels wrong, Remy."

"It's just a few more months," I argued. "Just... Dylan and I will be fine."

He blew out a frustrated breath. I didn't want to talk about my mom. She was gone and this time, she wasn't coming back. A few weeks ago, I'd come home from school and her bedroom door was wide open. All her clothes were gone. All traces of her vanished.

She'd left a note on the kitchen counter. *I met someone. He's different from the others. We need a fresh start and you know I hate being tied to one place for too long. I'll let you know when I get wherever I'm going. Goodbye, my babies. Take care of each other. You've been doing just fine without me for years so I'm not worried. Love, Mom xoxo*

She wasn't worried. Good for her. She got to sleep peacefully, her conscience untroubled, believing that we'd be just fine without her. She needed a fresh start, without us. As if we were a burden. Baggage she needed to unload before she could move on with this guy who I was sure was no different from the others. Rae St. Clair had lousy taste in men.

She'd sealed the note with an imprint of her red-painted lips and left us some cash, almost enough to cover the rent, but like everything else about Mom it had fallen short. Dylan called it the ultimate kiss-off. He crumpled the note in his fist and tossed it in the trash. After he'd stalked out of the kitchen and went for a run, I'd retrieved the note and smoothed my hand over the paper. It lived in my shoebox of memories now. The good, the bad, the ugly, and the beautiful. If I let myself dwell on my mom's actions, her abandonment, it would make me want to curl up into a ball and cry my heart out.

The only bright side to Mom's leaving was that Dylan finally had his own room.

But I didn't want to think about Mom or about Shane leaving to catch a plane for Australia at five o'clock tomorrow morning. Or about his duffel bag and surfboards packed and waiting by the door.

No. I wanted to live in this moment. Remember every whisper, every touch, every stolen glance. And when he was gone, I could dream about the future. Only ten weeks until graduation. Only ten weeks and one day until my eighteenth birthday. Even though we had already crossed every line, I knew he would still be relieved when I was of legal age. He hated sneaking around and I hated feeling like we were doing something wrong.

I lifted my head from his chest and checked the time on the bedside clock—twenty past twelve. He would be leaving in four hours and forty minutes. Careful not to wake him, I lifted his arm and slid out from under it. I got dressed in the dim shadows of his room and watched him sleeping for a few moments. His chest rising and falling, his breaths deep and even. As if he sensed the loss and realized I was already gone, he mumbled something in his sleep and rolled onto his side, his arm wrapping around my pillow. I took a mental snapshot I could carry around with me and pull out anytime I was missing him.

I didn't want to say goodbye, so I whispered, "I love you, Shane. See you soon."

On my way out, I stole one of his hoodies hanging on a hook in the hallway and pulled it over my head, threading my arms into the too-long sleeves, and burrowing my nose into the collar. It smelled like him. Like the sea. Like summertime. Clean and manly and intoxicating.

The street was quiet. The night air chilly. But I felt warm in Shane's hoodie. Unlike the other times before he left to go on tour, I didn't have those same fears. Like he'd forget me while he was away. I believed him when he told me that we would make this work. I meant it when I said I would wait for him. How could he even question it? There was nobody else I wanted to be with.

"If it isn't Shane Wilder's dirty little secret."

Ice froze my spine. My steps faltered, and I tripped over my flip-flop, stubbing my toe on the asphalt. I lifted my head to see that familiar smirk aimed at me.

Tristan Hart was leaning against his BMW, arms folded over his chest. I didn't have to look over my shoulder to know that he had an unobstructed view of Shane's apartment.

I swallowed hard and forced my feet to move. "What are you doing here?"

"The fun and games are over, Remy."

"Wow. You sound like a villain from a B-List movie." I tried to laugh it off, but dread filled my stomach.

"Get in the car, Remy. We need to have a little chat."

"Tomorrow at school works for me," I said, my tone breezy as if he was just paying me a social visit. I kept walking, my footsteps taking me to the metal staircase, my heart hammering in my chest.

A hand shot out, yanking my hair. I let out a surprised yelp. His hand covered my mouth and he dragged me by my hair and slammed me against his BMW, caging me in with his arms.

"What do you want from me?"

Wrong question, Remy. His erection pressed against my hip, leaving no question as to what he wanted. This was payback. When I had come back to school after Christmas break, after the first time I had sex with Shane, I'd decided that I wasn't going to put up with Tristan's shit anymore. He pushed, and I pushed back harder. He taunted and teased and threatened, and I had laughed in his face, telling him there was nothing he could do to me. I'd been vocal, loud and bold and defiant.

"We can do this the hard way or the easy way," Tristan said. "Your call."

I tried to shove him away. He laughed. "Let go of me, asshole," I gritted out.

"I want you and I'm going to have you."

So cocky and sure of himself. I laughed. "Haven't I made myself clear? There's not a chance in hell I'd ever be with you."

"Oh, I think there is."

"What are you going to do? Force yourself on me? Are you going to *rape* me, Tristan?" I was feeling cocky. Tristan was a lot of things, but he wasn't a rapist. Even he had lines he wouldn't cross. I'd studied him for eighteen months in this game of cat and mouse we'd been playing.

He took a step back, a smug smile on his face. "No. You're going to come to me of your own free will, little lamb."

"You're insane." I sidestepped him.

"What do you think would happen to Shane's surfing career if he got slapped with statutory rape charges?"

Statutory *rape*? "Shane and I are just friends."

"Just friends," he repeated. "From where I'm sitting, you are *very* close friends. Friends with benefits."

He had no proof. He couldn't prove a thing.

"My father is all about protecting his interests. It's all about the bottom line. Do you think my father shells out hundreds of thousands of dollars without expecting his golden boy surfer to deliver the goods? Not only does Shane need to win, he needs to show that he's a model citizen. He's a brand. And *you* are a liability to his career."

"So that's why you're doing this? Because you care so much about Shane?"

"I don't give two shits about Shane Wilder. But you do. You go over there at night, sneaking around under the cover of darkness. You let him fuck you, don't you? Or maybe you're the one who instigated it. Yeah, that sounds more like it. You're a dirty little whore. Like your mother. And come to think of it... your brother too. Must run in the family."

I tried to block out his words, the truth in them. Nobody could prove we had sex. He saw my hesitation though and he used it.

"If golden boy screwed up, my father would drop his ass so fast he wouldn't know what hit him."

"It's not statutory rape if two people are just friends. This is ridiculous. We're done here." I shoved past him. He grabbed my arm and yanked me back, his grip on my arm so tight, his fingers dug into my skin through the fabric of the hoodie. I'd have bruises tomorrow. Bruises from Tristan Hart's fingers. He shoved me into the passenger seat, scrolled through his cell phone and tossed it in my lap. "Maybe you should brush up on the law."

I picked up his phone and skimmed the words on the screen. The terms of statutory rape. Rape was such an ugly word. It shouldn't even be applied to what Shane and I had. Bile rose up in my throat and I swallowed the bitterness as Tristan settled into the driver's seat.

"Ready to play along?"

This couldn't be happening. This could not be happening. It seemed that the law wasn't too concerned about two teens fucking each other's brains out. It was the age difference that mattered the most. That's what I got out of it, anyway.

"I'd be willing to bet that he'd come clean," Tristan said, drumming his fingers on the steering wheel. "He'd never lie under oath, would he?"

A whimper escaped my lips. I hated myself for showing a sign of weakness. Tristan smiled smugly.

Shane wouldn't lie. He never lied. He believed that people had to be held accountable for their actions, and he would take the blame.

Oh God. What have I done?

What have I done?

"He has a promising career ahead of him. Do you want to be the girl responsible for ruining it?"

No. I didn't want that. Tristan had done his homework. Eighteen months of watching me had paid off. Somehow, he had seen right through my insecurities. Had figured out how to manipulate me. How to hit me where it hurt most.

Shane.

My fear of ruining something good.

Bullies preyed on people's weaknesses. But I wouldn't let this asshole ruin Shane.

His surfing career meant everything to him. It was his life. His dream. It had been stupid to pin my hopes on a future with him. Hope is such a dangerous thing.

My gaze drifted across the street to his house. He was sleeping peacefully, unaware of what was happening out on this street, in this car. For once, I wished I'd stuck around long enough to say goodbye. If I had stayed the night, safe and warm in his arms, I wouldn't be having this conversation right now. But Tristan would have found another opportunity. I saw him nearly every day. He knew where I lived, where I worked, where I surfed.

When your life is falling apart around you, there should be some warning. A crack of thunder. The jagged flash of lightning splitting the sky. But there wasn't. It was quiet. Nobody could hear the sound of my heart shattering. Nobody could hear me crying on the inside. That was how these things happened though.

And it was all because of sex.

Sometimes it was beautiful and soul-deep. Loving. Healing. Sometimes it was dirty and ugly. Sometimes it could be used as a weapon or a bartering chip.

"Now, are you ready to play along?"

I gritted my teeth, not answering him. He took his phone from my hand. His fingers moved on the keypad and he put the phone on speaker. A dispatcher on the end of the line answered. Costa del Rey Police Department.

"Hello. I'm worried about a friend of mine. She's seventeen and she's—"

I squeezed my eyes shut and forced out the word. "Stop."

"Just a moment, please."

He took the phone off speaker and held his hand over it to muffle the sound of our voices.

"If I do this, you'll leave him alone."

Tristan nodded. I had no way of knowing if he was telling the truth, but I couldn't sit here and let him tell the cops that Shane did something wrong. He didn't. I wouldn't let him pay the price. He had too much to lose. If Tristan destroyed Shane's career because of me I'd never be able to forgive myself.

Tristan got back on the line. "Turns out that my friend is okay. I'm sorry for taking up your time. I know you have more urgent matters to deal with."

I tuned him out as he wrapped up his conversation and then he cut the call and tossed his cell in the cupholder.

It was all so stupid but in the eyes of the law, what Shane and I had done was considered a crime. He could be arrested for it. Fined. Even put in jail. I tried to think of a different way out, but my brain was all jumbled, the fear of ruining Shane's career pushing out all my other thoughts.

I didn't want to be that girl. I didn't want to be responsible for the downfall of the person I loved. I had the power to stop it. Funny how I chose to look it as power. As if the power was in my hands.

"What do you want from me?" Everyone knew that the first rule of dealing with bullies is not to negotiate. Yet here I was going into negotiations.

"You can start by giving me a blowjob."

I didn't even blink, resigned to my fate but still, I had a tiny sliver of hope that it would turn out differently. "Why are you doing this?"

"Because I can."

Because I can. "Why me? Why did you choose me?" I was searching for a clue. What did guys see when they looked at me? Guys who weren't Shane. Guys who looked at me as a piece of ass that could easily be discarded when they'd gotten what they wanted. Maybe Tristan could enlighten me. Might as well get something out of this for myself, right?

The girl sitting in this BMW was the old Remy. The hood rat. The scrapper. Damaged goods. The Remy who Shane loved wasn't sitting in this car. It helped to separate the two.

"You have a lot of questions tonight, little lamb."

"I want answers before the big bad wolf eats me."

He laughed. It was boyish. And for a minute he was just a boy, and I was just a girl and we weren't locked in some crazy negotiation. Maybe in another lifetime we could have been friends. If I had grown up with them, privileged, above the law, secure in my place in the world, it could have been different. But I was me and he held all the power in his hands. He would use it to destroy me. Because that was what he did. If he couldn't control something, he destroyed it.

"I chose you because you look like you should be starring in a porn film. Your lips are fuckable. Tits could be a little bigger, but I can overlook that. Your ass makes up for it. Your attitude though... that's what clinched the deal."

"What's my attitude?"

"You give zero fucks." He slid his seat back as far as it would go, our little chat over. "Now. Where were we? Oh right. You were about to give me a blowjob." He unzipped his jeans and leaned back in his seat. "Get to work, dirty girl."

17

Remy

It had been three weeks and five days since I'd given Tristan Hart a blowjob. Three weeks and five days since Shane left for Australia. He was coming back late tonight. Could I just pretend that it had never happened? I stared at myself in the bathroom mirror and tried not to flinch.

Get to work, dirty girl.
Shane never has to know.

I'd shove it into that place where bad memories lived.

"Remy," Dylan yelled, banging on the door. "If you want a ride, you've got two seconds. I'm out of here."

I walked out of the bathroom and he was halfway out the door already.

The drive to school was silent because Dylan barely spoke to me anymore. I barely saw him these days. He was out every night doing God knows what and since most of his classes were at the community college, he rarely set foot inside the high school these days.

I slammed out of the pick-up truck he'd bought with money

he got from some unknown source and darted around Tristan and his jock friends standing by the door.

I'd been avoiding him since that night I had his dick in my mouth and planned on doing it for the foreseeable future.

Six more weeks. Only six more weeks and I was out of here.

I repeated the words like a mantra as I weaved through the students in the hallway and stopped in front of my locker.

I took out the books I needed for this morning's classes and replaced them with the ones in my backpack.

"Tonight," he said, his voice low in my ear. "See you at seven."

"For what?" I hissed. "You got what you wanted."

Tristan laughed. "Not yet. But tonight I will."

"What does that mean?"

"It means... I'm going to fuck your brains out."

I shook my head, trying to swallow down the fear. "No. We're done. That wasn't the deal."

"We're done when I say we're done." He held up his phone in front of my face. A photo of Shane in a HartCore jersey stared back at me. His white smile was wide, his hazel eyes looked green, and his hair was messy, tousled perfection. The caption under the photo said: Wilder is back in top form and secured the first win at Bells Beach.

Tristan smirked as he pocketed his phone, knowing he had me right where he wanted me.

Tristan tied a knot in the condom. So carefully. So precisely. My gaze followed him across my bedroom floor and out the doorway. Seconds later, I heard the bathroom door close and the toilet flush. Then the shower running. He brought his own shower gel in his gym bag, so he could wash off all traces of the dirty girl on the mattress. Tonight, I had removed myself from my body. Like I was watching it from a distance, and it wasn't really me. But now that it was over, I knew it hadn't been a dream. It had been real.

The scent of his cologne filled my nostrils. The soreness between my legs told me he'd been brutal in his assault of my body. Tristan had pounded into me over and over, chasing his own release with no regard for me.

He didn't care that it hurt. He didn't care about me at all.

I got dressed in the same tank top and ripped jeans I'd been wearing earlier. Then I lit a cigarette and sat with my back against the wall, staring out the window at the sunset. The sky was streaked pink and orange, a beautiful evening. A beautiful sunset. I blew the smoke out the window, poisoning the sweet spring air with toxic chemicals.

Funny how some things made you feel like crying. Like missing Shane. Or when Dylan occasionally said things that were so sweet a lump formed in my throat and my eyes stung with tears. Or when Shane told me he'd wait for me because I was worth it. He thought I was special. He told me he loved me. I could count on one hand the things in my life that have made me cry. And most of my tears have been shed for the people I love. My mom, Dylan, Shane.

Tristan Hart did not deserve my tears, so I gritted my teeth and dug my nails into the palms of my hands and I refused to let the tears fall. If I broke down, he would revel in it. I refused to give him the satisfaction.

I took another drag of my cigarette, feeling the nicotine course through my bloodstream. It made me lightheaded. I always said I'd never smoke cigarettes. I said I'd never do a lot of things.

I was a liar.

Over the past few weeks, I had tried to tell myself I wasn't that girl. I wasn't the girl who would allow a boy to bully and blackmail her in return for a blowjob. For *sex*.

I was not that girl.
Except that I was that girl.

Tristan returned to my bedroom, freshly showered, and plucked his jeans off the floor. He took his time getting dressed, the mattress dipping under his weight as he sat on the edge to put on his designer high tops. What did it matter if he had screwed me once or a thousand times? I was damaged goods.

My cell beeped with a message. It was sitting on the crate that acted as my bedside table. I didn't turn my head to look. I knew who it was. Shane was home. He'd texted a few times already, before Tristan arrived and I'd ignored his messages. What could I say? Tristan Hart is coming over to screw my brains out?

"You got what you wanted. Now leave," I told Tristan. I took another drag of my cigarette and kept staring out the window, at the palm trees and the backs of the terracotta-roofed houses as the sun dipped lower in the sky.

He laughed, but not in a boyish way. He laughed like a marauder who had raped, pillaged and plundered, and was about to burn the whole village to the ground. I should have known he wouldn't leave me in peace. "I wanted to see how far you would go, little lamb. I wasn't sure you'd fall for it." He scoffed. "You didn't actually believe that I would report Shane Wilder to the cops, did you? I don't give a shit if he screws the entire JV cheering squad."

I squeezed my eyes shut, hoping it would block out his words. That he would just shut up already. But of course, he didn't. He wanted to make sure there was no reasonable doubt left in my mind. Tristan loved nothing better than to watch me burn. He lit the match and threw it on the kerosene. I tossed my cigarette out the window. I'd become so careless.

"In case I need to spell it out for you, you've been played. Screwed. Fucked over. It's been fun, little lamb. Have a good life. Oh. Wait." He snapped his fingers. "You have no future beyond this shitty apartment."

He threw a few twenties on the mattress, the ultimate insult, a nod to the fact that he had treated me like a prostitute. I hurled my Converse at his head as he walked out of my room. It hit him squarely in the back. As he retreated down the hallway, I heard him laughing. Seconds later, the front door closed behind him and I let his words sink in, and the tears fall.

Everything I had done had been for nothing. I'd been played.

Why would someone go to so much trouble to ruin another person's life? You would think by now that a girl like me would stop questioning the horrible, ugly, crazy things people did.

After all, I was my mother's daughter. And I knew what I needed to do—set Shane free.

18

Shane

MY SEASON WAS OFF TO A GOOD START. I HAD SOME OF MY BEST heats in Australia. This was going to be my year. I could feel it in my gut. I was at the top of my game. My star was rising. Everything was right with the world, my dreams so close I could reach out and touch them.

As I showered, washing off the stale scent of travel, my thoughts drifted to Remy. On the eighteen-hour flight, I'd had plenty of time to think about our future. When she graduated, she could move in with me. We'd travel together, live together, spend our nights together. I had a few contacts I could put her in touch with. We had talked about her becoming a surfing photographer and being on tour with me would be the perfect opportunity for that, and for making surfing videos.

I toweled off and dressed in a T-shirt and shorts then chugged a bottle of water. Jet lag was a bitch and my body was still operating on a different time zone. I needed fresh air, exercise, and Remy. Not necessarily in that order. I shoved my feet into Vans and strode to my front door just as a knock sounded on it.

I swung the door open and my lips curved into a smile. "Hey Firefly. I've missed you."

Her smile was forced and didn't reach her eyes. "Hey Shane. How was your flight?"

"It was fine." I studied her face for a moment. She wouldn't meet my eyes. Something was wrong. Not only did she look less than thrilled to see me, her arms were crossed over her chest, warding me off, her shoulders rigid. "What's wrong, Remy?"

She gnawed on her lower lip, her eyes darting around, looking everywhere but at me. "We need to talk, Shane."

"Okay," I said slowly. This was not how I pictured our happy reunion. My stomach sank.

"There's something I need to tell you."

The first thought that entered my head was that she was pregnant. I'd always been careful, but accidents happened. Admittedly, it wasn't the best timing, but I didn't hate the idea either. We'd make it work. If she was scared, I'd let her know I'd be there for her every step of the way.

"Let's take a walk."

She looked over her shoulder. "Um... can I just come in? For a minute?"

I held the door open for her and she walked past me.

"There's no easy way to say this." She wrung her hands and paced the kitchen, her teeth gnawing on that poor lip.

I pulled out a stool for her. "How about if you sit? You're making me nervous."

She perched on the edge of her seat and I sat across from her, taking her hands in mine. "Whatever it is, you can tell me. You can tell me anything, Remy." I squeezed her hands, encouraging her to say whatever was on her mind.

She snatched her hands away and crossed her arms over her chest again. Not gonna lie, that hurt. She was pushing me away. Her body language screamed that she didn't want to be touched.

"I slept with someone while you were away."

At first, the words didn't register. I stared at her, unblinking, my breathing shallow as the words hit me and the meaning started to sink in.

"The fuck did you just say? Because it sounded like you said you slept with someone who wasn't me."

She nodded and swallowed, her throat bobbing. "I did say that. It just happened." She shrugged like it had been out of her control.

"How does something like that just happen? Who is he?"

Remy shook her head and gripped the arms of the chair. "It doesn't matter."

"It matters to me. Who the fuck is it?"

"Shane, that's not the point. He was just some guy."

Some guy. None of this made sense. My brain refused to accept it. "Were you drunk? Did he force himself on you?" There had to be a good reason. She would never do this to me. *Never.* I held on to my anger, my hands curled into fists, ready to rip the guy limb from limb for hurting her.

"No. It was my choice. I wasn't drunk. He didn't force me."

I searched her face for clues that she was lying. Her face was neutral. Nothing gave her away.

"I'm sorry, Shane."

Sorry did not fucking cut it. I speared my hands through my hair and held the back of my head, taking deep breaths so I didn't lose my shit and punch the wall behind her head.

"Why?" I asked, my voice deadly quiet. "Why would you do that?"

"Let's be real, Shane. This... us... it was never going to work. What was I supposed to do... tag along with you wherever you went? How long before you got tired of me? You have surfing, you have your career, and what would I have? I need to get a life of my own."

I laughed bitterly. Unbelievable. "So, your answer to getting a life of your own was to fuck someone else?"

She flinched at my word choice and tone of voice. Right now, I didn't fucking care. "I loved you. I loved you, Remy. I would have moved heaven and earth to make you happy. I would have done *anything* for you."

While I'd been planning our future, she'd been fucking some other guy. I couldn't even look at her face.

"Why would you do this, Remy? Were you trying to prove that you're just like your mother?"

"I *am* just like her. And it wouldn't have taken you long to figure that out. I ruin everything that's good. You should have known better than to fall in love with a girl like me."

"Go. Leave." My jaw clenched.

"Goodbye, Shane." Those were her final words before the door closed behind her.

Remy said goodbye.

After two years of fighting my feelings for her, of finally admitting I couldn't, and letting myself fall in love with her, it had only taken her two seconds to break my heart.

I slept with someone while you were away.

19

Remy

The pounding on my bedroom door wouldn't stop. *Bang. Bang. Bang.*

"Go away," I mumbled.

"Fucking let me in or I'm going to rip this door off the hinges," Dylan yelled.

I stayed where I was, lying on my mattress, staring up at the popcorn ceiling. My body was spent. I was too hollowed out and empty to care. Let him yell and threaten me all he wanted. I wasn't going anywhere.

Wood splintered, and the door flew open, slamming against the wall. Dylan's chest was heaving as he stalked across the room. I gaped and scooted back against the wall. The asshole had kicked my door in. "Get out of here!"

His eyes narrowed on me, taking in my red, swollen eyes and unwashed hair, the holey T-shirt and cotton boxers I'd been wearing for three days. Before I could stop him, he lifted me off the mattress and tossed me over his shoulder like I weighed nothing. I pounded his back with my fists. Undeterred, he carried me through the doorway, down the hall, and into the bathroom, keeping a vise-like grip on my legs.

"What the hell are you doing? Put me down."

I pummeled him with my fists and clawed at his back, my shrieks bouncing off the tiled walls. He didn't care. My brother was Iron Man. Holding me in place with one arm, he turned on the shower and held his hand under the water until he was happy with the temperature. Clothes and all, he unceremoniously dumped me in the bathtub.

The shower curtain snapped shut and he left me sitting there with the water pouring down on my head. All the fight drained from my body, and I just sat there with my eyes closed, letting the water wash over me. Cleanse me. Take away my sins.

"I don't know what bullshit is going on in your life, but you can't hide out in your room forever."

It had only been three days. That was *not* forever. He had no idea what bullshit was going on in my life because he was never home. "Says who?"

"Me."

"Who made you the boss?" It was childish and stupid. "Who cares if I go to school or not?"

"*I* care." His voice was low and angry, like that was something new and different. These days, that was his default mode.

"It's not like I'm going to college."

"You could if you wanted to."

"I don't want to." I sounded like a petulant six-year-old. Why were we talking about college? I had no plans for my future beyond this shitty apartment.

"We only have six weeks until graduation. Six weeks and one day until our eighteenth birthday. You're going to school and you're going to graduate with me."

"Dylan, I don't care," I said in frustration. "Can't you get that through your fat head? I. Don't. Fucking. Care."

"*I* care. I didn't do all this, so you could fuck off."

"Do what?" I screamed. "What did you do? You don't tell me anything." I whipped open the shower curtain and climbed out of the bathtub, sopping wet, my hair dripping, my boxers and T-shirt soaked through to the skin. "Tell me where you go at night. Tell me where you get all the money to pay the rent."

He shook his head. "I can't."

"Why not?" I screamed, shoving at his shoulders.

"Because I don't want you involved," he screamed right back at me. We stared at each other, our chests heaving, the water pooling on the tiles at our feet. The shower was still running, the bathroom mirror fogged up. "Six weeks and we're done, Remy. We didn't come this far for you to drop the ball now. We're in this together and I'm not leaving you behind." He wrapped his hands around my upper arms and shook me, his stormy blue-gray eyes pinned on mine. "I'm not leaving you behind. We made a promise to each other and I will *not* leave you behind. Do you understand?"

"Dylan..." I choked on a sob. It was too much. This was what love looked like. Two kids playing house. Two kids fighting against and for each other. Love was a verb. It wasn't just a pretty word that got tossed around all too casually. People were so quick to say the words, "I love you." But what did that mean? For some people, it meant nothing. Mom used to tell us she loved us all the time but she up and left without a backward glance. Dylan... he was still here. Through it all, he was still here when it mattered most. Hot tears streamed down my cheeks. His fingers dug into my arms, his grip too tight as if he was afraid to let go.

"I'm not losing you, too," he said. "I can't lose you, Remy."

His voice cracked on the words.

Oh God. Dylan. You would think that a broken heart couldn't break any more, but it could because mine was breaking all over again.

"Let go of me, Dylan. Please. You're hurting me," I whispered brokenly.

He released my arms and took a step back, his gaze still pinned on my face. Vigilant. Concerned. Scared that I'd vanish if he took his eyes off me. I could barely see his face through the blur of my tears, but I didn't need to see it. We looked so much alike, he and I. Our beauty was so sharp and jagged, you could cut your finger on our edges.

Slowly, I sank to my knees and wrapped my arms around myself, bending at the waist. It hurt so much. My sobs echoed off the tiled walls. I wanted to curl into a ball on the bathroom floor and stay there. My heart hurt. For my brother who was trying to hold all our broken pieces together. For our mother who abandoned us without a backward glance. For Shane... oh God. Shane. My ocean.

I loved him. Tragically and hopelessly.

"Do you know what a Siren is in Greek mythology?"

"Tell me."

"A Siren is an enchantress who lures the sailor with her voice..."

"And what happens to the sailor?"

"He shipwrecks on the rocky coast."

"I'll never sing for you, Sailor. I don't want to destroy you. I just want to love you."

"I was destroyed the first time I ever saw your face, Firefly."

I broke his heart, just like he said I would. But I broke my own too. I'd been merciless, my breakup with him swift and brutal. I told him I'd cheated on him, that I was too young to settle down with just one person. "It could never have worked," I'd said. "I'd just be trailing after you, like one of your pro hos."

And the look on his face... disbelief and then anger when he ordered me to leave. But I'd seen the hurt too, heard the pain in his voice when he asked me why... how... I could ever do that? To him? To us?

Dylan knelt in front of me and wrapped a towel around my

shoulders. "Remy. Come on. I'll drop you off at school." His voice was soft. Pleading. "You've never been a quitter. Don't start now. You can do this. I know you can." He believed in me. He was trying to give me strength.

Love was powerful. It could destroy you. It could heal you. It could soften the blows.

I peeled myself off the floor. I did it for Dylan. I did it because we made a pinky promise so many years ago, to never leave each other behind, no matter what. Now, he was making good on his promise.

I wiped away my tears and drew a shaky breath.

"You know you have to fix my door now."

He rolled his eyes, but his lips curved into an almost-smile. "I'll fix your door." He gave me the Boy Scout salute. It made me laugh. Dylan had never been a Boy Scout. Not even close. "Promise."

And I knew that he would fix my door. Because he promised he would. And Dylan, as it turned out, never broke his promises.

Life goes on even when we don't feel like we want to. Even when we feel like there's nothing left to hang onto, life goes on.

When Dylan pulled up outside Starbucks on Main Street, the tears threatened to fall again.

"Dylan, we can't afford... I don't need—"

"What do you want, Rem? I'll get you anything you want."

I didn't want Starbucks, but I didn't have the heart to tell him that. This gesture, it meant so much. He remembered how I used to feel bad for not being able to afford Starbucks. Not because I actually wanted Starbucks but because Sienna kept bringing me drinks. It was one of those poor kid insecurities, I guess. "Surprise me."

He hopped out of the truck and strode into Starbucks, a man on a mission.

I loved his guts.

I promised Dylan I would finish high school and even if it killed me, I would keep my promise. We'd been through worse. I could get through this.

I went to school and I went to work, and I read books instead of going surfing. I didn't take any photos. There was nothing I wanted to remember. Sometimes I went to the beach, and I swam but only at the pier, never the break where Shane surfed. Sometimes I just sat there, staring at the ocean that didn't feel like home anymore.

I missed every sunrise.

Life went on. Without Shane. And I told myself he was better off without me. Because it was true.

I used to love my job at Jimmy's Surf Shack but now I dreaded that too. It was just another reminder of the life I had before. I had to physically restrain myself from slashing a knife through every HartCore wetsuit and piece of surfing apparel in the shop.

"Do you want to talk about it, kiddo?" Jimmy asked one Saturday when I was restocking the shelves with sunscreen. The scent reminded me of Shane but then, what didn't remind me of him?

I shook my head. "There's nothing to talk about."

I didn't know how much Shane had confided in Jimmy. They were close, but I didn't think Shane would have told his dad about his sex life. Or about his relationship with me. Although Jimmy wasn't stupid. He'd drawn his own conclusions. Shane had taken me over to Jimmy's house for dinners and barbecues a few times and the three of us had hung out laughing and talking on the back patio until it got dark. Shane had kissed me once when his dad was in the kitchen and had kept his hand on my thigh all through dinner. Like it belonged there. Which it had.

"Funny," Jimmy said. "That's what Shane said when I asked."

He gave my shoulder a little squeeze. "If it's meant to be, you'll find your way back to each other."

"Do you really believe that's possible? Even if... you hurt someone so badly they'll never forgive you?"

"I didn't say how long it would take. I just said you'll find your way back."

My hand wrapped around the medallion hanging from the gold chain around my neck.

For Firefly, so you never lose your way home.

One time I ran into Shane at the grocery store. He was buying leafy greens, mangoes, and avocadoes. He ate avocadoes with a spoon. I'd never even tried an avocado before I met him. Dylan and I had a cart full of frozen pizzas and microwave meals. That said it all, really, just how different our lives were. Shane and I met in the peanut butter aisle. He was buying nut butter—the all-natural kind. Almond, I think. We were buying Skippy, with the added sugar and oil. I looked up and there he was, watching me. Our eyes met and for a few moments, we just stood there, staring at each other. He looked so good. With his golden tan, his honey-brown hair bleached lighter by the sun and saltwater. In surf shorts and a faded orange T-shirt that said Life is Good. Was it? Was his life good?

How unfair that he appeared to be thriving while I withered away. But this was what I had wanted for him. My sacrifice, my foolish choices and stupidity, couldn't all be in vain.

"Are you okay?" he asked. Even after everything I'd done to him, those were his words. Are you okay?

"I'm good. How are you?"

He shook his head and didn't answer.

I wanted to tell him the truth, all about Tristan, and what I'd done and why I'd done it and beg for his understanding. I wanted to throw myself into his arms and breathe in his ocean scent. But I couldn't do that to him. Shane deserved so much better.

So, I walked away without saying another word. Just as if my heart wasn't breaking and my world wasn't cold and lonely without him.

I rode my bike everywhere. To and from work. Late at night when sleep wouldn't come. Down quiet streets in sleepy neighborhoods, the air desert dry and warm, scented with forgotten dreams and broken promises.

Late one night, about a week after I ran into him in the grocery store, I was locking up my bike when his motorcycle pulled up in front of his house. I watched a leggy blonde climb off the back. He saw me watching. I knew he did. She wrapped her arms around his neck. Unable to look away, I watched him kissing her right there on the street like he couldn't wait until they got inside. His hands on her body. His lips on hers. His tongue in her mouth. And she was taking it all for granted.

I wanted to scream at her. *He's mine. You can't have him.*

To torture myself, I sifted through all my photos of him. I cried big, fat, silent tears. More tears. Would they never end?

At the lowest point in my life, I got scouted by a modeling agency. Tragic chic must be all the rage.

Funny how I never wanted to be defined by my looks. Funny how my mom's words had once again come true.

"A beautiful girl like you, you can have anything you want. You'll see. You'll see how far beauty can take you in this world."

20

Remy

DYLAN AND I SKIPPED OUR HIGH SCHOOL GRADUATION. NEITHER of us wanted to wear the cap and gown or go on the stage in front of all those people to accept our diplomas. Nobody would be in the audience to cheer us on anyway. Instead, we'd spent the day clearing out the apartment and packing up our belongings.

I tossed the pizza crust in the box and looked around the apartment that we'd lived in for two years. Now it was bare, and we were sitting on the floor, our duffel bags and liquor boxes packed and ready to go. It was our eighteenth birthday. Funny how I'd been counting down the months and days until it arrived, and now it hardly seemed to matter.

"Let's go up to the roof," Dylan said, holding a joint between his thumb and index finger.

"For old time sake." I smiled, remembering the night we'd gone up there for the first time, the night we'd moved in and our seventeenth birthday with Sienna. What the hell. I followed him to the door.

"You should end as you begin," he said as we climbed the stairs to the roof.

"You're getting philosophical in your old age."

Out of habit, I looked across the street. Shane was home. So close and yet so far away. Was he alone or did he have a girl with him? What did it matter?

"So, you're really going through with it?" Dylan asked, flicking his lighter. He inhaled, holding the smoke in his lungs and passed me the blunt.

I took a hit, hoping the high would blur all the edges and make me forget. Even though I knew it wouldn't.

I shrugged one shoulder. "Looks that way. I think it will be good." Modeling was a way out. It was money. I could support myself. It wasn't my dream but since when did that matter?

"I never thought that would be something you'd want."

It wasn't. At first, I thought it was a scam but then I'd Googled the agency, and they seemed legit. One of the big ones. I emailed them. Then I went to LA for an interview and test shots. "You have the look we want." Five-foot-nine, rail-thin with boobs that weren't too big or too small. A face they claimed was symmetrical. I was photogenic. I was versatile. I was, in other words, a chameleon. Just like Rae St. Clair.

"We've both done plenty of things we never would have dreamed of doing," I said, defending my decision.

"Yeah. I guess we have." He pushed his tattooed fingers through his dark hair.

"So... college, huh?"

He shook his head like he couldn't quite believe it himself. "Looks that way."

"I'm proud of you."

"Made it through high school without ending up dead or in prison. That's quite a feat for a St. Clair."

We were quiet for a few minutes, contemplating his words. In some ways, we had a lot to be proud of. We'd survived. Had practically raised ourselves. We hadn't given up. We weren't quitters. He had picked me up off the floor and kicked my ass when I'd needed it. I'd like to think that I'd done the same for him over the years. Our mom was never coming back, we'd reconciled with that, but no matter where I went or where he was, I knew we still had each other. It was something. More than something.

"Do you want to tell me what's going on?" Dylan said. His eyes narrowed as he took a hit off the joint.

The less he knew, the better. "It's complicated."

"Most things in our life are."

"Yeah, about that... how about you tell me what's going on with you."

"What do you want to know?"

He looked relaxed, like he was open to answering anything I wanted to know. Which seemed unlikely. So many questions were off-limits. I wasn't even allowed to mention Sienna's name around him.

The metal door flew open and my heart skipped a beat. Until I saw who was on the other side of it.

"What the fuck is going on?" She planted her hands on her hips and glared at me.

"The bitch is back," Dylan muttered.

"Dylan—"

He held up his hand and walked away. We both watched him leaving, the metal door closing behind him before Sienna slid down against the wall next to me. "I'm sorry," I said, apologizing for Dylan.

She huffed out a laugh. "He'll never speak to me again."

I wished I could tell her differently. Dylan held grudges. He'd been hurt but so had she.

"I thought we were friends." She sounded sad and I felt guilty for having ignored all her messages over the past couple months. "You just ghosted on me."

What a shitty friend I'd been.

"Are you okay?" I asked.

"I'm fine. No major drama. I'm home for the summer and I've promised to be a good girl." She held up her crossed fingers and rolled her eyes. "I got into USC."

"Congratulations."

"Yeah, yeah, whatever." She shoulder-bumped me. "I missed you."

"Missed you too." And as I said it I realized just how much I really had missed her.

"You suck at keeping in touch."

"I know. My mom left. She just disappeared one day. Left a note. That was it. We never saw her again."

"Babes. That sucks. God, I had no idea. Parents suck sometimes."

I laughed. We were quiet for a few minutes.

"And Shane?"

"Shane..." Shane. I took a deep breath and exhaled. I was going to tell her the whole story. It wouldn't fix my broken heart or change anything but sometimes confiding in a person made things a little bit better.

"Hey." She squeezed my hand. "You can tell me anything. No judgment, remember?"

I wanted to tell her. I wanted to confide in her. Maybe it was selfish. But I needed someone I could tell. And the only person I trusted with this information was Sienna. "You have to promise me that this will never go further. You can't tell anyone. Especially not Dylan."

"Why not?"

"Because... I don't know what he would do. I want him to go to college, not end up in prison. Shane can never find out. He can never know what I did." I held her gaze until she nodded, acknowledging that my secrets were safe with her.

"Whatever you tell me goes into the vault. Promise." She

crossed her heart and that was good enough for me. Sienna would never spill my secrets.

I took a deep breath and I started talking, feeling some of the weight lifting from my shoulders. Telling Sienna couldn't change anything but keeping it to myself had been hell.

21

Shane

EARLIER THAT DAY...

The sun was just rising and the last person I expected to see at this hour was leaning against my Jeep. I couldn't tell if he was just getting home from a night out or if he'd dragged himself out of bed and resented it. Either way, his usual scowl was firmly in place. He pushed off from my Jeep and crossed his arms over his chest, widening his stance like we were about to go a few rounds.

"Remy's leaving. She's moving to LA tomorrow. But you know what I think? LA is just temporary. She's looking to get as far away as possible. And I don't think she's coming back."

I slung my board into the back and slammed the door shut. He was blocking the driver's side with his body. "What do you want from me?"

"Do you love her?"

I laughed harshly. "That was never a question. She knew I loved her. *She* broke up with *me*." And fuck, it hurt. My chest tightened, and I rubbed it as if that would ease the ache.

"I didn't see you working to get her back. I didn't see you doing jack shit. Where the fuck have you been?"

Unbelievable. He was giving me shit. The guy had been mute for two years, barely acknowledging me and now he was laying into me like I'd done something to hurt Remy. When in fact she'd ripped out my heart, stomped all over it, and walked out the fucking door.

"Your sister has moved on. Why don't you talk to her about this?"

Dylan was still blocking my door. I folded my arms and glared at him.

"I've never seen Remy fall apart before. We've been through a lot of shit. Her more than me. But she's never broken down like that before. She wasn't eating. Wasn't leaving her bed. She's still a wreck. Because of you. She loves you. You deserted her like every other asshole in her life."

"She cheated on me," I said, my voice an angry growl. I hadn't meant to say that and instantly regretted it. Not cool.

He stared at me like I'd grown three heads. "She wouldn't do that. No. Fucking. Way. She would never have cheated on you. Don't you know Remy at all?" He shook his head like he was disappointed in me. "Maybe I gave you too much credit."

"Why would she tell me that if it wasn't true?"

"If she pushed you away, there was a reason. She doesn't believe that she deserves good things in her life. She thinks she's just like our mom. And she's not. If you really loved her, you wouldn't have let her go without a fight."

"You never wanted us to be together. Why the change of heart?"

"I'm losing her, and I don't know how to bring her back. But maybe you do. If you care about her at all, talk to her."

He was asking for my help. I knew that it had taken a lot for him to swallow his pride and come to me. Remy and Dylan didn't ask 'outsiders' for help.

Having said all he needed to, Dylan walked away. The St. Clairs were so damn good at turning your life upside down and then just walking away.

I scrubbed my hands over my face.

If it wasn't true, if she hadn't slept with someone else, why would she have told me she did? If she still loved me, why would she push me away?

Why did I have to fall in love with you, Remy? *Why?*

I had every intention of opening that metal door, crossing the roof, sitting down next to her and talking. Just talking. Like an adult. Like a sane man who was in control of his emotions. A sane man who had a handle on his feelings and could have a normal conversation. But that's where it all went wrong. When it came to Remy, I had no control over my emotions.

I did not, however, expect to be eavesdropping on the other side of the door, straining my ears to hear the conversation through the small crack.

It all started when I heard the words, "*Shane can never find out. He can never know what I did.*"

So, I didn't open the door. I stood behind it, and I listened. I heard it all. Every fucking thing she didn't want me to know.

It wasn't until she was done telling her whole sordid tale that I pushed open that door and walked onto the roof.

"Shane."

Sienna took one look at me, squeezed Remy's hand and told her to call if she needed her.

I raked my hands through my hair and held the back of my head. "Why, Remy? Why would you do that? Do you honestly believe I would *ever* want you to do something like that?"

"I don't know what you're—"

"Don't lie to me," I gritted out. "I heard everything."

"You were listening to my conversation?"

"Why, Remy? Why would you go along with that?"

"He threatened to call the police. He told me he was going to report you. And I was scared it would ruin your career."

I'd heard that part. I just couldn't believe she would have gone along with it. "And you thought that was more important... that I would choose my career over you? That I would choose a lie over the truth? Don't you know me at all, Remy? I never would have let you take the fall for me. That was all on me. *I* was the one who needed to take responsibility for my actions. All you had to do was talk to me and I would have—"

"You would have what, Shane? What would you have done?" Her eyes flashed with anger.

"I would have told the truth," I yelled. "I would have done whatever it took to make it right."

"Don't you see? That's what I didn't want. I'm the one who begged you to have sex with me. I'm the one who forced—"

I held up my hand. "Stop right there." I moved closer to her. "You didn't force me to do anything. I wanted you. Right from the start. I could have said no. I could have walked away. But I didn't. You never should have paid the price for my decision, Remy. If I'd known, I never would have let you. I should have been the one to deal with that douchebag. Not you."

Tears filled her eyes. "I was trying to protect you. I didn't want anything to happen to you because of me."

I closed my eyes and let out a breath, my stomach churning at the thought of everything she had done, thinking she was doing it for me. If I had kept it in my pants like I should have, she never would have been put in that position to begin with. This whole thing was my fault.

"I love you, Shane. It was always you. I never stopped loving you."

I pulled her into my arms and held her. She was crying, her body wracked with sobs. She was breaking in my arms. And I fucking hated myself. She'd been manipulated and played, treated like shit. *Again.*

She lifted her face to mine. "Do you hate me?"

I looked into her eyes. Her beautiful ocean eyes swimming with tears.

I hated that douchebag Russell. I hated that asshole who had bent her over the hood of a car. And I hated Tristan Hart. "I could never hate you. But you should have told me the truth. You should have let me deal with Tristan." There was no point in talking about what should have happened. It was over and there was no taking back what he'd done.

"You have a contract—"

"Fuck the contract. No money is worth that. He's not going to get away with this."

"Just let it go, Shane. Let's forget—"

I stared at her. Was she out of her fucking mind? "*Forget?* No. We're not going to forget what he did."

I strode to the door and jogged down the stairs. She trailed behind me.

"Shane. Wait. Where are you going?"

I didn't answer. She knew where I was going. I climbed onto my bike and took off before she could stop me.

I tightened my grip on the handlebars. I tried to breathe so I didn't lose my shit. I tried counting. I tried to find my fucking Zen. But all I could think of was Remy being used by another asshole. Because of me. If I had kept it in my pants, none of this would have happened. My jaw was clenched so tight it felt like it might snap.

"Fuck!" The more I thought about it, the angrier I got.

I wasn't thinking straight. Not when I rode my bike right across the Harts' manicured garden, leaving tire tracks, or when

I spun out by the pool behind their McMansion. Tristan was making out with some blonde chick in the pool and hauled his sorry ass out to greet me.

"The fuck do you think you're doing?" he asked, getting right in my face. I could smell the liquor on his breath. Tequila.

"What did you do to Remy?"

He laughed. The fucker laughed in my face. "If you ask me, I did you a favor, dude. She showed her true colors. She was ready and willing to spread her legs. The little slut. Aw, how far she went to protect—"

I slammed my fist into his fucking face before he finished his sentence. I wanted the smug bastard to pay for what he'd done to Remy.

Blind fury surged through me and fueled my punches.

I didn't even feel his fist slam into my face. From a distance, I heard someone shouting to stop, but I didn't. Couldn't.

"That skank's not worth fighting for. She wasn't all that either." He snickered, blood trickling from his cut lip. I lunged at him, and we both went down, my body landing on top of his.

I heard the thunk. A sickening sound as his head hit the rock fountain. And for a few seconds, everything was quiet. So still and so quiet. I released my hold on him and the world came rushing back.

"What have you done?" a woman cried. "Tristan. Oh my God. Tristan..." She was wailing, her body flung across her son's lifeless one. The girl he'd been making out with was crying, her hands shaking as she fumbled with her cell phone. I heard her asking for an ambulance and for the police.

I looked down at my bloody hands and flexed them.

What have I done?

What have I done?

Life could change in the blink of an eye. It only took me five minutes to ruin mine.

22

Remy

I FLUNG OPEN THE APARTMENT DOOR AND GRABBED DYLAN'S KEYS from the coffee table. "What the fuck?" he yelled.

I sprinted back down the stairs. There was no time to explain.

The engine turned over but then it spluttered and died. I gave it some gas, turned the key in the ignition and tried again. *"Come on, come on, come on."*

Dylan yanked open the door. "Move over."

"It won't start."

"Move over," he said again. "You'll flood the engine."

Accepting defeat, I slid along the bench seat. Whatever Dylan did, the engine started. "Where are we going?"

"Tristan Hart's house. It's—"

"I know where it is."

I didn't ask how he knew. Maybe he cleaned their pool.

"You planning to tell me what happened? Since I'm the only one in the dark here."

"Can't you drive any faster?" It should be a ten-minute drive but at this rate, it would take half an hour.

If anything, he slowed down. "What exactly are we going to do when we get to Tristan Hart's house?"

"*You* are not going to do anything. I need to stop Shane. He can't lose his sponsorship. Oh God, what if Shane beats him up?"

Not that Shane was violent. Maybe he'd just talk. Not that that was much better. What if John Hart was there and overheard? Or what if Shane confessed everything?

"Did he do something to deserve it?"

"He can't beat up Tristan. Shane is the poster boy for Hart-Core. He signed a contract."

"Fuck the contract." That was the second time I'd heard that tonight. "What did Tristan do?"

I sighed loudly. Everything I'd wanted to avoid had happened anyway. Everything I'd done, thinking I was somehow helping Shane, really had been for nothing.

Dylan pulled over and cut the engine. We were parked in a neighborhood that was miles from where we needed to be. "What are you doing? We need to get over there. *Now*."

"Not until you tell me what the fuck is going on."

"Seriously? You never told me about Sienna. You never told me a damn thing. You disappeared every night for the past few months. I never saw you."

"I'm here now." He leaned back in his seat, crossing his arms over his chest as if he was happy to sit here all night long, in no rush to get anywhere. "Start talking."

"Not until you start driving."

"I drive, you talk."

I looked around and cursed my shitty sense of direction. I wasn't even sure where we were. Dylan was too stubborn to give an inch and I knew he wouldn't go anywhere until I agreed. "Fine. Just go."

Now he was driving so slowly I was surprised we didn't get pulled over for going below the speed limit. "You're a pain in the ass."

"So are you. What did I miss?"

I checked the speedometer. He was going fifteen miles per hour. I could run faster than this.

He hit the brakes. "You're not talking."

I screamed in frustration and pushed the door open. Hopping out of his truck, I slammed the door and started walking. I should have just ridden my bike. My crazy brother raced past me and turned a hard right, blocking the street with his truck.

"Dylan," I screamed in frustration.

He rounded the truck and stood in front of me. "Remy. If you tell me, I promise I'll tell you everything you want to know."

We stared at each other for a few seconds. Finally, I nodded and climbed back in the truck. I gave him the Cliff Notes version.

"Motherfucker." He smacked the dash so hard I jumped in my seat.

Now he was driving like a freaking maniac, racing through town, his tires squealing as he cornered the turns. There was no middle ground with Dylan. There never had been.

"You shouldn't have kept this from me."

I laughed harshly. "That's rich coming from you. For all I know, you're banging every housewife in Costa del Rey."

"Who told you that?"

"Everyone knows about it."

"And you believed the rumors?"

"I don't know what to believe anymore, Dylan. You never tell me where you're going or how you make all this money."

"I was dealing drugs. Mostly pills. And then I got into the

underground fighting scene. I wasn't banging housewives. I was supplying them with drugs."

Was that any better? Peddling pills and fighting? "Why didn't you tell me any of that?"

"Why didn't you tell me what was going on with you?"

"I didn't want you to get involved."

"Exactly."

"And Sienna... did you love her?"

I never got the answer to that question.

"Fuck," he muttered.

I shoved the door open, and jumped out, racing over to Shane. His head was bowed, the blue lights flashing across his face.

"Shane."

His eyes met mine for a moment. And everything stopped. For a second, we were Shane and Remy. We were good. We were happy. Our dreams were going to come true. He wasn't handcuffed. He wasn't being taken away by police officers.

He closed his eyes briefly and my world came crashing down around me.

"No matter what happens to me, you go on with your life. Promise me you'll do all the things you dreamed about, Remy."

"No. *No.*" I grabbed his arm, hanging onto him as if I could stop the cops from taking him away. "I love you. I love you so much."

"You need to let him go, miss," an officer said, pulling me away from Shane. The other officer jerked Shane's arm and held his head down, shoving him into the back of a cruiser.

"Shane!" My eyes blurred with tears. *Don't take him away from me.* Not again.

There goes my world, I thought, as the police cruiser pulled away with Shane in the back seat. He wouldn't even turn his head. Wouldn't even look at me.

You are my ocean, Shane.

PART II

AFTER

23

Shane

Six Years Later/July

My muscles threatened to burst the seams of a white polo shirt and the hems of the ill-fitting khakis brushed the tops of my slip-on canvas shoes as I walked through the final door and into the sunshine. Stomach churning, I blinked at the onslaught of light and I tried to breathe. I was standing on the threshold of my new life, scared to venture forth.
Me. Afraid of the outside world.
"Good luck, surfer boy. Don't wanna see your ugly mug back here again."
I lifted my hand to acknowledge I'd heard the corrections officer's words and took a few more tentative steps as the door clanged shut behind me.
My dad was waiting for me outside the gate and pulled me into a bone-crushing hug. I squeezed my eyes shut, praying to God he wouldn't cry. I didn't even want him to speak, knowing

the words would make me lose my shit. Lose the shaky grasp I had on my emotions. He released me and sniffed, holding it together. *Just barely.* In silence, we walked to his van and climbed in. He tossed me one of my old T-shirts, soft and faded from wear, and a pair of shorts. I changed into them while he drove and then tossed the prison-issued clothes and shoes into the back of the van with the bag of personal belongings I'd walked out with.

My first taste of freedom in six years. My first foray into a world that had changed in the years I'd been gone. It should taste sweet, this freedom, but it didn't. Everything was so strange. Foreign. I felt like a baby bird taking its first shaky steps, trying to figure out if it was ready to fly.

Who was I now? And what the fuck was I going to do with the rest of my life?

I caught sight of myself in the side mirror and barely recognized myself. Scrubbing my hand over my buzzed hair, I stared out the windshield. The summer sun was blinding, the sky too blue, and everything around me looked fake. Radiohead's "Fake Plastic Trees" played on a loop in my head. God knows why. I'd never been a Radiohead fan. Someone I used to know loved Radiohead, especially that song. Of course, she had.

Two days after returning home and sleeping in my childhood bedroom, I told my dad I couldn't stay in Costa del Rey. He said he understood. I sold my quiver of boards, all but two, and my beloved Triumph. I emptied what little was left in my bank account and wrote a check for my dad. Small compensation for all that he'd lost because of me, but it was all I had so I forced him to cash it despite his protests.

I headed north, up the California coast, and I tried to forget.

But that was the thing about memories. Even when you tried your damnedest to block them out, they forced their way in, invaded your dreams and waking hours.

Karma. What a bitch.

24

Remy

Seven Months Later

Strips of black-sequined and metallic silver fabric crisscrossed over my breasts and white silk billowed around my legs as I strutted down the catwalk, hips swaying, a look of haughty disdain on my face. That was why I got paid the big bucks. I gave zero fucks.

Cameras flashed, music and lights pulsated, and the room smelled like money and expensive perfume. I stopped at the end of the runway and jutted out my hip. My eye caught on a Hollywood heartthrob and his girlfriend in the front row next to a Vogue editor and a rockstar—Bastian Cox. He winked at me and leaned in to say something wildly inappropriate to the Vogue editor. Her eyebrow arched. Just the one. But otherwise, there was no expression on her face. I smothered a laugh, pivoted and turned, and strutted past the models who had followed me down the runway. We were dressed alike, our hair slicked back, our eyes smoky and lips painted black. We looked like zombies, our skin ghostly pale under the spotlights.

It was Paris Fashion Week and Remy St. Clair was opening the show.

These days, I had so many different faces.

Who was I now?

Later that night, I was wandering the streets of the Latin Quarter. Paris in the winter was cold and gray, the air scented with crepes and garlic and butter. A busker was singing "Plastic Jesus" and I stopped to listen. Tossing some Euros into his guitar case, I huddled into my long cashmere peacoat and walked away, the music trailing after me.

Crossing over the Seine, I lit a cigarette on the bridge and stared at the gothic spires of Notre Dame through a film of smoke. My cell phone vibrated in my pocket and I fished it out, checking the screen before answering. Dylan.

I knew what he was going to say before the words were out of his mouth. I'd made him promise to tell me if and when it ever happened. I could feel it in my bones. Like a sixth sense. This was it.

"He's back." My brother confirmed what I'd already known.

And just like that, I knew what I needed to do next.

25

Remy

Four Months Later

"You're trending," Bastian said, scrolling through the social media updates on his cell. My own phone was turned off. Bastian was reading out a few choice comments for my entertainment. "Twenty-five-year-old supermodel Remy St. Clair is taking a break from modeling, citing mental health issues..."

Tuning him out, I stood back to survey the clothes hanging in my walk-in closet. I had more pressing issues at the moment. Namely, what should I pack for my trip to Costa del Rey?

"I'm scared," I admitted, turning around to look at Bastian who was lounging on my bed. He tossed his phone on the bedside table and lit a cigarette, leaning his back against my midnight blue velvet headboard to smoke it. I shoved his booted feet off my Egyptian cotton sheets and flopped down next to him. He handed me the cigarette and I took a drag, staring up at the jewel-toned crystals dripping from the chandelier, ribbons of smoke curling up to the ceiling.

"You should be scared."

I sighed loudly and took another drag before I handed the cigarette back to him. "I quit smoking."

"I won't tell Dr. Fran. I'd hate to ruin that exotic holiday you've funded."

I snorted. My therapist was a miracle worker and deserved every penny I've paid her over the years.

Bastian wandered over to the open window to smoke, and sat on the window ledge, looking out at the rooftops of Tribeca as the sun set over them. "Normally, I like it best when you're your tragically beautiful self. It makes you a better muse. But in this case, I'll make an exception and bolster your spirits," he said, in his East London accent. I couldn't count how many times I'd heard that Bastian Cox's voice made women's ovaries explode. He didn't discriminate though. He liked dick as much as pussy. "You're not the same girl I met seven years ago. You can handle this. Go you." He punctuated his monotone speech with a half-hearted victory punch in the air before his arm flopped back to his side.

I rolled my eyes. "That was pathetic. Don't give up the day job. You'd make a lousy motivational speaker."

He shrugged one shoulder. "I'm British. We don't do all the yahoo, heehaw, you go girl rah rah bullshit."

"You're all doom and gloom."

"That's why we get along so well. You speak my language." He flicked his cigarette butt out the window, the bastard. "Let's get pissed, eat our weight in junk food, and watch reality TV shows."

I snort-laughed. "The glamorous life of a rock star and a supermodel."

"*Ex*-supermodel. No more leafy greens and Artesian well water for you. Burgers and chips?" he asked, scrolling through his phone. When Bastian was home, it was easier to order in. Everywhere he went he got mobbed. The pitfalls of looking like a young Johnny Depp and being one of the biggest rock stars on the planet. But I was able to see past all that. From the first time we had met, I'd recognized a kindred spirit. Bastian and I were so alike, really, so damn vulnerable underneath it all.

"What the hell. I'll live dangerously."

After Bastian put in our order, he strolled over to my dresser, emptied my lingerie drawer into the suitcase at the foot of my bed, tossed in every bikini I owned and zipped up my bag. "There. Packed and ready to go. Tell Shane, 'You're welcome'. And tell Dylan I'm still pining for him."

With that, he waltzed out of my bedroom and left me laughing. "You're an idiot," I yelled as he let loose on a drum kit in the living room. Bastian wasn't even a drummer. He was a guitarist.

"I love you too," he said, driving his point home with a crash of the cymbals that reverberated off the walls of the loft.

My humor faded when I thought about Shane. Like I hadn't been thinking about him for seven long years.

Every. Single. Day.

I turned on my phone, ignored the social media updates, and texted my brother a reminder about tomorrow's flight details. His response was immediate.

Dylan: Got it the first time, Remy. I told you I'd be there. Chill.

Chill. Right. Easy for him to say.

I lowered the brim of my Lakers cap, avoiding the eyes on me as I waited for my bag to drop onto the carousel. Next to me, two middle-aged women were talking in stage whispers, snatches of their conversation drifting my way.

"She obviously doesn't eat. She probably does drugs..."

"They always call it R&R when they really mean rehab."

"Just like that rock star boyfriend of hers."

Get a life, people.

I cranked up the volume on my music to drown out their voices, my cell pinging with social media updates. I ignored them the same way I ignored the women who were staring at me. Judging me. I always tell myself it doesn't matter. They don't know me. But sometimes it still got to me.

In my periphery, I saw the women's jaws drop and their eyes widen. Silencing my music, I caught the last few words from my brother's mouth.

"...so I suggest you take your scrawny asses and bulging eyes over there" —he pointed to the opposite side of the baggage pickup area— "where I can't see you. And stop talking shit about my sister."

Having delivered his message, the women scurried away, and Dylan's gray-blue gaze met mine. He smirked as he erased the distance between us and pulled me into a one-armed hug.

"Got your back, Rem."

I smiled. "Always."

I stood back to take him in, looking for changes since the last time I saw him over a year ago. Last April, to be exact. We met in the desert and partied at Coachella. Unfortunately, Sienna was there too, and Dylan got his heart trampled on. *Again.* Forced to take sides, I chose Dylan. Sienna and I haven't spoken since.

It was still hard to reconcile this Dylan with the boy he used to be. Now, my twin was a tattooed bad boy in expensive clothes. The cuffs of his tailored black dress shirt were rolled up to his elbows, exposing the dark ink on his arms. Black jeans. Black leather designer high tops. An Omega Speedmaster on his wrist. Hair slicked back, Wayfarers on his head, he looked very LA.

His tattooed fingers rubbed the scar that split his left

eyebrow, his eyes darting to the baggage drop. "You bring a lot of bags?"

"One." I pointed to the black roller bag making its way around, a silver duct-tape X distinguishing it as mine. Classy, as always. You can take a girl out of the hood, but you can't take the hood out of the girl. He grabbed it off the carousel and we exited through the glass doors into the summer heat, walking in silence to the short-term parking garage.

The locks beeped on a matte black G-Wagen, and Dylan opened the hatch and stowed my bag inside. "Nice wheels." I climbed into the passenger seat, inhaling the scent of leather and new car. "I miss the rusty old pickup truck."

He snorted as he turned the key in the ignition, music blasting from his speakers—

"Daddy Issues" by The Neighbourhood. Hmm. Was he still hung up on Sienna? But then, who was I to judge?

The car was spotlessly clean. Expensive. Dylan had hit the big time when he developed an App while he was still in college. It was called EZ-Math. If you were stuck on an algebra equation or geometry question, the app helped you solve it. He sold it for millions and invested the money in a Tech start-up.

Dylan navigated the LA traffic, the eternal SoCal sunshine beating down on the windshield, and I drummed my fingers on my thigh, trying not to think of everything I had left behind—New York, my career, the new life I'd built—or whatever it was I was headed toward. Had I acted too rashly when I quit modeling? As soon as I'd gotten that call from Dylan back in February, I finished out my contract and didn't re-sign it. I could always go back to modeling, I rationalized. But it wasn't what I wanted anymore.

Being a human clothes hanger had earned me millions. It had gotten me out of a bad place and hurled me into a completely different world. When you had money, it was harder for the world to shit on you. But all that glitters is not gold. My self-esteem had taken a beating and my privacy had been invaded, two things I now coveted.

Dylan glanced over at me before returning his eyes to the road. "You back because of Shane?"

Shane. Seven years and I still dreamt about him, yearned for him, craved him. And now I'd come back to find out how the world had treated him. Badly. Unfairly. I wanted to find a way to make it up to him, even though I had no idea how that would be possible.

"I came back to make sure he's okay. And I came back because I miss you." I was telling the truth on both counts. Honesty was one of the things I'd been working on over the past seven years. I was a work in progress.

"Those women were right, Rem." Dylan scowled. "You're too fucking skinny."

I laughed. If only he knew how many times I had heard the opposite. I was worth more money and got more work when I was rail-thin with boobs. That was the look that photographers and designers wanted. Ribs and hip bones protruding? Perfect. Five-foot nine and able to fit into a size zero? You're just the body type we're looking for.

Dylan turned into the driveway of a two-story Spanish style white stucco house with a terracotta roof tucked into lush foliage and palm trees. The house wasn't flashy or huge. But not in my wildest dreams would I have ever imagined that he'd be able to buy a house like this—prime SoCal real estate.

"This is your house?" I asked stupidly. Of course, it was. He pulled into the garage and cut the engine, plunging us into silence. Three surfboards sat in a rack against the wall, and a few wetsuits hung from hooks but other than that, the garage was empty.

"It's mine."

"Are you sure your job is legal?"

He laughed but didn't answer as I followed him into the house and across the terracotta-tiled floor of the laundry room through a door to his kitchen—granite countertops, glossy white cupboards, and stainless-steel appliances without a smudge or fingerprint greeted me. Slack-jawed, I wandered through the rooms, all dark hardwood floors and clean white walls with black gothic-looking wrought-iron chandeliers hanging from wood-beamed ceilings. Black sofas, a dark wood coffee table and a plush Moroccan rug rounded out the décor and a flat-screen TV spanned the wall across from the sofas.

My jaw dropped at the view from the French doors that opened on to a Moroccan patio with mosaic black-and-blue tiles, a fire pit, and daybeds leading to a crystal blue swimming pool. The hilltops, canyon, and an ocean view in the distance provided the backdrop. "Dylan..." I turned to find him watching me, waiting for my reaction, and I knew it mattered to him what I thought. "It's incredible."

One side of his mouth curved up in an almost-smile. What would it take to get his real smile? We were on the move again. I followed him upstairs and down a hallway, black-framed black and white photos lining the walls. My steps slowed as I studied the photos as if seeing them for the first time. They were mine, I'd taken them—a cobblestoned Parisian alley in the snow, a hazy gray London drizzle blanketing the Thames and Tower Bridge, bare trees in Central Park, the sun setting over the rooftops of Tribeca from my loft window.

"You hung them on your wall." My voice was choked with emotion.

"They're good, Rem." He paused in front of the New York City skyline I'd shot from Brooklyn before moving on, carrying my bag by the handle instead of wheeling it over the smooth hardwood floors. That was Dylan though. He'd never taken the easy way out.

Pushing open the last door on the left, he carried my bag inside with me following close on his heels. He set my bag on a bench at the foot of a king-sized four-poster bed with plush white bedding, soft and downy, like a cloud. Mercury-glass lamps with white linen shades sat on dark wood bedside tables and a vintage Moroccan rug covered the hardwood floor, the vibrant colors faded with age. French doors opened onto a Juliet balcony with mountain and ocean views. It looked like a room in a boutique hotel.

"There's an en suite," he said, gesturing to a door next to the dresser.

"I just can't believe this. It's so nice. God, Dylan." Grinning, I smacked his arm.

"Kid from the hood made good."

And that was what this was all about—the house, the car, this life he'd created for himself. He'd been working his ass off since he graduated high school, trying to be 'somebody', as he'd once said. It wasn't just about the money. It went deeper than that, and maybe I was the only one who could fully understand it. He had never felt like he measured up, had never felt worthy of Sienna or her family.

I'm Sienna's dirty little secret.

"It's beautiful, Dylan." I looked around the room, trying to imagine him shopping for these items but I couldn't. "Did you design this yourself? I mean, did you choose all the furniture and..." I shook my head and laughed. "You *hate* shopping."

"I didn't do it myself. Not exactly."

I raised my brows. "How mysterious. Who did it?"

He ran a hand over his sleek hair. "It's my newest App. EZ-Design."

I was so impressed with everything he had done and accomplished at only twenty-five, that it rendered me speechless and for a few moments I just stared at him. "You're so smart, Dylan. How do you even know how to do all that?"

He shrugged one shoulder. "It's no big deal."

But it was. It was a huge deal.

"I'll order some dinner. What are you hungry for? Sushi? Vietnamese?"

"Are you going to order it on one of your apps? EZ-Food?" I teased. He shook his head and chuckled. "Sushi sounds good."

He nodded and moved to the door. "Meet you by the pool."

The bedroom door closed behind him and I flopped down on the bed, staring at the black wrought iron chandelier. Who was this designer version of Dylan St. Clair? He even smelled different. A subtle, spicy scent from his cologne or aftershave. Did he feel the same way about me? Like we were strangers, trying to get to know each other? After I changed into shorts and a tank top, I wandered out to the pool. The sun was setting over the hills—the sky streaked pink and orange—and Dylan was swimming laps, his strokes strong and sure. Unlike me, he could swim the fly. Show-off.

Sitting at the edge of the pool, my legs dangling in the water, I watched his tattoo-covered arms cut through the water, remembering the boy who had sung "Black" while he had floated in the ocean on our seventeenth birthday. I'd left Costa del Rey seven years ago and hadn't stepped foot in this town since. How funny that Dylan had chosen to make his home here.

I needed a cigarette. Then I remembered that I quit. I wanted to be the best version of myself when I came to Costa del Rey. I was trying. Every single day I've been trying to be a Remy St. Clair that I could be proud of. Some days I felt like I succeeded. Other days, I was still that screwed-up seventeen-year-old who let a boy use her because she didn't think she deserved anything better.

Dylan got out of the pool and toweled off just as the doorbell rang, as if he'd timed it perfectly.

We ate sushi outside on the Moroccan patio dotted with potted citrus trees, Moroccan lanterns hanging from the wood rafters, and I remembered a time when our idea of dinner was Spaghetti O's and hot dogs or frozen pizzas. After dinner, he smoked a blunt which made me want a cigarette even more. Music piped from his surround-sound speakers, transforming the space into an Ibiza club.

"I'm so proud of you, Dylan." My voice was soft and choked with emotion. Because I was there for all of it. All the years when we had nothing. And the years when we both lost our way.

"Proud of you too."

"So, tell me everything. Do you have a girlfriend?"

"Nobody special."

I translated that as: I hook up and kick their asses out the door because God forbid, anyone gets too close. He and Sienna were an on-again, off-again couple, and I'd lost track of how many times they'd tried to get it right over the years.

"Do you talk to any of these nobody specials? Or just your usual caveman grunts?"

"Talking isn't top of the list. They're too busy moaning and screaming my name to talk."

I rolled my eyes. "Too much information."

"You don't wanna know, you shouldn't ask, Rem-Rem," he teased. He was loosening up, the tension lifting. Over the years, whenever we'd see each other, it took a while until we got comfortable with each other again.

"Are you happy, Dylan?"

"Why would you ask that?"

"Because I care. Because you have this whole life I know nothing about."

"I can say the same for you."

"I know but..." I looked around at the pool. This used to be the stuff of our dreams and now he was living it, but I wouldn't say he looked gleeful. "Why did you buy a house and that fancy new car?"

I knew the answer, but I was looking for confirmation.

He was silent for a few moments. "Because I can. I don't have to wear shoes with holes in them anymore. I don't have to sleep on a shitty couch in a shitty apartment with no food in the cupboards."

"Do you like your job?"

"Fucking love it."

Then why didn't he look happy?

"I'm good, Rem. This is the life I want. The life I always wanted."

It was true. All he'd ever wanted was to make a lot of money and now it appeared that he was doing just that. "Do you ever get lonely?"

He exhaled smoke and leaned back in his seat. "I'm not like you."

"What does that mean?"

"You wanted to be loved. You wanted to belong to someone."

Not just someone. Shane. I had wanted to belong to him, be loved by him. To never have to say goodbye. My therapist, Fran Metzger, had helped me understand myself so much better. The way I'd craved affection. My abandonment issues. And the reasons why I'd never believed I was good enough. Dylan was my twin, we'd been raised by the same mother, had experienced so many of the same things, and I truly believed he had all the same needs and wants as I did but was filling the hole inside, patching up the cracks with money and material goods.

"Everyone wants to be loved, Dyl. Even you."

He shrugged. "Maybe."

"By the way, Bastian sends his love."

Dylan scrubbed his hand over his face and groaned. "That was fucked up."

"He's still pining over you." I sighed loudly, and dramatically. "You're the one who got away."

"Shut the fuck up," Dylan said, a laugh bursting out of him. He tossed a cushion at my head and I caught it, tossing it back at him.

Then I asked the question that had been on my mind ever since I decided to return to Costa del Rey. "Do you know where Shane is? Do you know what he's doing?"

"Last I heard he was working a construction job. I don't know where though."

I turned that information over in my head. It gave me hope that he was able to get a construction job. But it made me sad too. He shouldn't be working a construction job. He should be shredding waves. He should be on the Dream Tour.

"He could have been the world champion," I said. "He was *that* good."

"We could have all done a lot of things. There's no room in this life to think of all the things you could have done. You just have to live with what is."

With those final words of wisdom, Dylan disappeared inside the house and turned on his big-ass TV, leaving me alone on the patio. Some things might have changed but his social skills were still lacking.

Did Shane still surf at sunrise? Or did he wait until after work?

It took me three days to gather the courage to find out.

26

Shane

THERE WERE A LOT OF THINGS I'D MISSED WHILE I WAS IN PRISON, but surfing topped the list. Thank God the ocean hadn't deserted me. I was alone out here this morning. And these days, that was how I liked it.

I felt her watching me. I didn't know how I knew she was there. I was straddling my board, watching the horizon, my back to the beach. But I just knew. It was that heightened sense of awareness I used to feel whenever she was near me. I glanced over my shoulder and there she was, sitting on the beach like a mirage, her knees pulled up to her chest, arms wrapped around her legs, chin resting on her knees. For seven years I had tried to forget her. For seven years I had failed.

It felt like I'd been sucker-punched in the stomach. That was how it always had been, right from the first time I saw her. I dragged my eyes away from the lone figure on the beach and scrubbed my hands over my face as if that would help me clear the memories. I wasn't ready to see her. Not ready for her to see the mess of a man I'd become. So, I floated on my board until it was time to go, hoping she'd disappear. I didn't look at the beach to see if she was still there, watching me.

When I couldn't put it off any longer, I paddled in. She stood up, her eyes meeting mine for a split second before she turned and walked away. As I undid my leg leash, I watched her leaving. She walked differently now, more graceful, more practiced, her posture perfect, like she was used to being on a catwalk or being watched. When she reached the top of the staircase, she didn't even turn to look at me. Just kept going, disappearing behind the line of trees and scrubby bushes, and for a moment I wondered if I had imagined the whole thing. When I reached the parking lot, there was no sign of her.

I showered off the saltwater in the outdoor shower and changed into a T-shirt, cargo shorts, and dusty work boots. Securing my board to the roof rack, I climbed into the driver's seat as a black G-Wagen pulled in next to me. Dylan hopped out and circled his car, coming to stand by my window. Grudgingly, I rolled it down, not in the mood for chitchat. But then, Dylan had never been much of a conversationalist.

In the months since I'd been back in Costa del Rey, I'd seen him a handful of times, but we'd never spoken.

"You see my sister?"

"From afar."

He nodded and patted the roof of my Jeep twice before he backed away. *Nice chat.* I reversed out of the spot, my eye catching on the Firewire board he took off his roof rack. Fuck me. A Mercedes and a Firewire. All I could do was laugh at the way life had flipped the tables.

"Are you a surfer too?" a blonde girl asked me, her eyes raking over me from head to toe, a flirty smile on her face, as if she liked what she saw.

I gave her an easy smile. "Nah. I'm an ex-con."

She laughed as if I'd just told her a good joke. Travis shot me a look and shook his head, letting out a sigh.

"He's a surfer," Travis told the blonde. "One of the best."

I took another pull of beer while he talked shit. The party was low-key like he'd promised, a few people in the pool and others milling around, laughing and talking, music piping from the surround sound system. His house sat on a bluff, with views of the Pacific Ocean from the infinity pool. Travis Jones was a two-time world champion with endorsements and sponsorships that paid for his luxury lifestyle. He still worked hard. He was still driven and competitive. He was at the top of his game.

I didn't want to be here tonight. I'd been making excuses for months, claiming I was too busy to hang out with him whenever he was home, but he had threatened to disown me if I didn't make an appearance tonight. So here I was for old time sake, listening to him trip down memory lane and reel off the highlights of my career to some chick I didn't know. Daisy? Dahlia? It was a flower name. I think.

This was why I had been avoiding him. I didn't want to hear about what had been or what could have been.

"It's not too late," Travis said. "You can still—"

"Stop. Don't go there."

Travis knew why I couldn't even entertain that fantasy. That life was over for me. As further demonstrated when Cody Shaw joined us with a leggy brunette in tow.

"He lives." Cody gave me a one-armed hug and a few thumps on the back. Cody had never risen as high in the rankings as Travis, but he was still on the World Tour, still a pro-surfer. "Dude, you doing okay?"

"It's all good."

"That was some shit luck, man." He raked a hand through his spiky brown hair and blew air out his cheeks. "I don't even know what to say."

Say nothing. Not a fucking thing.

"When I heard about it, I was like... No way. Not Shane Wilder. Dude's chill. No way could he do that."

"What did he do?" the blonde girl asked, looking from Cody to me.

"Hey man, not cool," Trav said, his voice low, warning Cody to keep his mouth shut. But it was too late. It was out there now.

"Sorry, man. It was just the shock, you know." He looked at the brunette by his side and then the blonde who had scooted closer to Travis. "He's a good guy."

"I'm not a good guy," I assured the girls. "Not even close. I killed someone."

That was one way to kill the mood. The blonde's eyes widened, and we all stood around in awkward silence that I did nothing to fix.

"Jesus Christ," Trav muttered, dragging me away from the cozy little group to a quiet corner of the patio. "Did you really need to say that?"

"Just speaking the truth."

He scowled. Our friendship used to be easy. Now, like so many other things, we didn't know how to navigate the changes.

"You were always a better surfer than me. Everyone knew that. It's not too late. You can still—"

"Don't. Just don't fucking go there."

"You're still a stubborn ass."

I laughed, but the sound wasn't happy. He *knew* why I couldn't even entertain the idea. Every single odd was stacked against me. And yet he was acting like it was me digging in my heels. Why hold out false hope for something that could never be again?

He exhaled loudly. "I love you, man. I want you to be okay. If there's anything I can do, just say the word." His concern was genuine, and I knew he cared but it wasn't his problem. Travis ran his hand over his hair—he still wore it in a buzz-cut and looked much the same as he had seven years ago. "I miss you. I feel like I can't even talk to you anymore."

I took another pull of my beer, not commenting. He missed the Shane he used to know. Newsflash: that dude was gone. Travis was mourning our lost friendship. I was mourning every single fucking thing I'd lost. Pretty soon, that would be everything. Every. Fucking. Thing. So, excuse me for not being able to sympathize.

"Remy's back." Boom. How's that for conversation?

That shut him up for all of two seconds. I didn't have to look at his face to know he wasn't happy about it.

"Have you spoken to her?"

"Nope." For the past three days, she had come down to the beach and sat in her spot. This morning she had brought a camera. She had always wanted to be on the other side of the lens. Funny how life didn't always go to plan.

"Keep it that way. You don't need any more shit in your life to deal with. I won't sit back and watch her fuck you over. Not again."

"It wasn't her fault." By now, I sounded like a broken record. He had never believed that it wasn't her fault.

Did I hate her for what she did? I don't know. Maybe.

Did I blame her? No. It was all on me.

Did I still love her? Yes. Maybe. I didn't know anymore.

When it came to Remy, my heart and mind had always been at war.

She'd gotten under my skin, in my veins, in my fucking heart and soul and it didn't matter what she did or how many years went by, I still couldn't shake off the memory of her.

"I'm out of here." I finished off my beer and set it on a side table on my way out. "Happy Fourth of July."

"Shane, hang on."

"I need to get going. Sorry I said that shit at your party. It was a dick move."

"Forget about it." Travis was a good friend and I knew that all he wanted was for me to be happy, but I didn't know how to do that anymore, and I didn't want to drag down the mood of his party any more than I already had. "You wanna surf tomorrow?"

"Yeah. I'll be there."

The fireworks started as soon as I reached my Jeep. Instead of driving away, I sat on the hood, my back against the windshield, and watched them. Independence Day had taken on a whole new meaning.

27

Remy

I SLOWED TO A JOG WHEN I GOT TO THE PARKING LOT. I was late today, but it was a Sunday, so I figured Shane wouldn't be working and would spend his day surfing.

"Oh my God. Oh my God," a girl squealed. "It's Remy St. Clair."

Three teen girls who looked to be about fourteen or fifteen piled out of a minivan.

"Can we get a picture with you?"

I smiled. "Sure. As long as you don't mind that I'm all sweaty." I probably looked like crap, my hair plastered to my head and my face pink from the exertion of running. I'd started running seven years ago. I never used to run. That had been Dylan's thing. Now I ran a lot.

"We don't mind," a lanky brunette said.

I posed with them, smiling for the group selfies. The woman driving the minivan thanked me and apologized for the fangirling as one of the girls waved her off and said she'd text when they were ready to be picked up.

"Are you here to surf?" a petite blonde girl asked.

"I just came to watch."

"I would love to be a model," the lanky brunette said. "How did you get into it?"

They walked with me along the path to the beach, carrying their boards on their heads. Surfer girls were cool.

"I got scouted."

"Just walking down the street?"

"I was working at a surf shop," I told them as we walked down the stairs to the beach. "A woman came in and asked if I'd ever considered modeling."

"Well, I can see why. You're even prettier in person."

"Thanks."

We stopped at the bottom of the staircase and they looked at the ocean then back at me, taking their boards off their heads and exchanging looks. "Not to be rude, but why did you quit?"

"It's too personal. That's like asking her about her love life," the petite blonde said, nudging her friend and giving her the eye.

"I quit because I started to wonder who I was beyond a pretty face. And I thought maybe it was time to find out." There's some honesty for you, girls. I hadn't expected those words to come out but there they were.

They nodded as if they understood. Maybe they did. "I get it. I mean, we have friends who are so busy posing for selfies and trying to look perfect. Like that's all they care about."

"They're not even into surfing or anything. It's so lame." She pulled a duck face and struck a classic selfie pose that made me laugh. "That's how they look in every single photo. I kid you not."

"Well... see you around," the blonde said. "Thanks for the photos."

"Bye. Nice meeting you," I said. "Have fun surfing."

"We will," they shouted in unison as they jogged down to the water.

The beach was crowded, but I found a quieter spot further away from the staircase and lifeguard stand and laid out my towel on the sand. Stripping down to my bikini, I donned my ballcap and sunglasses and leaned back on my elbows, scanning the surfers in the lineup, easily spotting Shane. I wanted him to myself. Not happening today. Or maybe ever again. I didn't know who he was anymore or what I meant to him or if he even cared that I watched him every day.

Today he was surfing with Travis. I'd followed his career. Not closely, but enough to know that his dreams had come true. Shane belonged up there. Right at the top. But I could see now that Travis had surpassed Shane. Technically, at least.

Shane was still more exciting to watch though. Even though he wasn't competing, he still took risks. He still left it all out there. It was in his nature. I watched him fly across the wave, gaining speed, and launch off the lip, catching air. He kicked the board and grabbed the rail—*Superman*—reconnecting with the board before landing. God, I loved to watch him surf.

Shane paddled back out, and my gaze moved to Dylan. He surfed like he lived, attacking the waves like they had wronged him. I bet he was hard on his boards. His surfing had improved so much since I'd last seen him surf though. Seven years of living in SoCal with the ocean on your doorstep would do that. I was so focused on watching Dylan that I didn't notice Travis until he was standing in front of me. He dropped his board on the sand and sat next to me.

"Look at you, all incognito. Barely recognized you in that disguise."

I laughed a little. "How's it going, Travis?"

"It's all good. Living the life." Travis had one of those chiseled faces and ice blue eyes that made him look cold and unyielding. He'd never had Shane's warmth. His gaze flitted to me briefly before he gave me his hard profile again, his eyes on the ocean. Surfers were always watching the ocean.

"Looks that way. I'm happy for you."

"How's the life of a supermodel?"

"Busy. Hectic. Sometimes good and sometimes not so good. It had its perks."

He nodded, and I got the feeling that he didn't really give a shit if my life was good or bad.

Scooping up handfuls of soft sand, I let the grains sift through my fingers while I waited for him to say what was on his mind.

"Are you just passing through or are you planning to stay?"

"I'm not sure yet. But I won't be leaving anytime soon."

He nodded. "Right. Don't take this personally, Remy. But he's been to hell and back. He doesn't need any more trouble in his life."

Trouble. That was how Travis saw me. I couldn't blame him. He was just trying to look out for Shane, not trying to make me feel like shit. But it still hurt, knowing that all I'd ever brought into Shane's life was trouble.

"He's trying to get his life back together, but it's not easy. And now..." Travis ran his hand over his buzzed hair. "he's going through a hard time. Just do me a favor and stay away from him. If you care about him at all, just stay the fuck away, Remy."

Some things would never change. The universe had always conspired to keep me and Shane apart. But Travis had always been a good friend to Shane, so I couldn't fault him for speaking his mind.

I opened my mouth to respond but closed it again. Travis was already walking away, his board under his arm, his message delivered.

I watched him jog back down to the water and paddle out, getting in the lineup next to Shane. Even from this distance, I could see the pissed-off expression on Shane's face and then Shane paddled in and I knew this was it. After seven years, we were going to come face to face. My heart hammered against my ribcage as he walked toward me. I should leave. I should get up and walk away. Listen to what Travis said. But I couldn't move.

He'd gotten bigger, his muscles more corded. His face harder-looking. There was no warmth in his eyes, no easy smile on his lips. I couldn't read his face like I used to, couldn't guess what was going on behind those hazel eyes. We didn't know each other anymore. The world had changed us. But one thing was certain—he didn't look like a guy who was loving life, who could turn every day into an adventure.

The magic was gone. It made my heart ache to look at him.

I'd imagined this day so many times but now that he was actually right in front of me I didn't know what to do or what to say.

My breath whooshed out of my lungs as he lowered himself onto the sand next to me, sitting in the same place Travis had been only minutes ago. After all these years, he was so close. Close enough to touch. From the corner of my eye, I noticed the rigid set of his shoulders, the clenched jaw. I was too much of a coward to turn my head or look into his eyes. Too scared of what I'd see in them. Or what I wouldn't see.

All our unspoken words filled the empty space between us. Shouted into the silence.

I destroyed Shane Wilder's life and there was no coming back from that.

28

Shane

"Why are you here, Remy?"

"I just came down to watch the surfers."

Her voice was the same—low and husky. Sexy. The sound still went straight to my cock. Another one of her secret weapons. She had an entire arsenal at her disposal.

I couldn't look at her. Not really. It hurt too much. But I watched her in my periphery, my gaze on the ocean. I had seen enough as I'd walked toward her—she looked sleek and elegant in a black bikini that showed off her taut stomach and flawless caramel skin. Now, she was chipping away at the dark polish on her nails just like she always used to do when she was nervous.

There was so much to say, yet nothing at all. I wanted to ask her how the world was treating her. If she had fallen in love. If she had found someone else. If she was sleeping with that British rock star I had seen her with on social media. But I didn't ask any of those things. Maybe I didn't want to hear the answers. Her life was so far removed from what it had been, from the life I'd been living for the past seven years, that I couldn't relate. I'd seen her on a yacht in Monte Carlo, drinking champagne as the fireworks exploded above her head. At Coachella, partying with rock stars and models in their designer festival wear. She wasn't the Remy I used to know. The world was her playground now. Doors opened for girls who looked like Remy St. Clair.

The day I'd finally given in to my curiosity and Googled her, I'd been at an all-time low which was saying something for a man who had spent six years in prison. Seeing Remy on a catwalk, on the covers of glossy magazines, in London and Paris and Milan, had sent me spiraling down even lower. A bigger man would have been happy for her. A bigger man wouldn't have been so angry. It was what I'd always wanted for her. To get on with her life, put her past behind her, and find a way to be happy.

Did I want her to be broken? God, no.

But I'd come to learn that I wasn't a bigger man. I was angry all the time now. At John Hart who had gone after me with a vengeance, seeking retribution for his dead son. At Remy's piece of shit mother. At a God I didn't believe in. At the doctors who claimed there was nothing more they could do. But mostly at myself. I was holding so much anger inside that one of these days I was going to implode. The ocean was the only place where I felt some sense of peace.

Without surfing, I would be a lost soul.

"Why didn't you let me visit you?" Her voice was quiet, barely audible over the sound of the waves crashing against the shore and the voices around us, but I heard her as if she'd shouted the words.

"You know why."

"Because you hate me?"

How I wished it had been that simple. Hatred was cut and

dry. Clean. Simple. Remy and I didn't inhabit a black and white world, we were shades of gray. Did I wish I had never met her? Sometimes. But other times, most of the time, I missed the girl I used to know. "Why would you think I hated you?"

She swallowed hard, fighting back tears, her voice quavering on the words. "What else was I supposed to think?"

"You were supposed to think that I didn't want you waiting around and fucking up your life for me. You needed to get the hell out of here. And I was hoping you'd never look back."

"Shane... I would have been there for you."

"Well, there's your answer. I didn't *want* you to be there for me."

"You're so stubborn, thinking you know what's best. I didn't get a vote, Shane. That's you though, isn't it?"

I could call her out as a hypocrite, reminding her that she'd done the same thing when she caved to Tristan's bullying tactics, but I didn't want to go there. Not now. Not ever. "Yeah, I guess it is."

I stood to go. There was nothing left to say. I didn't even ask what Travis had said to her. It was none of my business. *She* was no longer any of my business. Instead of heading back to the water, I carried my board to my Jeep. It was a sad day when I wasn't in the mood for surfing.

I loaded my board and peeled off my rash vest, tossing it in the back. I'd shower when I got home. As I closed the hatch, a hand wrapped around my bicep. I closed my eyes and tried to breathe.

Don't get so close, Remy. Don't touch me.

She pulled her hand away, but my skin still burned from her touch.

"Need something, Rem?"

"Yes. I need you to turn around and look at me."

Reluctantly, I turned to look at her, my brows raised in

question. Her eyes roamed over my bare chest before she lifted her eyes to mine. Her aquamarine eyes were still the same. Bottomless tropical seas. I had seen them in my dreams more times than I cared to admit.

"Don't say anything. Just listen, okay?" she said.

I clenched my jaw, arms crossed over my chest, my gaze fixated on a spot over her shoulder, waiting to hear what she felt she needed to say. My face and posture didn't indicate that I was open to listening, but I stayed where I was which had to count for something.

"I want to... I can..." She stopped and took a breath. "Why are you making this so hard?"

I gave her a slow, lazy smile and threw in a wink for good measure. "Just my special talent."

She growled. Yes, she actually growled, her hands balling into fists. It was fucking fantastic, riling up Remy. Despite everything she'd been through and all the shit in her life, Remy hadn't lost her fire. Thank God. For a while there, she was so lost. So... broken. But she was strong. And she was resilient. I was happy that the world hadn't broken her spirit.

"I have money. And I can help you do whatever you want. I can help you make your dream come true, Shane. If you want to pursue a surfing career, I can—"

I held up my hand. "Stop. Right the fuck there. I'm going to pretend I never heard those words come out of your mouth."

She narrowed her eyes at me, her chest heaving, hands planted on her hips. "Why not? I owe you—"

"Fucking hell, woman. Stop. Talking."

I climbed into my Jeep, and slammed the door, rolling down the window when she still hadn't budged. "Move your pretty ass before I run you over."

I revved the engine. She stepped out of the way, her self-preservation instincts still intact, and I hit the gas, intent on putting her words and her face and her everything behind me as I peeled out of the parking lot, leaving her in my dust.

Why, Remy? Why did I have to fall in love with you? You would think that time and distance would have dulled the emotions. Dimmed the memories. But it was all crystal clear. Every memory, every snapshot imprinted on my brain. The good, the bad, and the ugly.

Time and distance hadn't stopped me from wanting her. But she didn't belong in my world. An ocean separated us and that was how it needed to stay. Again.

I grabbed the grocery bags from the passenger seat and walked around the side of the house. My dad was lying in the hammock, his eyes closed, the evening sun on his face. I halted in my tracks, the grocery bags hanging at my sides.

"I'm not dead yet," my dad said, his eyes still closed.

I exhaled loudly, my shoulders sagging in relief. "Don't fucking scare me like that."

"It's a sad day when a man can't sit outside and enjoy the sunset without getting told off by his own son."

I refrained from mentioning that it was hard to see the sunset with your eyes closed. It was a beautiful one though. A pink and red sky that promised a good day tomorrow, if you believed the sailors' lore. Red sky at night, sailor's delight. I had always preferred sunrises to sunsets. Maybe because it was the start of a new day, a symbol of hope instead of the end of something.

"Let's never say goodbye, okay? Goodbye is the saddest word in the English language."

Yes, Remy. Yes, it is.

I wasn't ready to say goodbye. I wasn't ready to let him go. Was anyone ever ready for something like that?

He rolled a joint while I got the barbecue going and tossed a salad together, before throwing two swordfish steaks on the grill. We ate at the table on the patio just like we had so many nights before. My dad picked at his food, eating a few bites of everything and I nearly cried like a fucking baby when I saw that he'd only eaten half of his swordfish steak.

I cleared our plates and tossed his uneaten food in the garbage disposal. There was no point stowing leftovers in the refrigerator. They went uneaten. After I washed up our dishes, I returned to the patio where he was smoking a joint, the scent of weed hanging in the air.

My eyes roamed over the small vegetable garden in the backyard that my mom had planted so many years ago, my thoughts drifting to Remy. She used to love that little garden.

I tipped back on the hind legs of my chair, my fingers laced behind my head and listened to the sounds of the neighborhood. A dog barking a few doors down, kids screaming "You're It" in a game of tag, the rumble of a motorcycle engine as it roared past. All the little everyday things I'd always taken for granted. The stars reeled in the sky, reminding me of all those nights with Remy on the roof. Our dreams, our hopes, our dirty secrets. Her midnight black hair shimmering blue in the moonlight. The softness of her skin and the feel of her lips against mine.

"If this is wrong, why does it feel so right?"

"You wanna talk about it?" my dad asked, his eyes closed as he inhaled, holding the smoke in his lungs before he exhaled.

"Nothing to talk about."

He chuckled. "Yeah, okay. So this mood of yours has nothing to do with Remy St. Clair coming back to town."

I narrowed my eyes on him. It had been two days since I saw Remy, and I hadn't mentioned it to my dad. "How did you know she's back?"

"Saw her earlier."

"Where?"

"She was down at the marina with her brother."

"What were you doing down at the marina?"

"Now I have to report my every move to you?"

I ran my hands through my hair and let out a frustrated breath. I didn't like him driving and unless he walked or ran the five miles to the marina, he had to have driven.

"Sam and I went out on his boat. We went diving."

"You went diving," I repeated. "Should you be diving?"

The answer was no. Fucking no he should not. "What if you had a seizure—"

"I didn't, Shane. I'm okay." His voice was firm but gentle. I gritted my teeth. "Look at me."

I eyed my dad, noting the color in his face. He was always tan. Had always spent time in the sun. He was gaunter now, but he still looked okay. If you didn't know him well, you wouldn't notice anything was wrong. But I noticed. "Do I look like I'm ready to die today?"

He didn't. Looking at him, you wouldn't realize he was dying. In some ways, that made it harder to process. He didn't look sick. Even though he'd lost weight over the last few months, he wasn't frail or haggard. He was out fucking riding on his buddy's boat, deep-sea diving.

"Did you talk to Remy?"

"She came over to me, yeah. She's back for you, Shane."

"Did she tell you that?"

He chuckled, seeing the humor in something I failed to see. "She didn't have to. I know she still loves you."

We sat in silence for a while, my dad smoking his joint, while I tried to process his words. Was it really love? Maybe she thought she still loved me, but she didn't know me anymore. I wasn't the same guy from seven years ago and it wouldn't take her long to figure that out.

"And I'm guessing you didn't tell her what you're going through?" I asked, eyeing him.

"Nope."

I shook my head. "You're a pain in the ass."

"So are you," he said, his voice affectionate, his smile warm.

My dad loved me. Always had. He was the least judgmental person I'd ever met and the best damn father anyone could ask for. In some ways we'd been more like friends than father and son. He had never disciplined me. Had always let me find my own way in life. But he'd been there whenever I had needed him. He had taught me to surf. Had nurtured my love of the ocean. I owed him everything and had repaid him by going to prison. All his hard work shot to hell. All his dreams for me destroyed.

Because of my actions, he'd lost everything too, and it killed me that he'd sacrificed so much for me.

He wanted his last months to be a celebration of life for as long as he could live it fully. I didn't know how to do that. I didn't know how to turn off the thoughts that someday in the near future he wouldn't be hanging out on the back deck with me, smoking a joint and shooting the shit. Sharing his life's wisdom, albeit warped at times, but always welcome.

Prison was a cakewalk compared to this. I was angry all over again. Angry at the world. Angry at the precious years I'd lost with him. Angry at him.

"Why didn't you tell me sooner?" I asked, my frustration so pent-up I wanted to punch a hole in the wall. Like that would solve anything. He didn't answer for a few minutes. He knew what I was asking. Knew damn well what I was talking about. I could have had more time with him.

"I wasn't ready to accept it yet," he said simply. He had always been honest with me, sometimes painfully so. Except the one time I had needed him to be. "I was still in denial."

I let out a ragged breath. He offered me the blunt. I shook my head.

"No more diving," I said, trying to exert some authority I didn't have. He wouldn't listen. Never had. Never will. He didn't listen to the doctors either, thinking he knew best.

"Don't worry about it."

"Don't worry about it? Yeah, okay. I won't worry about you collapsing or getting rushed to the ER. I won't worry that you're taking your meds and eating your meals. I won't worry about a damn thing."

"You're struggling, Shane. You barely have the money to keep yourself afloat. And I'll be damned if I'm going to sit back and let my son carry my burdens along with his own. You might think you're taking care of me by mollycoddling me, but I can tell you right now, you're not."

"Don't worry about the bills. I've got that covered." I sure as hell didn't. Every day they piled up. I had a mountain of bills, but I paid off what I could. The hospital and the doctors had set up a special payment plan for me. It sucked that you couldn't even get sick without accruing debt. Insurance didn't cover everything. I had been the one who begged him to get the operation, holding out on the slim hope that it would give him more time. Or that they'd be able to remove the whole tumor. He hadn't wanted to let them do a craniotomy. But he'd done it. For me. He'd suffered through rounds of chemo and radiation that made him weak and nauseous. That fucked with his quality of life.

Until finally, one day, he said he was done. He was going to live out the remainder of his life on his own terms which was what he had wanted to do from the start. How could I argue with that? It was his life to live as he chose, right to the bitter end.

While I'd been in prison, he had lost the business. The surf shop hadn't been running at a profit. Why? Because of John

Hart. It hadn't been enough to send me to prison for manslaughter. He'd gone after my dad too. I had deserved what I'd gotten. My dad had not.

Now, the house was all he had left, and I'd beg, borrow, and steal before I'd let him lose that.

"It's settled anyway. I'm going to work for Sam for as long as I can."

"*Work* for him?"

"That's what I said."

Sam took people out on snorkeling and diving expeditions. It did not sound like the right fit for a man with a goddamn brain tumor. The set of his jaw told me there was no point arguing. And who was I to argue anyway? Being on a boat, diving, snorkeling, made him happy. "Now that's settled, you wanna tell me about Remy?"

"Like I said, there's nothing to tell."

"There's nothing standing in your way now. Nothing to keep you apart."

Was he delusional? *Everything* was standing in our way. "Are you playing matchmaker now?"

"I want to see you happy. It's been too long."

"Yeah well, Remy's not the answer to your prayers. She makes me the opposite of happy so stay out of it."

"Whatever you say." His mouth quirked with amusement like he didn't believe me. My dad believes in soul mates. He believes in love that lasts forever even when the person isn't there. I knew this because he had loved my mom that way. He'd had a few women in his life since my mom died but he always said that a man only has one great love in his life. And he'd already had his.

"It's not too late for your surfing career, Shane."

Et tu, Brute? What was it with the people in my life? "Who's going to sponsor a convicted felon?" I sounded bitter. We've had this conversation before. He kept insisting that I needed to do something that makes me happy. As if it was that simple. "It's not what I want anymore."

It was a lie. I'd give my right nut to get back into it. But we couldn't afford it. The pro surfing gig was expensive. Even if I had the money, the pro circuit would never let a convicted felon represent the sport of surfing. What I had done went against the entire ethos of the sport. For me, surfing was sacred, and I would never sully its name more than I already had. The media had called me a 'disgrace' to the sport of surfing.

Except for the time I'd Googled Remy, about six months ago, I stayed off social media.

Truth was, even if I could go back to pro surfing, I didn't have what it took anymore. Not physically. Not mentally. Not emotionally. Thirty years old, and I was all washed up. Cue the pity party for one.

"There are other things you can do in the surfing industry."

"Can we just drop it?"

He sighed, but he dropped the subject and we sat in silence for a while.

"I just don't want to think of what might have been."

"I know," he said.

"I'm sorry."

I apologized all the time now. It didn't stop me from saying things I shouldn't, but I didn't want my final words to him to be something I'd regret for the rest of my life. My dad taught me that a long time ago, but I never really took it to heart. Now I knew what it was like to live with regrets. To spend years going over and over what you could have—*should have*—done differently. That was my penance. They call it prison for a reason. It's more than just being confined to a six by nine cell. Trapped in bricks and mortar. Your own mind becomes a prison if you let it. I'd done my time, but some days I still felt like I was in a prison of my own making.

"Wanna go surfing with your old man after work tomorrow?"

"Yeah. Sounds good."

He smiled, contentment on his face. He looked like he was at peace. Happy. And I wondered what his secret was. How had he found a way to be so fucking happy, even though life had screwed him over time and again?

29

Remy

I PULLED INTO A PARKING SPACE ACROSS THE STREET FROM THE fancy deli on Main Street where Sienna used to buy her school lunches—Caesar salads and those fudge brownies she loved. We couldn't afford it back then but now I could buy anything I wanted, the reality of that hitting me harder now that I was back in Costa del Rey. I made my way around the store, throwing food and drinks into my basket and I ordered salads and sandwiches from the deli counter—all of Shane's favorite things, and lunch for me and Jimmy.

My GPS led me to an address in Escondido that Jimmy had given me after I begged him to tell me where Shane was working. Unfortunately, he hadn't warned me what to expect. This wasn't a construction job. Quite the opposite.

I parked across the street from the demolition site, a lump forming in my throat as I stared out the window. I spotted Shane immediately, tossing debris and cinder blocks into the back of a dump truck. This wasn't where he belonged.

A hardhat covered his golden-brown hair, the ends curling

a little at the nape of his neck. The muscles in his arms and shoulders flexed and bunched under a sweat-stained gray T-shirt and his tanned, muscular calves were cloaked in dust like his work boots. There was no smile on his lips. No expression whatsoever. He was on autopilot, just doing his job. It was the saddest thing I'd ever seen. If he was at least building something instead of hauling away the debris from a demolished building, it would have given me a glimmer of hope. But no. That wasn't the case.

I was tempted to drive away and pretend I had never seen him. Instead, I took a deep breath and got out of my car. I knew it was a mistake even before I crossed the street, but I put on my brave face and strode across the street to the tune of a few catcalls.

"Hey baby, you looking for a good time?"

"Look at that ass. Shake it, Mama."

Shane turned his head and his eyes met mine. Hands balled into fists, he glared at the guys—that had been a big part of the problem. He'd always been so protective of me and it looked as if that hadn't changed. He strode over to where I was standing and hopped over the chain-linked fence, landing in front of me. Grabbing my arm, he walked me back across the street to my Range Rover and around to the side, so we were hidden from the guys' view. He took off his hardhat and speared his hand through his sweaty hair, his hazel eyes narrowed on me. Today they looked more brown than green. Probably because he was so far from the sea. I used to think that's what made his eyes greener. That and being happy. Which he clearly wasn't.

I could smell his sweat and his laundry detergent and him. God, I missed his scent. Even when he was sweaty and covered in a layer of dust and grime, he still smelled delicious.

"What are you doing here, Remy?"

I held out the paper sack from the fancy deli, feeling ridiculous. "I brought you lunch."

He planted his hands on his hips and looked up at the sky as if it held all the answers. Maybe he was counting to ten, so he didn't lose his shit. He looked like he was trying to lock it down and the effort was costing him a lot.

Why did I always have to be the thorn in his side?

I took a step closer. He crossed his arms, warding me off, the muscles in his arms flexing, his jaw clenched. So, this was how it was going to be. I sighed.

"It's just lunch, Shane."

"I packed a lunch, Remy. I don't need yours."

Ignoring the sting in his words, I dangled the bag in front of him. "Mine's better. Knowing you, you've got a PBJ and a gnarly brown banana in your lunch."

Obviously, that was a joke. I didn't think he had changed that much.

He chuckled. It was so good to hear. It reminded me of the guy he used to be. Standing in front of Shane Wilder still made me feel like a sixteen-year-old girl with a hopeless crush.

Please take the lunch I'm offering. Please love me.

Pathetic, I know, but true nonetheless.

I was still holding the bag in front of him, but he made no move to take it from me. I snatched it back. "Fine. If you don't want it, it's going in the trash." I sauntered over to a trash can and pushed the bag against the lid.

His hand shot out and wrapped around my wrist, pulling my arm back before the bag ended up in the trash. He took the bag out of my hand and I turned to face him. His eyes raked over me from head to toe, from the off-the-shoulder short cotton dress down my legs to the strappy, flat suede sandals on my feet and back to my face. I wondered if he liked what he saw.

He moved closer, shielding me with his body so the other guys on the crew couldn't see me. The air around us crackled with electricity, the hairs on the back of my neck standing up. I was holding my breath, my eyes drinking him in. His throat bobbed up and down as he swallowed, and I raised my eyes to his, watching his eyes darken. I knew that look—the wanting, the longing. We were trapped in this silent battle, neither of us moving or breathing a word, the sounds of the demolition site and the traffic on the street silenced by the thrumming of my pulse. My heart was beating so hard and so loudly, I was sure that he could hear it.

His gaze dipped to the compass necklace he had given me all those years ago. "You still have it," he said, his voice rough.

I nodded without speaking, not wanting to break the spell. Scared that anything I might say would come out all wrong. I ran my tongue over my lower lip. He watched the movement, his breathing ragged. The years melted away under the hot summer sun and for a moment we were right back where we used to be. Back to that place so many years ago, when he still loved me.

But he averted his gaze and took a few steps back, taking my hopes with him. "I need to get back to work."

I forced a smile and opted for a playful tone, trying to lighten the mood. "I'd stay and have lunch with you, but I've got a hot date with Jimmy Wilder."

A shadow passed over his face. "You're having lunch with my dad?" His voice sounded strained and I didn't understand it.

"Jealous?" I teased.

"Yeah. I am, actually." His answer surprised me and so did the softness of his voice. I didn't know how to interpret it. I looked over at the demolition site. At his dusty work boots. His bronzed skin covered in a layer of grime and dust. It was baking hot out here and he was working in the unforgiving sun, miles away from the cool ocean breeze. Miles away from the place he used to call his home. The ocean. A wave of sadness engulfed me. It felt like the sun had disappeared from the sky. I wanted to put it back, set the universe right again, but I didn't know how to do that. All the money in the world couldn't replace the magic.

"Why are you doing a job like this? There must be something else, something better..." I let my voice trail off. His eyes narrowed, the muscle in his jaw ticking and I knew I'd said the wrong thing. The absolutely worst thing I could have said.

"Not fancy enough for you, Rem? A little different from your glamorous life, huh?"

I let out a breath. "Shane. I didn't mean it like—"

"Thanks for lunch."

He stalked away, and I stood there, watching him go, my feet glued to the sidewalk.

"Show's over," he told a couple guys who were still watching, more out of interest now, trying to figure out what was going on. Good luck, boys. If you figure it out, clue me in.

"Hey Miguel," he said to a big Hispanic guy.

"Yeah, man?"

"Here you go. Lunch is on me today." He shoved the paper bag into the guy's hands and kept walking. He knew that I was still watching him. He wanted me to see that. Yet another offer of help he refused. It was just lunch but even that had been a mistake.

I climbed into the silver Range Rover I bought yesterday. It looked too new and flashy in this neighborhood. Like me.

I gritted my teeth in frustration and blasted my music as I drove away, the A/C on full-blast and Alice in Chains singing "Man in the Box." My taste in music hadn't changed.

For a guy who claimed he didn't hate me, he sure as hell acted like he did. Come to think of it, he'd never directly answered the question. I didn't blame him. I'd hate me too. But for a moment back there, I had seen something else in his eyes, a spark of the old Shane. Until I went and opened my big fat mouth and dissed the job he was doing.

Smart move, Remy.

What had I expected? That I'd waltz back into his life and he'd profess his undying love for me?

It didn't have to be like this. I could make his life better. But I knew he wouldn't accept any money from me. His pride wouldn't allow it. I'd just have to find another way to help him.

When I pulled into Jimmy's driveway, I sat in my car for a while, not moving. I'd always loved this weathered-gray shingled house. It had a good vibe. I took a few deep breaths, gearing up to face Shane's dad. It seemed that my life was just one long series of deep breaths, gearing up to tackle another one of life's problems, some I'd created myself and others that had been thrust upon me.

When I had seen Jimmy down at the marina, we hadn't really talked. He'd been hanging out with his buddy Sam and I'd been with Dylan on the way to lunch. He'd given me his usual smile. No judgment on his face. And had pulled me into a hug like he was happy to see me. But how would it be when it was just the two of us face to face?

Of all the people in Shane's life, Jimmy had the biggest reason to hate me. To blame me for what had happened to his son. No matter how laid back Jimmy was, there must be a part of him that wished Shane had never met me. I closed my eyes and took yet another deep breath before I grabbed the bags with our lunch and rounded the side of the house. Nobody ever used the front door.

Jimmy was in the backyard, waxing a board, and Jack Johnson was singing about home, the music coming from speakers on the patio. It felt like old times. Same music. Same Jimmy, barefoot in a faded raspberry Jimmy's Surf Shack T-shirt and Hawaiian flowered board shorts. He still looked like the quintessential surfer dude.

"Hey Jimmy. I brought lunch," I called.

"Did you now?" he asked with a grin that still looked the same. "I'll be done in a minute."

"I'll grab some plates from the kitchen."

"Good deal," he said absently, continuing with his task, like his mind was elsewhere.

It's nothing personal, I told myself as I carried the food inside.

The house hadn't changed much, and I took comfort in that. The wood-paneled walls were still painted white. A braided rug sat on the honey-wood floors, a blue and white striped sofa and two overstuffed chairs grouped around a driftwood coffee table. The photos of Shane surfing I'd had enlarged for Jimmy still hung in frames on the wall, but new ones had been added. I moved closer to inspect them, immediately recognizing them as my own. The pier at dusk. The In-and-Out. The sun sinking into the ocean.

My pulse quickened as memories assaulted me, my mind going back to another time. I wondered if Jimmy had made this gallery wall. Or if Shane had. My bet was that it had been Jimmy. If he was displaying the photos I'd taken, maybe that meant he didn't hate me.

I set my bags on the kitchen counter and took down plates from the kitchen cabinet. As I transferred the salads into serving bowls, my eye caught on a stack of bills on the counter, the top envelope from Jackson Memorial Hospital. I glanced out at the backyard through the sliding glass door. Jimmy was still waxing a board, his eyes on his work. I picked up the envelope and flipped it over. It had been opened. Reading someone's mail was illegal and wrong on so many levels. I went to return it to the stack when I saw the one under it. This one was from Dr. Bell, an oncologist.

They were addressed to Shane Wilder. They were none of my business. And yet, despite the voice in my head telling me this was all kinds of wrong, I read Shane's mail. There weren't enough deep breaths in the world to make this better. The words and the dollar figures blurred on the page.

I steadied myself, gripping the counter, Travis's words playing in my head.

"...*especially now, he's going through a tough time.*"

No. No, no, no. Not Jimmy. Please, God. Don't take him away from Shane. He lost everything, he couldn't lose his dad too.

I heard footsteps and then Jimmy was in the kitchen, his eyes darting to the invoices clutched in my hand. I'd been caught red-handed, too shocked to even try to hide the fact that I'd been snooping. With trembling hands, I stuffed them back in the envelopes and set them on the counter.

"Jimmy... what's wrong with you?" I asked, my voice a whisper as I searched his face for answers.

"Forgot about those." Jimmy stashed the invoices into a drawer and shut it as if that would make it go away.

"Jimmy?"

"You weren't supposed to see those. I'm not even supposed to see them. Shane takes them before I can open them."

"Jimmy..." I said again. Whenever I used to look at Jimmy, I could imagine Shane twenty years down the road. I'd always liked what I saw and that hadn't changed. But upon closer inspection, I saw the changes from the past seven years. His hair, greying at the temples, was short now. I hadn't noticed it the other day because he'd been wearing a bandana on his head. He used to wear his hair longer like Shane's. Was he thinner?

"It's okay, darlin'. How about this lunch you promised me?"

I swallowed down the lump in my throat, not even remotely hungry for any of the food I'd brought. But we carried it outside to the table and I picked at my food before finally giving up on pretending to eat. Jimmy had barely touched his. He was rolling a joint as if he'd done it hundreds of times before.

I looked from his hands to his face, really taking him in. He was seven years older, but to me he was ageless. He had lines around his eyes from squinting into the sun. From a lifetime spent in or near the ocean. His skin was tanned. He didn't look sick. Not really.

His eyes were brown, not hazel like Shane's and they were studying my face. He lit the joint and closed his eyes as he inhaled, holding it in his lungs before he exhaled. Then he opened his eyes again and he smiled. "This is some good shit."

Tears stung my eyes. I was two seconds away from losing it.

"Hey, hey. Come on. It's okay."

"You'll be okay? You're going to be okay?"

He took another hit of his joint, his gaze focused on the backyard. He didn't answer my question for a good two minutes. I watched a bee buzzing around the potted flowers on the patio. The backyard was like a mini-Paradise of exotic-looking flowers and palm trees. The vegetable and herb garden still flourished.

"No, darlin'," Jimmy said, finally answering my question. "But you're going to be okay. You and Shane." He said the words with so much conviction that I almost believed him. And I knew he was trying to convince himself as much as me.

"What's wrong with you, Jimmy?"

I held my breath, waiting for his answer. "I have a brain tumor. Glioblastoma Multiforme. Stage Four."

I squeezed my eyes shut as if that would help me block out the words. "But they can operate, right? They can remove it or give you radiation to shrink it?" I fumbled for the words. I didn't know the first thing about brain tumors. Except that it sounded bad. So, so bad.

"Afraid not," he said, with a soft smile as if he was trying to lessen the blow for me.

"But there must be something the doctors can do." I was grasping at straws, refusing to believe it could be true. Desperate for a remedy or a solution. He shook his head, letting me know there was nothing more the doctors could do. I sat in silence, trying to process this information. Why was this happening to Jimmy? How could the world be so cruel? Jimmy was one of the good guys in a world that had too few of them.

And Shane... oh my God, Shane. I slumped back in my chair and rubbed my chest, trying to alleviate the ache. Shane loved his dad so much.

"There's nothing they can do?"

"Nope."

"So now what?"

"I live my life to the fullest. Until I can't."

Until I can't.

"Hopefully, I'll be seeing my sweet, sweet hippie chick when I get to wherever I'm going."

His sweet hippie chick was Zoe, Shane's mom. That was supposed to be the silver lining in this shit cloud but for the people he was leaving behind it was hard to take comfort in that.

Jimmy was calmly smoking his joint while I was dying inside. "I'm so sorry. I'm sorry I didn't visit you or call you... I thought about you. So much. I wanted to keep in touch, but I was scared, I guess. I was such a coward."

"Don't do that to yourself. I never blamed you. It wasn't your fault, understand?"

It was though. It was all my fault.

"You're here now. It's all good."

It's all good. Was he high? Well, yeah, that was some good shit, apparently.

I thought about the bills on the kitchen counter and I knew that Shane and Jimmy couldn't afford to pay them. But I could. That was one way I could help Shane. Too bad if it made him angry. He'd have to find a way to live with it.

"Can I get you something? Is there anything you need?" I wracked my brain, trying to think of what he could want or need. If it was within my power, I would get it for him. I'd even be his dealer if he needed me to get him more weed. Whatever he wanted or needed, I wanted him to know I would be here for him.

"You and Shane. Both playing nurse. At least you're prettier to look at."

I forced a laugh, but it sounded hollow. "I don't know... Shane's awfully pretty."

"Tell me where you've been, kiddo. How's the world been treating you?"

I settled back in my seat, relaxing slightly. He might be dying, but he was here now, and he sounded like his old self. He didn't want me to mourn his loss while he was still very much alive.

"The world... well, I've seen a lot of it. I traveled to all those places I used to dream about."

"And how did the reality live up to the dream?"

I smiled. "Sometimes it did and sometimes it didn't."

"That's life, isn't it? What's your plan now?"

"I don't have one. I can be your nurse."

He chuckled. "Not ready for that yet. I've still got some living to do."

That was good to hear, but I was still trying to wrap my head around the reality.

"How about your photography?"

"That was just a hobby."

He shrugged one shoulder. "Do something you love, and the money will follow. Or not. Doesn't matter. Just be happy."

That was Jimmy's attitude. It always had been. It wasn't something I had ever fully understood. But maybe it was the right attitude. I wanted to ask him what had happened to his surf shop. But I was scared to bring it up. I had a sinking feeling it was another casualty of the whole mess I'd created.

"Why did you come back?" he asked, cocking his head as he studied my face. It was another gesture that reminded me so much of Shane.

"Dylan told me Shane was back. He told me he saw him... back in February. I was in Paris for Fashion Week when he called me." That sounded so strange, another world away. "Anyway, I'd been thinking about taking a break from modeling and I felt like... I needed to come back and make sure he was okay. Or... I don't know. Just *see* him. Confront the past, you know? So here I am."

He nodded like that was perfectly reasonable behavior. I came back for Shane. I came back to see if he was okay and now that I knew it was so much worse than anything I could have imagined, I wasn't sure what to do next.

"I'm glad you're here. You're just what Shane needs."

I laughed at his words. "I'm pretty sure I'm the last thing he wants or needs. He wants nothing to do with me."

Jimmy chuckled. "Sure he doesn't."

I cleared the table, telling Jimmy to sit down and relax when he tried to help. I needed something to do, something that might make me feel useful even though I was helpless. I couldn't heal Jimmy. I couldn't fix Shane. But I could pay their bills. So, I tucked them in my purse before I returned to Jimmy who was relaxing in a deck chair like he didn't have a care in the world. I wished I could channel some of his Zen into my own life.

"Do you need anything?" I asked, looking around the backyard for something to do that might be helpful but everything appeared to be in order. "Is there anything I can do for you?"

"*I* don't need a damn thing."

"What does Shane need?" I asked quietly.

"Someone to hold his hand and help him through this."

I would hold his hand and walk through fire with Shane. I would follow him to the pits of hell. If only he'd let me. But he hadn't let me back then and I didn't think he'd changed that much to believe he'd let me help him now.

"He needs to get back out there and start living again."

"He still surfs," I said, defending Shane.

"Uh huh. And that's an hour or two out of his day. The rest of the time he spends working or hanging out with me."

"He wants to spend time with you."

"I know he does. And I want to spend time with him. But he needs to stop hovering. He's like a helicopter parent."

I laughed. "Because he's worried. Because he loves you. So much."

Jimmy averted his head and nodded. "I know. And I love him. That's why I need to see him happy."

My heart hurt for Jimmy and for Shane. For seven years, I had tried to move on with my life. I had smiled for the cameras, strutted the catwalk. I had gone to parties at trendy clubs, traveled the world, dined at some of the best restaurants. But no matter what I'd done or where I'd been, I had never once stopped thinking about Shane. And I had never loved anyone the way I loved him.

What was hard though, was being back here and not knowing if Shane even wanted me in his life. That was before I knew about Jimmy. This changed everything. If I believed in fate, I'd take this as a sign. I was supposed to come back. I was supposed to be here.

I would do whatever I could for Jimmy. And I would try to help Shane. Even if he tried to push me away, I would be there for him the same way he'd always tried to be there for me.

Jimmy's eyelids were heavy, like he was fighting sleep, so I sat in silence for a while until he drifted off. When his breathing was deep and even, I ventured down the small hallway and used the bathroom. Then I opened the door to Shane's childhood bedroom and stood in the doorway for a moment. This was as bad as reading someone's mail.

I breathed in his scent as I looked around Shane's childhood bedroom. Everything was neat and tidy, the bed made, and the dresser top clear. Glancing over my shoulder to make sure nobody was watching, I opened the bedside table drawer, my heart sinking when I saw a box of condoms. Well, what did you expect? That he'd live like a monk? I closed the drawer, hating that the thought of him with another woman made my stomach churn. That old jealousy rearing its ugly head.

He was mine. *Mine.*

Except that he wasn't and never really had been.

I opened the dresser drawers, confirming that Shane's clothes were in them. Folded T-shirts and board shorts. Sweatshirts and jeans. I closed each drawer, telling myself I would stop after the next drawer. I shouldn't be in here. I shouldn't be searching for clues about the man I used to know. Touching his things. Holding his pillow to my nose and inhaling deeply as if it would bring him closer to me. This was stalker mode.

But I couldn't seem to stop myself. I wanted to know who he was now. I was searching for clues that would enlighten me. I opened the closet door and looked at the collection of shoes lined up on the floor—Nikes, flip-flops, Vans, work boots. Flannels, jackets, and hoodies on hangers, all of which I recognized. Nothing new here.

My eye caught on three shoeboxes on the shelf above the hanging rail. I knew I wouldn't find Nikes inside. I waited a few seconds, listening for signs of movement. The house was quiet.

No, Remy. Don't do it. You have crossed a line.

I did it. I pushed aside the beanies and baseball caps and pulled one of the boxes down from the shelf. Then I sat on the edge of his bed, took a deep breath and lifted the lid. Ignoring the twinge of guilt, my hands shook as I sifted through the photos. Some of them were taken with the Polaroid Jimmy had given me. Photos of Shane. Photos of us. Photos of me. Underneath the photos was a stack of letters I'd sent him in prison. The rest of them must be in the other two shoeboxes. I'd written him so many letters and had never once gotten a reply. I rifled through them. They'd all been opened. I had told myself that he hadn't received them. But he had. And here they were.

"The fuck are you doing in here?"

I startled. The box crashed to the floor, photos and memories spilling across the braided rug. I got on my hands and knees, trying to gather them up, return them to the box. Shane put his hands under my arms and hauled me to my feet. "Get out of my room."

"Shane—"

"Go." He pointed to the door, his teeth gritted.

"No. I'm not leaving." I planted my hands on my hips like I had the right to be here. Like I had any right at all to push back when I was clearly in the wrong here. But that was me, wasn't it? "Not until we talk about everything. You keep avoiding me. I was trying to find out who you are now."

He let out a harsh laugh. "So you thought the answer was to come into my room and go through my shit?"

"You cut me out of your life."

"What the fuck was I supposed to do, Remy? I was in prison for *manslaughter*."

Manslaughter. Such an ugly word. It had been an accident. Shane was not capable of killing anyone. "I never got to see you again. I never got to talk about anything...you could have let me visit you. Why wouldn't you let me see you?"

He stared at me for a moment and then turned me around, grabbed me by the shoulders and shoved me in front of the mirror on the back of his closet door. "Look at yourself, Remy. Take a good long look."

"I know what I look like." I knew every flaw too. They'd been pointed out over the years, spoken aloud as if I wasn't in the room.

"I don't think you do. I don't think you ever did. You were always so fucking oblivious to how you looked. To what it did to people when they saw you. To *men*," he added, his voice tight.

His fingers dug into my shoulders, his body vibrating with anger. With frustration.

"Don't go there, Shane," I warned.

"I thought you wanted to talk. Change of heart?"

I'd had seven years of therapy. I should be able to handle a conversation with Shane. "Fine. Let's talk."

"Not until you look at yourself. Take a good, long look."

I looked in the mirror, but I wasn't looking at myself. I was looking at him. Shane was gorgeous. He always had been. His muscles didn't come from working out in a gym. They came from manual labor and from surfing. They came from sweating in the hot SoCal sun. And his face... I had always loved it. The broad cheekbones and full lips. The square, firm jaw and the little lines around his hazel eyes from squinting into the sun.

I miss your face.

"Shane," I whispered. He was still holding my shoulders, but his grip had relaxed. His callused hands were warm against my bare skin. He leaned in closer, the heat of his body and his nearness making me dizzy.

"Remy." My name on his lips sounded like a plea or a prayer. I heard the desperation in his voice, felt his chest rising and falling against my back as I leaned into him, needing his strength.

Kiss me. Hold me. Never let me go.

"Shane. I've missed you. So much," I whispered.

He dropped his hands to his sides and took a step back. "I can't do this. Not again."

It felt like he'd poured a bucket of ice water over my head. I shivered, wrapping my arms around myself for protection. I was losing him again, before I'd ever gotten him back, the moment we shared too much for him.

He ran his hand through his hair. "I was in prison, Remy. Do you really think I would expose you to that? Did I need to know that guys were jerking off thinking about your face and your body? Trust me. They would have, and I would have heard about it. All. The. Damn. Time. They would have taken one look at you..." He stopped and exhaled, and I watched his face in the mirror, the pain etched on his features. His raw, naked emotions on display. All I wanted to do was comfort him, but he wouldn't let me. "You didn't belong there. I never wanted that for you. Not after everything you'd been through. It would have killed me to see you."

I swallowed hard, wanting to say something, anything that would make this better for him. He lowered his head and rubbed the back of his neck.

"Just go, Remy. Please go."

He didn't sound angry anymore. Just tired. Resigned. Like this was our fate and he'd decided to accept it rather than fight it. Maybe we were never meant to be together.

I nodded. "Okay." I nodded again. And then I walked out of his childhood bedroom, but I stopped in the hallway, my back to his room. "Why didn't you answer my letters?"

"I never read them," he said.

I shook my head. Shane wasn't a liar. Why was he lying about this? "But... they've been opened..."

"Not by me. Inmates don't get to open their own mail."

Another liberty that had been stripped from him. And yet, he'd kept the letters without reading them. All this time, and he still hadn't read them. "Why didn't you read them?"

I waited for an answer, not really expecting one. But still, I waited.

"It hurt too much," he said quietly. So quietly that I strained to hear him.

Without turning to look at his face again, I walked out of the house and I drove away. All I was to him now was a painful reminder of everything he'd lost. He wasn't the Shane I'd known so many years ago and I was no longer the same Remy.

It hurt too much.

30

Shane

"There must be some mistake."

"My records show that it's been paid in full," the woman said. "Will there be anything else today, sir?"

"No. Thanks." I cut the call and dialed the next number, somehow knowing it would be the same. It was. I stuffed the invoices back into my glove compartment and slammed the palm of my hand against my dash. Then I got out of my Jeep and kicked the tire a few times. No surprise that it didn't make me feel any better.

I got back in my car and drove to the marina.

The wooden walkway creaked under my feet as I strode to the end of the dock, in search of my dad. I found him hosing down the deck of Sam's boat. Two wetsuits hung over the railing which led me to the conclusion that he'd been out diving again. Of course, he was going to go ahead and do whatever he damn well pleased. That was him, wasn't it?

He looked me up and down. I was still wearing my work clothes. I was a sweaty mess of dirt and grime. The dust from the demolition site was clogging my throat. It was a beautiful evening, but somehow, I'd found a way to resent the sun for shining. I stared out at the water, the place that used to be my home but wasn't anymore.

"Something on your mind?"

I dragged my eyes away from the water and to his face. "You've been diving again."

It was a rhetorical question, so he didn't bother answering. He waited for me to get to the real reason I'd charged over here, not even stopping to shower. "What did you tell Remy? Does she know about..." I couldn't even bring myself to say the words. "The bills have all been paid."

He laughed, taking me by surprise. "I should have known." He was still laughing to himself although I didn't get the joke. "She wanted to help. She found the bills on the counter. I stuffed them in a drawer but too late."

I threw up my hands. "And now she's gone and paid the damn things. You weren't even supposed to open them. I told you to leave them for me—"

"You need the help. She wants to help."

"I don't need fucking help. Least of all from her."

"Stop being a stubborn ass."

"Since when are you okay about accepting handouts?"

"Sometimes you have to swallow your pride. This is one of those times," he said calmly, like we weren't talking about tens of thousands of dollars.

Un-fucking-believable. He was calmly cleaning the deck, not upset in the least that Remy St. Clair had paid our bills.

"Maybe you're okay with it, but I'm not accepting her money."

"What are you going to do? Throw it back in her face?"

That's exactly what I was going to do. I didn't want her pity. Or her guilt money. Or whatever the hell it was.

"Did you ever stop to think it will make her feel better? Are you really going to take that away from her? You're not the only one who lost something. She lost you. And the girl didn't have a lot to begin with. She was dealt a shit hand, but she never complained. Never sat around feeling sorry for herself. She loved you, still does. So, for once in your life, don't be a stubborn ass about this. Accept it graciously. And get on with your life."

Get on with my life. Like it's so easy to do that. The huge chip on my shoulder and all the baggage I was carting around was weighing me down. I was sinking under the weight of it all. Some days I felt like I was drowning. My dad was dying and there wasn't a damn thing I could do about it. Paying the bills had made me feel some small sense of control, like at least I could contribute. Try to put a dent in the massive debt I owed this man.

Now she'd gone and taken that away from me. Might as well chop off my fucking balls and call it a day.

"I don't need a babysitter or a nurse. I don't need you sitting around, watching over me every night."

Didn't he get it? I needed to be there for him the way he had always been there for me. Who was the stubborn ass now?

"When I'm about to die, I'll let you know. Until then, go do something meaningful. Or fun. Hell if I know. Just do something. I'm still alive and so are you. Start acting like it."

I stared at my father. The fuck? I scratched the back of my neck, still staring at him. He raised his brows, daring me to argue with him. Instead, I walked away. I had nothing left to say.

After I'd gotten out of prison last year, I'd been selfish. I'd driven up the coast, wanting to get away from John Hart and Costa del Rey, and the memories that came with being here. I rented a room above an old lady's garage in Bodega Bay. I was her handyman, taking care of chores she couldn't do anymore. Fixed her leaky pipes and repaired her front porch. Mowed her lawn. Bought her groceries. I surfed on rocky beaches, in the wild water of NorCal. It was the coldest summer I'd ever spent. I met a girl. The lady's granddaughter. A blonde pixie of a girl who looked nothing like Remy St. Clair. She was kind and she was good, and I was trying to reinvent myself. Trying to forget.

She told me she loved me. I couldn't say it back.

Then I got the call from the hospital, and I returned home.

There was a big difference between living and just surviving. I used to know how to live. I used to be pretty damn good at it.

"Now we're talking," my dad said, a big smile on his face as I stapled the plastic sheeting to the wood frame around the shaping bay I'd built in the garage. The fluorescent lights hung at waist level to highlight any imperfections, and my new tools lined the shelves—electric planer, block plane, surform, various grits of sandpaper.

"You've lost your parking spot."

"Small price to pay."

"Yeah, well, reserve that judgment until you see the finished product. It might be shit."

"It might be. But if it is, you can make another surfboard. And that one will be better. What are you thinking?" he asked as I set the EPS foam blank on the shaping stand.

"A seven-foot-six. Thick nose, low rocker, pintail."

My dad nodded his approval. "Good on the small, mushy waves but easily maneuverable on the bigger, steeper days."

"That's the idea."

He knew who the board was for without having to ask.

Over the next week, I devoted all my free time to shaping, glassing, and finning that surfboard. I lost all track of time, sometimes not stopping until two in the morning. I did so much sanding, the inside of the shaping bay looked like a snow globe. The perfectionist in me wouldn't stand for hills, bumps or dips. It had to be a smooth, solid curve from tip to tail. It took me six hours to shape the board. At least a hundred times, I ran my hand along the rail, then sanded. Ran my hand along the rail, more sanding.

Shaping was a skill and an art form, I'd come to learn. It was also highly addictive. By the time I finished glassing the board, I was hooked, and already thinking about the next board I wanted to make.

31

Shane

On Saturday morning, I was leaning against the back of my Jeep, waiting for Remy. She jogged into the parking lot and slowed to a walk, stopping in front of me.

"Why aren't you out there already?"

"I was waiting for you."

"If you're going to argue, you'll be wasting your breath."

I didn't say anything. I just stared at her. Her skin was covered in a sheen of sweat, her hands planted on her hips, chest heaving from the exertion of running. Her jet-black hair was pulled into a high ponytail, the style accentuating her sculpted cheekbones. What was it about Remy that made her so beautiful it knocked the breath out of your lungs just to look at her? The camera loved her. She was a chameleon. When I'd looked at some of her photos in magazines, I'd barely recognized her.

Over the years, she'd only gotten more beautiful, if that was possible. More polished. More refined. Even her running clothes looked like designer items, her running shoes top of the line. When she had shown up at the demolition site, she looked like she'd just stepped off a catwalk. The guys I worked with were still talking about her. Her ass. Her mile-long legs. Her tits. Her everything. It still stirred up the beast in me. Made me jealous of any man who wasn't me, for even looking at her.

I wanted her all to myself. Always had. Probably always would. But there was no place in my life for her now.

Why did you have to return to my world and turn it upside down again, Remy? Why do you make me want you all over again?

Remy averted her head, showing me her profile, also perfection. She was looking in the direction of the ocean even though we couldn't see it from here. "Where have you been?"

"Busy."

"Too busy to surf?" Her gaze returned to my face, her dark brows furrowed in confusion.

"I've been surfing. Just not here."

"Oh." Her shoulders sagged. "Shane, I don't want... if you're not surfing here because of me, I won't come here anymore. I'll just—"

"I have something for you."

"You... what is it?"

I took the boards off the roof rack—mine and the one I'd made for her. Yesterday after work, I'd tested it down at the pier. It was nothing compared to the money she'd shelled out, but it was something I could give to her. And lo and behold, I'd found something I enjoyed doing.

"You bought me a surfboard?" She studied the board—turquoise with black stripes.

"I didn't buy it."

"You didn't..." I flipped the board to the other side—glossy white with a signature: Firefly. Her mouth formed a comical O and her eyes widened. "Oh my God, Shane. This is..." Tears filled her eyes and she held a hand over her heart. "It's so beautiful."

I huffed out a laugh. "It's my first attempt. Beautiful is a stretch but hopefully it will—"

Before the words were out of my mouth, she threw her arms around my neck and hugged me tight. My hands found their way to her waist and upper back. Closing my eyes, I inhaled her scent. She didn't smell like green apple shampoo and summer rain anymore. But she smelled good. So fucking good. And she felt so right in my arms.

"Thank you." Clearing her throat, she released me and took a step back. "Sorry. I'm all sweaty."

I ran my hand through my hair, trying to pull myself together. "No problem," I said gruffly.

She ran the palm of her hand over the surfboard and I was jealous of an inanimate object. "It's so smooth. So perfect. I'm just... I can't believe you did this for me, Shane. It means so much to me. You give me the best presents." Her voice was soft, and she lifted her eyes to mine, all her emotions on full display. My chest tightened, and I took a deep breath. I hadn't expected such an emotional reaction, on her part or mine.

"It's just a surfboard."

"It's so much more than a surfboard but okay, we'll go with that. So, does this mean I get to surf with you?" Her eyes lit up as if the prospect of that was thrilling. The funny part was that she could have bought herself a board. She could have bought a Firewire or any damn board she wanted but she hadn't.

"The ocean doesn't belong to me, Remy. You're free to surf whenever and wherever you want."

She rocked back on her heels, her hands clasped behind her back. "I guess I was waiting for an invitation."

"That's not like you."

She flinched at my words that had come out sounding harsher than I'd intended but she recovered quickly and plastered on a fake smile. "I guess that's the new me."

The *new* Remy stripped down to a white bikini right in

front of me. The *new* Shane had the same reaction as the old Shane. My dick appreciated the view. My fingers itched to untie the strings, freeing her breasts from the triangles of fabric.

Millions of people had seen her in a bikini. Sad fuck that I was, I knew she'd been in the swimsuit issue of Sports Illustrated. But I couldn't even look at her in a bikini without getting hard. Without dying to touch every inch of her skin with my lips, and my mouth, and my teeth. Her skin. I could still remember the silky softness of it. The way her body had yielded to mine. The sound of her soft moans and whimpers.

She stuffed her running clothes and sneakers into her backpack and I locked it in the Jeep.

"I can carry my own board."

I shrugged one shoulder in response and carried both boards. We were silent on the walk along the trail, down the stairs and to the water's edge. Her toenails were painted a blush pink color that matched her fingernails. The soft, pretty nail color was disconcerting. She always wore dark polish.

"I haven't surfed since I left Costa del Rey," she admitted.

"Why not?"

"Because... surfing..." She let out a breath and shook her head, her gaze on the ocean. "I just didn't."

Because of me. She hadn't surfed because it reminded her of me. "Do you still remember how to paddle out?"

"I know how to paddle out," she scoffed.

"I don't know... those spaghetti arms are no match for these waves."

"These spaghetti arms? Ha." She made a muscle, all proud of herself. I laughed at her and she rolled her eyes. "Are we surfing or comparing muscles?"

"There's no comparison." I grinned and paddled out, leaving her to her own devices. That was how she was at her best. Her most resourceful. She needed to be challenged, to be told she couldn't do something, only to show everyone that she could and twice as good as everyone else.

I glanced over my shoulder, chuckling at the determined look on her face as she tried to paddle out to where I was, the waves intent on beating her back to shore. Straddling my board, I watched her duck-dive, relief flooding through my body when her head bobbed up, a smile on her face. That's my girl. She caught up to me and we floated on our boards for a while. It was a perfect day for surfing. Light winds. A west onshore breeze and that little bit of crumble on the lip that makes it easy to attack for airs, yet still clean on the face for carves.

She trailed her hand through the water. "I've missed you. I missed us."

I didn't say anything. What could I say to that? I missed you like a missing limb.

"I never got to tell you how sorry I was. I never got to tell you—"

"There's no point in dredging up ancient history. It's over. There's nothing to talk about." I clenched my jaw. "Subject closed. Don't bring it up again."

She let out an exasperated sigh. "Are there any topics we can discuss? You're so damn prickly."

"How about all the money you spent? You want to talk about that? I don't want your charity."

"It's not charity. How many times did you do the same for me and Dylan? How many times did you buy us groceries and pay our utilities, so they didn't get shut off? This was no different."

"It's a hell of a lot different." I watched a bead of water trail down the sun-kissed skin of her lower back and disappear inside her bikini bottom.

"Why? Why is it different?"

I scoffed. "Because I'm a man."

She laughed. "Oh my god, you're such an ass. Talk about a double standard."

"Less talk, more surfing. The next wave has your name on it."

"I just want to float and find my Zen." She closed her eyes and folded her hands as if in prayer. "You take it."

"Nope." Jarring her from her meditation, I turned her board around and gave it a shove. "Go! Paddle hard."

She lay on her belly and paddled for the wave—it was shaping up to be a four-foot to overhead on the outside peak. The lines were long, and it wasn't too big that it was closing out. But she hesitated, just that moment of indecision, and that cost her. The wave passed right under her before she popped-up, pushing the tail of the board up and the nose down. She was too far forward and did a nosedive into the ocean. I watched until she emerged and winced as the next wave slammed over her head. Retrieving her board and getting it underneath her, she paddled back out to me.

"That wasn't pretty," she said when she joined me, shaking water out of her ears. "It was fun though."

"Yeah?" I laughed.

Her face broke into a big smile and I read the joy on her face. "So much fun."

"Crazy girl."

"I need to keep my weight back, right? And I should have popped up sooner."

"Look at you, critiquing yourself."

"I learned from the best." She gave me a big exaggerated wink and I chuckled. Being out here with her, surfing together again, made me forget my problems for a while. It was too easy to fall back into the way things used to be, but I knew I couldn't do that.

"Let's see what you've got," she said, eying the same wave I was. Her eyes sparkled, her face lit up with a smile. This was the Remy I had imagined on my darkest days. The picture I carried in my memory. Seven years older but her smile, the real one that wasn't for the cameras, hadn't changed. She nudged my arm. "Go!"

After a couple hours of riding waves, she was starting to find her rhythm and her confidence again. I paddled back out to her and she gave me a big smile. "You've still got the magic."

"You know it, Firefly."

She gave me a soft smile at the use of her old nickname. I'd said it without thinking, slipping back into another time and place.

Surfing with Remy was one thing. Anything more would ruin me. I didn't for a minute believe that she would be happy to stay in Costa del Rey. Or that I could fit into her life now. She had gone on to bigger things. Her world had expanded. She was loaded with money, could go anywhere and do anything she damn well pleased. Once she figured out what she wanted to do next, she'd be gone. Even if she did stay in Costa del Rey, she was too far out of my reach now.

I shook my head, spraying her with droplets of water from my hair. She laughed and tried to shove me off my board, but I held my ground. "Watch yourself, sweet lips or you'll be drinking ocean water."

"I'm holding steady. You can't knock me off my board."

I laughed. "It would take zero effort to knock you off that board."

She raised her brows in challenge. "Prove it."

"I'm thirty years old, not thirteen," I scoffed.

"You're practically a senior citizen. You probably don't have the same strength you used to."

My hand darted out and I flipped her board. She tumbled

into the water and came up sputtering, pushing her hair out of her face.

"You play dirty," she said, laughing as she got the board underneath her again.

I winked. "And if memory serves... you loved it."

Her laughter died, and she stared at me for a few seconds, her tongue darting out to lick her lips. I averted my gaze. Why had I said that? I stifled a groan.

We surfed for another hour until it got too crowded to get in a decent ride. Remy chose to leave when I did, and we stood side by side at the outdoor showers, rinsing away the saltwater. We toweled off next to my Jeep, and I secured our boards to the roof. This part, surfing and all that went with it, felt so familiar.

"Come on. I'll give you a ride." Which was how this whole damn thing had started nine years ago.

"I can run home."

I sighed, sensing her hesitation. She wanted a ride, otherwise she would have taken off already instead of standing in the parking lot. "Get in."

She climbed into the passenger seat and directed me to Dylan's house. She was still shit at giving directions.

"Oh. You were supposed to turn left back there," she said, pointing back at the street we'd just driven past.

I rolled my eyes and turned around in someone's driveway, hanging the next right. Eventually, after a series of wrong turns, we reached our destination—Dylan's two-story Spanish-style house. I'd always liked this neighborhood with its views of the hills, the canyon, and the sea. The guy was only twenty-five and he'd gone from nothing to everything. The St. Clair twins had conquered the world. Good for them.

Which brought it home all over again, just how much our lives had changed and how far apart we'd drifted.

"Thank you," Remy said as I handed her the surfboard. "For the board and for getting me out there today."

"No problem." I climbed back into my Jeep and she came to stand by my open window.

"I'll see you tomorrow?" Her voice was hopeful. I didn't turn my head to look at her face.

"I'll be there."

She was still lingering outside my open window like she didn't want to leave. I watched her from the corner of my eye as I shifted into reverse. Her lower lip was clamped between her teeth. Those poor damn lips.

I remember those lips, Remy. I remember your kisses.

"Gotta run," I said. Yeah, I was being a dick. But like falling in love with Remy, I just couldn't seem to stop myself.

Her face fell in disappointment, but she plastered on that smile again. It must have been something she learned from the modeling gig. Smile and pretend everything is fine even when your world is falling apart. "Yeah, okay."

She took a few steps back and watched me reverse out of her driveway. As tempting as it was, I didn't even glance at her as I drove away. Being around her again was hard. Being without her was harder.

But then, nothing about me and Remy had ever been easy.

32

Remy

I DIDN'T NEED AN EXCUSE TO HANG OUT WITH JIMMY, BUT ON THE Monday after Shane gave me the surfboard, I came up with one anyway. "I thought the three of us could have dinner together. I bought some steaks. I know you guys don't eat meat that much, but you used to love steak sometimes, right?" I was blabbering like an idiot as I unpacked my bags onto the kitchen counter. "We can grill them. And I'll make a big salad. I wasn't sure what vegetables you had from your garden, so I bought some, but we can use yours." I stopped and took a breath, noting the amused look on his face. "In other words, I've just invited myself to dinner."

Jimmy chuckled. "I've worked that out. You're always welcome."

I wasn't so sure about that, but I didn't set him straight. Jimmy set two chopping boards on the counter and tomatoes, peppers and cucumbers from his garden. I took the knife he handed me and started chopping vegetables.

"Is steak okay? I could go buy fish or..."

"Do you want to talk about it?"

When I worked for Jimmy at the surf shop for those two years, he used to ask me that question all the time. Nine times out of ten I used to say no. Back then, I kept a lot of secrets. I hadn't wanted him to know about my mom or my relationship with Shane or what was going on with Tristan. And now... I didn't have a lot of secrets but my problem, of course, was Shane. I still couldn't believe he made that surfboard for me. It was a beautiful board and even Dylan was impressed. Since then, we surfed together twice but only because I drove down to the break and he was there. So, it wasn't like we were really together.

I added my chopped tomatoes to the bowl of mixed greens and set an avocado on the board. "There's nothing to talk about."

He chuckled and shook his head as he added his chopped cucumber to our bowl of salad while I ran the blade of my knife around the avocado, halving it.

"What's so funny?"

"You and Shane."

I didn't really see anything funny about me and Shane, so I steered the conversation away from me and Shane. "How was your day? Did you go out on Sam's boat?"

"I had a good day. And yes, I went out on Sam's boat."

"Good. That's good." I'd been reading up on brain tumors and I wasn't sure that was good. I could understand why Shane was worried about Jimmy. What if something happened to him when he was diving? The avocado half slipped out of my hand when I tried to whack the pit with the blade of my knife.

Jimmy nudged me aside and took the knife out of my hand. "You looked like you were about to lose a finger."

I leaned my hip against the counter and watched Jimmy remove the pit and the skin from the avocado. Bob Marley was singing "Three Little Birds" and the ceiling fans whirred above our heads. Jimmy and Shane had never liked air conditioning. They preferred to sweat out the heat rather than breathe artificial air.

"Shane's never been good at dealing with his emotions," Jimmy said, the blade of his knife slicing the avocado I'd mangled. "After Zoe died, he refused to talk about her. This went on for months. At first, I didn't notice. I was too caught up in my own shit. I thought he was okay, that he was handling it better than most nine-year-olds would. But he wasn't handling it at all. He was trying to block it out. Until one day, about six months after she died, he lost it." Jimmy shook his head, remembering back to when Shane was a kid struggling to come to terms with his mother's death.

"What did he do?"

"I couldn't find him anywhere. It was getting dark and his bike was gone from the garage. I found him down at the beach. The break where he surfs now. He'd snapped his board in two. Smashed it right on the rocks. I was furious, yelling and screaming at him for taking off without telling me and for breaking his board. He loved that board. It was his most prized possession."

"But he broke it. On purpose."

Jimmy nodded. "He was so angry with me and he didn't know what to do with all his anger."

"Why was he angry with you?" I couldn't even imagine Shane and his dad getting angry with each other. Their relationship had always been so easy.

"Because I wasn't there for him. I wasn't there when Zoe died. When I got the call about the accident, I was in Rio for a competition. I booked the first flight home. Thirteen hours on a plane. Zoe died before I got to the hospital and he'd been left to deal with that alone. Even after that, I wasn't there for him. Not in the way he needed me."

"I'm sure you did your best." And I was also sure that Shane would argue that Jimmy was always there for him.

"That's what I tell myself." He looked lost in his own thoughts, so I tossed the salad, not wanting to intrude on his memories.

Jimmy went outside to get the barbecue going, and I set the patio table for three, thinking about the story Jimmy had shared. When I'd first met Shane, I never would have guessed that he had a temper. He had seemed like a chilled-out surfer dude and most of the time, he had been chilled out with a positive outlook on life. But even back then, there had been things that set him off and made him angry. When he caught me riding my bike late one night with no lights or reflectors. The time he asked me for more information about Russell, as if he was planning to hunt him down and make him pay for what he'd done to me. The time we'd gone to In-N-Out for burgers and shakes (a cheat day for him) and some guy had bumped into me, knocking the shake out of my hand. Kind of like the Frappuccino incident at school. Shane chased after him and made him come back to apologize. And then there was the time down at the break when Tristan dropped in on me. It was all those little things that had prompted me to keep Tristan's bullying to myself. My rationale had been that Shane had too much to lose and couldn't afford to lose his temper with Tristan. Obviously, that had all ended in a catastrophic way.

But Shane reacted to all those things the way he had because of what happened to his mom. He had seen his mom get hit by a white van that took off without stopping and she'd been left to die. He believed that people had to be held accountable for their actions. On our very first date, he'd shared the most defining moment of his life with me. So, it didn't surprise me that Shane had broken his board or that he'd refused to talk about his mom. It was what he was doing now. Shutting down his pain instead of dealing with it.

I needed to be more patient with him. Or get him to open up and talk about it.

"What happened to Shane wasn't your fault, Remy," Jimmy said a little while later when he threw the steaks on the grill. "He made that decision to act on his anger. And he paid the price for it. But so did you."

When Shane went to prison for manslaughter, I'd lost my mind. *Six years.* Six years of his life stolen from him. It hadn't seemed real. I didn't know how I got through those first few months. It felt like a death. I used to wake up in the middle of the night crying, the thought of him in prison unbearable, a sick feeling in the pit of my stomach. And he wouldn't even let me visit him.

"Jimmy... I just... I feel so guilty."

"I know you do. But I'm telling you that you shouldn't. Shane doesn't blame you for that. He blames himself."

"Is that why he took that demolition job? To punish himself?"

"Maybe that's part of it. But he had a hard time finding a job after he got out of prison."

My stomach sank. My remarks about his job had been so insensitive. It was ironic, really. I'd once accused Shane of treating me like white trash, for looking down his nose at me. He never had. My accusation had been unjustified. And yet, what had I done to him? Made him feel like shit for doing a job he felt lucky to get. I hadn't stopped to consider how difficult it was for an ex-con to get a job. And it didn't help that John Hart owned half of Costa del Rey. He had a lot of power and influence in this town.

"The surfboard he made me is beautiful."

Jimmy smiled as he flipped the steaks—four thick T-bones. The fat sizzled and flames leapt up. "It is. He looked happy when he was making that board for you."

That gave me hope and brought a smile to my face. I lifted

my hair off the back of my sweaty neck and twisted into a topknot, securing it with an elastic.

By the time Shane came home, I was feeling better about everything and had forgotten that I was an uninvited guest. Jimmy and I were chilling out, drinking ice cold Coronas with lime wedges and tripping down memory lane. I loved hearing his stories about Shane's mom and about Shane's childhood. Up until Shane started school, he and his mom used to travel with Jimmy on tour. The world's best beaches had been Shane's playground since before he could even walk, let alone surf.

Shane stopped short when he rounded the side of the house and saw me and Jimmy talking and laughing. He planted his hands on his hips and glared at me. "What are you doing here?"

Just like that, my good mood vanished and so did all my lofty plans to be patient with him. I was tempted to punch him in the face, but I gave him a sweet smile instead. "Joining you for dinner. Is that okay with you?"

He didn't answer the question. I wasn't asking for permission anyway. Seven years apart had rendered him mute. Was it my imagination that we used to talk about everything and anything? His eyes darted to the salad and the steaks, and the three glasses of water with lemon slices on the table set for three. "I need a quick shower."

With that, he left his dusty work boots by the door and strode into the house, leaving me to stew over his personality transplant. I pressed the cold beer bottle, slick with condensation, against my sweaty forehead, and peeled my loose tank top off my body, trying to cool off. He was getting me all hot and bothered. I wanted to scream and shout, tell him what an asshole he was being, and just get it all out there. All the pent-up anger and resentment and frustration that he was bottling up instead of dealing with.

"I'm just what he needs," I told Jimmy sarcastically.

"I didn't say it would be easy, but you'll get there eventually."

Jimmy sounded so confident, like he truly believed that. "How can you be so sure?"

"I know Shane. I know how he acts when he's hurting."

"Like an ass?"

"Pretty much."

Shane was back five minutes later, freshly showered and barefoot in a faded T-shirt and shorts, bringing with him the scent of summertime and citrus. His blond-brown hair was damp and finger-combed. Messy and disheveled, the way I loved it. And even though I wanted to be mad at him, I couldn't stay mad because Shane disarmed me with a smile and a gentle squeeze of my thigh under the table. A nonverbal apology for his rude behavior. Heat spread through my body just from that simple touch and he smirked as if he knew the effect he had on me.

Shane ate enough to feed an army and even Jimmy ate most of his steak, so I considered the dinner a success, even though I hated the way Shane was making me feel.

At nine o'clock, Jimmy said he was tired and excused himself. I wasn't sure if he was making excuses, trying to give us time alone or if he really was tired. Shane watched him go before he turned his attention to me, not bothering to conceal his worry. He looked so tired, like he was carrying the weight of the world on his shoulders. The patio lights illuminated the dark shadows under his eyes that I'd missed earlier.

I stood up from the table and came around to stand behind his chair, placing my hands on his shoulders. "What are you doing?"

I didn't answer. My fingers kneaded the knots of tension in his rigid shoulders, and eventually, I felt him relax under my touch, a sigh escaping his lips.

"I'm putty in your hands," he said, with a little laugh and

then a groan when I continued my shoulder, neck and head massage. His eyes closed as I massaged his scalp and the base of his skull, working my way down his neck and returning to his broad swimmers' shoulders.

"I wish I could make it better," I said. I didn't even know what I wanted to make better. Him. Us. Jimmy. But none of it was within my control.

"I know, Firefly. Me too." His hand wrapped around my wrist and he pulled me around the chair, so I was standing between his legs. Clasping both of my hands in his, his thumbs rubbed the sensitive skin on the insides of my wrists and now I was putty in his hands.

He lifted his eyes to mine and I wanted to kiss away all the pain and the heartache. Fix everything that was broken. Give him back the six years of his life that he lost. Put the smile back on his face. But I didn't have the power to do any of that.

"I don't know how to do this," he said quietly.

My heart cracked wide open for him and then broke into a dozen pieces. "I'll be here for you if you let me."

His hands gripped my waist and he pulled me closer, pressing his forehead against my stomach. My body curled around him, my hands sliding through his thick hair and I held the back of his head. His hands slid down to the backs of my thighs, and I closed my eyes and cradled his head, feeling his soft breath through the thin fabric of my tank top.

We stayed like that for a few long moments, the crickets chirping in cadence and the moths beating their wings against the domed lights while I tried to hold his broken pieces together. Then Shane lifted his head and pushed his chair back to give himself space before he stood up and cracked his neck, those moments of intimacy vanishing into the night air like they'd never happened at all. "I'll walk you to your car."

My heart deflated, but I masked my disappointment. It was obvious that he didn't want me here and the whole "walking me to my car" offer was a joke. Shane strode briskly like he couldn't wait to get rid of me, ten paces ahead while I trailed behind, being made to feel like a second-class citizen. If I wanted to catch up, I'd have to jog. He'd always been so good at walking beside me, making sure I didn't feel like I was being left behind. Not anymore.

Gritting my teeth in frustration, I yanked on my seatbelt, annoyed that my hands were shaking. Damn him. I rolled down my window and called his name, halting him in his tracks. He stopped and turned around, raising his brows. "Did you need something?"

Infuriating. Internally, I was screaming, but I kept my voice even and measured. "I came back for you, but I'm staying for your dad. So, you'd better get used to having me around."

Without waiting for his reaction, I reversed out of his driveway, feeling smug and slightly vindicated. Remy St. Clair was not a doormat.

"So he made you a surfboard?" Bastian asked, trying to get the lowdown on my rollercoaster relationship with Shane Wilder. He didn't sound overly impressed by the gesture.

"Yep." I smiled at the barista and mouthed 'thank you' as she handed me my tall Americano.

"And?"

"And... we've been surfing together." I pushed the door open with my hip—every single time I got my nails done, I messed them up and today I was determined to preserve my stupid manicure, since nothing else could be salvaged—and strolled down Main Street.

"That's it? Just surfing? No angry sex?"

I rolled my eyes. "No."

"Why not?"

Cradling my phone between my ear and shoulder, I climbed into my Rover, set my coffee in the cupholder and slammed the door shut. "We haven't even talked. Not about anything real." I turned the key in the ignition and waited for the Bluetooth to kick in then tossed my phone in the cupholder and checked my indigo blue nails. All good. "There's so much we don't know about each other. We just... I don't know... I feel like we need to clear the air. Get it all out there."

"And then you can have angry sex."

"Why do I even talk to you?" My eye caught on two women walking down the street—a blonde and a brunette with designer handbags in the crook of their arm, eyes hidden behind enormous sunglasses. I slunk down in my seat and watched them through the windshield instead of pulling out of my spot. "Not all relationships are based on sex. He just needs a friend right now."

"So you don't want to have sex with Shane."

"I do. But he's not..." I let out a frustrated breath. "It's complicated."

I heard him take a drag of his cigarette and exhale, the sounds of New York traffic and a horn blaring in the background. "So, uncomplicate it."

Yeah, right. That was pretty funny coming from a guy who was so complicated he didn't even understand himself. The two women disappeared inside the nail salon and I let out a shaky breath. Dodged that bullet. One of them was Sienna's mother and the other one was Tristan's. They were still friends, getting manicures and pedicures together. This town was too small. No wonder Shane had tried to stay away. Last night at dinner, I found out that he'd gone to Sonoma after he'd gotten out of prison and he'd been up there for six months.

"My new album drops tomorrow," Bastian said casually.

"Oh God," I groaned. My head fell back against the seat,

and I banged it against the headrest a few times. Thud. Thud. Thud.

Bastian laughed manically. That was the trouble with artists. They used everything—your stories, your life, your heartache and pain and bittersweet memories, and they channeled it into their art. Then they set it free in the world and it didn't belong to them anymore. It belonged to the fans, to the critics, to the lovers and haters. Tomorrow Bastian would either be flying high or need to be peeled off the sidewalk. And I would be... I had no idea how I would be.

"Stay away from the nose candy," I said as I pulled out of my parking spot, the A/C on full blast, the backs of my sweaty thighs stuck to the leather seats.

He just laughed.

On that note, we hung up and I decided to go surfing. The cure-all for anything that ails you.

33

Remy

From the comfort of my poolside chaise lounge, I snapped photos of Dylan, capturing all the dark ink on his back and the full sleeves on his arms as he glided through the water, oblivious that I was stealing pieces of his soul. He'd always hated having his photo taken. Fifteen minutes later, he swam to the side of the pool and pushed his dark hair off his face, leaning his forearms on the pool's edge to catch his breath. Since I'd been out here, he swam twenty laps, but I suspected he'd been at it a lot longer. I snapped a close-up of his face and scrambled off my chair, darting away from the pool to protect my camera from the tsunami he'd unleashed.

"Watch the camera, asshat."

He splashed me again, but I was out of range and only a few drops landed on my feet. Just for that, I snapped a few more photos from a safe distance, using the zoom lens. Ha. That will show him.

After he got out of the pool, I returned to my chair and scrolled through the photos while Dylan ran a towel over his hair, making it stick up all over. I studied a close-up photo of his face, the high cheekbones, and stormy eyes fringed by lashes that were longer than mine, the permanent scowl firmly in place. "These are going in my beautiful collection."

He snorted and plopped down on the lounge chair next to mine, closing his eyes and basking in the last of the evening sun. I hadn't seen much of him in the weeks that I've been here. He always seemed to be working. Last night he hadn't come home at all and I wondered if he had a girlfriend or if he was still seeing Sienna who lived in LA. Not that he would ever confide in me. His personal life was still private, and I had no idea what he did outside work or who he did it with. Prying open Dylan and getting him to talk was still a chore, made worse after he'd let Sienna in and she had burned him. I didn't know the full story but the last time I saw them together, I could see that their relationship was toxic. Yet they kept going back for more.

Were Shane and I toxic? I'd never thought of us that way before but now everything had changed so much that I wasn't sure what to think.

"Why didn't you ever like Shane?" I asked.

"What makes you think I didn't like him?"

"Seriously? The dagger eyes. The attitude. You were never exactly friendly toward him."

"Guess not."

"Why? What did he ever do to you?"

He was silent for a moment. "Shane was the guy I wanted to be back then."

My brows shot up, but he didn't notice because his eyes were closed. "What do you mean?"

"He was this chilled-out dude. So cool, you know. An awesome surfer. I fucking loved to watch him surf. It was like… he was at one with the ocean. I've never seen anything like him.

Even now, he's still got that extra something that a lot of guys don't have. Not even Travis."

I swallowed the lump in my throat. I knew that. I'd always known that. It killed me that Shane was forced to give up the thing he loved most. But I never expected to hear those words come out of Dylan's mouth. It almost sounded like a case of hero-worship which was so unlike Dylan. It also surprised me that he'd watched Shane so closely.

"I admired him," he admitted. "It used to piss me off though. I hated it that he was always trying to take care of things. Like paying the bills and shit. That was my job."

"It wasn't your job, Dylan. It was Mom's."

"Yeah, well, she wasn't around, was she?" He sounded bitter. Hurt. I didn't think Dylan had ever gotten over Mom leaving us like that.

"No." Mom was in Santa Fe now. Or, at least, that's where she'd been the last time I spoke to her, about six months ago. She only called occasionally—when she was drunk and feeling low or when she needed money. Mom hadn't changed much over the years. She was still a drifter and still delusional enough to believe that if she moved to a different town or city everything would be different. Whenever she asked for money, I gave it to her because she was still my mother and I had the money. I didn't want her to end up homeless or dead in an alley somewhere. I suspected that Dylan gave her money too. Despite his insistence that he didn't give a shit about her, I knew he was lying. He cared. So fucking much. He hid his fragile heart under his tarnished armor of ink and defiance.

She once told me she was proud of us, that she knew we'd go on to do big things. In her own twisted way, she loved us, but some people just aren't cut out to be mothers. Sometimes it still surprised me that she'd kept us, and that she'd hung around as long as she had when it had always been clear that she'd rather be somewhere else, doing something different.

"I knew Tristan was bad news," Dylan said. "I fucking knew. But I didn't do anything about it. I just let you deal with your own shit because I was so fucked up with mine. It should have been me. I should have been the one to confront him, not Shane." His jaw locked, and his fingers curled into fists. Dylan always thought he could punch his way out of any situation, and that was why I hadn't told him about Tristan.

"No. Dylan. I didn't want either one of you to get involved. I wish I'd never told Sienna that night." I chipped away at the polish on my thumbnail then forced myself to stop and fiddled with my camera settings instead. "Why did Shane show up at the worst possible time? I mean, I hadn't talked to him in six weeks..."

"It was me," Dylan said quietly. "I went to talk to him that morning."

My eyes widened, and my gaze snapped to Dylan who was staring straight ahead. "What? *You* talked to Shane?"

He scrubbed his hands over his face. "Yeah."

"What did you say?"

"I told him to make it right. That you were a wreck." Dylan shrugged. "I guess he came over to talk to you."

Having dropped that little bomb, Dylan disappeared inside the house, leaving me to mull over that new information. I'd never known that. It made me feel even worse. If Dylan hadn't gone to Shane, he might never have come over, never heard what I told Sienna, and never gone after Tristan. But you couldn't think like that. What was done was done. You just had to deal with what was and not what could have been.

He returned to his seat, a beer in his hand and a cigarette clamped between his lips. I watched him light the cigarette and take a drag, blowing the smoke out of the side of his mouth and resisted the urge to ask for a drag. "I used to hang out with Jimmy sometimes," Dylan confided.

What? I sat up straighter in my seat, my head swiveling to look at him. My twin, the keeper of secrets. "When? You never told me that."

"You were gone. Shane was gone. I used to see Jimmy surfing. Or I'd stop by the surf shop. A few times I stopped by for dinner. I brought my own six-pack and hotdogs."

That made me laugh. Dylan was laughing with me.

"That's just... so weird." I laughed again at the thought of Dylan showing up at Jimmy's house with a six-pack of PBR and hotdogs. "Why don't you ever tell me anything?"

"I don't know." He squinted at something in the distance and took another drag of his cigarette. "I guess he was kind of like a father figure."

Dylan had this way of making me laugh and two seconds later, he'd say something that made me want to cry. I prodded him with more questions, but he was done talking. He'd used up his maximum word count for the evening and remained tight-lipped when I pressed for more information.

Dylan and I ordered pizza and started watching a movie —*Black Panther*. We set the pizza on the coffee table and ate it straight out of the box, not even bothering with plates. "That kitchen is just for show, isn't it?"

"It came with the house."

I laughed. Dylan texted throughout the movie and I went down the rabbithole, reading reviews on Bastian's new album. Rolling Stone called it "sparsely arranged, largely acoustic, and haunting... *Blue Ghost* shows clear-eyed, uncompromising strength in one of the most fragile-sounding sets he's ever made.... the songs address loss, letting go, and moving on..."

That's the beauty of music and lyrics. People can interpret the songs any way they want and inject their own meaning.

The doorbell rang as the credits on the movie were rolling. Dylan and I exchanged a look. "Expecting someone?" I set my wine glass on the coffee table and got to my feet.

Dylan checked his phone as if he needed confirmation. "No."

I elbowed him out of the way, trying to get to the door before him. Zero chill on my end. I knew who was on the other side of that door. "I'll get it."

Dylan was right beside me, a personal bodyguard ready to defend me from intruders. I opened the door and arched a brow, my cool composure the complete opposite of the butterflies invading my stomach. Dylan retreated, but he was still right behind me. "Hey Shane. Just in the neighborhood?"

He leaned against the doorframe and ran both of his hands through his hair, chuckling under his breath. It looked as if someone's hands had been running through it all night long. His hair was just rolled out of bed after sex messy and his hazel eyes were glossy, bloodshot drunk. "I don't know why I'm here."

"Hey Remy," a guy called, dragging my attention away from drunk Shane to the Prius idling in the driveway. A guy with a brown man bun hung out the open window of the backseat and waved.

"Oz," I said, his name finally coming to me. "Hey. How's it going?"

"All good. You've got my boy, Shane?"

I let out a sigh. "Yeah, I've got him."

"Good deal." He gave me the peace sign and I watched the Prius back out of the driveway then turned my attention to Shane who had somehow stumbled into the Bougainvillea next to the front doorstep when I'd taken my eyes off him.

"Oh shit." He got to his feet, rubbing the scratches on his arm, and glared at the innocent plant as if it had attacked him. Dylan was laughing, and I shot him a look that made him laugh harder. Grabbing Shane's arm, I dragged him inside and slammed the door closed behind him.

"Hi Firefly." He gave me the sweetest smile and tugged a

lock of my hair. Adorable drunk Shane had come out to play. "I could use a drink."

"Catch you later," Dylan said, heading toward the garage.

"You're going out?" I called after him.

"I have plans."

I didn't think that was true, but he left quickly, and in true Dylan fashion he didn't waste his breath on greetings or goodbyes. Neither did Shane who had stumbled to the kitchen and was banging around the cupboards.

"Where's the liquor?" he asked, slamming another cupboard shut.

I grabbed him a bottle of water from the refrigerator and pressed it into his hand. His brow furrowed, and I tried not to notice how adorable he looked with his disheveled hair and the puzzled look on his face like he'd never seen a bottle of water before. I reminded myself that I was mad at him and he was drunk.

Was I mad at him? I wasn't even sure anymore. Our relationship was in ruins. A total disaster. How naïve of me to think I could come back here and find a way to make things better.

"Water?"

"You love water," I said, picking up my glass of wine from the coffee table on our way out to the patio with him close on my heels. My palms were starting to sweat, and I needed something to do with my hands. Like slide them under his T-shirt and run them over his smooth golden skin and six-pack abs.

No. I didn't want to do that.

I flicked on the pool lights and dimmed the living room lights. Mood lighting, for what I wasn't sure. Shane plopped down on one of the patio sofas and propped his feet on the table. I sat on the sofa cate-corner to him. Getting too close seemed like a bad idea. He stared at the vines twisted in the rafters and the Moroccan lanterns hanging above our heads then out at the pool before his eyes found me. "Nice place."

"Yeah. I can't believe this is Dylan's life. It's so different from the way we grew up." But then, I didn't need to tell Shane. He was one of the few people who knew that. He had been there, and he had seen it all.

"You're so far away. Come closer." He patted the seat next to him then his lap. "This'd be better."

"I'm close enough."

"Are you?" He smirked.

We needed music. Or something. It was so quiet you could hear the crickets chirping and the hum of the motor in the swimming pool. I slid my cell phone out of my pocket and scrolled through my music. Nothing felt right so I hit random play. Mazzy Star's "Fade Into You" piped from the surround sound. Good enough. I tossed my cell phone on the table.

"Your music still hasn't caught up to the twenty-first century," Shane said, sliding further down on the sofa.

"I'm still stuck in the past." He didn't comment on the double meaning in those words.

"Firefly. Where've you been?" The corners of his mouth turned down and his eyes were so sad it made my heart ache. "How's the world been treating you?"

It used to be me asking him where he had been and what he had been doing. Begging for details of the places he'd traveled, of the adventures he'd had while he was away. Shane used to tell me about the waves he surfed, about the beaches and the food and the scenery. He used to tell me stories about Tahiti and Bali and South Africa. About the Great White that had come too close to the shore, so the officials had canceled his heats for the day. About getting towed out when the waves were too big to paddle out. He had surfed the big waves and he had traveled the world. Swam with dolphins. Cliff dived in Hawaii. Bungee jumped off a bridge in Australia. Once upon a time, Shane had been fearless. Once upon a time, Shane had been an optimist.

I toyed with the stem of my wine glass, not sure what to tell him. I'd wanted to talk to him about everything but not like this. Not when he was drunk. I didn't know how much he'd remember tomorrow.

"I live in New York City. In a loft in Tribeca. I used to try to picture you there, but I never could. Maybe that was why I liked it."

"So you could forget me?"

"No. I never forgot you. It was just easier to be in a place with no memories. I think you would have hated living there. It's too crowded for you. A concrete jungle. And not close enough to the ocean."

"Do you live alone?"

"No."

He nodded like he already knew that and fiddled with the dials on his watch. Shane wore a watch now—a diver's watch—he never used to wear one. Funny how he'd chosen to keep track of time now that his dad was running out of it.

"You live with a rock star." He swept his arm in the air and let it fall to his side. "Everyone wants to be a rock star. Sex, drugs, and rock and roll. Tell me about your rock star boyfriend, Remy."

"I live with a friend who happens to be a rock star." Bastian wasn't a rock star when we met. He was still a struggling musician, playing seedy clubs and bars in LA.

"Are you sleeping with this *friend*?"

"Bastian and I... we're not... it's not like that." We had almost slept together once in LA when we were both really drunk but thankfully, Bastian had passed out and it had never happened. Sex with Bastian would have ruined our friendship. Ruined me. For Bastian, sex was just physical. He was a hit and run kind of guy and saved his emotions for his music.

"What's it like then?" he asked, his eyes on the pool that glowed under the lights.

"This is what you want to know? After seven years apart, you want to know if I'm sleeping with Bastian."

"Yep," he said, popping the P. "That's what I want to know, Remy."

It pissed me off that of all the things he could have asked about me, that was the only thing he really wanted to know. "How many girls have you slept with in the past year?"

"One." He held up his index finger and waved it in the air like a flag.

One. One girl who wasn't me. I wasn't expecting it to hurt as much as it did, but I should have known better. I'd always hated the idea of him with other girls. I hadn't even planned to ask but now I was going down this path too. "Did you... do you love her?"

"I've only loved one girl. She was the siren and I was the sailor. We all know how that story ended." Loving me had been a curse, not a blessing. "Do you love the rock star?"

Honesty was my new thing, and I didn't want to lie to Shane. I'd promised myself I wouldn't, so I chose this opportunity to tell the truth. He probably wouldn't remember this conversation anyway. "Yes. But not the way I loved you. I love him as a friend and I care about him. He was there for me when I was really messed up and we've been through a lot of tough years together, *as friends*. And no, we're not sleeping together."

I wasn't sure what he wanted to hear. I wasn't sure why this was the road we'd chosen to go down. Was he angry that I had gone on with my life without him? I took a sip of my wine, tempted to chug it. He moved on to his next line of questioning.

"Do you like modeling? Does it make you happy?"

"I quit. Right before I came here."

"Why did you quit?"

"So I could eat whatever I wanted." I made it sound like I was joking even though there was some truth in it.

"You gave up modeling so you could eat?" His eyes raked

over my body, but I couldn't even tell if he liked what he saw. I was wearing a tank top and cotton harem pants with a batik print that I bought in Bali. I had pictured him there, surfing on the beaches and sitting in outdoor cafes, chatting with locals and surf bums. I'd visited temples and wondered if he still believed in reincarnation. Or if he still believed in anything at all. *Those* were the questions I wanted to ask him. I had spent seven years chasing the memory of us, and I hadn't been able to move on with anyone else. Because he was always there. In my head. In my heart. In my dreams.

"Kind of." I shrugged one shoulder. "It started to get to me... having all my flaws and imperfections pointed out. Having to keep my weight down."

He started laughing. Then he laughed harder. "That's ridiculous."

"Which part?"

"All of it, Remy. The whole fucked-up story." He leaned his head against the cushion. "You're skinny and flawless and you look so damn good. Better than my dreams. Better than all my memories. And you know what?"

"What?"

He cocked his head and closed one eye. "I liked you just the way you were."

And I liked you just the way you were. The past tense wasn't lost on me.

"And now? Do you still like me?" Asking that question made me so vulnerable, all my old insecurities rose to the surface.

"I don't know you anymore, Remy. You're a supermodel. You live with a rock star..."

"I'm still me."

"Maybe it's me then. I'm not me anymore. Or... I'm not..." He waved his hand in the air. "I'm not the guy you fell in love with. Whoever that guy was he's gone."

But he was in there somewhere, I knew he was. Every now and then, I caught glimpses of him when we surfed together. It gave me hope. I felt like an excavator, trying to dig up relics from the past and expose them to the light. I hated this. I hated it that we couldn't talk to each other the way we used to. There was so much built-up resentment and anger and hurt.

"Did you..." I took another gulp of wine, steeling myself for my next question. Really, I should have gone for something stronger. Tequila, maybe. "Did you do okay in prison?"

I winced. What did that even mean? How could anyone 'do okay' in prison, especially a guy like Shane who had known the good things in life. A good person who had killed someone by accident. In a horrible twist of fate, a fistfight had gone so terribly wrong. Shane hadn't grown up on the streets and I always thought that would have made it so much harder for him. He'd never been a thug or a lowlife like some of the scum of the earth I'd met. Like Russell. Or the crackheads and dealers I'd run across in the shitty neighborhoods I'd once lived in.

"I did just fine. Kept my head down. Did my time. Got to catch up on all my reading."

"So, nobody gave you a hard time?"

He narrowed his eyes. I didn't know why I'd asked that or why I was asking these questions except that Shane was pretty and I'd heard what goes on in prison. Oh god, if anyone messed with him, that would kill me.

"Stop fucking talking about it, Remy. It's over. Done. Put it behind me."

I released a breath. "Sorry."

"Just wanted to hear your voice..." His eyes closed. "That's all I wanted and now you had to go and bring up... all that shit."

I thought I could handle this, handle him, but I couldn't. Finishing off the rest of the wine in my glass in one big gulp, I stood up and breezed past him. I needed more wine for this conversation.

His hand darted out and wrapped around my wrist. He reeled me back and yanked me into his lap, his reflexes still working just fine despite his drunkenness.

"What are you doing?" I tried to scramble out of his lap, but he held on tighter and wouldn't let me go.

"Remy. Stay here. Don't leave me." It was the tone of his voice that made me stop struggling. Raw. Tortured. "Need you."

His eyes were hooded and lust-drunk. He slanted his mouth to mine and his tongue parted my lips, sweeping inside my mouth. I closed my eyes and wrapped my arms around his neck, deepening the kiss. He tasted like tequila and limes and all my favorite memories. His hand slid under my tank top, over my stomach and ribs, and cupped one of my breasts. He pinched the nipple and I let out a little moan, swallowed up by his kiss. He pinched my nipple again, harder this time and heat pooled between my legs, my body writhing. My heart was hammering against my chest and my breaths came out in little pants.

"I don't know how to stop myself from wanting you," he said, his voice hoarse.

I never want you to stop.

His hand tangled in my hair and we kissed like we were starving, our kisses greedy and hungry, never enough, our hands trying to touch everywhere at once. Somewhere in the back of my head, a warning voice was telling me that I should put a stop to this. Shane was drunk and didn't know what he was doing. But I didn't stop it.

My fingers fumbled to unbutton his jeans and he unhooked my bra with one hand, freeing my breasts. We broke apart long enough to rip off each other's clothes and then our lips and hands found each other again. He lifted me up, my legs cinched around his waist, and my mouth fused to his. My back hit the sofa cushions and I stared up at him through my lashes as he knelt over me, nudging my thighs apart and settling between them.

"Miss me?" he asked with a mischievous grin.

Before I could form a response, his finger tunneled inside my walls and I bit back a whimper. The blood rushed from my head like a wave and shot straight to my core. He pulled out his finger, watching my eyes as he sucked the wetness from it.

"I remember the taste of you."

"I remember everything," I whispered, watching his eyes darken.

I reached down, aligning him at my entrance and he thrust forward, sinking inside me in one fluid motion. Buried to the hilt, his head dropped down to my neck, teeth biting my soft skin and grazing my collarbone.

He pulled back and grabbed my leg, putting it over the back of the couch, so he could go even deeper. Then he moved, hard and deep and fast, making me crazed by the sensations tearing through my body. My nails dug into the small of his back, whimpers and moans ripped from my lips when he rotated his hips and drove into me, hitting a sweet spot he remembered so well. Sweat dripped from his face, our bodies slick with it, and I could smell the alcohol seeping from his pores, but I didn't care. I wanted him. So badly. I *needed* him. This. Us. I wanted everything he had to give me, even though I knew it wasn't enough.

I pulled his head down to mine, sinking my teeth into his bottom lip. He growled, the sound sending a jolt straight to my core.

My walls tightened around him and he pressed his finger against my tight bundle of nerves, causing me to cry out and buck my hips. "That's it, baby. Come all over my cock." I exploded, his name escaping my parted lips as my body shook uncontrollably. Shane followed shortly after, grunting as he pounded into me, the orgasm seeming to go on and on.

Afterward, we lay spent, boneless on the sofa on the Moroccan patio by my brother's pool, until the beating of my heart slowly returned to normal. Idly, my fingers played with his hair and stroked his back and I tried not to think about the fact that he only came over here because he was drunk.

He lifted his head from my breasts and gave me a lazy, half-drunk smile. "I've missed this."

This. Not you. Not us. This. He'd missed the sex.

Without warning, he pulled out of me, giving me no time to adjust to the loss, an emptiness that shouldn't feel as devastating as it did. Hot, silent tears leaked from my closed eyelids.

What was wrong with me?

"Baby," he mumbled, and I wondered who the hell baby was because it wasn't me. "Oh shit."

Shane peered down at me, his expression so serious I panicked for a minute.

"What's wrong?" I asked, lifting my hands to his face and rubbing my thumbs over his cheekbones. God, I loved his face. I loved his everything.

"I didn't use anything."

"It's okay. I'm on birth control."

His eyes narrowed, and his voice was an angry growl. "Why? Are you sleeping with the rock star?"

"No. I already told you I wasn't." I didn't need him coming over here drunk and stirring up all these emotions. He was the one who had slept with someone in the past year without giving me a second thought. Shoving him off me, I scrambled out from under him.

34

Remy

I gathered up my clothes from the ground, and pulled on my tank top and underwear, tossing Shane's clothes in his general direction.

"You know what's funny?" he said, not sounding amused in the least. "You come back here... uninvited... with your designer clothes and your expensive car, flaunting your money and rock star lifestyle... rubbing it in my face..."

I spun around to face him, anger surging through me and making my whole body shake. "I came back for you and I'm not flaunting my money. I was trying to help you."

He pulled up his jeans and advanced on me, getting right in my face. "The last time you tried to *help* me, I ended up in prison for six years."

I gaped at him, rendered speechless by his words and the harsh tone of his voice. This was happening. We were finally going there. Unable to stop myself, I rose to my own defense. "I tried to stop you. I never wanted you to go after Tristan—"

"You lied to me, didn't you? You told me he didn't hassle you at school. What else did you lie about?" His eyes narrowed to slits, and his jaw clenched.

He hates me.

That thought knocked the air out of my lungs.

"You're drunk. I'm not having this conversation now." I grabbed my phone from the table, and walked inside the house, turning on the lights as I went. "You should go," I said, hating how my voice shook. "I'll call you a Lyft—"

He turned me around and walked me backward. My back hit the wall and he flattened the palms of his hands on either side of my head, caging me in.

"I. Loved. You. I told you we would have found a way to work things out. There was nothing I wouldn't have done for you. Nothing I wouldn't have done to be with you. Instead of telling me the truth, you broke my fucking heart." Years of pent-up anger bubbled to the surface and erupted like molten lava. Heat and tension rolled off him in waves.

"I broke my own heart too. I thought I was doing the best thing for you." I wanted so much for him to believe that. I raised my eyes to his, and I flinched at the flash of anger in his eyes.

"If you had one ounce of faith in me, you would have let me handle it."

"I was tired of you always having to rescue me. Always playing the white knight." My protests sounded so feeble now, but I was telling the truth.

"Excuse me for giving a shit about you." His nostrils flared, and I could smell the beer and liquor on his breath. He smelled like sweat and sex and his own heady scent. "Was I supposed to apologize for that?'

"No. You were supposed to let me help you for a change. And you were supposed to stay out of it."

"Explain to me how you fucking Tristan was supposed to help me." He laughed incredulously. "Did you think that was all you deserved? Why would you let him do that to you? Why, Remy?" His voice was low and steely, and cut me to the core. "Did you fight him? Did you punch and kick? Or did you just lie back and take it?"

I struggled to break free of his hold, fighting off the memory of that night with Tristan. Shane pressed the length of his body against mine and cupped my jaw, tilting my face up to his. Unshed tears swam in my eyes and distorted my view of his face. A face I loved but didn't recognize.

"You can fight me, but you couldn't fight him? Why didn't you fight, Remy? Why didn't you tell him you didn't give a shit what he said? It was my responsibility to take care of you. My responsibility to take the fall. In the eyes of the law, you were a minor. Too young to give your consent."

A whimper escaped my lips. "That's not how it happened. You know that."

"How long... how long had he been hassling you?"

"What does it matter?" None of this mattered anymore. We couldn't do anything to change it.

"For once in your goddamn life, tell the fucking truth, Remy," he shouted. "It. Matters."

I took a deep breath and averted my head. "He targeted me in eleventh grade. He said he wanted me... that I was a whore just like my mother. I told him he would never have me. Is that what you want to know, Shane? Why did you have to go after him? I tried to stop you." Tears streamed down my face and I couldn't stop them from falling. All our dreams. Our whole future destroyed because of Tristan Fucking Hart who was now dead. How could any of that have happened?

"Why, Shane?" I squeezed my eyes shut, going back to a time and place that had become the stuff of my worst nightmares. "Why did you have to go after him?"

Shane staggered backward, swaying on his feet, reeling as if the reality of everything that had happened was just hitting him now. "Because he hurt you. And I thought you were worth fighting for. Were you, Remy? Tell me. Were you worth fighting for?"

When had Shane learned to be so cruel?

That was the thing about the ocean. It was wild and unpredictable. It could be dangerous, showing no mercy. Shane once told me that it was a mistake to turn your back on the ocean. The thing you love most could destroy you. And Shane... he was still my ocean.

I sagged against the wall, my legs shaking, and watched the emotions play across his face. He looked so sad and so lost right now—bereft—and all I wanted to do was make it better. Rewind the years and go back to a time when he loved life. When he loved me.

"Remy, how did we get here?" he asked, his voice raw with emotion. His head dropped between his shoulders and he rubbed the back of his neck. I couldn't bear to see him in pain.

Closing the distance between us, I wrapped my arms around him and I held him tight because I didn't know what else to do. "I'm sorry. I'm so sorry."

I kept repeating the words over and over, my tears running down my face and soaking his bare chest. His arms wrapped around me and he buried his face in my hair. We held on to each other as the world spun around us and Pearl Jam's "Better Man" piped from the speakers. We were so broken. How could I have ever believed we could fix this? What we'd once had together—the good parts—was nothing but a distant memory. But when he'd been mine, it had been the best thing I'd ever known.

Shane's hands slid down my back and he hooked his hands around the backs of my thighs, lifting me off the ground. My legs cinched around his waist and he started walking. Carrying me across the living room and up the stairs, his gait drunk and unsteady. But still, I trusted him to carry me. I knew he wouldn't drop me. I knew he wouldn't stumble and fall. I had always trusted him. With my life. With my heart. With the secrets of my soul.

"What are you doing?" I asked, pulling back to look at his face.

"Where's your room?" I told him—last door on the left. "Just for tonight. You can make it better, Remy."

I don't know how to make this better.

He tossed me on the bed, ripped off my panties and tossed them aside. Then he undressed, and he fucked me. That was how it felt. Just sex, without love. The only difference was that I still loved Shane. I loved him hopelessly and tragically.

35

Shane

"I WANT TO DIE AT SEA," MY DAD SAID OVER DINNER.

"Why are you talking about dying?"

"I want you to know my final wishes."

I pushed my plate away, not hungry anymore.

"What are your other final wishes?" Remy asked.

True to her word, she still showed up for dinner every night. If I had thought it was hard to be around her before I showed up at her house drunk, it was nothing compared to this tension. I hadn't even planned on going out that night. I didn't socialize in Costa del Rey anymore. But Oz had called when I was on my way home from work after a particularly shitty day on the job. All day I'd been thinking about Remy and I'd been thinking about my stint in prison. It had been the one-year anniversary of my release and I was no closer to getting my life back together than I had been a year ago. In fact, everything was so much worse now.

While we'd been at the bar, I'd overheard some people

gossiping. I'd never paid any attention to idle gossip but now that it was directed at me, it was hard to ignore.

I was the pro-surfer who had killed Costa del Rey's golden boy. I was the guy who had 'lost his mind and bashed Tristan Hart's head against the rocks at his own home.' Without provocation, according to the gossip mill.

Fuck my life.

So, one beer had turned into five or six and one tequila shot had turned into too many. Next thing I knew, I was standing outside Remy's door, wanting her to make everything better. Heal my broken heart. Find the pieces of me I'd lost somewhere along the way. Bring some light into my darkness. It hadn't gone to plan. Drunk ideas always seemed so good at the time but typically turned into the next morning's regrets. So, that was where we were. Between a rock and a hard place.

"Don't hang on to the house for sentimental reasons," my dad said, sharing his final wishes on a beautiful summer's evening when death didn't even feel like a remote possibility. "It's real estate. Sell it. Buy what you want and live wherever the hell you want. Got that?"

I nodded. "Yeah, I got it."

In theory, these things were so easy to agree to, but I didn't want to think about any of it. I didn't know what was harder, losing my mom so suddenly and unexpectedly or knowing that I was going to lose my dad. I should be taking this time to prepare for the day he wouldn't be here but when I had told Remy that I didn't know how to do this, I was being honest. I *really* had no idea how to do this.

So, I cleared the dinner dishes from the table, stopping Remy and my dad from trying to help. More uneaten food from my dad's plate going in the garbage. I stacked the plates in the dishwasher and wiped down the countertops, the sound of my dad and Remy's laughter drifting through the open glass doors as I joined them on the patio again. I needed to man up. Face this shit.

"Jimmy?" Remy said.

My gaze snapped to her and then across the table to my dad. I'd obviously missed part of the conversation.

"What's wrong?" I said, worry creeping in as I studied his face. He looked at me blankly then shook his head, trying to snap out of it.

"Nothing. Just forgot where I was going with this conversation." He chuckled to himself and lit a joint. It wasn't funny, so I couldn't laugh with him.

His short-term memory was slipping. I'd been noticing it over the past few weeks. He'd remember a story about something that happened twenty years ago but completely forget why he'd come into the garage or the kitchen. Or if he'd eaten breakfast that morning. He blamed it on age. I wasn't convinced. Remy had offered to be his chauffeur. Big surprise, he shot her down.

"Talked to Dylan today," my dad said, relaxing in his chair, his face tipped up to the evening sun.

"About what?" I asked, my curiosity piqued.

"He's working on a new app."

"He is?" Remy huffed. "God, he doesn't tell me anything. What kind of app?"

My dad held up his joint. "Cannabis. For medical purposes."

I sank back in my chair and laughed. Then I laughed some more. That guy. He had his finger in every pie. "He'll own half of Costa del Rey by the time he hits thirty."

"I'm pretty sure that's his goal in life," Remy said matter-of-factly.

I hadn't told Remy or my dad that Dylan made me a business proposition. I wasn't sure how I felt about going into business with Remy's brother. Or if it was even something I could consider. I had no capital, and no bank would ever give me a loan, but he was willing to invest his money on a long shot. I told him I'd think about it, but it was more of a brush-off than a promise.

I wasn't in the habit of making promises these days.

I still wanted Remy, that hadn't changed, but I was scared to let myself love her again. I'd lost so much already, and if I let her in only to lose her again, my heart couldn't handle it.

We were in limbo, caught between our tumultuous past and our uncertain future. What did I have to offer a girl like Remy St. Clair? I worked manual labor for a demolition company, slept in my childhood bedroom, and couldn't even get a bank loan because I was a convicted felon. She was rolling in money with the world at her feet, living with a rock star in New York City.

I had nothing left to give her. Not even myself.

"It's not going to work," my dad said later, after Remy left and my dad and I were still sitting outside on the patio.

"What's not going to work?" I asked, watching the moon being chased away by the clouds.

"You can't keep lying to yourself."

"What are you talking about?" I knew what he was talking about. My dad had this uncanny ability of getting to the heart of a problem without being given the details. His observational skills were still on point.

"Remy. You still love her. She still loves you."

"I don't remember you getting so involved in my love life in the past."

"I never did. I always stayed out of it. But times have changed. I refuse to die until I see you happy."

As if he had the power to decide when he would die. That was optimism taken to a whole new level. And with that, he stood up, clapped me on the shoulder and left me alone on the patio.

I retreated to my shaping bay in the garage—I'd painted the walls midnight blue—and trained the lights on the board I was making. It was for Dylan St. Clair, of all people. I'd watched him surfing. He was a goofy-footer and charged hard. Dylan had actually spoken to me and communicated his needs. He wanted something fast that would turn hard and fit into the tighter transitions, so that was what I was going for. The board I was making for him, a shortboard—five-foot-eight—would be snappy and maneuverable. Skatey when you wanted to generate some speed, but you could step back on the tail and hammer some vertical wall.

By the time I stopped working, it was after midnight, and I had a missed call from Remy.

I called her back, watching the stars reel in the night sky from my spot in the hammock that used to be mine. The hammock where I'd had countless phone conversations with Remy not to mention all the other things we'd done in this hammock back when we were still trying not to cross lines. Nine years ago. Eight years ago. Seven years ago.

"Hi."

"Hi."

We both laughed and then we were quiet for a few moments, just listening to the sound of each other's breathing.

"What's on your mind, Firefly?"

"You. What else?"

"What about me?"

"Can you... will you come over?"

I scrubbed my hand over my face. "Why?"

"Dylan's not home. He's gone to Cabo for a long weekend. With Sienna."

"They're still together?" I asked, surprised.

She huffed out a laugh. "Who knows? He doesn't share much. He said it's complicated."

"I can relate."

Remy didn't comment on that. "I just thought... maybe we can spend some time together and... I don't know..."

"What would we do with our time?"

"Oh, you know... things."

I stifled a laugh. "What you're trying to say is that you're horny and this is a booty call."

"Just forget it. It was stupid—"

"I'll be over soon."

"You will? Oh. Okay. See you soon then." I was about to cut the call when she said my name.

"Yeah?"

"Would you bring some ice cream?"

I laughed. "I'll see what I can do."

When she opened the front door, I handed her a bag of mangoes.

She pulled the handles apart and stared into the plastic bag. "Mangoes?"

"They're better for you and you can suck the juice off my fingers after I feed them to you."

Blushing, she turned away, taking the bag of mangoes with her. I reached behind the Bougainvillea where I'd stashed the bag of ice cream and met her in the kitchen. The ice cream, as it turned out, wasn't necessary, so I stowed it in the freezer.

"What are you doing?" I asked as she stripped off her T-shirt and flung it in my face. I caught it and dropped it to the floor, following a trail of discarded clothes and her perfect lace-covered ass to the swimming pool. With her back to me, her wild waves of midnight black hair glowing blue in the pool lights, she dropped her panties and kicked them aside. Looking over her bare shoulder, she gave me one of her Mona Lisa smiles before she dove into the pool.

Apparently, I was game because I pulled my T-shirt over my head and pushed down my shorts. My dick was calling the shots. I might have been drunk the other night but not so drunk I'd forgotten how good it felt to be buried deep inside Remy. I also hadn't forgotten all the things I'd said to her and later regretted.

Butt naked, I dove into the pool and swam underwater in search of Remy. She was a sitting duck, treading water in the middle of the pool. Wrapping my hand around her ankle, I yanked her under. She flailed, her arms windmilling, and tried to use my chest as a wall to push off of with her other foot. I released her ankle and caught her around the waist, pulling her against me as we surfaced, with Remy spluttering and her hair plastered to her head.

She twisted out of my hold and swam to the edge of the pool, gripping it with her hands. Trapping her in my arms, she turned around to face me. My erection pressed against her stomach, making it painfully clear just how much I wanted her. She wrapped her legs around my waist, and her arms around my neck.

"What are we doing, Remy?" I asked, partly out of curiosity but mostly for self-preservation.

"I thought it was obvious."

"Explain the rules of the game so we're clear."

"Sex and surfing. That's all I want from you. It's simple. Anyone can play."

There wasn't anything simple about us. "You want sex with no strings attached?" I asked for clarification.

She nodded. "Bingo."

"I call bullshit."

Her dark brows raised. "Call it what you want. Are you up for it or not?"

"Well, I'm obviously *up* for it."

"Yeah, I can feel that. We've had sex on the beach. How about sex in the pool?"

My fingers dug into her bare ass cheeks. "Would I be your first?"

She gave me a wicked grin. "Wouldn't you like to know?"

"New rule of the game. I ask a question, you answer honestly."

"Does it go both ways?"

I nodded. "Yes or no questions only."

She tapped her chin. "Okay. That's a yes."

"Game on." I turned us around and flung her off me. She flew into the air and hit the water with a splash.

"What the hell," she shouted when she bobbed to the surface.

"If you want me, come and get me." I draped my arms across the pool ledge and waited to see what her next move would be.

She glared at me then swam to the opposite end of the pool and levered herself out. In all her naked glory, she sauntered around the perimeter of the pool, hips swaying, her posture perfect, a look on her face that I'd never seen before. Predatory. She was coming for me. Her wet hair partially covered her breasts and my gaze drifted south, over her taut stomach, hips and pelvic bone, and down those long legs that had been wrapped around my waist only minutes earlier. She was the most beautiful thing I had ever seen in my life and I couldn't take my eyes off her. All the blood rushed out of my head and straight to my dick. It was hard as stone, bobbing on the surface of the water.

I had no clue what we were doing, but it felt dangerous. Therefore, I was in. Old habits die hard.

She towered above me, giving me a prime view of her beautiful pussy. I needed to be inside it but not in a pool. Hated to burst her bubble, but that wasn't happening. The whole lube thing, or lack thereof, made it far less enjoyable than one would suspect. I'd figured that out the summer I was sixteen and we didn't need to repeat my stupid mistakes. I snagged my T-shirt from the pool deck and laid it out at her feet.

"Sit," I said with a flourish of my hand.

Remy sat on the edge of the pool in front of me, her legs dangling in the water. I lifted one of her legs out of the water and planted her foot flat on the deck and then the other. Nudging her knees apart, I slid my hands under her and pulled her toward me until her bottom was at the very edge, right in front of my face.

"What are you doing?" she asked.

"Eating my dessert." My tongue dipped into her soft folds and then I feasted.

We were one week into this arrangement, and I was under no illusions that this could actually work or that Remy would be happy with this for much longer. Whatever we were doing felt temporary. She'd given me the keys to her brother's house and late at night, I'd slip into her room under the cover of night, climb into bed behind her and slide inside her. Even when she was still half asleep, she'd reach for me, her mouth seeking my mouth, kissing and sucking and biting. She was always so ready for me. Wet and warm and eager.

I'd fuck her and then I'd leave her, never staying the night. It was easier to pretend that it was just fucking, with no emotions attached but we both knew better. She didn't ask me for any promises. Didn't ask me for a damn thing. Which made me feel like a dick. I knew Remy, and I knew that down deep, she hadn't really changed. So, I knew this was hurting her, and I knew she wanted more from me.

But I wasn't sure I could give her more.

Knocking softly to let her know I was here, I eased open her bedroom door. Her queen-sized bed was empty, and I followed the sound of raised voices to the open French doors. Firefly was sitting on the balcony, her legs tucked under her chin, a glass of wine in her hand. She held a finger to her lips as I lowered myself to the ground across from her. From here, we had a partial view of the pool and every word of the argument going on below us was amplified.

"...same old shit every fucking time, Sienna. You're twenty-five years old and you're still letting your daddy call the shots."

"That's not true. I just have to handle the situation—"

"It's not a fucking situation. It's a family wedding that I'm not invited to. Nothing has changed. Nothing ever will."

The sound of something smashing against the tiles made Remy suck in her breath and close her eyes. "Oh Dylan," she whispered.

"Dylan, stop. Please," Sienna cried. "I love you."

"You don't love me," Dylan shouted. "You never have. I wasn't good enough for you when I didn't have money. Now I have money and I'm *still* not good enough."

"I'm doing you a favor. You would hate every minute of it. It's a formal occasion. You'd have to wear a tux and socialize with my family and—"

"And I guess the asshole your daddy chose to be your date is good at all that. Why are you even with me, Sienna? If I embarrass you so much. Don't your rich country club boyfriends fuck you like I do? Is that why you keep coming back for more? A bit of rough on the side, is that it?"

"No. I love you and I can't lose you. I want to get back what we had."

"You had me. You had all of me. But you broke your promise."

"I couldn't... my parents threatened..."

A chair flew into the pool, another chair swiftly on the heels of the first one and I could only guess who had hurled them. Remy muttered something about the Titanic while the scene downstairs raged on. We shouldn't be eavesdropping on this conversation. I tried to coax Remy inside, but she stubbornly refused to budge.

"You're acting crazy, Dylan."

"You make me fucking crazy. You said it would be different this time. Lies. All. Fucking. Lies. Why do I believe anything that comes out of your lying lips?"

"I shouldn't have come over. You're such an ass."

"I'm an ass yet you're the one who has broken every single promise you've ever made to me. Fuck it, Sienna. I'm done."

"Dylan!" Sienna screamed over the sound of wood splintering.

Remy and I exchanged a look, and I stood up, heading for the door. "I've got this."

She was right on my heels as I jogged down the stairs and stopped in front of the open French doors, surveying the graveyard of broken planters and spilled earth. Two chaise lounge cushions floated in the pool, the wood frames capsized. A teak table was smashed against the pool tiles, one of the legs broken off. Shards of pottery crunched under my Vans and I stopped, holding up my hand to stop Remy from venturing any further in her bare feet.

"I'll clean it—"

I wrapped my hands around hers and pulled her to her feet. "I'll take care of it."

"Shane?" I turned to look at Sienna as she walked toward us, her pale hair glowing in the pool lights. She wiped the tears off her face and forced a smile. "Hi. It's good to see you. Sorry about all this. I just... Dylan and I were... we keep trying, you know?" Her thin shoulders sagged. "I messed up. Again."

"It happens."

She drew a shaky breath and nodded, her eyes darting to Remy. "Remy. I'm so sorry. I fucked up our friendship and..." Her shoulders shook, and she started crying, covering her face with her hands.

Remy pulled her into a hug and Sienna held on to Remy like she was her lifeline. Remy's eyes met mine over Sienna's shoulder as she stroked her hair and tried to comfort her. This scene looked so damn familiar.

"I'll go talk to Dylan."

Remy nodded, and I left her to take care of her friend. Following the scent of smoke and the cherry glow of a cigarette, I found Dylan at the far edge of his property. Sliding down against the glass fence onto the grass next to him, I eyed the cuts and bloody knuckles on the hand wrapped around the neck of a scotch bottle. He took a drag of his cigarette and tipped back his head, exhaling a plume of smoke into the night air.

"I bought this place for the view," he said, jerking his chin toward the hilltop view of Costa del Rey spread out below us and beyond that the Pacific Ocean shimmering under a silver moon. He took a drag of his cigarette and passed me the bottle. I took a swig, feeling the burn and then another one before I handed it back to him. "My booze is more expensive. My clothes, my car, my fucking house..." He laughed humorlessly. "But I'm still white trash. I'm still the asshole who breaks shit and punches walls when I get angry."

I leaned my head back and looked up at the stars reeling in the sky. I knew from experience that breaking shit and punching things—or people—didn't solve anything. Neither did lashing out verbally and trying to make them hurt as much as you were hurting.

"Love hurts," I said, rubbing my chest as if it would alleviate the tightness, the ache that never seemed to go away.

"Like a motherfucker." He lifted the bottle to his lips and chugged. "I guess you'd know all about that. You still love my sister?"

I huffed out a laugh. This was the second real conversation

I'd ever had with the guy and it was the second time he'd asked if I loved his sister. "What do you think?"

He side-eyed me then looked straight ahead and took a drag of his cigarette. "I'll take that as a yes."

We were quiet for a few minutes, lost in our own thoughts. Dylan stubbed out his cigarette on the grass and tossed it over the fence, and we passed the bottle back and forth in companionable silence.

"I'm sorry about your old man. He's a good guy."

I nodded to acknowledge I'd heard him. "I hear you're his supplier."

"I do what I can to help the cause," Dylan said with a laugh. "He was smoking some bad shit."

"When was this?"

"Before you came back." I eyed him. "Jimmy never told me he was sick. Remy did."

I rolled out my shoulders, trying to relax. These days I was so tense, so tightly wound, it was ridiculous. "You should stop by the house for dinner sometime. He'd like to see you."

"You'd be cool with that?"

My brows raised in surprise. "Why wouldn't I be?"

He shrugged. "Not like you and I were ever friends."

"I've never been your enemy."

Dylan exhaled loudly, his gaze on the view. "I didn't want Remy to get hurt. That's what all that shit was about. She hates being left behind and I thought you'd... I didn't think you'd stick around. Whenever you used to go away, she was scared you'd never come back."

"She told you that?"

"She didn't have to. I know Remy."

"What do you know about Remy?" Firefly sat next to me on the grass and drew her knees to her chest.

Dylan got to his feet and stood in front of Remy. "I know that you should have minded your own fucking business."

"If you told me what was going on in your life, I wouldn't have to eavesdrop on your conversations."

Dylan scowled and shook his head, looking over his shoulder toward the house. "Where's the princess?"

"She went home. Are you okay?"

"Yeah. I'm fine." He strode away, disappearing into the shadows, leaving me and Remy sitting under a towering palm overlooking the lights of Costa del Rey.

Remy sighed and leaned back against the fence, chipping away at the polish on her nails. "I don't know why they keep going back for more. All they ever do is hurt each other. Underneath his moody, broody exterior, Dylan is vulnerable. He never believed he was good enough. Never thought he deserved someone like Sienna. But it's not true. He deserves so much better. He needs someone who fights for him the way he fights for the people he loves. Someone who keeps their promises just like he does. Dylan hides it well, but he has such a big heart. If only Sienna had handled it with care. He would have given her the world."

Remy turned her sad face toward me and I knew this was just as much about us as it was about Dylan and Sienna. I was doing this to her. I was making her miserable. All I'd ever wanted was to make her happy, to see her smile. To protect her from the bad shit in her life. But I had failed on all counts.

"I don't know how to fix us or make things right," she said.

"Some things can't be fixed. Sometimes you have to start over."

"Is that what we're doing? Is this the new us? Am I just a willing body to you?"

"No. You're so much more. You always were."

"It hurts."

"I know," I said. "I'm sorry. I never meant to hurt you. I'm just trying to get my life back together and it's hard," I said, being more honest than I'd been with her since she came back.

I wanted to talk to her the way we used to talk. Back when I could tell her everything. "It's so fucking hard."

"I'm so sorry. For everything that happened," she said. "I just want to be here for you. I *need* to be here for you. Please don't shut me out. I'm still that same girl, you know? The girl who doesn't like to say goodbye. The girl who's scared of being left behind."

"I know. I know who you are."

"Am I being stupid, fooling myself into thinking that there's still a chance for us?"

I didn't have any answers for her. I was just as lost as she was right now. "Let's just take it one day at a time."

I reached into my pocket and handed her the set of keys she'd given me. She took them from me and wrapped her hand around them. "I guess that was a bad idea."

"A good idea but not for us."

She exhaled loudly and nodded. "Guess not. I wanted it to work. I wanted sex with no strings attached."

It would have never worked for us. Even our first kiss had strings attached. I stood up and held out my hand. She took it and I pulled her to her feet, checking that she'd put on shoes before I walked her back to the house, past the chairs and cushions still floating in the pool and around the ruins on the patio that Dylan hadn't bothered cleaning up.

I left her with a kiss and no goodbye. Remy hated goodbyes.

36

Remy

"We know we're not good for each other but it's like an addiction. We can't quit each other. But I think this time... I think we really have to call it quits. It just hurts too much."

Sienna's eyes were puffy from crying and she was pale under her tan. Loving Dylan had taken its toll. On her and on him. How long could you try to hang onto something that just wasn't working?

"I'm not the girl he needs," she said, her voice sad. "I wanted to be. I tried."

She leaned her shoulder against mine and we looked out at the ocean through the rough wood railings, our legs dangling over the side of the pier. This was the beach where I'd learned to surf. I could still envision Jimmy teaching me and Dylan how to paddle out and do pop-ups on the sand. Dylan had listened to everything Jimmy told us to do and had followed his instructions, without complaining or making any smart-ass comments. This was the beach where I'd surfed with Shane all those mornings when I was just learning, and he was so patient with me, making little comments that turned me into a better surfer without making me feel like an idiot. This was the beach that we'd ridden our bikes to on our seventeenth birthday, drunk and high and nauseous from cupcakes, with Sienna on Dylan's handlebars.

Memories were such a bittersweet thing.

The beach was quiet at this early hour, and I watched the seagulls dip and dive over the water and listened to the sound of the surf as I drank my coffee next to the girl who used to be my best friend.

"I wish it could have been different for you guys," I told Sienna, and I meant that sincerely. "I wish it could have all worked out."

"I know, babes. I'm sorry you had to choose sides. That's why we never wanted to get you involved. He's your twin. I knew where your loyalty would lie."

"I love you too though," I said. "And I know Dylan... he's not always easy. Why does love have to hurt so much?"

"It shouldn't. It doesn't always."

"You had good times, right?"

"If we didn't have good times, we wouldn't have kept going back for more."

I sighed.

"So... you and Shane? What's the deal?"

I sighed again. "We tried the whole sex with no strings attached gig."

Sienna snorted. "How did that work out?"

"Not so great. I mean, the sex was great. But the rest of it sucked." I had too many feelings for Shane and sex without love just made me feel too empty.

"It doesn't work with someone you already love. Someone you have a history with. It's like trying to put a Jenga tower back in the box."

I puzzled over that one for a minute. "Is it really though?"

She laughed. "Or like... when you get an inflatable for your pool and after you blow it up, you try to..."

"Fit it back in the box?"

"Exactly."

We were both laughing too hard to worry if that made sense. Sienna wiped the tears from her eyes and smiled at me. "I miss you, babes."

"Miss you too."

But we both knew that we'd never be as close as we used to be. Our friendship would never be the same. Too much had happened. Too much history, and too many times when I'd been forced to choose Dylan's side over Sienna's. I would always choose him, even when he acted like an ass or shut me out, he was my soul twin and Sienna had known that from the start.

We talked for another hour, about her job as an events coordinator and my modeling career which I hadn't missed at all since I'd come back. It was funny how easy it had been to walk away from modeling. Now I just had to figure out what I wanted to do with the rest of my life.

After I left Sienna, I took a drive up the coast and listened to Bastian's new album, playing the title song "Blue Ghost" on repeat. Was that really me? I'd like to think it was the eighteen-year-old Remy that Bastian had first met in LA and that I'd come a long way since then but some days... I wasn't so sure.

"Got you covered, Jimmy. I brought the good shit." Dylan produced a bag of weed and tossed it on the patio table in front of Jimmy. His contribution to our Sunday evening dinner.

"I was hoping you'd bring a six-pack and some hotdogs," Jimmy teased.

"Well, you can't always get what you want," Dylan said,

cracking open a beer from the six-pack I brought and putting up his feet on the patio table like he owned the joint.

I shoved his feet off the table and they hit the ground with a thud. He scowled at me but kept his feet on the ground and leaned back in his seat to drink his beer in the summer sun. It was odd to see Dylan here, talking and joking with Jimmy, looking perfectly at ease in a place that I'd come to think of as a second home. With a man who was like family to me.

Shane and I took over the food prep and stood side by side in the kitchen, skewering the vegetables we'd cut into chunks for our kebabs.

"I've been reading your letters," he said conversationally.

The mushroom cap slipped out of my fingers and the point of the wooden skewer stabbed my index finger. "Ow. Shit."

"Slippery suckers," Shane said, guiding my finger to his mouth and sucking away the drops of blood, his eyes on mine. Today his eyes were green.

"You're drinking my blood."

"Mm." He released my hand and I stared at him for a beat then moved over to the sink and washed my hands. Drying them on a towel, I returned to my spot in front of the chopping board.

"So... how many have you read?" I asked, stabbing a cherry tomato.

"All of them."

My head snapped up. "All of them?"

He smiled. "Every single beautiful word you wrote."

I gave up all pretenses of helping with the dinner prep and leaned my hip against the counter, studying his profile. "Are you okay?"

Shane stacked the kebabs on a tray to take out to the grill and then he turned to face me, and he looked different to me somehow, a little bit more like the old Shane. Like some of the weight had lifted from his shoulders. Or maybe I was imagining it. He gave me a soft smile and cradled my face in his hands, his eyes locking onto mine.

"I'm sorry I didn't read them sooner. I did miss you. I did think about you. Every day. Every hour. You were always with me. And I never hated you, Remy. I never could. I hated myself. For leaving you. For ruining the future we could have had together." His thumbs brushed away the tears falling down my cheeks. "Forgive me."

"Shane, there's nothing to forgive." I wrapped my hands around his wrists.

"One day at a time?"

"Okay," I whispered.

He held me against him, and he bent his head to kiss me. I melted into him as my fingers tangled in his hair. My mouth opened to his and our tongues met, exploring the taste of each other. Inhaling each other's scent like a forgotten memory. It was a forever kind of kiss, and I thought that this was how it should have been the first time we saw each other again. It didn't feel like a goodbye. Not at all. It felt like a promise.

37

Shane

"What made you want to get into demolition work?" I asked Miguel when we stopped for our lunch break. Let's face it, it was a valid question. What kid dreams of cleaning up the debris from a demolished building? Yet, the dude was always cheerful. Acted like there was nothing he'd rather be doing than hauling away broken cinderblocks and rusted pipes.

He gave me a funny look. "Pays the bills. Keeps my wife and kids fed with a roof over their heads. What more could a man want?"

What more indeed. What was a man if he couldn't even provide for the people he loved? If he couldn't protect them from all the shit in the world?

"You know what you gotta do?" Miguel said, making himself more comfortable, settling in for a chat on the tailgate of my Jeep.

"Enlighten me."

"You need to lay off that tofu shit," he said, eying my lunch —tofu, brown rice, and leafy greens.

I laughed and cast an eye at his lunch—leftover fried chicken and some other fried food I couldn't identify.

"You think I'd be happier if I ate fried chicken?"

"Couldn't hurt to try," he said, wiping the grease off his fingers with a lemon-scented wet wipe, no doubt supplied by his wife.

"Huh." My eyes wandered to the graffitied wall next to my Jeep. *Jesus Saves. Drugs Kill. Fuck You, Cocksucker.* Getting mixed messages here.

I wiped the sweat off my forehead with the back of my arm and chugged a bottle of water while Miguel imparted more of his wisdom.

"You need to pray," Miguel said. "Whatever you need, God will hear you."

"Will God answer my prayers?"

"Maybe He will and maybe He won't."

"What's the point in praying then?"

"You gotta keep the faith."

On my way home from work, Remy's song came on the radio. I call it her song because Bastian Cox was singing it. Not only was the song about her, she had obviously told him about the blue ghost fireflies and he'd used it in his lyrics. She hadn't even mentioned the song to me and I wasn't sure how I felt about it or the other songs from the album that I ended up downloading after I got home and showered. A Post-it note on the refrigerator informed me that my dad had gone to dinner with a few of his old surfing buddies. *Don't wait up*, he'd joked. *I might get lucky.* The man was a comedian. I chuckled to myself as I crumpled up his note and tossed it in the trash. Then I retrieved it from the trash and flattened it out on the counter, smoothing my palm over it. I added it to my shoebox of memories and letters.

I had lied to Remy. Not all of her letters had gone unread while I was in prison. In the beginning, for the first six months, I read every letter she sent. I'd read them so many times I knew them by heart. Her letters were funny and sweet and selfless, a heartfelt attempt to buoy my spirits rather than dwell on whatever she was going through. I'd even penned responses, but I'd never sent them. I wanted her to live and to move on and to do big things, not stay stuck in the past, thinking about someone who could no longer give her a future. With five and a half years left to serve on my sentence, I had stopped reading her letters. I'd told myself that I was doing it for her, that it was in her best interest to cut all ties with me. And at the time, I'd truly believed that.

But now that I'd listened to "Blue Ghost", it dawned on me that this Bastian guy had gotten to see another side of Remy that she'd kept hidden from me. If the lyrics were really about Remy, which I suspected they were, she hadn't moved on with her life at all.

I decided to go surfing to clear my head and sort out my feelings about the song, and about Remy. As I stood at the top of the staircase leading to the beach, there she was, floating on her board. She turned her head, her eyes seeking me out as if she'd been expecting me. By the time I paddled out to her, I was seeing everything more clearly. I didn't know what had changed, but something inside me shifted. I'd been so selfish and so self-absorbed, only dwelling on my own problems and not thinking about how my actions and careless words have been affecting Remy. Sometimes it's the people you love the most that you end up treating the worst. And I loved Remy. I had never stopped loving her. But I'd stopped believing that I was good enough for her.

She gave me her Mona Lisa smile and I gave her my real one. "If it isn't the Blue Ghost, haunting my dreams. How dare you star in all my dreams, Firefly?"

She sat up on her board, the one that I made for her, those ocean eyes locking onto mine. "If it makes you feel any better, you always stole the show in mine too. You heard Bastian's song," she guessed. I nodded. "What did you think of it?" She gnawed on her bottom lip, waiting to hear what I thought.

I looked out at the horizon. The sun was starting to sink into the sea, but we still had another hour or so of light to surf by. "It's a beautiful song," I said. "It reminds me of you. But I hope you weren't sad for seven years. I never wanted that for you." I turned my head to look at her. She was so sad and tragic and beautiful, like all her stories without happy endings. "I wanted you to be happy."

"I know," she whispered. "But the world was so cold and lonely without you."

"Firefly. I'm here. Right beside you."

"If I hadn't come back, would you have looked for me?" She shook her head. "Don't tell me. I already know the answer."

"I thought I was doing the best thing for you. I thought you'd be happier without me."

"That's such a load of bullshit. I never took you for a coward."

"I'm just being honest. My life has changed. Drastically. I have nothing to offer you anymore."

"How can you even say that? *You* are enough, Shane. It doesn't matter if you're working a demolition job or you're a pro surfer."

"I have no money, no prospects, no future to offer you. I've got nothing."

"You're such an idiot. Is that what this has been about?" She threw her hands up in the air. "Is that why you've been treating me like shit? Because of *money*? All I've ever wanted was you. God, you're so infuriating. I want to punch you."

Her hands curled into fists and her eyes blazed with fury.

I laughed. I didn't know why but it struck me as funny. She smacked my shoulder.

"It's not funny." She growled in frustration and punched the water. It made her look like a toddler throwing a tantrum. That made me laugh even harder.

She glared at me and I pretended to cower. Thinking she'd catch me off-guard, she tried to shove me off my board. When that failed, she took off, paddling hard for a wave. I was still laughing loudly enough for her to hear it. Which pissed her off even more. She popped-up on her board and flipped me two middle fingers which would have looked badass if she'd managed to keep her balance. I shook my head and clucked my tongue as she pitched over the nose and tumbled into the water. She came up spluttering, her hair plastered to her head, her middle finger in the air.

It was fucking fantastic.

I caught the next wave and did my arrogant little hair flip move for her entertainment. "I hope you faceplant," she shouted as I zipped past her, riding that sweet spot. Why she was still hanging out in the impact zone getting slammed by waves was anyone's guess.

God, I loved her.

We paddled back out, side by side. Her arms might be thin, but they were toned, and she had fierceness and determination on her side. We were nose and nose when we returned to the lineup. She gave me a triumphant smile. "Spaghetti arms, my ass."

I chuckled and straddled my board, admiring the view. Remy's back straight, head held high, the last rays of evening sun setting her skin aglow. She'd always been a warrior. Strong and brave and true. She'd never given up on me even when there had been times I'd given up on myself.

"I'm tired of being sad," Remy said, stretching her arms over her head, her face tipped up to the sun, her lips curved into a smile. Midnight black hair brushed the top of her bikini bottom and her long, graceful neck was arched. So delectable, I was tempted to take a bite out of it.

"I'm tired of being bitter."

"And angry?" She arched her brows at me.

"And angry."

She sighed. "I'm hungry."

"Let's surf for an hour and then I'll take you for tacos. Afterward, I'll feed you a mango."

"I'll suck the juice off your fingers." Her tongue swept out to wet her lips.

"Fuck surfing. Let's go for mangoes."

We got the tacos to go and ate the mangoes first.

We banished sad and bitter, and life started to be good again. Little by little, I recovered pieces of myself that I thought I'd lost somewhere along the way. Slowly but surely, Remy and I started to find our way back to each other and our days fell into a rhythm. Mornings, Remy and I surfed together. She spent her days taking photos of all the beautiful and ugly and interesting things and was teaching herself graphic design.

"Why graphic design?" I asked one evening over dinner when she'd brought her laptop over.

"I'm designing a logo for your new business venture." She winked at me. "Branding, baby. I'm going to help you make it a success."

"Really. And what business venture is this?"

"Firefly Surfboards." She grinned, and my dad rubbed his hands together, "Now we're talking."

By day, I worked at an ugly job that I'd grown to appreciate in a weird way. Demolition work wasn't my lifelong ambition and certainly not my dream, but I took some measure of satisfaction from doing an honest day's work for honest pay. I told

Miguel that surfing was my religion, and I worshiped at the altar of Remy St. Clair. He wasn't sure how to take that. Nobody at the demolition site knew what to make of my attitude adjustment. I'd been out of prison for just over a year now and while it wasn't yet a distant memory, the bad memories were starting to fade. They didn't have their claws sunk in so deep anymore. I was beginning to remember how it felt to be an optimist and how it felt to live rather than just survive.

I'd once heard that if you wanted to learn how to live, you had to learn how to die. My dad was still living his life to the fullest. He tired easily and had short-term memory lapses, and headaches he denied having, but he was still here. Larger than life. Living in the moment. In the evenings, we had dinner together and we talked about life and surfing. For us, they were one and the same.

Whenever I had free time, I shaped boards in the garage. Sometimes Remy hung out with me and sometimes my dad did. Dylan popped in occasionally, and every now and then he even talked. A few times Travis stopped by and wanted to get in on the action.

"You know how I surf. You know what I need," Travis said, sanding down the rail opposite the one I was sanding. "Make me a board."

Why the hell not. I agreed to take a stab at making a board for a world champion. He agreed to stop giving me shit about Remy.

August was a good month. Remy and I were happy. As happy as two people with a lot of excess baggage could be.

38

Remy

"Ready?" Shane asked with a grin.

I returned the grin. "I'm up for anything." Except for walking in these swimming fins. They slapped against the boat deck as I made my ungraceful journey to the platform on the back of the boat. "These things are hard to walk in."

He laughed. "They're not made for walking."

"Tell that to a duck."

Shane laughed harder and pulled the mask over my face, reaching around to tighten the rubber straps to make sure no water could get in. "How's that?"

I gave him a thumbs up and he pulled down his own mask. "No matter how tempting it is, don't touch anything," Shane cautioned.

I nodded, and he squeezed my hand. "I want to keep you safe, trouble."

"Thank you, lover. I appreciate that."

"Hold on to your mask and snorkel when we jump in."

"Got it." Without a second thought, I held my breath and

jumped off the back of the boat, with Shane following closely behind me. Sam's boat was anchored near a cove and I'd been promised wild and wondrous things, so I was eager to explore. It was just us today—me, Shane, Jimmy, and Sam. They'd gone diving ahead of us and if Shane was worried about his dad, he hid it well. He looked happy, like he was loving life, and looking forward to the next adventure.

Breathing through the tubes, masks face-down in the water, we floated along, only moving our feet to propel us forward. My hands were safely tucked against my body to resist the temptation of touching anything. The water in the cove was warmer and so much bluer and clearer than the break where we surfed. You could see straight down to the ocean bottom.

At first, all I saw was plant life and small coral reefs but the further we went, the more sea life we encountered. Schools of fish swam right past us, not bothered by our intrusion, and sea stars floated by. Shane grabbed my hand and pointed to an octopus. I got so excited about the octopus and the stingray I spotted on the ocean's bottom that I dove down, wanting a closer look. I'd forgotten what Shane had told me about breathing through a snorkel when diving. My lungs compressed, squeezing my chest and suffocating me. I couldn't breathe. Lightheaded and dizzy, I panicked, and I flailed. I was going to die in the blue waters of a cove off the coast of Laguna Beach.

Arms wrapped around me and Shane pulled me to the surface, my head emerging from the water. He was behind me, or under me, like a life raft. He reached around and removed my mask and snorkel. "You're okay. I've got you. Just breathe, baby."

I breathed. In. Out. In. Out. Until I calmed down.

"Are you okay?" Shane asked, his voice tinged with concern.

I nodded against his chest and took another fortifying

breath. "I'm good. I just got excited about the octopus and then I panicked."

He held onto me a while longer, floating on his back with his arms wrapped around me. It was still and peaceful, the afternoon sun red under my closed lids and for a while, I was just happy to breathe and hang out like this, the threat of my imminent death well and truly behind me. Snorkeling was fun but after experiencing that pressure on my chest and the feeling of suffocating, I had no interest in learning to deep-sea dive.

"Do you want to go back to the boat?" he asked, his brow furrowed. We were face to face now and he'd taken off his mask and snorkel. There was an imprint on his forehead from the mask and my finger traced it, chasing a bead of water.

"No," I said quickly. "I want to see everything."

He smiled, that chilled out beautiful smile I remembered so well. His eyes were green today. Jade green.

My panicky moment a distant memory, I smiled at him. I was smiling so hard my cheekbones ached.

"What's that smile for?" He pushed a strand of wet hair off my face and tucked it behind my ear, the backs of his fingers brushing my jawline.

"That smile is for you. Thank you for bringing me out here today."

"Thank you for reminding me how it feels to make you smile."

"How does it feel?" I asked, my eyes flitting over his face.

"It makes me feel like a god."

"You've always been godlike in my eyes."

He huffed out a laugh. "Just a mere mortal." He pushed his hand through his hair and looked over his shoulder at the entrance of the cave then back at me. "I wanted you to see it. I knew you'd love it."

My eyes lowered to his mouth and he bit his bottom lip. I

didn't think he understood what that did to me, that sexy little move.

"We're almost at the cave. The tide's low enough to swim to the other side."

"Huh?"

He chuckled. "Ready?"

"Yep. Let me just give this a spit and polish." I spit into my mask which was kind of gross, but supposedly the best way to clear the fog and swished some water in the mask to rinse it before putting it back on my face. Then we were off, exploring the cave and the underwater landscape around the cove with its reef rock spires inhabited by sea snails. We ventured further into open water and spotted sea bass and some sharks, the harmless kind, according to the resident expert on Great Whites. I dove down a few times after that first time and started to get the hang of it, enough so I didn't panic or feel like I was going to black out at least. For me, the highlight of the snorkeling trip was the dolphins. I loved those things.

By the time we returned to the boat, I was happy and relaxed and chilled out. Jimmy and Sam had already come back and were lounging on the cushioned bench seats in the late afternoon sun, in no hurry to get anywhere. I could understand why Jimmy loved getting out on a boat, diving and snorkeling. There was a whole other world down there. Shane and I chugged bottles of cool, sweet water and then he wrapped an arm around my shoulder, pulling me closer to him on the seat across from Jimmy's while Sam steered us back to the marina. I captured Jimmy in a dozen photos and tried not to think of a time when I wouldn't be able to see his smiles in real life.

Jimmy stood up and leaned forward, holding out his hand. Knowing what he wanted, I passed him the camera and leaned into Shane's side again. I was wearing a turquoise bikini and he was bare-chested in surf shorts. My ocean-damp hair was wild and wavy, whipping around my face in the breeze. We smiled for the camera and Jimmy kept snapping photos. I looked at Shane and he looked at me and we smiled at each other. He lowered his head, his mouth close to the shell of my ear and whispered, "So fucking beautiful" and then he pressed his lips against the sensitive skin just below my ear and I melted.

Best. Day. Ever.

When we docked at the harbor, I wrangled my windblown hair into a topknot and threw on a cotton dress over my bikini. Stepping into my flip-flops, my sea legs carried me to the back of the boat. Shane hopped off the boat onto the dock and held out his hand to me. Even though I didn't need his assistance, I took his hand and let him help me off the boat. He pulled me against his hard chest and wrapped his arms around me, kissing my lips. A soft, sweet kiss that tasted like the sea and like hope and possibility.

"I'm glad you came back," he said, his voice low and rough. He kissed the corner of my mouth and my jaw and the side of my neck and I forgot all about how cruel and distant he had been. "My world was so cold and lonely without you too, Firefly."

"Shane," I breathed. My heart was so full I thought it might burst.

"Remy." He smiled and wrapped his arm around my shoulder as we walked along the dock, the evening sun on our faces. My skin tingled from the sun and saltwater and I felt like I was glowing from the inside.

We were Shane and Remy again. But this time, we didn't have to sneak around because of my age, and we had nothing to hide anymore.

The four of us went to a seafood restaurant at the marina and sat at a tall table on the outside deck, overlooking the harbor and the ocean beyond it.

I was drunk on mojitos and high on life. We ate a mountain of king crab legs, watched the sun set over the water, and kept the drinks coming long after we'd finished our dinner. Jimmy and Sam, who reminded me of Jeff Bridges in *The Big Lebowski*, regaled us with tales of their wild youth. I was laughing so hard my stomach hurt.

Alcohol blurred all the edges, and I was viewing the world through a hazy, rose-tinted filter.

39

Shane

I watched Remy laughing with Sam and my dad and filed it away in my good memories collection. My dad looking healthy and relaxed after a good day of diving, his eyes sparkling with humor. Remy in her pretty white dress, with her caramel sun-kissed skin and ocean eyes. Tendrils of hair escaped the messy topknot, the long, graceful column of her neck exposed. Who knew that necks could be so sexy?

Heads swiveled when she walked by, and I couldn't blame people for wanting to take another look. The face that had graced so many glossy magazine covers was even more beautiful in the wild. Makeup-free. Messy hair. No airs or graces, she was stunning.

She caught me watching her and slid off her tall stool, leaning into my side. I wrapped my arm around her and buried my face in the crook of her neck, breathing her in.

"I love you," she whispered in my ear. Instead of waiting for a response, she sipped her mojito and directed her smile across the table at my dad and Sam. They were re-telling a story I'd heard a million times, but I still loved it.

"... so we're out there floating on our boards, talking smack, and we see this little blonde thing carrying a Malibu on her head. She was tiny with white-blonde hair all the way down her back and so damn pretty..."

"Beautiful," my dad corrected him. "She was beautiful."

"Yeah, she was," Sam said. "So, of course we both got to watching, wondering if she'd be able to paddle out let alone ride the thing."

My dad chuckled and shook his head. "Put us to shame."

"She rode her first wave in and me and Jimmy are ogling her, drool dripping down our chins, like the fourteen-year-old idiots we were. By the time she paddled back out and joined us in the lineup we were both in love." Sam took a pull of his beer, his eyes glazed over with memories. "We were caught in a bit of a triangle."

My dad snorted. "She never loved you. There was no triangle."

"Only because you followed her around like a lovesick puppy." Sam puffed out his chest. "I was too cool for that."

We all laughed at that one.

"I swept her off her feet with my charm and witty banter," my dad bragged.

"They were glued to the hip from then on out," Sam said.

"Yeah, we were. Me and my sweet, sweet hippie chick. Then Shane came along, and life was good. So fucking good."

"Good times, good times." Sam sighed. He and my dad still looked like surf bums—Sam with his long brown hair pulled back in an elastic, sporting one of his usual butt-ugly Hawaiian shirts and a muddy tan, and my dad in one of his faded-out T-shirts with that chilled-out expression on his face like he'd just had a good day of shredding. Old buddies who went way back and shared a long history.

Today had been so perfect, so good, that neither of us wanted it to end. Except for the scare when Remy had panicked underwater, it had been one of the best days I could remember in a long, long time. Remy was brave and strong, and that scare hadn't deterred her in the least. That was one of the things I loved most about her. Her resilience. The way she bounced back from things so quickly, with a new resolve to try it again and do better next time.

The long day had taken its toll on my dad and he and Sam left twenty minutes ago, insisting that we stay and enjoy ourselves, so Remy and I had ordered more drinks. Now I wished we had gone home with my dad and Sam.

I used to see Tristan's face all the time. And now I saw it again, from our table at the marina. John Hart's dark eyes bored into me and his jaw was locked. If looks could kill, I'd be six feet under. I used to be his poster boy, the face of his brand. I used to wear his logo on my jersey, the HartCore sticker on my surfboards. When I used to see him in town, he'd stop and shake my hand, clap me on the shoulder and tell me that I needed to keep on winning.

"*Everyone loves a winner, Shane. Winners sell wetsuits and T-shirts and ballcaps. Losers rack up credit card debt. Nobody is going to sponsor a loser. No more repeats of Peniche.*" He shot me a finger gun. A finger gun. What a douche move. It took all my restraint not to roll my eyes or laugh. "*What can I expect from you in Australia?*"

I humored him. I didn't win for him. I did it for myself. Becoming the world champion had been my dream since I'd won my first surfing competition when I was ten. "A win."

And I had won in Australia. I had done what I'd set out to do. He'd called to congratulate me after my win at Bells Beach. Neither of us had been aware of what was going on between Remy and his son. Now, seven years later, John Hart and I locked eyes across a restaurant and all I could see was Tristan's face.

Sweat beaded on my forehead and my heart was beating too fast. *I need to get out of here.*

My conscience... it was so fucking loud. It drowned out the voices around me, the music and the clinking of silverware, and the sound of the water lapping against the boats in the harbor. I felt my chest tighten, and if I didn't know better I'd think I was having a heart attack. I took a few breaths through my nose and rubbed my chest trying to alleviate the pressure.

My stomach churned, and I wanted to get Remy out of here. Grab her hand and run away with her. To Fiji or Bali or Tahiti. Keep running without looking back. Anywhere but here, where the eyes were accusing and the time I'd done for my crime didn't seem to matter. How could it? I couldn't bring his son back from the dead.

Facts had gotten muddled—Tristan's drunk girlfriend and his mother had been the only witnesses. That night I had known I wouldn't stand a chance. I knew I was going to prison. I knew I would be found guilty because I was guilty. I took someone's life. My lawyer told me there was no proof of what Tristan had done to Remy. It also hadn't helped my case that I'd been having sex with a minor or that Tristan's friends had come forth and said they saw me 'physically assault' Tristan the day he'd dropped in on Remy down at the break.

The odds had been stacked against me. John Hart was rich and powerful and wouldn't rest until he'd gotten his pound of flesh. I had accepted a plea bargain. Better than dragging Remy into court. I was advised that the prosecution would dig up everything they could on Remy—her messy home life and our relationship. I didn't want that for her. If I was going down, I had no intention of taking her with me. It had been my decision to go after Tristan, and I had always believed that people needed to be held accountable for their actions.

Remy placed the palm of her hand on my cheek and turned my head toward her, searching my face. "Are you okay?"

"Yeah. I'm fine."

Her brow furrowed, and I wrapped my hand around her wrist, rubbing the delicate skin with my thumb as I lowered her hand from my face, kissing it before I released it. "It's all good. Let's get the check."

"Okay," she said slowly.

I signaled for the bill and threw down some cash, trying to hustle Remy out of there. But it was too late. John and Amanda Hart stopped in front of us, impeding our progress. They looked like they had just stepped off a yacht. He was wearing khakis, a white button-down shirt and navy blazer. She was wearing wide-legged white pants and a blue shirt knotted at the waist, a designer handbag in the crook of her arm. I didn't know why their outfits and physical appearance were the first thing I noticed but they both looked impeccable. Her hair was styled to sleek perfection, her makeup expertly applied.

Remy tucked her arm in mine and wrapped her hands around my bicep. I didn't know if she was hanging on to me for strength or trying to give me some of her own strength. This was the first time I'd come face to face with the Harts in the six or seven months since I'd come back to Costa del Rey.

What was the proper etiquette for a situation like this? There was none.

"If you'll excuse us, we were just leaving," Remy said, tugging on my arm, trying to get me to move.

"Excuse you?" Amanda Hart bit out, her face twisting into something ugly. She advanced on Remy, getting right in her face, and pointed her finger in accusation. "We know all about you, you little tramp. Paige told us everything. We know how you went after Tristan, you shameless little hussy."

Remy released my arm and took a step forward, her chin lifted in defiance. She was so fucking beautiful and strong and brave at this moment. "Whatever she told you, it was a lie. Tristan was the one who came after me."

Amanda laughed harshly. "She said you would say that. We looked into your background. We know all about you and that mother of yours. You act all high and mighty, but you crawled out of the gutter and that's where you belong."

My jaw clenched, and I tried to take deep breaths through my nose. *Find your fucking Zen, Shane. Don't let them provoke you. Don't lose your shit. Not again.*

I pushed Remy behind my back. "Whatever you have to say, say it to me. Leave my girlfriend out of this. I'm the only one who deserves your venom."

Amanda took the opportunity I'd presented and unleashed her fury on me. "I hope you rot in hell," she hissed. "You killed our son."

"I'm sorry. It was an accident." What else could I say?

She lunged at me and I held my hands up in surrender, letting her shove at me and pound my chest with her fists. Her nails scored my skin and black mascara tears coursed down her cheeks. I could smell the wine on her breath and I knew that she was drunk.

"Stop this," Remy said, and I could hear that she was crying and was standing beside me now.

"Do you think that saying you're sorry or a letter of apology will change anything?" Amanda cried. She spit in my face, the ultimate insult, and I wiped it away with the back of my hand, dropping my arms to my sides. Amanda's face crumpled, and her shoulders shook as her sobs became louder.

John Hart stepped in and wrapped his arms around his wife, pulling her against his chest. Amanda covered her face with her hands, her shoulders sagging as she wept for her dead son in front of the man who had taken him away from her.

"I thought I made myself clear when I told you not to set

foot in this town again," he told me, his voice low and his eyes hard.

I looked around at the crowd we had drawn and curbed the words that were on the tip of my tongue. *Go to hell. You've gotten your pound of flesh. You can't banish me from my home.* Instead of responding, I put my arm around Remy's shoulders and steered her away from the crowd, leaving John Hart to console his wife. I didn't blame Amanda Hart. If I had come face to face with the person driving the white van that had killed my mother, I would have reacted the same way. Probably worse. I didn't blame John Hart for wanting to send me to prison either. An eye for an eye. But dragging Remy into it was where I drew the line.

Remy came home with me and we showered together in the outdoor shower. She dressed in one of my T-shirts and crawled into bed with me, resting her head on my shoulder and her hand on my heart. I stared at the ceiling in the darkness of my room and stroked her shower-wet hair that smelled like citrus shampoo.

"Tell me something good, Remy."

"There's only one you and you are not replaceable."

I wrapped a lock of her hair around my fingers, remembering the story about the farmhouse she lived in and the cat she had to leave behind. "I always wondered if you got another cat."

"No. I would have had to say goodbye too often. Too sad for words."

"Like missing the sunrise."

"Or the ocean."

"Or your smile."

"Or your big heart. I think I fell in love with you the very first time I saw you. You were wearing a faded blue T-shirt and black surf shorts with a blue design. You were barefoot with a golden tan and messy surfer hair that I wanted to run my fingers through."

"You were wearing cut-off Levis with a ring from a Skoll can in the back pocket. Beat-up white Chucks and a swim team T-shirt from a college you didn't go to. It was maroon." She rolled onto her back, and I propped my head on my elbow, peering down at her face. Her lips curved into a small smile, her eyes on mine. "Your hair was wavy and wild, halfway down your back and I imagined it wrapped around my fist as I kissed your bee-stung lips."

"Your nose was peeling." She traced her finger over my nose. "I thought it was adorable."

"Your dark nail polish was chipped. I thought it was sexy." I pressed my lips to her wrist.

"I stared at your hand on the gearshift. It was vein porn. You have the best hands."

"I couldn't keep my eyes off your mouth, wishing it was my teeth gnawing on that plump bottom lip." I kissed the corner of her mouth. "I wanted you from the minute I saw you walking out of your apartment. I saw you first."

I hooked my hands under her T-shirt and gently pulled it over her head, tossing it on the floor.

"I loved you first. And last. And always," she said, tugging down my boxers. I undressed quickly and climbed between her legs.

My lips traveled from her jaw to her ear and I whispered, "I love you, Remy. I've never stopped loving you."

"Say it again."

"I love you." My hands slid up her thighs, her sides, her neck and into her hair. "I love you."

My Firefly. My forever.

I reached for her hand and entwined our fingers, resting

our joined hands next to her head on the pillow and then I glided inside her, allowing our bodies to say everything that our words couldn't. Nine years of loving her. The cold and lonely years. The pain and the heartache. But even after everything, here we were, our love stronger for all that we'd gone through.

"I'm sorry," I whispered, my forehead dropping to hers. "For everything."

She touched my face. "You're my ocean, Shane. I'd never turn my back on you."

Her legs wrapped around my back and I thrust harder, stroking in and out, blinded by my love for her. She called out my name. She told me she would love me forever. Her nails dug into my back, her body curving away from the mattress as she pulled my head down to hers and our lips met.

Love tasted like the sea, like tears and hope and possibility.

Love tasted like Remy.

By the next day, photos of us were all over social media. Remy had tried to hide it from me, so I didn't find out until Monday at work when one of the guys mentioned it. Later that day, my boss Raymond, called me into his office—a trailer on the demolition site and he fired my ass.

By Tuesday, it turned into an all-out war with the Harts leading the charge. As if just the sight of me had stirred up new animosity. What more did they want from me? I'd given them my pound of flesh. I'd sent them letters of apology from prison. I had let Amanda Hart spit in my fucking face. My father had lost his business and soon he would be gone. He didn't need this shit in his life. Remy and I had lost each other, and for years, I had lost myself. Now, she was being dragged into this mess because the Harts had decided it wasn't enough, they wanted more. They felt it was somehow within their rights to publicly shame her.

Enough was enough. Remy and I had found our way back to each other and we weren't going to let outside forces drive us apart. Not again.

"Now we're talking," my dad said, rubbing his hands together when we shared our plan of action with him. It was becoming something of a catchphrase for him. *Now we're talking*. Turns out my dad was more of a fighter than I'd given him credit for. "I'm proud of you. And for what it's worth, if someone had done that to your mother, I would have done the same damn thing."

I didn't know if our plan was the right course of action but when your name and your reputation and everything you had worked hard for all your life was being shit on, sometimes there was only one clear line of defense. Tell the truth.

40

Remy

Two Weeks Later

"Let them talk," I said, draining the rest of the champagne in my flute as our car stopped outside the drop-off entrance to the Hollywood Bowl. Bastian had sent a car to pick us up, suspecting we wouldn't show up unless he forced the issue and plied us with expensive alcohol. "They don't know us."

"You don't care?" Shane asked before he knocked back the rest of the whiskey in his tumbler.

"I only care if it upsets you."

"Fuck 'em. If you're okay, I'm okay."

And I was more than okay. I was downright giddy. We tumbled out of the ridiculous car Bastian had sent—a stretch Hummer with a fully stocked minibar and a driver who looked like Ringo Starr—a little bit tipsy but not drunk. Shane was wearing frayed cargo pants with the hems rolled up, a plain white T, and the straw fedora I took off my head and placed on his. He looked effortlessly cool and gorgeous.

I flicked the brim with my fingertip. "You look jaunty."

"You look badass." He gave me a playful smack on the ass and a wink.

What I looked like was a grown-up version of the girl he met, in ripped denim shorts, a black skull tank top, and an Army jacket. He slung an arm around my shoulders and guided us to the outdoor amphitheater. "The beach bum and the queen of the catwalk."

"The god on a stick and the alley cat."

"Put your claws away," he said. "You'll hurt someone."

"My sharp tongue already did."

"You're my hero, Firefly." He dipped his head and kissed the corner of my mouth. I fisted his T-shirt in my hands and backed him against the wall. We kissed like it was the end of the world, our hands roaming and our tongues tangling, an island in the sea of people streaming past us in search of food and drinks.

Love tasted like whiskey and warm sunshine and the sea. I was drunk on his kisses and high on his scent. I lifted my eyes to his hazel greens, dark with lust, and hooded with desire. His grin was slow and lazy, and he swept his tongue across the lower lip I'd just been sucking on.

I cocked my head. "What are you thinking about?"

"Baseball. And a museum I went to on a grade school field trip..." I pressed my body flush against his. He groaned, and I laughed, grinding my body against his erection to torture him.

"I'm wet, if that's any consolation."

"Not helping," he said, laughing. "Fuck. This is painful. Look what you do to me."

I took a step back and we both looked down at the source of his pain. Not going to lie, I wasn't sorry in the least. Unable to keep from laughing, I shielded his body with mine, giving him a chance to readjust himself in his cargo pants. Then we swaggered to our seats in the Pool Circle right down in front of the stage.

I bumped my hip against his and we took our seats on folding chairs. I was halfway in his lap, our arms around each other, my legs slung over his thighs. We were Shane and Remy 2.0. There was something to be said about giving zero fucks. And there was a lot to be said about telling the truth. It was liberating. After the backlash we got from those photos on social media and the trash talk from the Harts, we refused to take it lying down. One of the perks of being a model and being friends with a rock star was that I knew people and I had contacts.

With the help of Bastian's publicist, I set all those wagging tongues straight. The Harts filed a lawsuit against me, but they dropped it when Shane and I went to speak with them, taking our lawyer with us. We'd tried to be as respectful as we could of Tristan's memory, and we'd kept the details vague. Nobody needed to know the whole sordid tale.

In some ways, I felt bad for the Harts but at the same time, it was unfair for Shane to shoulder all the blame and get all that backlash and vitriol aimed at him. Tristan's death had been an accident and Shane had not gone over there, unprovoked as they'd claimed. The beauty of social media was that there was always a new scandal or a juicy bit of titillating gossip to eclipse the last story. So, in time, I knew the interest would die down and nobody would remember our twenty seconds in the spotlight.

But there had been a few positive developments over the past couple weeks and although we had to wade through a lot of shit to get to this place, I thought we were stronger for it. The surfing community had rallied around Shane and even though he said he could never compete again, it meant a lot to him that his former competitors and fellow surfers had come to his defense.

Sometimes you had to use your voice. It could be a powerful tool.

Bastian took the stage and the crowd went wild, seventeen thousand fans screaming his name. Worshiping him. Hanging on to every note and lyric as if it was their lifeline. He left his heart and soul, sweat and tears on that stage. For his art, Bastian would bleed himself dry. After his live performances, he was always emotionally drained but fueled by adrenaline. A high when you're feeling low. A dangerous drug for anyone, but especially for Bastian. His highs were manic, his lows laid him out for days or weeks at a time.

He was beautifully broken and damaged, and up on that stage, he looked every inch the rock star, from his tangle of dark hair to his skinny black jeans and beat-up motorcycle boots. He was skinny but cut, sweat coating his bare chest and abs, his shirt having been flung into the audience and caught in the hands of a girl who buried her nose in it and cried with joy.

Shane and I didn't get caught up in the feeding frenzy. We listened to the music, our arms wrapped around each other as Bastian sang about a girl who was just as broken and damaged as him. He sang about a girl with a ghost-sized hole in her heart who was haunted by the memory of the boy she loved. Hopelessly. Madly. Tragically. Bastian put lyrics and notes to my pain and heartache, and he created magic, turning something ugly into something that was heartbreakingly beautiful. That was his gift, even though sometimes he felt as if he'd been cursed.

"If committing manslaughter doesn't say love, fuck if I know what does," Bastian said by way of greeting when he climbed into the back of the Hummer after the show. After he'd rubbed his sweaty chest all over my tank top and gave me a smack on the ass when I complained that I'd have to smell him all the way home.

"Someone needs to put that in a Hallmark card," Shane deadpanned.

Bastien howled with laughter and lit a cigarette, bumping his fist against Shane's. "Good to meet you, mate. Glad you finally got your head out of your ass. Saves me from having to play fairy godmother."

Shane chuckled and wrapped his arm around me. He knew that Bastian wasn't a threat and that all we'd ever been was friends. "You'll have to find yourself a new muse."

"Who knows? It might be you, Golden Boy," Bastian said with a wink.

"Golden Boy?" Shane muttered, raising his brows at me. I just shrugged. I should have mentioned that Bastian goes both ways and was a shameless flirt.

"Enjoy the show?" Bastian asked, his leg bouncing as he took a deep drag on his cigarette.

"It was great. You were great, Bastian," I said, meaning it. Because he was. Bastian was gifted. So freaking talented it wasn't funny. But even now, five years after hitting the big time, he still needed that reassurance.

He blew his smoke through the moon roof and settled back in his seat. "You two want to hang out and party?"

I shook my head, knowing that Shane was worried about leaving his dad home alone for too long. He'd texted a few times, only to get Jimmy's reply to stop worrying and enjoy the concert. But still, we both worried. "No. We need to get home."

Bastian asked the driver to drop him off at the Chateau Marmont and he let all his 'people' know where to be when he arrived. He led a weird life in the spotlight, hounded by fans and groupies, but Bastian was always lonely. Especially in a crowd. He never really knew who he could trust either. I was one of the few people he let into his very small circle of trusted friends and I'd never taken his friendship for granted.

"Are you ever coming back to New York?" he asked before he got out of the Hummer.

"If all goes well, no."

He gave me a smile. "Love always wins, yeah?"

"Yeah. You'll find your one."

"Not in this lifetime. Goodnight Cinderella." He kissed my cheek and shook Shane's hand, telling him to take care of me before he hopped out of the car and got whisked away by his manager and his entourage of bodyguards. I watched him through the window as he stopped to sign autographs. Bastian's story was a Cinderella story too. Once upon a time, he came to LA with dreams and empty pockets. Now he was a rock star, with the money and the fame and all that went with it. None of that could buy happiness though.

The Hummer navigated the LA traffic homeward-bound, and Shane leaned back in his plush leather seat looking all chilled and relaxed. A few minutes later, he side-eyed me. "Have you ever had sex in the back of a stretch Hummer?"

"Never."

He grinned. "Another first."

He undressed me in record time, and seconds later, in nothing but a black lacy bra and suede ankle boots the color of the desert sand, I was straddling him.

Three orgasms and a glass of champagne later, I sprawled out on the seat with my head in Shane's lap, and woke up when the car stopped in front of his house. Jimmy was lying the hammock, the patio lights still on as we rounded the back of the house. I squeezed Shane's hand as we ventured closer and we both sighed in relief when Jimmy's eyes opened. When he saw us standing there, he gave us a little smile then closed his eyes again and drifted off to sleep. We stood there for the longest time, neither of us going inside the house. I had the strangest feeling. Like this was the end. And pretty soon it would be time to say goodbye.

Two days later, Jimmy had a seizure. And then another one when he got to the hospital.

41

Shane

Two Weeks Later

Sam passed me the bottle of whiskey and I took a swig, passing it to Remy. Leave it to my dad to get us all out to sea on a boat. It was peaceful out here. The moonlight glowing on the water. The boat rocking back and forth in a steady rhythm. If it weren't for the occasion, I would probably enjoy this. But here we were, waiting for my father to die. Death was so goddamn final. I found it hard to believe or accept that by the time we headed back to land, I'd never hear the sound of his voice again.

We might be out here for days or for hours. Could he really predict his own death? Yet he seemed to know that it was close. That he wasn't going to live much longer.

In the end, it had all happened so quickly. One minute we were talking and laughing, and the next minute, he was all disoriented and his words made no sense. After the two seizures, we brought him home from the hospital instead of putting him in a hospice. Remy hired two nurses and I didn't argue with any of the money she shelled out for my father's care. Pride be damned. This was for my dad. He slept a lot, he wasn't in pain, and his sense of humor was still intact during his lucid moments. Today he had told us that it was time and even if he was wrong, we weren't about to argue with him.

So, we got him on a boat, just like he'd wanted and upon Remy's insistence, we took it a step further and set him up in the hammock on the deck in the space between the seats. Not the easiest feat but we did it and now here we were, 'celebrating' the end of my dad's life.

I didn't know how much my dad heard but we talked to him throughout the night. We told stories. Recounted memories. Sam and I talked about my mom. Remy talked about working with my dad in the surf shop and about the time he taught her to surf. Our words flowed. We laughed at some of the funny stories and smiled at some of our memories. We talked about the sea and about surfing. About the stars in the sky and the friends who had stopped by to see my dad and what they had meant to him in his life. His surfer buddies. His former employees from the shop. A few friends who had known my mom.

There were times throughout the night when he was lucid. We held his hand. We tried to decipher his garbled words.

Sea... love... son... Zoe...

"He's telling us he wants us to be happy," Remy said. "He wants you to be happy."

"I'm happy," I said. "You were the best father any guy could ever ask for. I hope you know that. I hope you know how much I love you."

And I thought he heard me and understood. I thought I saw him smile. I wasn't sure, but that was what I needed to believe.

Jimmy Wilder passed away peacefully at six twenty in the

morning on the first of October. Three weeks before the anniversary of my mom's death. Silent tears streamed down Remy's face and Sam's eyes were red-rimmed from crying.

My eyes were dry, my heart heavy as we headed back to shore.

42

Shane

OVER A HUNDRED SURFERS GATHERED ON THE BEACH FOR MY dad's paddle-out, and I spotted Miguel hanging back on the fringes of the group. Dude was built like the Incredible Hulk so blending in wasn't an option. It was the first time I'd seen him away from a demolition site. Instead of dusty work clothes and a hardhat, he was sporting a gray button-down shirt and slacks, his dark hair slicked back with styling products.

"I came to your church," Miguel said when I made my way over to him to shake his hand with Remy in tow. "Not to surf. But to pay my respects."

"Thank you. That means a lot to me," I said sincerely. It was two in the afternoon on a Friday which meant he'd taken off work to be here. "This is Remy. Remy. Miguel. We used to work together."

"I remember," Remy said.

I winced, reminded of the time I'd given Miguel the lunch that Remy had brought for me. He'd taken one look inside the bag, scrunched up his nose at the salad containers and passed it back to me. I'd ended up eating the lunch, but she never knew that because I never told her. I was still in my asshole phase.

"Thank you for coming," she told Miguel, gracing him with one of her genuine smiles. It was blinding. Miguel looked a little star-struck for a minute. Couldn't blame him. Remy's wetsuit fits like a glove, hugging every curve of her body. Curves I loved that she didn't have when she first came back to Costa del Rey. Wild jet-black waves of hair fell down her back and around her shoulders, framing her perfect face.

"It's my pleasure," Miguel said, pulling himself together.

We moved on to the others gathered on the beach and I shook hands and clapped shoulders, fist-bumped a few old friends and thanked everyone for being there. Then I gave the nod and we all paddled out together, slipping under the waves and over the choppy water, orchid stems clenched in our teeth and leis around our necks. The orchids and leis were Remy's contribution and I was pretty sure she'd wiped out the entire stock of orchids on the west coast or Hawaii or wherever she'd ordered them from.

It took a while for so many of us to get into the right position, but eventually, we formed a wide circle in the calmer water out beyond the breakers. I sat up on my board—my dad's favorite orange longboard—and looked around at the circle of surfers. Remy was right beside me just like she had been since the day my dad died. Before that, even. She wasn't a quitter, and she hadn't given up on me even when I'd given up on myself. Dylan was on her other side. We were besties now. Not really. Dude barely spoke. But over the past two weeks, we'd been hanging out together. I guess I hadn't realized how close he and my dad had gotten while I'd been in prison. For Dylan and Remy, my dad had been the only real father figure in their lives and his death had hit them hard. During the first week after my dad died, Remy cried a lot. I'd find her in the vegetable garden, pulling weeds and crying. Making a salad, butchering an avocado, and crying. When I took the knife out of her hand and told her she was going to lose a finger if she kept it up, that made her cry harder. Last week, she threw herself into a project and yesterday she presented me with a photo album that brought tears to my eyes. She'd enlisted Sam's help and he'd dug up photos from forty years ago, thirty years, twenty, and her own photos up until the day he died. There wasn't a single photo in that album where my dad wasn't smiling or laughing.

Travis was on my other side, his brother Ryan, Cody, and Oz and Sam in the circle. A few silver surfers who had a good twenty years on my dad, and the locals who surfed this break every day.

We were all out here to celebrate Jimmy Wilder's life. A paddle-out is a beautiful Hawaiian tradition, and I couldn't imagine a better way to honor a surfer's memory. A better way to honor my dad's life, a man whose passion for the ocean had lasted for all of his fifty years.

Over the past two weeks, I'd made peace with my dad's passing. I missed him like hell and I always would, just like I still missed my mom after all these years. But a few weeks before he died, he told me he had no regrets and I took solace in that.

"*I've lived a good life. I've loved, and I've been loved. What more could a man want?*"

What more indeed.

I turned my head to look at Remy and her eyes locked on mine. For a few seconds, it was just the two of us out here, sharing an intimate moment. She gave me one of her beautiful smiles, and it made my heart ache. The afternoon sun lit up her face and her aquamarine eyes rivaled the blue of the ocean. But it was her strength and her courage and her indomitable spirit that shone the brightest. "Are you ready to say goodbye, Firefly?"

She shook her head. "This isn't goodbye. He still lives on. In the ocean. In here," she touched her heart and then placed her palm over mine. "And here."

I clasped her hand in mine and brought it to my lips, placing a kiss on it. Then I released her hand and the ceremony began.

With a patrol boat in the distance shooting water from a canon and spectators watching from the beach, we threw our sunset-colored petals into the sea and splashed water.

Hands joined, we raised our arms above our heads, whistling and howling. After a while, I led a roaring chant that seemed to echo off the bluffs: *Jimmy. Jimmy. Jimmy.*

It was loud, and it was joyful. For a few minutes, out here on the ocean, a place I'd always considered to be my home, there was no anger or bitterness or sadness or pain. Only love.

We pointed our boards toward the sky and beat on them like drums.

Then, we surfed.

I swear that I could feel my dad's spirit vibrating through my body as I rode those waves. He was with me—in the ocean and the grains of sand, the brushstroke clouds skittering across the blue October sky. Remy was right. This wasn't goodbye.

But it was time to let go and move on. From the old life I'd been clinging to, grieving the loss of, and the dreams that had died the day I got locked up in prison. As Sam told me the other night when he stopped by for a few beers, "A good sailor knows when it's time to readjust the sails."

And that was what I had to do. Readjust my sails and take a different course.

Since I'd lost my job on the demolition site six weeks ago, I'd thrown myself into shaping, glassing, and finning surfboards. I had a whole rack of them in the garage and a few commissions to fill. I needed the money, still a touchy subject for me and Remy. But I also needed a purpose. A new dream. A new future. With any luck, I'd be pursuing those things with the same girl.

Remy, Dylan, Travis, and I stayed at the break, surfing long after the others had paddled in. The sky behind us was red with the promise of a good day tomorrow when we rode our last wave in. As I undid my leg leash, I saw him standing on the beach watching me. A lone figure in khakis and a navy blazer with a crisp white dress shirt.

Our eyes met and held for a few seconds then he tipped his chin and he turned and walked across the sand, carrying his expensive Italian loafers in his hand. I stood and watched him go, my feet sinking into the wet sand. I didn't know what to think. Maybe it was his way of acknowledging that we'd both lost so much. Or maybe he had come to pay his respects. My dad and John Hart used to be friendly acquaintances, and Jimmy's Surf Shack had been the exclusive supplier for Hart-Core surfwear in Costa del Rey. John Hart had always liked my dad. Until he decided to fuck with him. When he disappeared from my sight, I tipped my head up to the sky.

Thanks, Dad.

I chuckled under my breath, amused that I thought my dad had some hand in this. As if he'd sent a sign that everything would be okay.

"What was all that about?" Travis asked, jerking his chin in the direction of the staircase that John Hart had just climbed.

"A truce?" Remy asked, her voice hopeful. She wanted to stay in Costa del Rey. I knew it without her having to tell me. Now that she was back, she didn't want to leave Dylan, but she would. For me. I knew that too.

"John Hart won't cause you any more trouble," Dylan said confidently. He made it sound like he had inside knowledge.

My gaze swung to him and my brows raised. "Why's that?"

"Rich people are back-stabbers who prey on others' misfortune." With that, he tucked his board under his arm and strode away. As if that explained a damn thing. Dylan St. Clair was a puzzle wrapped in an enigma.

Remy chased after him and grabbed his arm, halting him in his tracks. "What are you talking about?"

Travis and I caught up to them, curiosity getting the best of us.

"Explain," I said.

He exhaled loudly like explaining himself was an imposition and we were meant to read his twisted mind. "Sienna's dad—Simon Woods—had something on John Hart and was holding it over his head." Dylan held up his hands. "I don't know what. Don't care either. But they were partners in a lot of their business deals and holdings. Now Simon Woods is the majority shareholder. John Hart isn't poor. But his finances have taken a beating. He'll be too focused on this feud with Simon Woods to give a shit what you're up to."

"Karma. What a bitch," Travis said, sounding downright cheerful.

I shook my head. "You're cold, Ice Man."

Travis just shrugged. Remy remained silent and gnawed on her lower lip. A tell-tale sign that she was nervous or unsure.

I suspected she was just as conflicted as I was about that news. Did John Hart deserve to lose more than he already had? Honestly, I didn't think he did. But that was life, wasn't it? Sometimes it knocked you on your ass and then it kicked you in the teeth.

But harsh as the world could sometimes be, I was ready to get back to the business of living, not just existing. Remy and I had spent so much time dwelling on the past that we hadn't discussed the future. Or the possibility of one together. She'd brought a bag to my house two weeks ago and was living out of it. She hadn't even unpacked it, as if her stay was temporary.

Back in July, my dad had given me another piece of advice. Unsolicited, might I add.

"If a man is lucky enough to find his one true love in this whole big crazy world, he hangs on and he doesn't let go. Not even when it gets hard. Especially not when it gets hard. Fight for her. She's worth it."

43

Shane

"The first time I ever tried sushi was with you," Remy said, slathering wasabi onto a piece of salmon sashimi and popping it into her mouth. Her eyes watered from all that wasabi.

I chuckled at the memory. "I remember. And now look at you. Sushi for lunch. Heavy on the wasabi."

She grinned at me across the island in her brother's kitchen —gleaming stainless-steel, glossy cupboards, and black granite countertops. I'd popped by unannounced. It had been two days since the paddle-out and Remy and we hadn't gotten a chance to talk. We hadn't seen much of each other at all. She was trying to keep me away, scared of what I might do or say.

Her hair was in a messy topknot and she was wearing one of my old T-shirts that I'd forgotten about. "Where did you get that T-shirt?" I asked, eyeing the slogan: Live Hard, Die Shredding.

"I stole it." She cleared her throat. "Before you left for Rio that one time..."

That was about eight years ago.

"You wore it on our first date. I used to sleep in it. I didn't wash it for about a year." She laughed at herself then shook her head. "That sounds really gross. But I didn't want to lose your scent, you know?"

"Remy—"

"Well, my, my, my... hello, sugar." The scent of cigarette smoke filled the air and I ran my hand through my hair before I turned to look at Rae St. Clair.

I hadn't seen the woman in seven or eight years, but she still looked the way I remembered her. She was wearing a crop top and a strip of red leather that she was trying to pass off as a skirt. On a thirteen-year-old girl the outfit might look cute. On a grown-ass woman it looked ridiculous. Especially when she'd paired it with black stilettos. She'd turned up unannounced at Dylan's house the night of our paddle-out, and Dylan had called Remy for backup. It surprised me that he hadn't kicked her ass out of his house. But here she was, with her matching red lips and nails, her eyes narrowed as she sucked on her cigarette. "You're even sexier now that you're an ex-con."

Remy sighed. "Mom. Please don't."

She waved her cigarette at Remy. "I'm on my best behavior. Just speaking the truth. He was just a boy back then but now... well, he's all man." She winked at me and slid onto the stool next to me, blowing her smoke in Remy's direction. That was her though. She didn't give a shit about anyone but herself.

I took the cigarette out of her hand and snuffed it out in Remy's soy sauce, after confirming that the sushi had all been eaten.

"Well, that's not very friendly of you." She pouted and crossed her legs. I averted my head before I saw too much. Too late. I'd have to bleach my eyes to get rid of the sight of her red lace thong.

"What brings you to town, Rae?" I asked, attempting to sound pleasant.

"Do I need a reason to visit my babies?"

The same babies you abandoned when they were seventeen and left to fend for themselves even before you walked out. Hell yeah, you do.

"Do you have a reason or is this just a friendly visit?"

"You've always been so judgmental," Rae said, rolling her eyes. "Don't think I forgot about that time you manhandled me."

"I didn't—" I took a few deep breaths. In. Out. In. Out. Find the Zen.

"What are you talking about? What is she talking about?" Remy asked, redirecting her question to me when Rae just shrugged in response.

I shook my head. "It doesn't matter. It was a long time ago."

I knew that wouldn't fly with Remy, but I thought I'd take a stab at it anyway. Remy stood up and crossed her arms over her chest, her eyes darting from her mom and landing on me.

"It. Matters. What happened?" I heard the accusation in her voice and didn't appreciate it, although I suppose it was understandable, given my track record.

This goddamn woman. Was it too much to ask that we'd never have to see her again? Obviously, the answer was yes. She was like a bad rash. Just kept coming back every time you thought you'd gotten rid of it.

"Why do you think I left town?" Rae said, pointing her finger at me. "It was his fault."

I exhaled loudly, and stood up, putting some distance between myself and Rae before I grabbed her finger of accusation and snapped it in two. Leaning against the counter, I crossed my arms and glared at her. "It was your choice to leave. I simply told you the truth about something you should have known about. Something you should have done something about. *You* were supposed to be the adult. Not Remy. Not Dylan."

"Shane... please tell me you didn't... oh, my God, what did you say to her?"

"He was making false accusations. That's what he did." Rae snorted out a laugh. "Russell was crazy about me." She tossed her hair over her shoulder. "He'd never go after my own daughter. The whole thing was ridiculous."

"Shane, I told you that in confidence. Why would you discuss that with my mother?"

I stared at her. "You're asking me why? Are you fucking kidding me? Why *wouldn't* you discuss it with your mother?"

"Because Dylan and I took care of it. We handled the situation," she gritted out. "What did you do... hunt down my mother and just spill all my secrets?" She threw her hands in the air and then planted them on her hips.

I lowered my head and rubbed the back of my neck. This was not something I'd ever wanted to discuss with Remy or even share with her but now her mother had brought it up within two seconds of seeing me again. "That's not how it happened."

"Well, I'm waiting to hear how it did happen." She tapped her foot on the tiled floor, her eyes flashing with anger. When no words came out of my mouth, she raised her dark brows to prompt me into loosening my lips.

I narrowed my eyes on Rae. Most likely, she'd conveniently forgotten exactly how it had all come about.

"Why don't you make me one of those fancy coffees, baby?" Rae waved her hand at Remy, shooing her away.

"Dylan showed you how to do it," Remy said, her gaze still on me.

"Honestly." Her mom huffed. "You kids are so damn difficult. Can't even make a cup of coffee for your own mother."

My hands curled into fists and I wanted to scream at the woman and tell her that she didn't deserve her kids' generosity much less a cup of coffee. Instead, I gritted my teeth as she sashayed over to the coffeemaker and made her own damn coffee, making a big show of banging around in the cupboards until she found a suitable mug and then checking every drawer until she found the pods for the Keurig. Remy lost her patience and ended up making the coffee for Rae who disappeared for a few seconds only to return with a pack of cigarettes. She returned to her seat, so her daughter could wait on her and lit another cigarette, throwing a smug smile in my direction. An ex-con who had been through anger management sessions should not be entertaining the notion of wringing a person's neck or wishing them bodily harm.

"Why don't you tell Remy what *really* happened?" I said when Remy set the mug of coffee in front of her mother.

To my surprise, she told Remy the truth. "I didn't know you were in love with him."

Remy closed her eyes. "Please tell me you didn't—"

"I saw him one night when I was coming home. He was riding a motorcycle, weren't you?"

I nodded and waited for her to continue the story. One I'd like to forget. But here we were, almost eight years later, revisiting another bad memory.

"I wanted a ride, that's all. But he said no."

"You were drunk." Obviously, that wasn't the only reason I'd said no. But I could tell from the expression on Remy's face that she understood without my having to spell it out.

"I followed him up the stairs to his apartment."

"And then what happened?" Remy prompted.

Rae took a drag of her cigarette and a sip of coffee before she spoke. "It was all harmless. I can't remember the details."

Nobody needed to remember the details or even discuss them.

"Did you... God, Mom... did you make a play for Shane?"

"What does it matter? It was a long time ago. He shoved me away. I do remember that part quite clearly."

"I didn't shove you," I said, forcing myself to remain calm and reasonable. "I removed your hands from my body and I put some distance between us." The woman had palmed my cock through the fabric of my jeans. She had also grabbed my ass and rubbed her tits against my chest. The only reason I hadn't told Remy was because I hadn't wanted her to feel embarrassed. Which I knew she would have been. Remy wasn't responsible for her mother's behavior.

Rae ignored my reasoning. "Then he made all those false accusations about Russell. Told me I needed to start acting like a mother. As if he had any right to tell me what to do." She laughed as if the mere notion was ridiculous.

"I'm sorry," I told Remy. "I never meant to say anything. I was just..." I let out a breath, remembering how angry I'd been. "I wanted her to be held accountable for what had happened to you."

She swallowed hard and lowered her head, her hands gripping the counter as if she needed the support to hold her up.

I went to her side and put my arm around her shoulder, trying to pull her close and comfort her. She shrugged me off and took a few steps away from me, her chest heaving, her eyes on her mother.

"I can't anymore with you, Mom. Do you know why Tristan Hart targeted me? Why he bullied me? Because of you," she said, her voice shaking with anger. "It was because of you. That's how it started."

"Now you're just making things up. You can't blame me for every bad thing that happened to you. I didn't even know Tristan Hart," Rae said dismissively, waving her cigarette in the air. Ash fell onto the counter.

"You came to our school. To meet with the guidance counselor. Do you remember that day? Tristan was the guy you came on to. He told me I was a whore. He told me I was just like you. And for a long time, I think I actually believed that I didn't deserve anything good. And Shane... he was the best thing in my life. But I ruined his life. I crushed his dreams. I destroyed him. Because of me, he lost precious years with his father. Years he'll never be able to... You need to leave," she said, pointing at her mother. "You need to get out of this house. *Now*."

"I'm not going anywhere." She took a final drag of her cigarette and added it to the other one floating in the soy sauce.

"Rae, your daughter—"

Remy grabbed my arm, forcing me to look at her. "No, Shane. You're not getting involved. Not this time. This is between me and my mother and Dylan. Please leave."

I shook my head. "I'm not leaving you to deal with this—"

"I'm not asking you. I'm telling you. You need to leave." Her voice was strong, her back ramrod straight and she had that look of defiance in her eyes. Without waiting for my response, she pressed a key on her cell phone.

"Dylan. I need you to come home. It's important. Please."

Her mother turned on the waterworks. I rolled my eyes. The woman was so predictable, but this time Remy didn't fall for it. She didn't try to comfort her mother. But she was kicking me out. Not happening. I wasn't going anywhere.

I leaned against the counter, my arms crossed over my chest like I was planning to stay all day. Which I was. And the next day. And the day after that.

"I asked you to leave."

"Too bad, Firefly. You're stuck with me. I'm not leaving your side. I get that you feel it's a family matter. You and Dylan can deal with your mother but I'm going to be here. For you. Whether you like it or not."

She opened her mouth to protest then closed it and came to stand in front of me. "But I... you heard what I just said... how can we ever... you and I can never get past what happened. It was stupid to think we could." Her smile was sad.

Oh Firefly. You underestimate us. I'm going to give you one story with a happy ending and that story is ours.

"You're wrong. I'm with you for better or worse." I cradled her face in my hands. "I won't leave you because it gets too hard. Or because we sometimes say things that hurt each other. The past is behind us. We can't fix it or change it. But we're not going to let the past destroy our future."

Her eyes widened, and I heard her intake of breath as if she couldn't quite believe what she'd heard. "You want a future with me?"

"That's all I want. It's all I need. Just you."

"I love you," she whispered. "So much."

"Good. Because I love you too. So fucking much." I was still holding her face in my hands. I rubbed my thumbs over her cheekbones and pressed my lips to her forehead. I wanted to kiss her and carry her out of the kitchen and to the bedroom but that would have to wait. I hadn't planned to make these proclamations in front of Rae St. Clair, but life didn't always go to plan so fuck it. I wanted Remy to know what she meant to me. "I don't want to live another day without you. I never want to say goodbye again."

She leaned into me and wrapped her arms around my neck, holding on tight. It would have been a touching scene if not for her crazy mother's crying and the sound of the door banging against the wall. Dylan strode into the kitchen and Remy pulled away, turning to face Dylan, her back leaning against my chest. I wrapped my arms around her to let her know I was planning to keep my promise.

"What happened?" he asked, his eyes darting from me and Remy to his mother who was wiping away her crocodile tears. She stood up and flung herself at him, wrapping her arms around his waist and shedding fresh tears on his black V-neck.

"You can't turn me away. I have nowhere to go." She pulled back and peered at his face, her eyes pleading with him. I couldn't tell what he was thinking. Dylan's face didn't give a lot away. But his shoulders were rigid with tension and the muscle in his jaw was ticking.

"You have an apartment. I pay for the damn thing. What do you mean you have nowhere to go?" He extricated himself from his mom.

"Wait. You pay for her apartment? *I* pay for it," Remy said.

Dylan sighed and shook his head, dropping his head between his shoulders. I'd never seen him so defeated. "I'm sick of your bullshit. Just so fucking sick of it. I'm done." He sounded weary and wouldn't even look at his mother. "Get your shit and leave."

It took twenty minutes to get Rae out of the house but would have taken a hell of a lot longer if Dylan hadn't packed her stuff and tossed it in her car, physically removing her from his house. He hadn't even asked Remy what happened, but he must have known that whatever it was, it had been bad enough for Remy to want her mother gone. Remy and Dylan supported each other and fought for each other, no questions asked. For all the shit they'd gone through in their lives, or maybe because of it, their bond was unbreakable. They would always side with each other.

After Rae left, Dylan, Remy, and I sat down and talked. It was the first time Dylan had ever included me in a family discussion. Progress. I guess he had finally realized I was here to stay.

"Do you want to run away with me?" I asked Remy, pulling her back against my chest. Her body fit into the curve of mine and she let out a contented post-orgasmic sigh.

"I'd follow you to the ends of the earth. Where are we going, lover?"

"Tahiti, Bali, Hawaii... anywhere we want." I kissed her hair. It glowed blue-black in the moonlight coming through my bedroom windows.

"And what will we do in Tahiti, Bali, and Hawaii?" I could tell by her light, teasing tone that she thought I was joking.

"Surf. Live. Love. Take photos. Make surfboards. Chase new dreams. And when we get weary of traveling, we'll come home."

She turned to face me, her eyes searching mine in the shadows of my room. "You're serious."

I retrieved the ring from my bedside table, took her left hand in mine, and slid it on her finger. Once again, this hadn't gone to plan. I hadn't meant to do this at night, in bed, in the dark. But hey, sometimes you just had to be spontaneous. "Will you spend the rest of your life with me, Firefly? Will you be my forever?"

Her mouth dropped open and for a few long moments, she just left me hanging. I was starting to sweat, thinking this wasn't what she wanted before she finally put me out of my misery and went for the surprise attack.

"Yes!" She pushed me onto my back and climbed on top of me. Wrapping her arms around my neck, she kissed me so hard and so fast, it knocked the breath out of me. When she came up for air and stared down at my face as if seeing it for the very first time, I laughed. "A million times yes."

Life was good. So fucking good.

EPILOGUE

Remy

ONE YEAR LATER

I moan and close my eyes, my lips parting for another slice of heaven.

"Mmm. Delicious." Shane sweeps his tongue over my lips and licks my chin, catching the mango juice that's dribbling down it.

His hands grip my waist and his perfect lips kiss me on my neck. My collarbone. My breast. He takes it into his mouth and sucks my nipple. I untie the belt of my short kimono robe and try to disrobe, impatient and frustrated that he hasn't already done it. My back arches and my legs circle his waist. I'm trying to pull him even closer, my hands simultaneously tugging on his hair and holding the back of his head. I throw my head back and grind my hips against his, trying to get the friction I need. My panties are soaked and they're probably leaving a wet patch on the kitchen counter. I'm so freaking horny it's not even funny. Lately, I've been blaming it on our morning mango feeding sessions but we both know that's not the real reason.

"Shane," I pant. "I need you." It comes out like an angry growl.

He chuckles, keeping up his maddeningly slow pace, teasing one nipple with his mouth, his tongue circling it and his teeth nipping lightly while he squeezes the other nipple between his fingers.

I'm rocking against him, my nails digging into his shoulders and scraping his scalp. Torture. Pure freaking torture.

He releases my nipple and pulls back, his hands sliding down my sides and over my belly, his lips following the same path. "Your mommy is greedy, isn't she?" His lips press against my sun-kissed skin and he keeps talking like the baby can hear him and understand every word. He has whole conversations with our baby and normally I find it adorable but right now that's not what I want.

"Less talk, more action," I say.

He's talking about mangoes and surfing. I think. I'm not really sure because it's falling on deaf ears. I'm too busy grinding my body against his to care what he's saying.

Then he stops talking and lifts his head, his eyes wide. "Did you feel that?" he asks in a hushed tone. I nod. I'm holding my breath, and we're both looking down at my stomach. I felt it. He presses his hand against my skin and it happens again. The baby is kicking. It's just a fluttery feeling in my stomach but we're both so in awe that for a few seconds we're just staring at my stomach with big-ass smiles on our faces. I wipe away a tear. Hormones suck.

"I love you so much," I say, wrapping my hands around the back of his head and pulling him toward me. "But if you don't give me what I want, this baby will be fatherless." I narrow my eyes, trying to look like I actually mean it.

He just laughs and lifts me off the counter. Then he carries me out of the kitchen and to our bedroom, although I'm not sure how he can see where he's going because I have my tongue inside his mouth and my hands on the side of his face to lock it into the position I want. Instead of tossing me on the bed like he used to, he lays me down gently as if I'm made of precious glass. Then he slides my underwear down my legs and tosses them aside, skimming his hands up my legs and nudging my thighs apart.

His tongue barely touches my clit when I come apart, my hands fisting the sheets.

When I come down from my orgasm high, Shane is watching me with a bemused expression.

My eyes travel down his bare chest and down to that V and the happy trail that leads to... boardshorts?

"Why are you still dressed?"

He laughs and scrubs a hand over his face. Then he laughs even harder for no apparent reason. I cross my arms over my chest and wait for him to pull himself together.

"It's because I look like a double-wide, isn't it?" I raise my brows in accusation. "I'm taking trailer trash to a whole new level."

"You're insane," he says, his gaze raking over my body in appreciation. "I love this body."

"Prove it."

Finally, *finally*, he takes off his boardshorts and climbs between my legs, kneeling over me. Worry creases his brows. "Maybe you should be on top—"

I wrap my arms around his neck and pull him down on top of me. "Just do your job and nobody will get hurt."

"You're insatiable," he says, guiding himself into my entrance. But *just* the tip.

I growl in frustration. "You're infuriating. If you're not up to the job, I'll find—"

He shuts me up with a dirty kiss and buries himself inside me to the hilt. Now we're talking.

The baby must be happy that I'm happy because our little bean is having a field day in there. "I'm pretty sure he's swimming the fly."

"I'm the father. What do you expect? I have strong swimmers."

I snort, and he hits a spot that makes me cry out. All he has to do is touch me and I detonate. It's ridiculous. The orgasm rocks my whole body, and I feel like I'm riding a killer wave. It's such a rush and I barely hear Shane telling me he loves me before he shudders and collapses on top of me, bracing his arm at my side to hold up most of his weight. He's always worried he'll hurt me or the baby which he won't.

He rains kisses on me and I close my eyes and breathe him in. I love this man so much. With every cell in my body. My heart is so full that some days I feel like it might burst. And those damn emotions. Or hormones. My eyes are welling up again. But Shane and I... we have been to hell and back and I'd like to think we deserve this slice of heaven.

My eyes wander to the photos on the wall in our bedroom. The one that always draws my eye is Shane surfing a gigantic wave at Teahupo'o—the wave looks like a wall of blue-green glass and Shane looks so small in comparison. I hadn't been able to get close enough to do the photo justice, but it's a memory I'll never ever forget.

Tahiti was the first stop on our travels. The day he'd ridden that wave, my heart had been in my throat. It had taken every ounce of my self-restraint to bite back the words on the tip of my tongue. *Please don't do it. Don't risk your life for a cheap thrill. I can't live without you.*

But he had done it, and it had been the ride of his life.

Traveling with Shane for those six months taught me how to live. He found his smile again. The magic and his capacity for joy came back, and every day had been a new adventure. We followed the sun and chased the waves, traveling to the most beautiful beaches in the world. We didn't simply exist, we *lived*. Fully and without restraint. We loved, madly and deeply. We surfed. It really was like a religious experience. Shane prefers to think of surfing as a spiritual thing. It's not just a sport, it's a life choice. I felt it deep in my soul.

Six months ago, we got married in Bali on a beach at sunset. It was beautiful. A perfect day surrounded by our small circle of nearest and dearest. Luckily, Bastian managed to fly under the radar and nobody cottoned on to the fact that he was there until the ceremony was over. Then we flew back to Costa del Rey with Dylan, and we bought our cool little coral-pink beach house. We painted the walls. Hung photos. Planted a garden. We started a business—Firefly Surfboards. It's doing well. Shane is perfecting his craft and works closely with guys surfers like Cody and Travis to shape boards based on his knowledge of how they surf. It's a real collaboration between a surfer and board shaper, and Shane loves his work. It makes him happy which is all I ever wanted for him. Money isn't everything, but Shane is still weird about taking my money—as in, he flatly refuses to take it—so I invested my money from modeling in a trust fund for our future children. I'm still taking photos and they grace the walls of our home and the business. I'm also getting better at graphic design, and I do all the branding and social media for Firefly.

When we found out we were having a baby four months ago, it made our life complete. Nobody will ever love this baby the way we already do. I always tell Shane that this baby will be so damn lucky to have him as a dad. He says the same goes for me. I hope so. I hope I can be a good mother. Nothing like my own. Dylan and I haven't heard from her since he kicked her out last year. I suspect it's because we stopped giving her money. It makes me sad that that's the only reason she really kept in contact. But with Shane's help, I've been letting it go. He said she never deserved us, and now that we're about to become parents, I can't understand how any mother could ever abandon their kids the way she did us.

With another kiss, Shane pulls me off the bed and ushers me into the shower. We're big on water conservation around here and nobody does a more thorough job of soaping every inch of my body than Shane does. I reach up to push it off his face and he gives me that chilled-out beautiful smile I love so much.

He's my endless summer. With his golden tan stretched over bone and sculpted muscles and his disheveled golden-brown hair falling into his eyes.

"I love you, Firefly."

"I love you more."

Life. You never know what's coming next. It doesn't always go to plan but sometimes it turns out better than your wildest dreams. I've spent a decade loving Shane and I hope I get to spend many more decades loving him. Someday we'll get to tell our children the story of Shane and Remy and it will be an epic story with a happy ending.

Oh yeah, we have a cat too. Her name is Pearl. Like Pearl Jam. Or the pearl in the oyster. Whatever. She has a name and sometimes she even graces us with her presence. Shane doesn't completely trust her, but Pearl always seeks him out first and likes to sleep on his head. I'm pretty sure I was a cat in my former life.

Shane

Four Months Later

When I enter the waiting room at Jackson Memorial, Dylan's eyes fly open and his gaze snaps to the doorway. Even from a distance, I can smell the alcohol seeping from his pores. He looks like he hasn't slept in weeks and his hair is sticking up all over the place. He stands up, scrubbing his hands over his face and attempts to smooth out the creases of his rumpled black shirt. It's hopeless. He looks like he's just rolled out of a dumpster.

"Is Remy okay?" His concern is real and his eyes flit over my face, seeking answers. "You look like shit, man."

I snort. "When's the last time you looked in the mirror?"

He shakes his head and exhales loudly. Let's just say he isn't taking the news of Sienna's engagement too well. "Is she okay?" he asks.

I smile because I can't help it. She's amazing. Tired, but amazing. I'm pretty sure my hand is broken. She squeezed it so hard I could feel the bones disintegrating under her grip. She's stronger than she looks. But it was a small price to pay and nothing compared to what she's just gone through. "She's doing great. It's a boy."

Dylan's face breaks into a huge-ass grin like I've never seen before. Dude is smiling. For real. "No shit. I have a nephew." He shakes his head like he can't quite believe it, his smile softer now. It's a good look on him. "Can I see him?"

I quirk an eyebrow at him. "After you take a shower. You smell like a distillery."

"Fair enough."

A flash of blonde hair streaks past and Scarlett skids to a halt in front of me. She hands Dylan a cup of coffee which he takes from her but doesn't acknowledge. Ignoring his rudeness, she looks at me expectantly. "Well?"

I deliver the news she's come to hear, and she does a little happy dance. Then she claps her hands and squeals in excitement, stomping her Doc Martens on the floor. Scarlett is not normally a squealer, but she and Remy have gotten really close and she's been so excited about this baby you'd think she was Remy's little sister, instead of Sienna's.

"You're too fucking loud," Dylan mutters, rubbing his temples with his tattooed fingers.

She plants her hands on her hips and glares at him. "You should be thanking me."

"For what?"

"Picking up your drunk ass and bringing you to the hospital. And I just traipsed all over the hospital to get you that coffee, asshat."

"Why would I call you?" he asks, his brows furrowed.

She rolls her eyes and huffs. "Seriously? You don't remember?"

I watch this little exchange and maybe if my wife hadn't just given birth I'd be interested in finding out what's going on with these two. But right now, I really don't care to speculate on whatever might be going down with my brother-in-law and his ex-girlfriend's little sister who also happens to be our surfboard artist. Actually, I'd *really* rather not know.

They're squabbling about something, but I tune them out and leave them to it so I can return to Remy and our baby. His name is Kai James Wilder and he's perfect if I do say so myself. Remy looks over at the doorway as I enter and gives me a big, beautiful smile that knocks the air out of my lungs. For a minute, I just stop in my tracks and stare at her holding our baby who's already latched onto her breast. Greedy little guy. Like father, like son. I chuckle under my breath, but my humor evaporates, and it hits me all over again how much I love her. How much we've gone through to be together. In the end, it was all worth it to get to this place. We have a lifetime of love and living ahead of us and I don't want to miss a single minute of it.

"Firefly," I say, my voice choked with emotion when I lean over to kiss her forehead, making sure not to disturb Kai who looks like he's in a state of Nirvana. Can't blame him. "You're my hero."

"And you're mine. Always. And forever."

Life is good. So. Fucking. Good.

Did you know that Dylan has his own book? Sweet Chaos is available now: mybook.to/SweetChaos

ACKNOWLEDGMENTS

To my daughters who put up with my crazy on the daily. A big thank you for your unending patience and your unwavering support. You and my writing give my life meaning.

A huge thank you to my beta readers—Aliana Milano, Petra Gleason, Monica Marti, Annie Dyer and Pernilla Burton—thank you so much for your time, your thoughts, and your encouragement, and for your attention to detail. This book is so much better for it.

Ellie McLove, thank you for the editing and for putting up with my shifting deadlines. Najla Qamber, thank you for creating this gorgeous cover. You are such a joy to work with, thank you. Thank you, Jessica Ames for the interior design and the quick turnaround. To Ena and Amanda at Enticing Journey for arranging the promotions and being so organized.

To all the book bloggers who took the time to read and review and share, thank you so much! I appreciate you and everything you do for the indie community. To the Rambling Roses, thank you so much for all your support.

And finally, a huge thank you to the readers. I couldn't do this without you and I'm so grateful to each and every one of you for reading my words. If you enjoyed reading Shane and Remy's story, please consider taking a few seconds to leave a short review. They mean so much to indie authors.

Thank you so very much.

Emery Rose xoxo

ABOUT THE AUTHOR

Emery Rose has been known to indulge in good red wine, strong coffee, and a healthy dose of sarcasm. She loves writing about sexy alpha heroes, strong heroines, artists, beautiful souls, and flawed but redeemable characters who need to work for their happily ever after.

When she's not writing, you can find her binge-watching Netflix, trotting the globe in search of sunshine, or immersed in a good book. A former New Yorker, she currently lives in London with her two beautiful daughters.

Keep in Touch

For all the updates, sales and new release info subscribe to Emery's Newsletter: https://bit.ly/2StluHc
    Facebook Group: http://bit.ly/2ISyS5y
    Facebook: http://bit.ly/2IDPHRj
    Instagram: http://bit.ly/2KPVgJf
    Twitter: http://bit.ly/2PBE8Kk
    Bookbub: http://bit.ly/2kJpoOR
    Amazon: http://bit.ly/EmeryRoseAmazon
    Goodreads: http://bit.ly/emeryroseGR

ALSO BY EMERY ROSE

The Beautiful Series

Beneath Your Beautiful

Beautiful Lies

Beautiful Rush

Love and Chaos

Wilder Love

Sweet Chaos

Lost Stars

When the Stars Fall

Made in the USA
Monee, IL
12 June 2025